THUNDERBIRD

Savage Law: Book 5

THUNDERBIRD

Savage law: Book 5

KIRBY JONAS

Cover design by Birgitta Bright

Howling Wolf Publishing
Pocatello, Idaho

Howling Wolf Publishing
1611 City Creek Road
Pocatello ID 83204

For more information about Kirby's books, check out:

www.kirbyjonas.com
Facebook, at KirbyJonasauthor

Or email Kirby at: **kirby@kirbyjonas.com**

Manufactured in the United States of America—*One nation, under God*

Publication date: May 2019
Jonas, Kirby, 1965—
Savage Law 5: Thunderbird / by Kirby Jonas.

ISBN: 978-1-891423-38-3
Library of Congress Control Number: 2019904296

To learn more about this book or any other Kirby Jonas book, email Kirby at kirby@kirbyjonas.com

To Henry Ford, the pioneer

And to *Wakinyan Tanka:* Thunderbird

CHAPTER ONE

♦ *1973* ♦

Salmon, Idaho, Savage residence
Tuesday, January 23
5:10 A.M.

The smell of whisky made her gag until she almost threw up. They were holding her down, laughing. One man on either side of her thirteen-year-old body, both of them drunk, bruising her slender arms with the brutal force of their grip.

But *he* was not so drunk. He was sober, and lustful, and furiously angry, and he stank from two weeks without a bath. He didn't have a lot of whiskers, but those he did have burned her cheeks, her chin, her lips. He kissed her, a savage, violent kiss. He sat up on her abdomen and grabbed her face and squeezed it so hard it hurt, then slammed her head against the ground, again and again and again.

He was growling words at her, but their garbled sound could not penetrate the blood in her ears. She only saw his horrible face, when she was brave enough to open her eyes, and she felt his tobacco spit spray her face each time he spoke.

He clawed at her shirt, tearing it, ripping it open wide. He said the first words she could understand, with bits of chewed tobacco driving into her cheeks like pin points, and one of them striking her in the eye: "I told you never t' tell nobody, didn't I! An' you did anyway. This time I'm gonna give you somethin' t' help you remember: When I tell you t' keep your mouth shut, I ain't just playin', you little whore!"

And then he dug a jackknife out of his pocket and started prying open the blade.

Maura PlentyWounds woke up on her feet, screaming and flailing her arms around. She spun in a circle, looking for the men who were holding her down. She could never let them hurt her again.

There was no one else in the room.

Oglala, South Dakota
Pine Ridge Reservation of the Lakota Nation
Tuesday, January 23
5:23 A.M

Leland Iron Rope awoke with sweat streaming down his face and barrel chest—streams of sweat numbered near as many as the long, curly, ugly hairs around his large nipples—which equaled perhaps thirty, if he ever took time to count.

He stared up at the ceiling, trying to decide where he was, and if this time the little demon girl with smoke-blue eyes was really in his room with him. Darkness so completely engulfed the room even with his curtains tied open that the white ceiling was a dark, nearly fathomless gray. There were no street lights in this tiny settlement of Oglala, so on moonless nights, or on cloudy ones such as this, Leland Iron Rope's bedroom generally was paradise, for one who sought undisturbed sleep.

But tonight, it was the full darkness itself that made it so disturbing. Even awake, he could not shake the hateful gaze of those baleful blue eyes from his mind. She didn't say one word, as she had said no word in real life when he was sitting on top of her and giving her his brand. Yet the things she said with those deadly obsidian points in the stormy blue water of her eyes was plenty. She abhorred him. She wanted him dead. So he tried to stop lusting over her, and he tried to will her dead too.

Throwing off the heavy covers, he swung his feet to the cold, oily-feeling floor. Putting his elbows on his knees, he buried his eye sockets against the heels of his hands and tried to chase away the last of the bad sleep spirits with a rough massage. Finally, he sat up straighter, rubbing at his chin. The lack of extensive facial hair was a trait of his people, but there was enough on his chin to act like sandpaper on the palm of his hand and his fingers. It felt good, because at least it felt real. He had had a dream. Only a dream, from an overactive imagination. The girl was gone, and she would never more plague his life.

A lamp flipped on in the hall, and he heard ponderous footsteps, the tread of a big person who had just come out of a deep slumber. A silhouette appeared around the doorframe. The silhouette owned long hair, normally worn loose, but now in braids, for sleeping.

"Dad . . . You all right?" The words were slurred, but the voice was a strong one, the voice of a warrior. The voice of a man he was proud to call his son—although he would never have told him that.

"Yeah, I'm fine. Just a bad dream."

"Yeah? You sure bin havin' a lot o' bad dreams lately."

Leland Iron Rope sat there for a while mulling over his son Asa's words. "I reckon so, yeah."

"Somethin' change for you?"

Leland shook his head, running the claws of his thick fingernails through greasy shoulder-length hair. "No. No, nothin'. I don't know what it is. I think we gotta stop puttin' so much wood on the fire at night."

The silhouette of Asa Iron Rope nodded. "Yeah. An' if you'd roll up that buffalo hide an' put it in the closet where Mom used t' keep it I think you'd be happier too."

Leland sighed. "Nah. It's good medicine, the buff hide. Maybe I'll sleep on top of it."

"Okay. But it's gettin' old wakin' up t' you hollerin'."

"Hollerin'?" Leland looked up at his only son, trying to make out his face in the dark. "I was really hollerin'?"

"Yes. That's what woke me."

"Yeah. Well, I don't like it neither."

"It's about that girl again, ain't it?"

"Don't you talk about that girl," Leland snapped. "We don't talk about her in this house."

Asa nodded. He knew more about the girl from rumors whispered in town than he would ever learn from his own father. Sometimes he wondered if his father had any shame over what he had done, or anger at the girl, or any emotion at all. But when he had dreams like this, that woke him up pouring sweat, then it seemed that answer was clear.

"You go back t' sleep," Leland told his son as he struggled up off the bed, his fifty-six year-old joints creaking and crackling. "I won't sleep no more, an' then I won't dream no more."

"You gotta sleep, Dad."

"I'll sleep in the day. Nightmares never come t' me in the daylight."

Asa's shadow nodded again. "Well, I'm goin' back t' bed."

Leland reached Asa as he was turning away to walk back down the hall. He wanted to clap his big, strong boy on the shoulder, but Asa never let him get that close anymore.

Leland traipsed outside, where it felt like the temperature couldn't be much over twenty, and stood in his bare feet, with only his worn-out jeans on, relishing the ice-cold air that swirled around him. He felt like his people of old, except for living in this square house, which those old people would never have agreed to. They would have died first.

In the distance, a dog was barking, and that made his own dogs, his big, muscular rottweilers which had followed him out into the cold, gather around him and begin to whine. A strong smell of cottonwood smoke permeated the air, and his nostrils. A horse whinnied somewhere, and he wondered what had disturbed it. Horses didn't often call out in the night.

He ran his hand back through his oily hair, then let it fall again, and tickle his shoulders. The girl. Where was the girl? So many years had passed. She could be dead. She should be, anyway. Nobody wanted her, and nobody cared about her. And that damn baby. That baby too, it must be dead. So why had the girl begun to come to him now, haunting his dreams? Perhaps that was it: She had left the world recently, and it was her ghost that came to him in these dark, moonless nights. It was time to go see the shaman, Emery Afraid of Lightning. That old man would know what to do, and for a small donation he would banish this bad spirit, the shade of the yellow-haired girl, from the Iron Rope house forever.

Salmon, Idaho, Savage residence
Tuesday, January 23
2:00 A.M.

Coal Savage didn't even have the sound of Slugger Janx screaming to haunt his memories. Unlike Hollywood portrayals, his friend Slugger had gone over the edge of the Salmon River cliff with complete grace and poise, and from the start of his dive to his landing hundreds of feet below there was no sound from him at all.

There was only that haunting, echoing raven cry.

Coal lay in bed that night, after all the weeping in his house was done. Broken inside, he stared at the ceiling, feeling the warmth of Dobe's body as he lay snuggled up against his right side, breathing warm on his arm. He ached for Slugger, and he ached for a human race that seemed only in the case of brothers in arms to be able to come together as one family.

All the day before, he had put off the phone call he dreaded so much, the call he had to place to Slugger's parents in Louisiana. Of all the things he had to do as sheriff, perhaps those death notifications were the worst. Slugger's parents had trusted him completely. They had been certain he would provide a safe place for their boy. And now he was gone forever.

There was no way to remove Slugger's silent passage to the Promised Land from his mind, but Coal tried. He forced his mind to thoughts of Annie Price, and of Kathy MacAtee and her girls. He needed to be with an adult, someone he could open up to besides Connie, who had already heard enough. And opening up meant it had to be a woman, because men—most men—could not speak to each other honestly about the things that affected them deepest.

Kathy would be the obvious choice, because right then Coal felt very weak, in every way, and Kathy had three built-in chaperones who would be sure to keep them safe.

But he could not choose Kathy. There was someone else who had seen the same horror Coal had, who was suffering as much as he was.

In the morning, he had to go to Maura, who was sleeping just downstairs, in his mother's room. The two of them had to be together. If any sanity could be preserved at all, they must find it as one. All too often, it seemed tragic moments were what bonded him and Maura together the strongest.

With that thought in mind, Coal slept at last.

*   *   *

He awoke with a start. He thought he had heard a scream. Dobe was up too, sitting up on the bed, staring at the door. Shadow stood in front of the door, looking a question back at Coal. She fancied herself the guardian of the house. She needed to go check to be sure everyone in her care was safe.

Coal wanted to get up. His groggy head just wouldn't let him. He lay there watching Dobe, who seemed to tower over the top of him as a promise that no harm could ever come to him, not as long as there was a breath of life in that dog.

No other sound came, and in half a minute or less Coal faded back to sleep.

Because Dobe and Shadow remained restless, he was back awake twenty minutes later and downstairs grinding freshly roasted coffee beans while Connie and Maura were out feeding the horses. It would be a particularly strong brew today, for he had slept but little, and he had plans of a long road ahead.

After his first cup, Coal threw everything he could muster into a thirty-minute extreme workout for his chest and back. He came back upstairs, smiling into the kitchen at Maura, who sat at the bar on a stool next to Connie. She appeared to be lost in thought, or perhaps preparing to bare her soul to his mother. She gave him back a broken, close-mouthed smile.

With a heavy heart, Coal unplugged the phone and took it upstairs with him, plugging it back in in his room. At last the time had come, and he placed the one phone call he most wanted not to make. The meek voice of Martha May Janx, mother of his friend Slugger, answered in faraway Louisiana, sounding just as far away as she was. His voice caught for a couple of seconds, and she said hello again. He introduced himself, and silence fell again.

When he hung up the phone, he felt sick. Martha May's voice had gone even more distant-sounding, ever quieter, before she said a polite goodbye. She didn't say thanks. For anything. He guessed he hadn't done a thing to thank him for when it came down to it. Gathering the phone, his clothes and boots, feeling numb, he went back downstairs.

Taking a quick shower, shaving, and trimming his overgrown mustache and sideburns, Coal went back into a kitchen filled with the aroma of maple bacon. He sat down on the other side of Maura. No one spoke. It wasn't an atmosphere for words. The only sound was the *clickety click* of Shadow and Dobe's toenails as they patrolled the kitchen on crumb duty.

Connie got up and refilled Coal's coffee cup without asking. She never drank the stuff, but before handing it to him she held it to her nose and breathed deeply of its aroma. Coal looked at Maura, unable to bear the thought of breaking the emotional silence. He gestured at her with his cup, a question in his eyes. She gave him a blood-shot gaze for a moment, then allowed herself a brisk nod. Seeing the exchange, Connie went to the cupboard after another cup.

Reaching over as Maura took her cup from Connie with a little smile and a mouthed, *Thank you,* Coal gave the woman's shoulder a gentle rub, then let his hand fall away. He looked over at Connie, then back again at Maura. Was all this quiet, and the palpable pain in the room, because of Slugger, or had he missed something?

Eventually, the silence had to be broken, and Coal figured he had the most important thing to say. He put his hand on Maura's. "Can I talk to you for a minute outside?"

With only a glance at him, she got up listlessly and walked toward the front door, coatless. The thermometer said it was only fifteen degrees out, and she had already been out in it to feed the horses, so she knew it wouldn't be comfortable, but she didn't seem to care. She opened the door, and Coal followed her out, snatching his own coat from the tree beside the door.

She stopped and turned to him, giving a little smile as the coat he was holding up registered on her mind, then standing patient as he went behind her and helped her into it.

He stepped back around to the front of her and reached out without a word to draw her in to him. They stood that way and forced themselves not to cry. Or perhaps Maura had run out of tears in the night.

Finally, he leaned back. "Hey. Is it safe to assume you're supposed to work today?"

"I was. I called Mr. Beller and told him what happened. I said I'd try to get through the day anyway, but he ordered me off work until I felt ready to come back. Nice, huh?"

"Real nice. He's a good man."

"What did you need to talk about?"

Coal looked at her. He hadn't built the courage to break down and tell her all that was in his heart. He didn't have the strength to tell her how Slugger's death, and especially the way it had happened, was tearing him apart. He couldn't talk about how hopeless Slugger's choice to go out that way had made the whole world feel. He had to make it seem like this was all about her.

"I want to go away."

She stared at him, her eyes jumping back and forth between his. Her expression bordered on panic.

"What? Why? Where?"

"You're missing 'how,' but you sound like a list of questions my teacher used to hand out to help us start a book report." Coal smiled but couldn't laugh. Maura managed a silent laugh, but sadness held her face a prisoner as she dropped her chin down to her chest, then finally forced herself to look back up.

"What are you doing, Coal? I don't think you should go." He wasn't very smart about women, but he was guessing she really meant she didn't *want* him to go.

"I was hoping I could talk you into going with me."

Again, she mined his eyes for a sign that he wasn't playing with her. "Wait—are you serious? With you where?"

"I don't care. I don't know. Just somewhere. We're leaving. And we'll come back when we come back."

This time she actually released a real laugh, but a laugh of incredulity. "What about my horses? And Chewy and Dart? And . . . And you can't just walk off your job like that, can you?"

He took both of her shoulders in a firm grip. "Listen. Since I came back to this valley, I've been put through the ringer. I've been shot at, beaten up, watched several friends murdered, almost lost two girls I really love, because of our pathetic legal system . . . Then I almost had to throw one of my best buddies in prison, and now this with Slugger. This county owes me a vacation. They can't expect any man to keep dealing with this kind of strain day after day without a break."

"So what about me? My horses and dogs."

"We're going over there right now and bring them all back here. My mom and the kids will take care of them—there's no worry there. And then I guess I have a few phone calls I have to make."

He had the couth not to say it, but he would take special joy in telling Deputy Jordan Peterson that he was not taking this little vacation all by himself.

CHAPTER TWO

Coal sat at his desk making "one last phone call", with Maura half asleep on the chair she had dragged from the front of the desk and put beside his. She looked sweet and innocent in her sleep—two things she quite often didn't portray in her waking state. Part of him wanted to take her home and let her go back to bed. She must have had as long and haunted a night as he had, for not only had she grown fond of Slugger as everyone else had, but he was sure she wasn't accustomed to people taking their lives right in front of her.

Without telling him anything specific, while Maura was showering Connie had confided in him that she had already started having nightmares, and he was afraid those would get worse as time went on. The one thing his mother had hinted at was that the nightmares might have nothing whatsoever to do with Slugger, and that troubled him more than anything, because in that case there was no way he could help her. Still, he kept telling himself it would be best if any nightmares she was going to have hit her in the next few nights, when he could be there to comfort her. Coal's biggest surprise of all was not to hear Connie preaching to him about his planned getaway with Maura. In fact, she had spoken about it as if they were man and wife.

In his head, Coal checked off the list of people he had intended to call. Flo was last. Oh! And he had to contact the interim State policeman who was taking Willie Stinger's spot until after his hearing. The officer needed to be warned that his call volume could be going up with Coal gone.

Flo answered the phone in her sweetest possible morning voice.

"Hi, Flo."

Oh! Hello, Coal. Hey—how are you doing?

"Better than yesterday."

I hope so. I was sure sorry to hear about your friend.

They spoke for a little while about that, and the depth of her heart was evident even through the phone line. Finally, he broke the news to her that he would be far out of radio contact for at least a few days and that the state policeman would be handling any calls where Jordan needed help.

Oh! Coal, that reminds me . . . Someone called yesterday and left a message for you. A young man named Grant? I guess he's an officer from the western part of the state somewhere and he's here to meet you.

"Wait. Really? He's here?"

Yes. I guess he volunteered to help look for your friend yesterday, and everyone was gone when he came back afterward.

"Okay. Bob Wilson told me about some outside guy helping in the search, but I didn't realize it was him. Did he leave a contact number?"

No. But he said he'd try to get you today.

Coal sighed as he hung up. Mr. Grant Fairbourne had better prove to be one patient man if he intended to take the job of deputy here, because he wasn't going to find Coal for days.

Reaching over, he took Maura's arm and shook her gently. "Hey. Miss Sleeping Beauty."

She dragged her eyes open and smiled at him. "You're trying to get me in bed again, aren't you?"

"Ha! I don't work that way. What am I supposed to call you so you don't think that—ugly step sister?"

She laughed, her swollen eyelids almost closing her eyes all the way over, but she didn't have a wisecrack to answer him.

"You're really out of it, Maura. Are you sure you feel like going with me?"

That exploded her eyes open wide. "Yes! Coal, I'm fine. Sorry I was dozing. I guess I won't do *that* again." She seemed a little hurt. "Do you still *want* me to go?"

"I wouldn't have asked you to if I didn't. Why don't you run out and get the car warming up? I'm going to make one last call to the state officer and then we'll be out of here."

He handed her the keys to the LTD. He had told Jordan he would be in the pickup until they returned, since Coal didn't plan on doing any off-roading, and he wanted the most comfortable highway ride he and Maura could get—with a good radio and tape player to boot.

He was close to hanging up with the state policeman, an older man by the name of Gentry, when the outside door opened again, and Maura came back in. Only this time she was tailed by a tall, dark-haired man not much younger than she was.

Coal said goodbye to Officer Gentry and stood up. His reaction to the appearance of Maura's tag-along probably revealed his growing impatience, and he didn't believe he cared. They were already an hour behind in his travel plans—if such they could be called.

"Can I help you?"

The man stepped forward, smiling. "Yes sir, I hope so. My name is Grant Fairbourne. I wrote you last week?"

Inside, Coal let out a sigh, but he didn't let Fairbourne see it. All right. He did need a new deputy, so all desire to rush out of town aside, he at least had to be polite.

"Yeah. Yeah, Grant, I got your letter. I actually did try to call you but didn't get any answer, and I meant to call back, but things kind of blew up around here."

"I know, sir. I'm sorry to hear about your friend. I was part of the hunt yesterday."

"So I hear. I appreciate you jumping in on that."

"Nothing you wouldn't do, I'm sure. I'm sorry to pop in like this, but my family and I drove over from Caldwell because I was hoping to get an interview with you before anyone else could snatch up the job. My folks live in Challis, so I thought we'd kill two birds—"

"With one stone," Coal finished. Grant gave him a grin Coal already knew he could get used to.

Coal gave out another sigh, this one audible. "Well . . . You kind of caught me at a bad time. We were just getting ready to head out of town."

"Oh." Grant looked over at Maura. "I'm sorry, sir. Is this your wife?"

Shaking his head, Coal smiled. "No, no. This is a good friend of mine. Maura? Grant." They shook hands.

"It's really nice to meet you, miss." Fairbourne turned hopeful eyes back to Coal.

"Grant, how long do you plan to be here?"

"Uh, well . . . I'm only on my days off. And I might be able to get one extra, but then I have to get back to work—so I have to leave by Thursday afternoon, tops."

"All right. Well, we might still be gone then."

Although he tried to hide it, Fairbourne appeared almost crestfallen. He looked back and forth between Coal and Maura, searching for anything he could say to turn the tide.

"Say, you went on a church mission, right? Isn't that what I read?"

"Yes, sir. To Monterrey—Mexico."

Coal had just wanted to check to make sure. Otherwise, he really wanted to swear at all this inconvenience.

"Great. A God-fearing man. Maybe you can whip this place into shape."

Grant laughed. "I'd love the opportunity to try. So I know you're on your way out, but . . . Is there time for that interview?"

"You still speak any Spanish?"

"Yes sir. Fluent. And it's Mexican Spanish, so I could interpret for most of the farm workers around the—"

"Listen, Grant," Coal cut him off, "I'm really sorry to be abrupt, but . . . I don't know if my other deputy will be coming back. You understood that, right?"

"Yes sir. But I've been wanting to come back here for so long I had to take a chance."

"So this could be a one or two month job. Maybe three. Four. I don't know. And then if Deputy Mitchell is able to come back to work and the budget won't handle another position . . ."

"Sir, I decided I'll go back to guiding hunts over in Challis for a while if I have to. Until you have a full-time opening here, or one comes up in Challis. I really want to bring my family home."

"You're hired."

Fairbourne stared at him. "Excuse me?"

"I said you're hired. Raise your right hand."

Fairbourne's hand shot up. Coal quoted him the oath as nearly as he could recall it from his own recent swearing in and made him repeat it back to him. When he was finished, he thrust his hand out, and the younger man grabbed it.

"Thank you, sir. Thank you so much." If the man had been a puppy Coal was afraid he would have peed himself. He was practically shaking all over.

"You're welcome. Now I know you'll have to give your employer a couple of weeks or so, right?"

"Yes, I guess I need to."

"You need to. I know what it's like suddenly being short of manpower. We'll suffer another couple weeks. But since you're already here . . ."

He went over and picked up the keys to the pickup Todd Mitchell had been driving. "That brown pickup in the back lot is what you'll use until Deputy Mitchell comes back" —he didn't dare tell Fairbourne how much he hoped Todd *would* come back— "so you might as well get to know it. And you saw where the keys go. Another thing: I can't really pay you until you're actually done with your other job and up here fulltime, but are you interested in getting a jump on the job and getting familiar with things around here before you head home?"

Grant's eyes leaped around the office, trying to take it all in. "Yeah! You bet."

"Do you have something to keep you busy until two or three?"

"Sure. I'll be with my wife and kids."

"Great. Come back up here at—well, let's say three. I'll have a guy waiting here to train you. His name's Jordan Peterson—big guy, almost my size. He'll take good care of you. And I'll warn you right off—you'd better learn fast how to make a good cup of coffee, or you're going to last about one day."

Fairbourne laughed. "Don't worry. I don't drink it, but most of my department does, and when I was the rookie . . . Thick and black as tar, right?"

Coal grinned. "You're going to do all right."

The three of them left the jail together, and Coal called Flo on the radio as they drove to the end of the driveway at Courthouse Drive and stopped. He asked her to give Jordan a call and have him to the jail by three and to be ready to show a new deputy some of the ropes, and then, feeling only a little bad about turning such an important duty over to a guy who was still learning the job himself, he headed down off the Bar.

When they reached the turn-off to Highway 91, he stopped in the middle of the road.

He looked at Maura, struck by her already attentive blue eyes. "If I don't tell this car where to go, it's going to go wherever the road goes. You know that, right?"

"Will you be behind the wheel?"

"I hope so."

"Then I don't really care where the car goes."

CHAPTER THREE

Coal had to admit his first instinct in life was always to head for Montana, and since Maura didn't have a preference, that was just what he did. He had planned ahead on just about one thing, the most important thing possible on any worthwhile trip: An eight track tape of Marty Robbins was protruding from the deck. Now he pushed it in. The first song playing was "Big Iron." It was going to be a great trip.

There had been so many times when Coal's whole family was packed into Connie's Chrysler, or, in other cases he had a crowd in the pickup cab, so it had become normal for Maura to sit right next to him, and for her leg to be pressed against his for an entire drive. Today, however, she didn't have that reason, and she started out the trip sitting next to her own door, a world away. She seemed to be studying the scenery with great interest: the mountains, the river, the animals, the old barns and cabins and crossbuck fences along the highway. The stuff of picture postcards made to tell people back home what a piece of paradise a traveler was in. It all seemed to fascinate Maura even more than usual this bright morning. With all the fresh snow still frosting it like a gigantic, complicated cake, Coal couldn't blame her. It had a special beauty today.

Coal didn't know if Maura had thought about scooting over. But he killed twenty minutes hoping she would. Her resolve—or was it apathy?—outlasted his.

"Hey."

She looked over, her face calm. Her eyes asked, *What?* but her voice said nothing.

"Are we still friends?"

Her lip corners lifted slightly.

"There's still a seatbelt in the middle."

No change in her expression. On any normal day, she would have made some wisecrack. But Slugger Janx had leaped to his death in front of them only twenty-four hours ago. Levity was not something anyone would find today in the LTD.

Unbuckling her seatbelt, Maura slid closer. She dug out the middle seatbelt and fastened it, then looked down and saw the half-inch between them. Apparently, two feet was fine, but half an inch was not to her liking, so she shoved her hip closer until he couldn't have slipped onion skin paper between them. And that was fine. He didn't have any onion skin paper anyway.

Taking his invitation a step further, Maura put her hand on his leg, waking things in him that needn't be awake at the start of a long road trip. And thus, they drove to North Fork, made the right turn to head up Lost Trail Pass, and listened to Marty Robbins croon his "gunfighter ballads and trail songs". Just shy of the Continental Divide Coal turned east onto Highway 43, and they went coasting through their first stretch of the Beaverhead National Forest, in the Bitterroot mountains of Montana.

It was an idyllic day, with a dim three-quarters of the waning gibbous moon hanging still, ethereal, in the calm blue sky, like a wonderful promise of good fortune. Sunlight sparkled on snow that was heavy enough up here to bend conifer boughs down like rainbows drained of the color spectrum, and against that snow, which presented itself in tones of blue and purple in the timbered shadows, now and then they could pick out elk, either bedded down or browsing.

Once out of the mountains, they stopped to eat in the little ranching community of Wisdom, hardly a burp in the landscape, and here Coal found out he and Maura had somehow gotten permanently magnetized to each other, for even inside the restaurant she sat so close to him she nearly had to eat with her left hand.

Talk was limited, and with the noon crowd of local ranchers and cowboys making more than enough noise for everyone, he didn't push it. He had plenty to think about, and certainly Maura did too. They would have all the time they could ever need to open up before this trip was over. He would make sure of it.

They drove out of Wisdom through what Grant Fairbourne would probably refer to as God's country—and he would be right. It was a wonderfully lonesome landscape, with ranches speckling the snowy range at wide intervals, and a lot of open country for livestock and wildlife to graze. But eventually they climbed back into the Beaverhead National Forest, shooting along through the deep timber. In spite of the temperature outside, in this corridor Coal couldn't resist rolling his window down. He started to reach for the fan switch, to turn the heater up for Maura, but she lay a dissuading hand over his.

"Let's let it be cold for a while."

He sighed, contented. Maura was more like him than either of them would admit.

Forty to fifty-five mile an hour winds, the speed of the car, drove the perfumed scent of the pine, fir, and spruce into the close space inside. Maura beside him, a long, smooth road ahead, and the aroma of conifer forest. Coal had made it to heaven.

The bustling mining community of Butte, although pretty and historic, was only a place for Coal to change directions. Now he headed almost due east, through a land of golden and amber meadows of grass and the haggard brown remnants of wildflowers knifing into stands of black timber. Maura gave his leg a hard squeeze out of surprise and delight when a massive mule deer with his trophy-size rack not yet discarded, and sitting upon his head like the finest of crowns, darted across the road in front of them.

At Bozeman, just three hours after departing Wisdom, Coal took a detour through downtown. He couldn't pass here without letting Maura see the huge, rearing plastic palomino that turned on a carousel over the western wear store. That giant stallion Coal referred to as "Trigger" was nothing short of a landmark for him and the children.

After the slow cruise through Bozeman, it was only another half hour to the cowtown of Livingston, which, lacking the university atmosphere that existed in Bozeman, was much more to Coal's liking.

They stopped here for a sandwich, and Coal let Maura have his right side this time, just to see if he could fumble through his meal left-handed as gracefully as she had. Apparently, his comments in the car that morning had made Maura decide to imitate Velcro all day, and he was pretty sure that was fine by him.

He polished off his roast beef and toast before she did, then leaned back and surveyed the room. Two old cowboys sat at a table across from them. Relics of a bygone age. The leathery creases in their necks and cheeks, and around their faded eyes, were trail maps of all the places they had been, and their almost feeble, battered hands seemed barely strong enough now to cut beefsteak. To Coal, it felt tragic. The cycle of life had almost reached its final curtain for those old boys, and they would take a lot of the West with them when they were gone.

Coal turned away from thoughts of growing old. "How are you doing?"

He had picked the moment right after Maura took a huge bite of her sandwich, so she turned and made a disgusted face at him. He started laughing and couldn't stop until she finally choked down her bite and scalded him with her eyes. "Thanks. Great timing."

Coal wiped tears from the corners of his eyes. "I know. Sorry. Are you okay? You've sure been quiet all day."

"You too."

"That's because I *know* how I am. I was wanting to hear from you."

She held his eyes for a while, then finally dropped her gaze to her plate. After a moment, she turned her head to look out the window to her right, but her left hand fumbled its way off her lap onto his leg and lay there, perhaps trying to comfort him, but more likely herself. He realized he had opened a window for her emotions to come through.

At last, she looked back. "Coal, this seems really stupid."

"What?"

"I'm an EMT. I've seen people hurt. I've seen them die. Old people. Little kids. Animals. What's different about this?"

Coal drew a deep breath. "Slugger was pretty easy to get fond of, I guess. At least if he knew you were on his side. What a hellcat he could be if you weren't, though!" He chuckled. "Tell me this: Are you saying all those other deaths never affected you?"

She sat there silent for a long time with thoughts bounding around inside her eyes. Then those thoughts began to grow calm. She began slowly to nod.

"No. They did. You know what it is?"

"Tell me."

"I think I used to hold it all in because I didn't have anyone to talk to about it. Ronnie Davis is too hard to open up to, and Jay's so quiet you don't know for sure what he's thinking. And the people I worked with in Ra—" Abruptly, she stopped herself from whatever she had been about to say. She sat there in thought. "Does that make any sense?"

"Sure it does. I guess I used to do that too. At least until I found Erin."

He had just a moment to think of Erin, back in Washington, D.C., and to wonder where her life might have taken her since their painful, hurried goodbye, and if she had found some kind of peace since then.

Pushing Erin's gentle memory aside, Coal continued, "But that kind of silence—keeping things to yourself—that'll rot your insides out."

Maura laughed. Not a happy sort of laugh. "Oh, well that explains my insides then."

When they left Livingston, the big timber eventually faded away from the roadsides, leaving them crossing still almost due east over snow-swept rolling hills and prairie with a scattering of big, unruly pines. The wonderful, sparkling blue Yellowstone River snaked along beside the highway to their right. They paralleled the Yellowstone almost all the way on into Billings, arriving some two and a half hours later because Coal took it slower than any of the other traffic on the highway, as he had done the entire trip.

The Billings Hotel was a historic landmark, built out of red brick and rearing stately and beautiful two tall stories over the old part of town. Coal parked the Ford in front and looked at Maura. "You ready to stretch your legs, or would you rather just stay here until I check in?"

"I'll go with you. I know how men are: I'd better make sure you don't do anything dumb."

He laughed and clapped her on the thigh. "You got me pegged there."

Inside the old lobby, musty-smelling but mingled with the scent of Lemon Pledge furniture polish, Coal took a look around at the beautiful, dark old wood and tile. The ornately carved check-in counter, stained dark red but having turned nearly black, looked like something straight out of *Gunsmoke.*

A heavy-set, middle-aged man with a blond, groomed mustache and make-your-community-proud sideburns smiled at them over the top of the counter. "Welcome. You folks have a reservation?"

"No sir."

"One room?"

Coal's eyes flitted like a leery house fly toward Maura, then off and away. "No, we'll need two."

Maura's hand came up on the counter in front of Coal. "Hold on a second, sir. Coal, can I speak with you?"

Bewildered, he apologized to the clerk and followed her over to where a couch and some soft easy chairs welcomed weary travelers.

"Why two rooms?"

He stared at her, clamping his mouth shut when he realized it was open. "Uhh . . . Okay, what's the punchline?"

"I'm okay to be in the same room with you. Or I'll pay for my own room. You're not paying for mine."

He shrugged. "I guess it's up to you. What's your preference?"

"Can we talk without making fun of each other—just for this once?"

With a little laugh, he said, "Okay. Just this once."

"I don't want to be alone tonight. Okay?"

"I guess. So one room, two beds?"

"Coal . . . Fine, I guess if you feel like you have to."

"Maura." He spoke her name flatly. "You must really hate me."

She read the teasing look in his eyes and giggled. "Yeah, that must be it."

"I'm getting two beds."

"I said—do what you have to."

He sighed and searched her eyes and wondered what reasons this woman thought he had brought her here for. Walking over to the clerk again, he dropped his wallet on the countertop, and flopped down his hand, with two fingers splayed out.

"One room, two beds. A long ways from each other," he added, looking over at Maura with raised eyebrows and a mock look of sternness.

"But only one set of covers," Maura told the clerk with a wink.

The clerk finally laughed. "You folks are too much. Well, the beds are unfortunately already made, ma'am . . . or *miss*. Any arrangements you two decide to make once you're in there, that's purely your business."

Although it seemed Maura's intention was to try and make the two men uncomfortable, now she was the first to turn red. She laughed to cover her embarrassment, walked over to the sitting area, and plopped down in one of the chairs.

Coal could feel her eyes on him the whole time he was filling out the registration papers.

CHAPTER FOUR

Oglala, South Dakota
Same day

At the front of the dilapidated, boarded-up general store where once he had sold his dyed quill work on pieces of leather, old Chessie Bad Milk stared at both shattered halves of his cane where they lay yards away along the corroded decades-old sidewalk. He wished he had inherited the cane his father used to have leaning behind the door of their shack, which they convinced him was made of a bull phallus. He was pretty certain Asa Iron Rope could never have broken that one. Chessie's father had taught him more than once how hard and unbreakable it was.

There was a time in the old days when the young people of the Lakota nation honored their elders. Older men were referred to as *Grandfather* and older women as *Grandmother,* and they were terms of high respect. Now all was beginning to change. To brutal young men like Asa Iron Rope and his friends, nothing was sacred. And no one was safe from their idea of "having fun."

Under his shapeless once-black hat, Chessie's badly thinning hair was dark gray, light gray and yellow-gray threads, all wound and twisted, kept from falling apart by months of grease that came from his own scalp, from food, or even from motor oil. Any oil was good enough, if it did the job. His only mirror was the window of a car he might pass, or the windows in structures around the settlement, but with his finger he could feel that the creases through his face were sometimes knuckle-deep—and especially if he used the finger he had sliced the tip off years ago cutting up a melon. Chessie had grown old, and an unfortunate meeting with a delivery truck two years ago had rendered him mostly crippled. Now he was a target for all the bad boys on the Pine Ridge Reservation. He was only fifty-eight years old, but he had already passed the life expectancy for a man here on the Rez by more than a decade.

The skies were gray, with a thin sheet of cloud, more like a film, that barely concealed the sun. It had been a dry start to winter, and not extremely cold, but among their other fun, Asa Iron Rope and his friends had torn off his coat and thrown it far down the street. And without a coat even thirty-five degrees would kill an old man who was as thin as a praying mantis.

Far down the sidewalk, Chessie could see two forms standing in front of the church. Among other things, age had taken much of his eyesight. But from what he could see, these figures were smaller than men. And he could see the shadows of their eyes. They were watching him.

It took a few minutes of the two beings swiveling their heads to look all around them before they ventured down the sidewalk, which more closely resembled a mountain trail now, after the decades of rotting and spalling and heaving in the cold and heat.

The faces came clearer: a couple of the more decent citizens of this wide spot in the road called Oglala. They were young Joseph and Billy, who were joined together by identical tragedy: Their mothers had died in car accidents—neither of the deaths connected—and their fathers had both been taken by the bad liver disease. The boys had been fortunate enough to be adopted into the home of ancient Lakota humanitarian Maybelle Littlebrave, who had taken in many young people over the years—and had saved many lives.

"Hau, young boys," Chessie hailed. "You wanna help a old man?"

Joseph and Billy didn't need to be asked. Already, one was splitting off to go after Chessie's coat. The other came on, closer and closer until Chessie recognized Joseph, who had the unfortunate last name, passed down through generations, of one simple word: Afraid.

Joseph crept on, now very leery of his surroundings. The creases in Chessie's face deepened as he smiled, thinking maybe Joseph had well earned the name Afraid. But then Chessie sure didn't blame him—not with the way the Rez was today.

"Hau, Grandfather. You okay?"

"I will be. If mebbe you c'n get me a board or somethin' I c'n walk with. An' that coat would sure be good. It's colder than I thought out here."

That last part didn't need to be said, for Billy was walking over now with the coat, and he crouched in front of Chessie. "I'm sorry about those men, Grandfather. Grandmother Maybelle says they don't know no good."

"You sure she didn't say they don't know no better?" asked Chessie as he gratefully took the coat from Billy's outstretched hand.

"Oh, maybe. Maybe they don't know no better. But our friend Paul says they just ain't no good, an' that's that."

"I don't disrespect Maybelle Littlebrave," said Chessie, "but I think maybe Paul is right. Did you boys see what happened?"

"Yes, Grandfather," Joseph replied. "If I was bigger, I would have come down here an' showed them how to treat you right."

Chessie laughed, touching the sore place on his cheek where he could tell some of his paper-thin skin had been torn away. "Well, I ain't hurt much. It's no big trouble. I sure wish I had my cane back, though."

"It's okay," said Billy with a grin. Billy's last name was Pierre. It had been passed down from one of the many French trappers who had come through the area a century ago and taken a wife among the Lakota. "Grandmother has two canes. I know she'll give you one."

It ended up that Billy was right, and Chessie should have known he would be. When Maybelle made her way out of the church and saw them gathered together, she hobbled down on her two canes to see if everything was all right.

"Yer too old t' be settin' on the cement," ancient Maybelle said, her eyes glinting through the folds of her eyelids like polished obsidian.

"Yep. I was waitin' for you."

Maybelle seemed to have used up all her smiles. Or maybe she was too old and tired. Maybe too discouraged by how the people of the Rez had become. But at least she tried, and her eyes almost completely vanished in the attempt.

"I got two o' these," she said, raising up both canes and shaking them. "An' see? I don't hardly need them, neither one."

"I'll make you a new one," Chessie promised. "I'll carve it out of a piece of chokecherry, if we c'n find it." And he would. Unless the bad liver disease took him first.

*　　*　　*

After taking their luggage in the room, Coal and Maura left to take a walking tour of downtown Billings. Historic buildings and impressive architecture were something Coal had always loved to study, but right now they were the last things on his mind. Maura was here with him, the world was all very far away, and they had a single hotel room—which had not been his intention coming here. He wondered if he would be strong enough to make it through the night.

They ate supper at a quaint little mom and pop café lit mostly by kerosene lanterns, for ambience. They were playing Herb

Alpert and the Tijuana Brass very softly in the background, and wreaths of cigarette smoke drifting around from the other patrons made it feel a little like they were dining in a prehistoric cave.

Afterward, they had a good two hours of daylight left, so they went down and wandered the north bank of the Yellowstone, stopping now and then to toss rocks into the water and watch the ripples being carried away downstream.

Coal would have liked to sit for a while and watch the river roll by, but it was around forty-five degrees, the vegetation on the banks was moist, and they had nothing to sit on. So when it looked like they had half an hour left before dark, and the sun was starting to set in the western sky behind them, they turned and headed back to the car.

Maura boldly reached out and took his hand. Finally. He smiled at her and watched the sun set in her eyes.

Back in their room, Coal took off his coat and helped Maura off with hers, and then he hung them both up in the closet. "Do you want to watch TV?" the woman asked. "The marquis outside said it's colored."

"You choose. I'm not much for it, but I guess this is supposed to be a vacation, right?"

"We can talk if you'd rather do that. Or just sit quiet."

"We've been doing a lot of that already—the quiet part."

Maura drew a deep, chattering breath and walked close to him. Reaching out, she took his hands. "Can I tell you something? I hope it doesn't sound bad."

"What?"

"I think I've realized today that I don't really need to talk about Slugger. It's felt good to just be with you all day. To know you're probably thinking the same things I am. Does that make any sense?"

He smiled. "It does. I've been thinking the same thing."

"I do wish this world could be a kinder place though. I don't know why people are so cruel to each other."

A shake of his head was all he could answer.

"Will you hold me tonight?"

He searched her eyes. He realized one of the reasons he was having a hard time replying to her was that his heart was racing, and now it sped up even more—Corvette speed.

"You're sleeping in that bed over there, right?"

She lowered her eyebrows, giving him a mock angry frown. "Am I? Really?"

He dropped her hands, reached out, and took her by the shoulders, pulling her to him. "Come here." They stood for a long time wrapped in a soft embrace. "Maura, I don't want you ever to think I'm one of 'those' guys."

"I know you aren't."

"Just don't forget that. Ever."

A few minutes later, Maura decided to go shower. She picked up everything she needed and headed for the bathroom, and Coal thought he heard the door shut. He got up to wash his hands in the sink, which was outside the shower and toilet room. As he turned the corner, his shocked eyes fell on Maura, standing there still in her Levi's, but down to only her flesh-colored bra on top.

He stared at her. She stared back. Neither moved until Coal whirled away, stumbling back to the darkness and safety of the room.

"I'm really sorry about that," he said to the plastered wall.

Maura said nothing back.

When the shower water was running behind a closed door, Coal got up off the bed again and washed his hands. He took off his shirt in front of the mirror and thought about Maura, about what he had seen, and what she hadn't tried to conceal—an ugly scar down the very center of her chest.

Going back to the bed, he pulled off his boots and socks but left his jeans on and got into the farthest queen-size bed. He heard the shower room door open a little later, and he thought he could hear the faint sound of Maura running a brush through her wet hair. He lay paralyzed. Petrified. He thought of Annie. Of Kathy. Of Erin. He thought of beautiful, joyful Laura on their wedding day, and disillusioned, drug-addicted, and broken Laura's body, being rolled away from him on a gurney.

Of all the things someone could say of Coal Savage, there was one thing they could not: that he was a philanderer. He had given himself fully to one woman, and that was Laura. So he waited in the half-dark for Maura, and he tried desperately to think of what he would tell her when she came to him.

CHAPTER FIVE

Half-dark became full dark when Maura came out of the bathroom and switched off the light. A few seconds later, she turned it back on and looked around the corner, her eyes falling first on the closer bed, then sweeping to the other one and making Coal out under the covers there.

"Why the far bed?" she asked.

The first thing to Coal's mind was his answer: "Did you want this one?"

For quite a few seconds she stood there, one hand on the section of wall that served as a divider between the bedroom area and the bathroom. Finally, leaving the light on, she walked over and sat down on the other bed, facing Coal. She was wearing a long blue shirt and what appeared to be pajama bottoms.

"Is that what you want?"

Coal struggled up out of the bed and sat on the edge, knowing their relationship from here forward could change in drastic ways depending on what he said and did tonight. He couldn't lie there looking apathetic to her.

"What do *you* want? I'm a man. You can't ask me what I want at a time like this."

"I already said. I want you to hold me."

His heart was pounding, and those words didn't help. He stood and held out a hand that was almost trembling, and she rose and came to him. They met in no-man's land between beds, and once again he took her in his arms.

"Did you want the light on, or off?" he asked.

"Maybe leave it on."

He nodded. "Maura, I have to tell you something. I've never been with anyone but my wife."

After digesting this for a while, she said, "That's okay."

"I need you to understand what I'm trying to say."

She buried her face deeper in his chest. "I need you to want me, Coal."

He almost laughed. "Well, you've got that part sewn up."

"Promise?"

"I promise."

"Then if you only want to hold me all night, that's okay. As long as I know how you feel."

He turned and laid back the covers, and she crawled in. He went around the other side because he was used to being on the left, both with Laura, and now with Dobe, and old habits die hard.

Snuggling up against her and drawing her tightly in to him, he wondered if he had any clue yet how long this night was going to be.

He lay there listening to her breathe, and then, minutes later, listening to her cry, while she tried not to let him know.

In time, she sniffled herself to silence, and half an hour passed, but neither of them slept a second. "You saw it, didn't you?"

Coal froze. He knew she was referring to her scar, but he thought about playing it off. And then he remembered how much Maura liked blunt honesty.

"I did. I didn't mean to."

Another long stretch of silence. "Were you going to ask me how I got it?"

"No."

"Why?"

"I thought you would tell me if you felt like it."

"Do you *want* to know?"

He had to think about that. "I'm not sure. Would it change anything between us?"

Her silence this time was almost devastating. He almost
wanted to sit up and confront her. But still he waited.

"If I tell anyone about it, I want it to be you. But I don't know
what will happen to me if I do."

He had no answer for that until she probably started to wonder
if he had gone to sleep. Then he told her, "I'm here if you ever
decide to talk about it. But I'll never bring it up again."

She snuggled back so she was even closer to him, like his personal torture machine in the flesh. He lay thinking about clouds,
and seashores, and forests, and icy cold showers. His arm went to
sleep long before he did, but, in time, he too was gone. He remembered dreaming, and even in his dream he knew he still wanted to
be awake.

An hour or two later, Maura woke up swinging and crying out.
Coal flew off the other side of the bed, bewildered. He watched her
standing between the beds like a fighter, ready to take on anyone
or anything that approached her. Finally, a light came on in her
eyes. He knew when she looked at him that she was Maura
PlentyWounds again, awake and alert.

Her face contorted in pain, she rushed around to him and fell
against him, and he held her while she cried, knowing some kind
of devil was here playing with them tonight.

At last, he got into bed, lying on his back, and she lay across
him as he had done with her so long ago in his mother's room.
Mercifully, his body had forgotten its craving for her now.

She finally said, "They were here. Right in this room. And last
night too—at your house."

His answer was to pat her back. If she wanted him to know
who "they" were, she would tell him.

"His name was . . . Leland Iron Rope."

It was a strange-sounding name, but he guessed no more odd than PlentyWounds, or TrueBear. "Who was he?"

"The man who . . . hurt me. The man who made them . . ." Here, she stopped, and again her tears flowed free.

There was no more talk.

Wednesday, January 24

"Last night I was a monster," Maura said.

Coal leaned up against his pillow, at the head of the bed. Maura lay on her back beside him. "You weren't a monster."

"I was. I'm so sorry, Coal. I should have given you some kind of warning."

"There was no reason to."

She gave a laugh and wriggled up so her back was against the flat of the headboard with his, then frowned at him. "No *reason?* You had no way to know what you were in for last night. That's a reason."

"Okay. So can I ask you something about this?"

She looked back and forth in his eyes and finally gave an almost indiscernible shrug.

"Do you always have these nightmares?"

This time she shook her head, and adamantly. "No. Not for a long time."

"What brought them back? Something to do with me?"

"No, Coal. No. This is nothing to do with you."

He believed that she believed this. Beyond that, he didn't know. "How can I help it stop?"

"I thought it *had* stopped. I came to Salmon, and I thought I left it all behind. But now I guess I don't know how to stop it. I'm afraid I never will."

"Sometimes you have to face your fears head on."

Her eyes filling up with fear, she jerked her head back and forth and jumped up out of bed, whirling to face him. "No. No, not something like this. You don't have any idea how bad it is. There's no way you ever could! Don't you ever even try to suggest that."

"All right. I won't."

"Sorry, Coal. Do you want to take me back home?"

"Hey. We're on a getaway, remember? Give it a chance."

In the shower a few minutes later, he thought about that. A chance? What were he and the woman doing here? By being on this trip they were risking everything they had together—all the fun, all the sarcastic banter, all the companionship. And for what? Maybe for a regular guy he could answer that. But for Coal Savage, who had never been with anyone but his wife and whose life seemed to have begun and ended with her, what was this trip really all about?

He dried off and dressed in the bathroom, so that when he came out he already had on everything except his boots. Maura was sitting on the bed watching *Captain Kangaroo* on the pathetic little TV that sat glued to the top of the dresser at the foot of the bed, its forlorn rabbit ears sticking up, with one of them bent almost sideways. The Captain appeared to be in the middle of a nasty eastern Montana blizzard. It was black and white.

"I thought the sign said 'colored TV'."

"I did too. The outside is brown—I guess that's color."

Coal grinned. He knew that at least for the moment he had his old Maura back when she looked him up and down and said, "So I don't even get to see you in your underwear?"

"Right! You saw me with my shirt off, I saw you in a bra. Now we're almost even."

She threw her pillow at him.

After breakfast, they headed down the road, Coal with a specific destination in mind he was keeping as a surprise from her. After Hardin, they headed almost due south, and it was only ten-thirty in the morning when they pulled off the highway at a little place called Garryowen and went to visit the site of the Battle of the Little Bighorn—the fabled "Custer's Last Stand".

Maura was quiet all the way through the gate. Once they were inside, she looked around them at the dead grass, and the sagebrush jutting out of the prairie snow. "I've never been here before."

"It's a lot nicer later in the year."

She went quiet again until they stood surveying all the markers on Last Stand Hill, where Custer and his last little group of men had fallen. Coal had always had a fascination with one of Custer's officers, an Irish captain by the name of Miles Keogh, whose horse, Comanche, was the famous "only survivor" on the side of the Army and who had led many parades carrying his saddle and Keogh's backward-facing boots until his death fifteen years after the battle. He meant to take her to the place they said Keogh had fallen.

"You realize that my ancestors were killing yours right here, don't you?"

The comment took Coal by surprise. He looked over at the woman and studied her for a moment. "You know, last I remember you have more Irish in you than Lakota. Seems like your ancestors were killing each other."

This got a frown out of her, and that surprised him. Did she really identify so much with her Lakota blood, which he remembered her telling his mother had started getting diluted way back with her paternal grandfather? For some reason, he had never caught this side of her. In fact, considering all of the bad it seemed like she had experienced with her full-blooded Lakota husband, Nyle TrueBear, from what she had told him, he was a little surprised she would want to identify with her Lakota blood at all.

Either way, between that little conflict in their minds, and the feel of the ghosts that seemed to haunt the Little Bighorn, they drove away from there two hours later with a sober feeling in the car.

Some time later, they crossed over into Wyoming, paralleling the mighty Bighorn Mountains for a while, passing incredible country that in any season of the year would take the breath away. They ate dinner in the town of Buffalo, another historical place Coal always loved to visit, and the weather had turned so nice that they stood on the bridge over Clear Creek, which ran right through the heart of town, and watched the wide, icy waters for a long time.

It was here Coal finally decided to ask her, "Hey, back at the battlefield, it seemed to make you a little ticked off when I mentioned how you were more Irish than Lakota."

She stared at him for a moment. "I wasn't *ticked off,* Coal. It's just the opposite. If I could go back in time and erase every drop of Lakota blood from my body I'd do it today."

CHAPTER SIX

Coal headed east after Buffalo, and they were driving for five minutes before Maura caught the change in direction. When she started looking around, she suddenly seemed to realize what road they were on. She turned to Coal.

"Hey, where are we going?"

"East."

"Oh. Well, I thought maybe we could go south."

This was Maura's first real input into where Coal drove on this trip. "Okay. Any particular reason?"

"No, I've just never been that way."

"So how about we get to Gillette, and then we can head south. I was looking at the map earlier, and if we do that it will take us through a place called Thunder Basin National Grassland. That sounds kind of neat, huh?" Or at least it would have if it hadn't been January.

After several moments' thought, she drew her shoulders way up almost to her ears, in a long, lazy shrug. "Yeah, sure. And then where does it go?"

"A little town called Douglas. I've heard of it before, in a song by Eddy Arnold. I always wondered what kind of a place it was."

"Then I guess we're destined to go," she said with a smile, and she leaned far over on him, took his biceps in her hand, and closed her eyes.

It was an hour and a half through a vast, rolling country of sagebrush and dirt to Gillette, and here, true to his word, Coal turned due south. For the last several miles before Gillette, Maura had seemed nervous, constantly reading road signs, fidgeting, and looking around. After he made the turn, she settled back down, snuggling into him even closer than before, if possible.

The Thunder Basin Grassland, to Coal, was remarkable, even though what would have been beautiful greens now lay dormant and had turned to yellows, browns, and grays. It seemed a piece out of the nation's past, before all the over-grazing had destroyed so much of the range and turned it to tumbleweed and prickly pear.

A feeling of peace seemed to come over Maura as well, and although she didn't say much about the grassland, her sharp eyes scanned it constantly, and now and then she would let out a big sigh. He wondered if something primeval, deep in her genetic makeup, was calling to her. In times past, grass country like this would have drawn her great grandparents' nomadic people with a promise of bison a-plenty, the Lakota's very source of life.

As the grasslands turned at last once more to dominating sage, she squeezed his arm hard again, leaned her head over, and it wasn't long before he could tell by the sound of her breathing she was asleep.

By the time they got to Douglas, which turned out to be another quaint little cowtown from straight out of the Wild West, they had had a seven-hour day, thanks to Coal's choice to drive fifty-five miles an hour and an hour for lunch.

Maura shrugged her shoulders to staying in Douglas or moving down the highway another hour or so to Lusk, so Coal, wanting to get a step farther ahead, drove on.

Lusk was a pleasant surprise, showing off a neat little down-town area where a wonderful collection of mostly red or orange brick buildings with tall windows, beautiful facades, and decorative parapets proclaimed the little town to be of perhaps more value than it really was.

But value, like beauty, is in the eye of the beholder, and in spite of its lack of looming mountains, Lusk, in its structure and ambience, reminded Coal a little of Salmon, so to him it was a beautiful place.

They got a room there, then spent what remained of the afternoon walking through shops and eating at a locally owned restaurant that specialized in some of the best pork barbecue Coal had ever tasted.

Coal went to bed shirtless, but with his jeans on again, belt included. Maura laughed as she snuggled up to him and faded off to sleep much quicker than the night before.

Around three in the morning, she woke up crying. And Coal could get nothing out of her, so he just lay there and held her until they both fell back to sleep.

Thursday, January 25

The ice of the world outside could be felt right through the hotel's windows when Coal woke up too early the next morning, but the skies were once again clear. He put on his shirt and stood at the window, surveying the quiet gray street below. He had to admit that for obvious reasons he was glad the weather kept holding. But at the same time he dreaded the drought the West was in for this summer if snow didn't start to fall soon.

Maura had had a restless night, and he wondered how she would hold up today. But he had places he still wanted to go, and at the same time he knew they couldn't avoid going home forever. So, with Maura lying there in sleep, which had finally, mercifully, been granted her, he went and took a shower, even though he knew it couldn't be much later than five-thirty. He was determined to make an early start today.

After his shower, he snuggled up for a last few minutes with Maura, nuzzling her neck to try and wake her up. Considering the

volatile way she had been waking up the last two nights, he hoped
that wasn't a dangerous move. He used that possibility of danger
as an excuse to hold onto her tightly.

But the bad spirits must have fled from Maura, and when she
came awake it was with a slow, lazy yawn. She raised her shoulder
against his nuzzling and his tickly mustache and pressed her head
back against him. "Mmm . . . Wow, you're better to wake up to
than the dogs."

She giggled, and he laughed with her. "I sure hope so. I'm not
sure I even know how to take that."

Reaching back, she put her hand on the back of his head and
pulled his face deeper into her neck. "Yes you do."

He kissed her neck, and she pulled away and rolled over to face
him. "I bet my breath smells like a cow," she said, smiling and
making her sleepy eyes close almost over.

"Good thing I like cows."

She laughed, at the same time pretending to be offended.
"Wow. You don't have to agree so fast."

He smiled. Her face was less than a foot away from his. His
heart was pounding, and all of a sudden he felt short of breath.
Leaning closer, he saw her lips part, just before his own met them
in a soft kiss. Softness soon led to something more passionate, and
soon his fingers were twisted in her hair, drawing her close to him,
and her hand pulled insistently at the back of his neck. He never
even noticed her breath, whether it smelled like a cow or like pep-
permint gum.

Coal felt like he was on the verge of caving in when without
warning Maura's hand was on his shoulder, and she eased him
back from her and drew in a deep breath. "Wow." She looked up
at him, her eyes full of wonder and wanting. "I guess whatever my
breath smells like didn't bother you."

He laughed. "I guess not."

"You *do* still want me, don't you?" Her question was voiced more like a statement.

Another laugh. "I guess I'm too obvious."

"Good. What time is it?"

"Twenty to six, maybe."

She rolled her eyes. "You're like a cowboy in the Old West, aren't you? *Get up!"* she quipped. *"We're burnin' daylight!"*

Coal reared his head farther back from her in pleased amazement. "Wait—you know John Wayne?"

"Ha! Of course. I've seen them all. Apparently, you haven't hung around with me enough."

Coal laughed, and they talked about John Wayne's recent release, *The Cowboys,* from which Maura had taken her quote. Coal's boys still called the movie *John Wayne and the Cowboys,* even though his name in the movie was Wil Anderson. The movie ended up being somewhat of a tear jerker, and all four of his children were crying when tough old Wil Anderson succumbed to the wounds inflicted upon him by the evil Bruce Dern and was buried on the lonely prairie on the way to Belle Fourche, South Dakota.

Maura's demeanor once again changed, about the time Coal mentioned South Dakota. She got quiet and reserved, and he knew the romance was over for now. That was for the best anyway.

She got up and gathered her clothing, heading for the shower and leaving him lying there in the dark, contemplating life.

*   *   *

Standing in front of the mirror, Maura peeled off her pajama bottoms and her underwear. She stood for a long time looking at her torso through her long shirt, thinking as hard as her heart had started to pound she might see it throbbing right through the soft cotton fabric.

Angrily, she swiped at the tears that had started to well up in her eyes. She was a grown woman. She had moved on. She was tough. Everyone said she was. Coal included. There was no reason she should be living in her past. And yet it seemed like every night her past came to live with her.

She grabbed her brush and started jerking it through her tangled hair. It caught and tore out of her hand, flinging to the floor, where the hard plastic handle broke in half. She swore and stared at it. Snatching the brush half off the floor, she made do with it, finishing her hair . . . stalling.

At last, fighting back her tears, she grabbed the sides of her shirt and slowly drew it over her head. Her eyes were transfixed on the mirror. The angry scar glared back from where it ran down her breastbone, and at the bottom of it, centered directly between and at the bottom of her breasts, was a little loop, making the scar resemble a noose. She stared at it until she couldn't see it anymore through her tears, then folded to the floor and leaned up against the wall, reaching out to draw her legs close to her body. She didn't know how clean this floor was, and it didn't matter. She had no strength to rise. She hugged her legs to her body, and in complete and painful silence she wept.

Later, as she washed, she thought of all that had been done to her as a girl. The violence she had lived through. The torture. The mental and emotional anguish, the physical pain, the loneliness. She wanted the strength to destroy something. Anything that got in her way. But she couldn't. The very thought of *him* paralyzed her with unreasoning fear, which went far deeper even than the hatred.

As always, she scrubbed hard at the places he had touched, all the places where his skin had been against hers. But it didn't help. Even as she was rinsing, and all the soap ran away, the filthiness remained, even where her skin was rubbed nearly raw. It would always remain.

*   *   *

They ate breakfast in silence in the hotel restaurant. Coal knew something had changed in Maura since their kiss. He wondered if he would ever learn what it was. One thing was certain: He had always seen a haunted look behind Annie Price's eyes, but he had come to learn that Maura PlentyWounds was every bit as haunted as Annie—perhaps more so. Her eyes just didn't show it the same.

He ate his potatoes and steak and tried not to look at her, because she didn't seem to want him to. He dreamed of going back in time, finding her demons, and taking them away from her before they could leave her this sad and afraid and broken.

The sleep Maura had missed in the hotel caught up to her on the drive, as Coal had guessed it would. She actually lay down this time, as much as she was able to, and put her head on his leg, with her feet bunched up against her door.

He was driving east, over the border into Nebraska, thinking without talking it out with Maura that he might drive all the way out to Sioux City, Iowa. But then, just before the town of Chadron, an unfortunate road sign said that turning north would take them to Custer State Park and the Black Hills, along with Mount Rushmore. So, with no input from the slumbering woman, he turned north on Highway 385, headed for South Dakota . . . and destiny.

CHAPTER SEVEN

Near a little place called Pringle, in some beautiful country in the Black Hills National Forest, Maura woke with a start. She sat up, staring around outside with disconcerted eyes. She finally stifled a yawn and looked over to see Coal grinning at her and her swollen eyelids. She smiled back, and the yawn came again, this time full-force.

"Where are we?"

"Coming up to some place called Pringle? It's in the Black Hills."

She stared at him, then turned to scan the country again, her face whitening. Her eyes shot back to drill into his. "The *Black Hills?* What are you doing! Why are we here?"

"Whoa! Whoa. Are you okay?"

"No! I'm not! Why are we here?" She ran her eyes again over the timbered mountains around them. "We're really in South Dakota?" Her eyes said she really knew it, down deep. She was just waking up and getting her bearings to be sure.

"Yes. I thought we'd go up and see Mount Rushmore."

"Stop the car!" she practically screamed.

"Maura!" he snapped back. "What the hell?"

When she jerked her seatbelt off and started across the car seat for the door, he slammed on the brakes. Before the car was all the way stopped, her door was open, and she stumbled out on the road, throwing her arms around in an agitated manner.

A car was coming up behind them, so Coal had to drive forward with the passenger side door hanging open until he could find a wide, grassy spot on the side to pull most of the way off the asphalt. He got out and turned around to see Maura some fifty yards away. She was marching south as fast as she could walk.

Leaving her door open, he took off down the road at a run. Luckily, it had warmed up to the middle thirties, so his lungs were able to handle the run they hadn't been prepared for. As he got close to Maura, she turned and saw him, and then she took off at a trot too.

He caught up to her and grabbed her arm, spinning her around to face him. "Maura—" She struck him in the side of the head, faster than a rattlesnake.

"What are you doing? Why did you take me here?"

Confusion flashed through his brain, at once trying to decide if she had really hit him, and then to figure out why she was so afraid of South Dakota.

He grabbed her by both upper arms and practically yelled into her face: "Maura! Stop it! Just stop!"

She jerked back out of his grasp, staring as if she hated him. She flung her hands up, then down. "I am *not* going up there. You take me back to Salmon—*now!"*

Coal's trip of a lifetime was plummeting into a nightmare from hell. He stared at this woman he suddenly realized he knew nothing about. Many things raced through his mind to say, but he didn't know what would set her off. Unfortunately, even his silence was a catalyst.

She screamed at him to go turn the car around and come back, and he yelled back at her to stop screaming and tell him what was going on. She hit him, this time on the chin, and with her fist.

Holding his chin and staring his shock at her, he wanted to go get the car and keep driving north. Leave her standing out here in the middle of nowhere to find her own way back home. His chin was throbbing. That girl's fury made her strong. But it was the adrenalin flooding through him that hurt the worst—and the shock and confusion. He had no idea what had just happened, or why.

This time before speaking, he backed away. "Maura, you damn well better tell me what's going on—right now."

She stared at him, throwing hate his way like he had never seen in her before. Finally, she whirled again and started walking south. This time he didn't follow.

He went back to the car, shut her door, then got in and started it up. Letting it idle and warm back up for a while, he tried to figure out what to do. The back of his mind was filled with dread at the thought of the long, long road back home to Salmon after this incident, because once he got calmed down enough he knew he couldn't simply leave her out here. He had to take her back. But any magic he had felt with her, any connection, all that was gone now. Gone in one big, howling firestorm of a tornado. He doubted it could ever come back. And the worst thing was not even knowing why.

Rearview mirrors can lie, so he finally turned around to see if Maura was really as tiny as she looked in his mirror. She was. And as far as he could tell, she was still walking.

He drove a ways up the road to find a place to turn around, then headed south. By then, Maura was already maybe a mile away.

He was half a mile from her when he saw a car approaching from the south, and in time it stopped by Maura, and she stopped too. He was two hundred yards away before he realized there was a red light globe on top of the car, and he swore.

Pulling abreast of the car, a South Dakota state patrolman, Coal brought the LTD to a stop. The officer, who had been standing in front of Maura writing in a little notepad, looked over at Coal and didn't see the badge on the side of the LTD because his own car was blocking it. Maura didn't look at all.

"Can I help you, sir?"

"Yeah. Hey, I'm Sheriff Savage, from Salmon, Idaho," he said to set the officer at ease. "She's with me."

In some surprise, the man looked at Maura. "You're with him?"

Without looking over, her arms folded tightly across her chest, she gave a brisk nod.

"Well, I don't know what's going on with the two of you," said the officer, "but it's pretty cold out here. And this isn't that great of a road to be traipsing along in the middle of winter anyway—or ever, for that matter. You know the Pine Ridge Reservation isn't that far from here. Why don't you go get back in the car, ma'am?" Maura stared the other way. She folded her arms even tighter. "Ma'am?"

Repeating that last word must have been a trigger, and Maura dropped her arms and marched around the front of his patrol car, walking to the passenger side of the LTD. Instead of getting in front, she threw open the back door and climbed in.

Coal wanted to get out and speak to the officer, but then he decided he was probably never going to see him again anyway, and really, none of this was any of his business. He raised a hand in farewell, said thanks, and drove down the road.

At the first good wide spot he could find that would accommodate the entire car, Coal pulled over. He put it in park and left it idling, for the heater. Then he reached down and flipped the radio on. They were barely picking up an AM station, and an advertisement for Coca Cola was running, with some people singing about how they would like to "buy the world a Coke,' to the tune of "I'd Like to Teach the World to Sing." It ended, and a deejay introduced Conway Twitty singing, "You've Never Been This Far Before."

The song's title, whatever the words might be, seemed ironic to Coal. He laid his head back against the seat, feeling the tension in the car and trying to draw huge breaths in without sounding like he was. He needed to calm himself back down in the worst way.

They sat there for a good half hour before either spoke, and then it was Maura. He had determined to stay there until dark if he had to, but he wasn't going to be the one to break the silence. His guts told him Maura needed some time to think.

"Are we going to go?"

He reached up and adjusted the mirror so he could see her. For a while, he looked at her, but she wouldn't look at him after one fleeting, angry glance.

"Go where?"

That sent her into another long spell of silence. And then: "I want to go home."

"I wanted to take you to see Mount Rushmore. And this neat place I've been reading about called Bear Country, USA, that opened up last August."

"I don't want to be in South Dakota, Coal. Don't you understand?"

He whirled around on his seat so he could look at her. "Hell no. I *don't* understand. How could I? Why don't you at least give me *something?* Otherwise, this trip has been a big waste of time— and worse."

Her face hardened even more. She went silent. He went silent too, and returned to sitting there listening to the radio play Donna Fargo, singing, "The Happiest Girl in the Whole USA," another song he found terribly ironic in the moment. He had always kind of wanted to slap Donna Fargo whenever the song came on, especially when it got to the part where she sang, "zippity doo dah, thank you, Lord, for making him for me," but the feeling had ramped up ten-fold at the moment. *No one* could be that happy!

A dozen more songs and irritating commercials for things like McDonald's and Head and Shoulders shampoo had played and ended as they sat there, an occasional car passing them and two of the drivers stopping to see if everything was all right. Finally, Maura opened her door and got out, stood outside the car for half a minute making whatever decision she was trying to make, then opened the front door and climbed in, staying far over on her own side.

"Can we go?"

"Where are we going?"

She looked over at him, her lips contorted. "You want to go north, Coal, then let's go north. Turn the damn car around."

"Why?"

"Are you stupid? Turn it around, I said. I want to go north."

"But you don't."

"I do. Can you just turn it around?" Her voice had softened, but almost indiscernibly.

Coal put it in drive and slowly spun it around, only having to back up twice to be headed north again.

Without looking over, he said, "Hey. I don't need to know everything that ever happened to you, Maura. But I need to know *something*. Don't you think you owe me that?"

"You know I lived in Rapid City before."

"You don't talk much about it, but yeah, I knew. So what?"

"Well, that was after the Rez."

"The Rez?"

"I lived on the Pine Ridge Reservation before that. It's where I was born. My family was there for generations."

"Okay." A feeling of huge relief was seeping into Coal's insides, even as his face continued to throb where she had struck him. She was talking! He wasn't sure he had ever wanted to hear her voice again, but now he did.

The car was traveling fifty miles an hour. She stared at the road ahead, then finally snuck a glance at his speedometer. "You know you're never going to get far driving like this. You want me to drive?"

He almost smiled, pressing down farther on the gas. "I think I'll be okay."

"Coal?"

"Yeah."

"Do you remember in Idaho Falls when we took the girls to the counselor?"

"Of course. How could I forget?"

"And I acted bad?"

He recalled that vividly, the confusion he had felt, the embarrassment. And some of the same anger he had felt today, only without the physical pain.

"Yeah. Okay, I remember." He was starting to feel guilty for his anger, but only a little. Sure, he remembered there had been pain in her earlier years, but how could he have known the whole state of South Dakota would trigger it?

"I can't get past South Dakota," she said softly, as if reading his mind. "Even the words make my stomach hurt. I swore I would never come here again."

"But now we're here. I'll turn the car around."

She reached out and put her fingers on his arm. "No. No, Coal. Let's keep going. Even if we go back, we have to drive right past the road that goes to the Rez."

"Oh. Well, I don't want to see you upset anymore."

"I'm all right. Let's just go. I know you were excited about Mount Rushmore. Let's go see it."

"You're sure. You won't hate me tomorrow."

That got a little smile out of her. "No, I won't hate you tomorrow." Tears erupted in her eyes, and he saw.

"Hey. What's wrong?"

She wiped at her cheeks, looking away, as the tears spilled over.

"Come on, girl. What's going on?"

"I hit you, Coal. I hate myself for that, and I'm really sorry." She forced her eyes over to his. "Will you forgive me?"

"I'll never for*get*. My face is going to hurt for days. But of course I forgive you."

She tried not to giggle, but a little one escaped her. She scooted close to him and put her cheek on his arm, her hand on his leg. "I'm really sorry. I'm so embarrassed."

"Nothing to be embarrassed about. Shoot, Cassius Clay has nothing on you—oops! Sorry, forgot. It's *Muhammed Ali.*" The famed boxing champion had changed his name in the mid-sixties, claiming Cassius Clay was his "slave name", when it seemed to everyone on the outside that he was doing it just to escape the draft and going to Vietnam. The trivia that rattled around in Coal Savage's head. He smiled at himself.

* * *

There was snow around Mount Rushmore, so they walked carefully. A few minutes in, Maura stopped him. "Hey." He turned and looked at her. "Will you hold my hand?"

He was glad to. As angry as he had been earlier, his chest had filled up again with feelings for this woman. They held hands the rest of the way up to where the faces looked down at them in grandeur. It was unimaginable what the sculptors had gone through to bring those faces so realistically to life, carved out of the side of a mountain.

After seeing the heads of the presidents, Coal was ready to drive on up through the rest of the Black Hills, visit Deadwood, then head out through Spearfish and make his way back toward Wyoming and Montana.

He told Maura the plan and she only nodded. They drove to Deadwood, although it was far out of tourist season. The history of the place was incredible. Coal could imagine gunfighters and miners filling the town to overflowing, gambling games going full-tilt at every saloon in town, and the deadly poker game where Wild

Bill Hickock himself, going blind at the sad young age of thirty-six, took a bullet to the back of the head from a murderer at the Number Ten Saloon.

When he went to drive out of town, Maura stopped him. "Coal, will you drive the other way?"

"Back the way we came?"

"Yes. For a while."

"Then what?"

"Then . . . I want you to take me to Rapid City."

CHAPTER EIGHT

Coal turned to the right, following Maura's wishes, instead of heading for Spearfish and home. He only got a couple of miles, however, before realizing that he might have been born yesterday, but yesterday some forty-two years ago.

At the first turn-out, he pulled over and stopped, and Maura whipped her eyes over at him with a big question in them he had every intention of answering.

"What are you doing?"

"What am *I* doing? I think a better question is what are *you* doing."

She gave a little shake of her head and leaned a bit back so their faces weren't so close together. "I'm not sure what you're asking."

"All right, let me explain it to you. Not that long ago, I got hit. Twice. And they weren't play hits. They were serious, noggin-busting hits. I'm still sore and have a headache."

Her expression saddened. "I said I was sorry."

"Yes you did. And I forgive you. But I told you I wouldn't forget it, and I won't. I don't want it happening again. So we've got to talk this out, and if I'm not satisfied with what you say, I'm going to turn this car around and start for home."

"Well, I don't know what you want me to say."

"That's because I haven't gotten to the main part yet. It took something pretty bad to make you hit me—especially like that. We've been through a lot of things together, and we've traded a lot of barbs. Most of them were in fun, but not all of them, not at first. But in all those times you never hit me or even acted like you wanted to. I'm not asking you for all the details of your past. I won't pry that deep. But what kind of guarantee do I have that something that upset you so bad a while ago that you would hit me like that when I really hadn't done anything to deserve it won't come up again? I can take a hit pretty good. As good as any man, I think. But taking it from you makes me pretty sad. So?"

"So . . . I still don't know what to say."

"Tell me why we're going to Rapid City when a couple hours ago you would have rather walked home before you would even agree to stay anywhere in the entire state."

Maura's eyes filmed over with tears, which she struggled to blink away, obviously angered that she couldn't control them. When she went to reply, her chin was shaking. "You told me I had to face my fears head on. Or something like that."

"Yeah, I remember saying that. And you told me in no uncertain terms that it was too much for you to do."

"Okay. But when I was here before, I was alone. Now you're here with me. I've decided I need to try."

"I can't protect you from everything."

"I know." Her chin quivered again, and she swiped at her eyes. "I know. I don't expect it to be easy. I just think . . . It might be my last chance to get over what happened."

"You've got to be sure, or I don't want to go."

"Coal, I can't be sure of anything. Only that I want to try—because you're with me."

He finally let out a long sigh. One thing about Maura PlentyWounds: When she made up her mind about something, there was no changing it.

With one long last look at her, he put the car back in drive and pulled out onto the highway. They were Rapid City-bound.

It took something over an hour to get to Rapid City from Dead-wood, in part because Coal kept his foot light on the gas. He wasn't in any hurry to get there, not when he could see how much more distraught Maura was growing almost by the minute.

By now, she was up as tight against him as she could be without crawling right up on his lap. And he had adjusted the rearview mirror just right to see her in it without her realizing he was observing her, so he had seen how in the last ten miles she spent almost more of her time with her eyes shut tight than with them open.

Still five miles shy of where the last highway sign said was Rapid City, Coal pulled over. Maura's eyes jerked open, and she swept the area, then looked up at him. "Are we okay?"

He put his arm around her and squeezed. "You tell me, Maura. Are we?"

She searched his eyes. She said nothing.

"We still have five miles to go. I can still turn around right now if you tell me to. We'll find a room in Deadwood or somewhere for the night, or we can keep on driving until we're back in Wyoming. Tell me what to do."

"Keep going."

"That's your final word. You're not going to go crazy on me."

Slowly, she shook her head back and forth. But in her eyes, beyond the fear and dread, it was plain: She could not afford to speak a promise she wasn't sure she could keep.

"Okay. You're going to be fine, all right? I know you will. It's just something you need to face. We'll get through it together." He leaned down and kissed her on the forehead. The gesture, which had been totally impulsive, brought a teary smile to her. Judging by the rest of her face, these were tears of happiness.

He pulled back onto the highway again, this time keeping his arm around her.

They soon passed the city limit sign, and almost instantly Coal noticed Maura breathing a little faster, more shallowly. He hesitated for a bit but finally decided he might be able to help her.

"Try to take really deep breaths. Hold them in for a second or two—longer, if you can." He had said he wouldn't pry, but he ached to know what was torturing this girl. He had only ever seen her being less than stoic or humorous or displaying grit and backbone one, maybe two times. Now she seemed reduced to a lost little girl.

To her credit, she tried to breathe the way he said. It worked for a little while as they slowed for the in-town speed limit, but every few minutes she would start breathing fast and shallowly again and he would give her a squeeze to remind her.

They had made it through the majority of the downtown area without a word from her, and he was starting to wonder if she weren't waiting for him to say something.

"Any place you need to go in particular?"

Shivering as if she were once again walking coatless along a wintertime highway, she scanned her surroundings. Finally, she raised her hand to point at a sign that said MAPLE STREET. Her voice shaking, she said, "Can you turn left there?"

He followed her direction and found the car rolling along a quiet street with homes that were mostly humble, some perhaps overly so, and with few trees to speak of. Maura quaked more and more as they puttered along the worn-out old street. He had had to take his arm from around her to operate the car safely, but she was still tight against him, and the thought of what must be going through her mind was driving him insane.

Soon, she said, "Can you slow down a little?"

He looked down at the twenty-two miles an hour on the speed-ometer but obliged her with seventeen. She was staring at the right side of the street, so it seemed whatever she sought was there.

"Okay, stop."

Thanks to their speed, he was able almost instantly to bring the car to a stop. Noticing an empty place at the curb, he pulled forward far enough to park, then followed Maura's tear-filled gaze to a great big old house that must have stood at this corner, the corner of Maple and Denver, for many decades. It was a building of bal-loon-type construction, made of hand-hewn gray stones, a daunt-ing three stories high, counting the full attic, which featured one lone window in the center of a green mansard roof. A big double door was central in the bottom story, a vacant-eyed window to ei-ther side, and three more on the second story. By the look of the peeling paint on door and window frames, and the curling asphalt shingles, Coal guessed whoever lived here had given up caring about upkeep, or else it was abandoned.

He studied the solemn-looking structure, which at one time must have been quite a show home. Then he turned his eyes to Maura, who was quivering all over. He waited for her to find her voice.

After a few minutes, she ran a sleeve over both of her wet cheeks, then slowly slid her hand over and took Coal's in a grip that seemed unnecessarily strong.

"This is where they left me. They shouldn't have put me here, Coal. I was only thirteen years old."

Her voice sounded odd, almost robotic. And although they were the only two people in the car, it felt like she was addressing somebody else besides him. He fought for soothing words. Or should he say anything at all? He found himself asking God for help.

He braved a question: *"Who* put you here, Maura?"

She stared at the building, transfixed. It was at least a full minute before her eyes blinked a few times to show that her brain was trying to register what he had asked. "My people. A man. Somebody I didn't know. My mother said I had to go away forever, so my father took me with him to the mercantile to use the phone. He . . . He called that man. I remember his name."

Here, she stopped. "What was his name?"

"Mr. Redshirt. That's all: Redshirt. He picked me up. I was sitting in the dirt in front of the house with a paper bag I had all my things in, crying because my mother pushed me out the door and didn't even tell me goodbye. Mr. Redshirt came in a long black car that smelled like bad gas and grabbed my arm and dragged me to it. He threw me in the back seat and drove me here."

Coal realized he was breathing shallowly himself, and in rapid breaths. He forced himself to breathe deep. The pain and fear this place had caused Maura was sculpting her face. It was spilling over onto him.

"Who lived here?"

"A white woman. A big woman. To me she was big, anyway. And ugly. Mrs. White." Here, she almost smiled, but it was a wooden expression. "The other girls used to laugh at her name, because most of us were Lakota, and her name was White."

Coal held still. Partly because he had no reason to move, but perhaps in part because something about this whole scene made him wish to be invisible. He even wished he weren't here at all.

A dam had broken inside Maura. Things flowed out of the holes. Haunting things. She spoke of a tiny girl who was twelve but who had the appearance of a six-year-old. Tilly Bourdon was her name. A girl with a French name but whose skin was darker copper than all the others. And the other girls made fun of her because she came to the house with a big belly, and while she was there it kept getting bigger and bigger. Just like Maura's.

Tilly cried. A lot. Mrs. White would yell at her to stop, but she wouldn't, so she would lock her in a coat closet that had a hasp on the outside of it, and a big old rusty padlock. There was no light inside except what came under the crack of the door. Mrs. White would let Tilly out when she knocked on the inside of the door and could prove she wasn't crying anymore. Sometimes it was an hour. Sometimes several.

One morning when Maura woke up earlier than normal, she saw some men wheeling a gurney away. In a way that was never explained, Tilly Bourdon had died during the night. No one was ever allowed again to speak her name.

"All those girls are gone now," said Maura, in a breathy voice. "All . . . gone."

"Is this still that kind of place?"

Slowly, Maura nodded her head. "A home for girls no one wanted. Yes, I think so. When I lived in town it was. They tried to make me come here on the ambulance one time, to take away another girl who died, no one knew how. I couldn't see to drive. I had to get out, and my partner took the wheel and left me standing in the street. That was my last day working the ambulance until I moved to Salmon."

Coal felt an emotional opening, and he took it. Putting his arm around her, he drew her tightly in to him.

"What about Mrs. White?"

"She's gone. Some other woman was here when I left. Mrs. White died. I saw it in the paper. So I went downtown and had a man buy me a bottle of wine, and I went back to my house and drank all of it, while the boys were asleep in their room."

"And your husband?"

"Already gone. He found a woman even whiter than me. No Indian in her at all. They went to Deadwood and built a house. She had a lot of money."

Maura still seemed to be speaking like a robot. It reminded him of the creepy movie from the year before called *The Stepford Wives*, where most of the wives turned out to be robots. A chill ran down his spine.

"Hey. Have you had enough of this place?"

She nodded. "Yes. Except . . ."

"What?"

"Maybe I can go see the room where I slept." Her voice broke on the last word.

"Maura. Are you sure you want to do that?"

She nodded. He guessed she was unable to speak.

CHAPTER NINE

Coal sat there holding Maura for half a minute more before she raised her face to him and looked in his eyes. "Is that all right?"

He shrugged. "Hey, let me tell you what I think. For me, it would be the right thing to do. It's the same reason I started catching and playing with rattlesnakes when I was eleven or twelve—because they scared me to death. I have to face my fears down. So for me, it's right. But I can't speak for you."

She thought about his words. Her voice came stronger: "I want to be like that."

"Then let's go."

He opened the door after checking to make sure no other traffic was coming down the street. She slid out behind him and stopped with the door still open to stare at the front door of the big house. She was starting to tremble again.

"Okay. I'm ready."

He wasn't as sure of her as she tried to sound, but he wasn't going to question her at this stage. They walked together up the long, cracked sidewalk, up two concrete steps and onto a little stoop as broken as the sidewalk. Coal let her knock.

They waited. No one came. She knocked again. Nothing. He was about to kick it with the toe of his boot when she surprised him by doing just that. He laughed.

"What's funny?"

"Great minds think alike," he quipped.

It was obvious by now that no one was here. He looked at Maura. "Where would they all go?"

"Nowhere," she replied. "We never got to go anywhere. Not even to school. Anything we learned we had to learn right in this house."

Turning, he stepped off the porch and went to the left window, putting up a hand to take the glare off it. The home was empty. A few wrinkled newspapers and other debris littered the floor, and one broken lamp was tipped over in a corner. Nothing more but ugly old tan carpet and cobwebs.

He went back up on the stoop and told her. She stared at the door. "That can't be. Where did they take all those girls?"

He had no answer.

"I wanted to face it," she said quietly. "Now I'll never know if I would have been strong enough."

Looking both ways along the sidewalk, Coal told her, "Don't watch me." And then he picked the lock—an exceedingly easy old-style mechanism. Turning the knob, he pushed the door open, and it squealed in protest, not stopping until it was all the way back against the wall.

She looked up at him. "You could make a good burglar. Something you learned at the FBI, right?"

He jumped one shoulder up. "Maybe."

Motioning for her to go in first, he watched her. She didn't move. He took a big breath. "I'll go." And with that, he stepped inside.

The front room had the dank, musty odor of a place that had been abandoned for some time. Along the walls lay a sporadic trail of mouse droppings, and along the same walls, especially by the windows, a scattering of what he decided were the torn-off wings of moths. They must have died, and the mice had eaten their bodies. The corpses of house flies also littered the place, probably far too many to be from one, maybe even two years of the place standing empty.

Coal pressed the door shut after Maura walked in. She instantly folded her arms across her chest, and her head went on a swivel. She walked from the entryway into a big room on the right, apparently at one time either a parlor or perhaps the dining room. He decided on dining room when he saw six big spots on the wood floor that were darker than the rest of the floor. Before he could say anything, she volunteered: "This is where our table sat. We ate all our meals here."

He nodded. She went to the kitchen, where there was a broken plate on the floor. Maura stared at it for a moment, then almost ran to it and crouched down. She picked up the biggest piece and stood back up with it. Her eyes had filled again with tears. "We ate on these. But they kept breaking, until there was only one left. I was the oldest one here by then. This was my special plate. All the rest were plastic."

She turned the broken chip of plate over and over in her hand, studying its whiteness and the tiny red and green flowers painted on it and glazed over. At last, she reached around and put the piece in a back pocket.

A staircase of deep chocolate wood led upward, and Maura looked at it for only a moment, then started up. The second stair screamed at her as if in pain. She stared at it, took a deep breath, and reached back for Coal's hand. He gave it to her, and on they went, straight up.

The stairway spilled out into an open area with four bedrooms surrounding it. There was one brown fabric sofa against the far wall, a piece of furniture so torn and faded that it had apparently had no value to the owners. Like an unwanted orphan, it was left behind. Abandoned.

Trembling, Maura walked to it, then stopped. Tears slowly began to wind their way down her cheeks. She squeezed Coal's hand.

"What is it?"

She shook her head, holding him at bay until she could find her voice. Finally, she said, "My friend used to sit right here with me and teach me how to read." She dropped his hand without warning and brought both hands up to her face, a motion of self-comforting. A sob broke from her. "Molly . . ."

"What happened to her?" Coal asked when it seemed like Maura had said all she was able to.

"A man came one day. We were reading. I remember it was *The Last of the Mohicans.*" She stood still for a moment, lost in a memory. After a while, she began to speak, and it took him a few seconds to realize she was quoting from the book:

Chingachgook grasped the hand that, in the warmth of feeling, the scout had stretched across the fresh earth, and in an attitude of friendship these two sturdy and intrepid woodsmen bowed their heads together, while scalding tears fell to their feet, watering the grave of Uncas like drops of falling rain.

"That's out of the book?" asked Coal after a long moment of quiet reverence and amazement.

Maura nodded, tears standing in her eyes. An unexpected sob chattered out of her. "I had been reading it to Molly for weeks—to show her how well she had taught me. There were only two paragraphs left before the end. And then . . ." Her voice broke, and she stood there trembling. Trying to find her voice, she walked closer and stroked the arm of the dusty sofa. "She was sitting right here when he came up the stairs. We could hear him coming, and the stairs creaking. That second stair, it always made that screeching noise like it did just now. It seemed like forever before he came in sight. A big ugly man. Fat. With broken teeth. He pointed and said, 'I want that one', and then he came and grabbed Molly by the wrist and dragged her out of the room. The rest of us stood. I guess we were paralyzed. We knew someone would come for us the same way."

Maura was suddenly weeping, and Coal took her in his arms. After several minutes, she was down to sniffles. "I can see all of them. It's like they're all in here still. Like they never escaped."

When she had gotten control over herself, she walked over to one of the open doors and leaned against the doorframe, looking slowly around the empty room. The only thing there now was one hanger, bent and forgotten on the floor of the closet.

Suddenly, she walked over to the outer wall, where light shone through the single window. Bending over, she caught a loose edge of a mop board and pried it outward from the wall. Something rolled away from the wall, and she reached down and picked it up, clutching it in a tight fist. She bunched her lips and walked back over to Coal, opening her hand.

A small, shiny marble lay like a magical black pearl in the middle of her palm. She stood there nodding for quite some time before she could speak, and Coal waited.

"Nora Sue gave this to me, and I hid it. She said to always think of her whenever I held it, and she . . ." Her voice cracked once more. ". . . she would always be there."

"Who's Nora Sue?"

"My sister."

Walking away from Coal, Maura dragged the fingers of her left hand along the wall as she went, like a blind person feeling her way. Coming along behind her, Coal saw her whole body start to shake as they neared the only door that was shut. At last, quivering all over, she lowered her hand and touched the doorknob, jerking her fingers away. She returned them to rest on the middle of the door, bowing her head, and for a long time Coal could tell she was holding back her tears.

He waited as long as he could. "What is it, Maura?"

She sniffled, raising her head but not turning to look at him. "It was in this room I gave birth to my baby. My Emmie Lee. And then they came and took her away from me, and I never saw her again."

CHAPTER TEN

After leaving the abandoned girls' home, Maura showed Coal where she had gone to reside after Nyle TrueBear came and got her from the home, when she was sixteen, and took her to live with him. It was only after several years living together that he had been talking to some of his friends and had decided to take her to the first church he could find—an Episcopal church down the street— and have the pastor make them man and wife. She was never sure what prompted that move. He never volunteered any answer. And the only good things he ever gave her in more than a decade to- gether were her two sons, Ty and Sky, both of whom came along after Maura and Nyle had been together for more years than Maura wanted to remember.

Beyond that, he gave her cuts and bruises and an even bigger helping of emotional scars, along with a driving desire to fly like a prairie falcon—fast, and away from Nyle TrueBear, South Dakota, and any past she couldn't erase from her mind.

In those years with Nyle TrueBear, she exhausted every means she could find and afford to locate her baby girl, but there was never a sign of her anywhere. Finally, with no energy left and no money, she gave in to fate. But she would never lose all hope. Emmie Lee TrueBear was out there, somewhere. Alive. Maura needed to believe that. Her little girl would now be twenty-one years old.

The motel Coal found them was cheap in price, but it was clean. On a marquee outside (the place wasn't important enough for a neon sign) it said nothing about a TV, colored or otherwise, and, true to that implied word, there was none. There was only one bed, a worn-down queen, but the sheets were so clean and fresh they were stiff and still had creases in them where they had been folded.

Maura went straight to the bed, pulling down the bedspread, which had a horribly psychedelic green, red, and yellow swirly design on it, and the stiff, thick, white sheets, pressing a pillow up against the wall and sitting down against it, fully dressed down to her Lucchese cowboy boots—cow*girl* boots, she liked to correct whenever Coal referred to them wrong.

She sat there quiet and staring, rolling the black marble from her sister Nora Sue back and forth between her hands. The little chip of porcelain plate lay like a tiny, sad keepsake on top of her right thigh.

Out of boredom, Coal found a Bible with a shiny gold cover in a drawer, not the typical Bible from the Gideons which haunted so many motel rooms, but an actual King James Version, and he sat down on the one lonely chair in the room to thumb through it reading snippets of various chapters. Every now and then he would look over at Maura, sitting there with her shiny marble, now probably much shinier than it had been in ages, and he would see her lips moving. She was mouthing some words that he eventually realized were the quote she had given him from *Last of the Mohicans*. He had to wonder if that had been word for word. If so, he was duly impressed. That moment when her friend had been taken away must be seared into her memory.

Once Coal realized he wasn't going to get much in the way of conversation out of Maura, he settled in to reading Bible passages in earnest. Someone who had apparently been drinking too much to walk—or draw—a straight line had taken the liberty of underlining certain passages in blue ink, and Coal found one of those in chapter three of Ecclesiastes. Of course it was a passage he had heard many times, or at least parts of it. But he never ceased to find it interesting.

Verse three went: "To every thing there is a season, and a time to every purpose under heaven."

Of course most devout Christians could quote much of what followed, and even Coal, who believed in God but was by no means any great student of the Scriptures, could name many of the main words in the passage. The theme went all the way from its beginning at verse one to verse eight, and there were many words that struck home to Coal: *a time to heal; a time to love; to embrace, to dance, to laugh, to keep silent, to speak . . . a time of peace.*

As he reached the end of the passage, something came to him: This might be good for Maura to hear. Getting out of the chair, he went over and propped his pillow up against the worn-out headboard, as she had, and sat down by her.

"You okay?"

She looked over at him and managed a kind smile. "I think so. Just . . . a lot of sad memories. It's been hard to come back here."

"I know. I knew it would be rough on you. Hey—I found something in this Bible I want to read you. It seems sort of peaceful— you know?"

"Okay." She smiled again, not a huge smile, but one that let him know she had made it through day one, and survived. She closed her fist over the shiny black marble, enshrining it in her warm hand.

He read her the verses, and for twenty seconds or so she only sat there. By the time he stopped reading, she was crushing the little black marble tight in her fist, and her lips were pressed together.

"It actually says there's a time to hate? And kill?"

The question shocked Coal, and he looked up at her. Were those the only two words she gleaned, out of all that was good and hopeful in those verses? Hate, and kill?

"Yeah, I guess it does say that."

"Ecclesiastes comes after Exodus, doesn't it?"

He shrugged. "Yeah, why?"

"Because if it does, it seems like what you read contradicts the Ten Commandments. I never thought about that."

Coal didn't know whether to chuckle or be offended. He had intended to bring a feeling of peace to Maura with the words he read, not make her start thinking it was all right to circumvent God's laws. But then he realized she was right: It did seem like a big contradiction. How was he supposed to reply?

"It also says there's a time to love," Coal pointed out.

She looked him directly in the eye. "And hate . . . and kill."

She had brought her other hand up, and the tips of her fingers were pressed through the fabric of her blouse against the ridge of the ugly scar on her chest.

CHAPTER ELEVEN

Oglala, South Dakota
Friday, January 26

Leland Iron Rope remained awake half the night. His first nightmare ended with the girl crouched over him, a butcher knife in her hand. Its tip burned into his throat. His bed was soaked with sweat, and he threw off the bison hide and rolled to the side—and almost off onto the floor.

His son Asa thumped down the hall faster than normal and shot his disheveled head around the corner. "Dad! What the hell?"

"Go to bed!" Leland snapped. "It's nothin'."

Asa didn't move. The darkness in the room was too much, and the light behind him too bright, to make out his face, but Leland knew he was staring. "Go on, I said! Get."

Asa backed away and retreated to his room. Leland stood in the half-dark, blinking his eyes, wiping the sweat off his face that seemed just as quickly to bead up again. He turned to the collection of pine boards he had nailed together and dubbed a nightstand, grabbing a pack of Saratogas off the top of it and fumbling for a lighter. A couple of strokes from his callused thumb made the little flame come up, and he puffed his cigarette into life and drew deeply. This thing with the nightmares, this had to stop!

In the morning, he was meeting with Emery Afraid of Lightning, the old shaman who somehow had skirted around the life expectancy of a man on the Rez of less than fifty years and crept along to something more like the life expectancy of a tortoise—although he looked even older than that.

Emery would know what to do. He had been chasing bad spirits off the Lakota people for more decades than over half the denizens of the Rez had been sucking this dusty air.

Leland stood and stared out the window, caressing his protruding belly, which he had allowed to go so much to fat. Sometimes he was ashamed of it. But at least it meant he always had enough food. And that certainly was not true for many on the Rez. He ran a hand back over his hair, gazing into the night. But it was so dark that only his own silhouette gazed back at him from the window glass.

He sat up against the wall, but this time with an eagle feather fan clutched in his fist. It was his good medicine. He would keep her from coming back this way, until Emery Afraid of Lightning could perform a ritual that would make it permanent. He heard the yapping of Coyote, the wily old trickster, singing his chants from the distance, and then he drifted down again into that world of chaotic, disturbing dreams.

Early in the morning, she came again. This time several people stood behind her, faceless, soundless. But he knew who they were. They were her family—all hypocrites. This was not his fault! These nightmares were because of choices *they* had made, not him. He hated those people, the PlentyWounds. If those many years ago they had given the girl to him as he asked, none of this would be happening now. She would have been here with him now. Or, more likely, she would be buried, somewhere in the sacred Black Hills, where her ghost could no longer haunt him.

He thought of their other daughter, just younger than the one with the yellow hair. He had tried to make arrangements for her as well, but they said she was too young, and they got all indignant and religious on him and said they didn't need any more of his alcohol. But he had shown them. He had shown them real good.

Asa didn't bother coming to check on him after the second dream, and Leland was just as glad. He rose from the disturbing dream and put on a red plaid wool shirt, then got a bottle of cheap wine out of the cupboard and went barefooted to stand out in the dark and watch the stars, puffing on Saratogas and sipping straight from the mouth of the green bottle. Sleep was not his friend. He would stay awake, like a watchman on the hunting trail or the war-path. He would wait for tomorrow, for Emery Afraid of Lightning to make him clean of bad spirits.

Rapid City
Friday, January 26

Maura PlentyWounds was a little girl. A lost little girl. A strong-willed, hot-blooded, unscrupulous man could very likely have talked her into anything that night. But of course Coal never tried. He could never have faced himself again. He held her through the night, except for the times when she was thrashing around so bad he had to get up and sit in the chair to wait for her to settle down again. The rest of the time, he held her, and intimate relations were the farthest thing from his mind.

Early in the morning, she had the first nightmare that finally woke her all the way into alertness. She sat shivering in the dark, her knees hugged up close to her chest, and Coal's arm around her shoulders. It took half an hour before she could speak.

"They came to my dreams. All of them." Coal wasn't positive she was speaking to him, or if she was speaking to someone in her shadow world of dreams. "They never said anything. They were just there. Nora Sue . . . She had no mouth, but she tried to talk to me with her hands, and I couldn't understand. Her eyes . . . They were full of so much pain."

"It was only a dream," Coal tried to soothe her.

"No. Not only a dream. This was much more."

Coal tried for a while longer to ease Maura's worries. Finally, she rolled over onto her other side, away from him, and pulled the blankets tight around her. A glance over at the clock showed Coal it was five-thirty, and sleep was as likely for him in this room as the appearance of a ten-foot armadillo, so he got up, showered, and shaved.

He had to get Maura away from South Dakota. Whatever she had felt she needed to face, she had faced it. It was time to go home and forget all this. He wished he had never suggested any of it.

He came back out and pulled his boots on, then flipped the chair around so he could watch the approaching day.

Maura got up and went to the bathroom so quietly he didn't know she was up until he heard the shower come on. He jerked around to see the bed sitting empty. With a sigh, he folded his hands in his lap. Deep, tarnished silver was materializing in the sky over the lights of Rapid City. He prayed for good weather, heading home. Good weather, and an end to Maura's dreams.

Coal didn't want to start up anything bad again, but they were already here in Rapid City. If Maura was going to think of anything else she needed to see here, or do, it had best be now, before they were well on their way home.

They had eaten breakfast in a noisy café that didn't invite any talk between them, and now they sat in the car, the heater struggling to get warm enough to take the chill out of their seats. Outside, the wind was howling hard, moving the car around. It had been so long since Coal had felt winds like this.

Good for their travels, but a bad omen for the coming summer, the skies once more promised no moisture, and the weatherman on the country radio station confirmed it, then turned the airwaves back to the morning deejay, who presented them with Loretta Lynn singing, "Your Squaw is on the Warpath." Coal quietly shook his head. Songs on the radio sometimes had the worst timing.

Trying to keep Maura from noticing the silly song, Coal asked, "Is there any other place you'd like to go before we head home?" Inside, he cringed at his own words. He mentally had his fingers crossed that she would give him the answer he had hidden behind his Door Number One: *No, I want to go home.*

Instead, the answer she softly gave him was behind *none* of the doors he would have presented her.

"What was that?" he asked because she had spoken so softly and because he so fervently wanted to pretend he had heard her wrong.

"I want to go to Oglala."

Coal clenched his teeth, blinking his eyes exaggeratedly to clear sleep from them. "That's on the Sioux reservation." He voiced this as a statement, not a question.

"Lakota," she corrected.

"The Lakota reservation. Maura, I don't think that's a good idea." He had a dozen reasons why, but he hoped he wouldn't have to give any of them, for fear of turning her back into a raving fiend who wanted to deck him.

"I'll go alone."

"But I'm driving."

She looked at him with what he could only describe as an expression of sharpness. Challenging. And then turned back into the raving fiend.

"Then I'll walk." With that, she flung the door open.

"Hey! Maura! Get back in here. *Maura!*" The second *"Maura"* bounced harmlessly off the closed car door, his shout almost lost in the reverberations of metal on metal.

Coal hastily threw off his seatbelt, opened his door, and jumped out. She was already walking up the sidewalk. "Hey! Maura, come back here and let's talk."

She kept walking, and he started swearing—the cure for all that ailed him. An older couple emerged from the café, and he wanted to tell them he was sorry for swearing, but he had meant every word of it.

Reaching back in the car to snatch the keys out of the ignition, he slammed the door as hard as she had and started down the sidewalk after her. Maura's pace was resolved, but not overly fast, and he caught her with a minimum of trotting. He grabbed her arm and swung her back around, flinching in expectation of having to dodge another angry blow. Luckily, although her hands were in fists, they stayed down along her thighs.

"Maura, you're not even giving me a chance," he told her stone face.

"Because I knew you wouldn't want to go."

"Yesterday you didn't want to be in South Dakota at all."

"Everything has changed. I have to go. And you're not going to stop me."

"Do you understand what could be waiting down there for you?"

She stared at him as if he had **STUPID** written in huge letters on his forehead. "Do *I* understand? What kind of a question is that? I'm the one who *knows* what's there."

Good point. So maybe STUPID *should* have been written on his forehead. Even tattooed there.

"Do you understand what's waiting for me back home if I don't go?" she asked then. "You're the one who said I needed to face things. So I guess I thought about it too long, until I realized you were right. Now I'm facing them."

He stared into her eyes. They were set. She was waiting for one or two wrong words out of him before she would turn and walk away again. His heart fell as he thought about the road that lay ahead of them and wished he knew everything that was in this woman's head—not to mention everything in her past.

"I'll take you to Oglala. But I sure don't want to."

She almost smiled and almost wept. At least that was how he read the expression on her face. "I don't either." She stepped around him and walked back to the car.

*   *   *

On the radio, Elvis Presley was telling them in song to "clean up their own backyard", as the blue LTD shot down Highway 79 to Hermosa on one of the straightest stretches of road Coal had ever seen. Here, they turned directly east, then after a while abruptly southeast, on Highway 40. In time, they made an almost straight turn south to the little roadway stop of Redshirt, then hit another length of barely improved road that looked like what the dictionary would define as a "straight line: the shortest distance between two points".

Coal's guts felt worse and worse as they went. There was one point in the drive when he even wished he had never suggested this trip, or at least that he hadn't asked Maura to come along. As strongly as he had ever sensed it in his life, his insides told him they were headed for certain doom. Whatever Coal and Maura had been before this trip, they could never be again when it was over.

They came to a tee in the road, where turning west would point them toward a place with the charming Western-sounding name of Buffalo Gap, and east led toward Rockyford. Coal slowed way down and looked over at Maura. She gave him back a level gaze.

"Please understand, Coal. You were right. I need to face my past. I have to see some people. My sister Nora Sue, and . . . There's this little woman who saved my life. I'm sure she's gone by now, but I have to know. I have to see where they put her."

He continued driving, but much more slowly. Mostly, he was studying her. She felt it and looked at him again, almost smiling as some memories that for a change must have been good flooded her thoughts.

"You would have really liked Maybelle Littlebrave. Sometime I'll tell you about her—and what she was to me."

He nodded and smiled. "Okay, Maura." He felt like hell, but she seemed to have found strength deep inside of her, and somehow some kind of peace. For that, he was happy.

It was almost an hour and forty-minute drive to Oglala, because Coal dreaded going there, and accordingly he drove like a hundred-year-old man. With winter, the country was broken and gray, with rocky, alkaline looking hills to their left and flat, grassy rangeland all around, the kind of country the United States government tended magnanimously to put Indians on and tell them they were "gifting it to them until the end of time". They made a hard dive south, then another, just as hard, to the east, on a road designated as 18.

And then they were coasting into the windswept, dusty, brow-beaten village of Oglala, South Dakota, *population 100*. Coal's heart fell as he looked around. Maybe his fear of this place was not for fear of the place itself. Perhaps it was the shame of knowing how he and his kind lived, while this place sat nearly in their back yard, one of the poorest spots in the entire country.

When he looked over, Maura had tears in her eyes. He reached out and took her hand, hoping it would still be welcome. It had the effect of forcing her tears down her cheeks.

"I grew up here," she managed in a breaking voice. "This was home to me."

He scanned the trailer houses with their sand-scoured, wind-gnawed siding. His eyes fell on homes—he thought of the word loosely—constructed of plywood, some lucky enough to have tar-paper tacked on them, some of which hadn't even been torn loose—yet. The only reason he guessed these were homes was because of vehicles parked outside them. Slat-sided scrub horses and cattle stood in mud-packed pastures with eyes shut and tails tucked, rumps thrust back against a howling wind that beat their shaggy, often muddy hair back and forth. Dogs peeked out from under the few porches in town—if "town" it could be dubbed.

Here and there a sheet of tin on a roof would raise up in the wind, then rattle or slap back down with a *clang*, and other than the purr of the Ford's engine and the wind past its frame that was about the only sound.

Coal remained speechless. He had never seen such a place of utter, devastating poverty. His heart had never hurt more for an entire community, not even in Korea or Vietnam.

He looked again at Maura. He wanted to ask if he could turn the car around. He wanted to be gone. He felt like a glaring red pimple on the face of this homely place. Although not a soul was in sight, he imagined suspicious, jealous eyes peeking from every window at his beautiful car. One of the world's wealthy had stumbled into their realm, and they would want to know why.

They were out the eastern side of the scramble of slapdash structures in less than a minute. "Keep driving if you want to see where I learned to swim," offered Maura. Coal didn't want to. He didn't care what she had done here, or what she had learned to do in what location in this horribly poverty-stricken place. He wanted to take her back to her safe, now almost wealthy-seeming trailer house life in Lemhi County, Idaho. Right then it seemed like the other side of the moon.

But because he was still too shocked and numb to pull over, they kept rolling, slowly, through the tone-less prairie until Maura pointed out the right window with her thumb. "Oglala Lake. It's really a reservoir."

Coal stared out at the wide stretch of water, which was smutty gray under the overcast sky. "You learned to swim in that?" She was lucky she hadn't caught some nasty disease.

"Yeah. That's the only decent swimming pool around here in more than a hundred miles."

He only grunted. She had an odd concept of "decent."

All of a sudden, she reached over and grabbed his leg, her claws digging in. "There." She tried to go on speaking, but her voice faltered. He stopped the car in the middle of the road. It seemed pretty safe since he hadn't seen a moving car in miles. He sat in the road, his hand over hers, holding it, trying to give her whatever comfort he could while she tried to find her voice.

"There's a car there," she said, almost in a whisper.

He looked at an early sixties Ford Futura that squatted beside what some kind-hearted people would have excused as a house and thought how sweet Maura was herself to use the term "car". The collection of rust didn't *have* a dent—it *was* a dent. Its assortment of hammered-out parts had an aura of once having been red, before a few thousand scouring dust- and sandstorms and eight or ten brutal winters had sanded all paint into submission, and its headlights stared out at them like sad, tired, almost worried eyes, waiting— perhaps praying—for death.

"What place is it?" He felt like she wanted him to ask.

With a tight voice, and tears coming fast, she managed to say, "Maybelle Littlebrave lived there. And me too—when I ran away and she hid me. I would have died if she hadn't cared. She was really the only brave person in this whole place."

"I guess I owe her too."

It took a moment for his words to register on her, and she looked over at him and tried to smile, but he was positive that through her tears she couldn't see him.

"We could go knock, if you want to see it closer."

Maura squeezed his leg harder. "I wouldn't know what to say if someone's home. Coal . . . You don't know how it is out here. They'll think I'm white."

He almost laughed. To anyone but her and others who knew her as a child, she *was* white. Other than perhaps a little more pronounced cheekbones than a run-of-the-mill Caucasian, with her blond waves and smoky blue eyes she looked as white as anybody else—even paler of skin than Coal. And the reality was that she had only a fourth Lakota blood running in her veins.

"We don't have to," he agreed. "Would you rather go?"

"No, I want to see it."

Of course. Coal sighed. "Okay. I'm going to pull in there. It looks like the driveway" —he used the word as loosely as the skin on a Shar pei dog— "goes all the way around, so I'll pull around so we're facing back to the road—in case they come out wanting to shoot your lily white— Uh, hiney."

Somehow, a giggle escaped the woman, and Coal was more than a little surprised: He had thought her fresh out of all laughs, giggles, grins, and even amused smiles.

"Okay, can we?"

He had said he would. So he didn't reply, just turned the wheel and rolled through the ugly gray clay and sand that pretended to be a yard for this hodgepodge of boards and pieces of tin that people around here most likely referred to optimistically as a house but any of Coal's sheds would be embarrassed to stand beside. He went all the way around the back, thinking that as barren and un-dressed as this "house" seemed to be he wouldn't be surprised to see its bare butt protruding out the back wall. He had to hold back a laugh at his own warped humor, for he was pretty sure his expla-nation of that image would not register as humorous on Maura.

Back on the other side, he stopped alongside the Futura and thought he would get out and see its headlights close over, or tears roll out from under them in embarrassment at the beautiful car that had come for a visit. An ache throbbed deep inside Coal for these Lakota people and how they lived. It was all he could do to keep using his twisted sense of humor to chase away his shock at seeing this kind of poverty in his own country.

As Coal got out, Maura was already opening her door. He frowned. He wanted her to get in the habit of letting him open her door, he guessed for the sake of being old-fashioned. But it was probably the last thing on her mind today.

She walked around the front of the car and stopped beside him, looking over the house. Suddenly, her face contorted, and she brought a hand to her mouth and sobbed. He was proud of her for getting herself under control quickly, though, and with a big, self-strengthening breath, she knuckled her eyes and started forward.

She rapped on the door with one knuckle. He figured that was in part because the whole house couldn't have been twenty feet from one side to the other, and partly because she was afraid the door would fall in if she knocked any harder.

A feeble voice came from inside the house, a sound Coal judged to be mostly human, as opposed to possibly feline. So they waited.

After forty seconds or so, they heard a rattle inside, and the partial sheet of plywood that masqueraded as a door was lifted slightly upward—probably to keep it from dragging on the bottom—and it swung in.

Coal had to lower his eyes a long ways to meet the shaded black marbles that peered out from the unreasonably wrinkled visage of a woman of ancient days. Maura froze, her mouth open partway to speak. The old woman holding the door stared up at her. *Way* up.

Then Maura broke into tears.

CHAPTER TWELVE

Once Maura broke down, it took only seconds for recognition to flood over the old woman's face as well, and her hands flashed to her cheeks. "Oh, my little white Peta!" she said, repeating it three more times. Somehow, tears made it down the bags below her eyes and the gauntlet of crevices in her cheeks and tumbled off the wrinkles in her jaw to the floor. "You really came back to me! I can't believe you came back to me."

The old woman stepped forward and threw her arms around Maura with such emotion Coal thought he might have to step out, to keep them both from seeing how this heartfelt reunion was affecting him.

Movement flashed in the corner of his eye, and he turned to see two boys somewhere between ten and twelve years old stop at the end of the house, staring at him. Obviously, they could hear the old woman and Maura sobbing, because they kept glancing that way, but it was as if Coal's sudden appearance before them had them petrified.

Not knowing what else to do, and believing it was an inopportune time to speak, Coal looked at the boys, managed a lame smile, and shrugged. Putting up his hands as if to say, *I don't want anything to do with all this female drama,* he backed away from the door into the yard.

Now, far enough away from Maura and the old woman hopefully not to disturb them, he took a few steps and stopped in front of the boys, both of obvious American Indian blood. He spoke in a quiet voice. "Hello, boys. I'm Coal."

"Hello," said the less suspicious looking of the two, but he didn't volunteer a name.

"Hello," stammered the second one, who seemed both in looks and timidity to be slightly the younger of the two.

Coal thought about holding his hand out to shake, but he had a feeling the move would only scare them, so he refrained, then turned uncomfortably away from them to wait for Maura to recover. It seemed pretty evident that this old woman was the same one she had been certain would be dead.

It was a full two minutes before Coal looked up toward a movement at the door. Maura had emerged and was gazing at him, digging happy tears out of her eyes with her fingertips. She beckoned him over with several quick waves of her hand. He gladly made for the door, away from the scrutiny of the boys, not minding when he heard them both follow because it seemed obvious they belonged here and because at least in the house they would have the old lady to keep them occupied.

They all went into the entryway of the beat-up board shack, which smelled of cottonwood smoke, greasy fry bread, and beans, and Coal lowered his eyes to the diminutive woman who, in spite of her age, still had silver-laced jet-black hair capping off the myriad wrinkles. If Coal had thrown down a couple hands full of dry grass clippings, then traced a line where each blade fell on the woman's face and neck, he believed he might come close to matching the intricate puzzle of crevice, gully, and chasm that told of the years, the trials, and the toil she had endured.

She wore all the way to the middle of her thighs a faded brown shirt sprinkled liberally with little yellow flowers, paired with an ochre-colored skirt with what seemed a hundred pleats, sweeping all the way down to the tops of her moccasined feet—which in fact was a very small distance.

Maura took Coal's elbow in a gentle hand. "Coal, this is my grandmother I told you about: Maybelle Littlebrave. Not my real grandmother, but in Lakota it is a term of respect: *Unci,*" she spoke the word for grandmother in a voice and accent he had to be looking at her to know came from her throat. "Unci, this is my friend Coal Savage."

Looking at his belt buckle instead of his eyes, the old woman gave a little bow and what might have passed for a smile in some circles. He didn't feel like she was unfriendly, because of a sparkle in her deep-set black eyes. She beckoned him forward.

"Come and sit. *Peta*, you come too."

Maura smiled and nodded, turning to Coal and saying in a low voice, "Her name for me is Peta, which means 'fire'. Fire-in-her-Eyes is what my uncle called me, but Unci shortened it to Fire."

Coal laughed. "Pay-dah?"

"Yes. It is spelled P-e-t-a."

"Fire-in-her-Eyes, huh? It sounds like they had you pegged even way back then."

It was precisely six of Coal's long strides to where a prehistorically blue and white sofa he had no desire to sit on was pushed up hard against a rear wall, probably to hold it up. Out of deference, he turned with Maura and sat, knowing if the house caught fire he might burn to death before he could manage to claw his way back out of this collection of fabric, wood, and one-time springs that was more human trap than couch. It didn't take much imagination to picture a truckload of scavenging Lakotas patrolling some filthy, dusty dump around Rapid City, finding this treasure of a discarded sofa, and carting it back here for Maybelle Littlebrave as a gift. The three soft chairs may have been a product of that same trip, and none of them should have had human beings sitting down in it, but Maybelle and the two boys did it anyway. Gallantry aside, Coal would have had a hard time choosing between this furniture and a cactus.

It was hard for Coal to understand everything Maybelle said without concentrating all his energy. He was fairly sure he had seen she only had maybe enough teeth left that she didn't have to count them on more than one hand, and her lips looked like she had just eaten a whole lemon. Between those two flaws and a voice that he guessed would rather speak in her native tongue, comprehension for any stranger would be a chore.

But she managed to do all right introducing the two boys, Joseph Afraid, the more timid of the two (tragically ironic, in light of his name), and Billy Pierre. They were both scrawny-looking boys, but their bone structure proclaimed their predisposition to grow into impressive men, if only they had the proper nourishment at this stage of their lives.

Maura, not knowing anything about Coal's interest in the lore of the so-called "Old West", felt she needed to explain where the surname of Pierre came from, since Billy looked every bit the full-blooded Lakota Joseph did, and far more so than she did. Coal already knew all about the French trappers who had ranged the mountains and plains of the West taking wives among the native people, but he nodded and smiled. He could see that, just for this little window in time, Maura was in her glory. He sure wasn't going to be the one to take anything away from her moment.

Not bothering to ask whether Coal and Maura were hungry, Maybelle served them bread, beans, and something she pretended was coffee, but tasted more like she had poured a little brown paint, some motor oil, turpentine, and a few yard weeds into a vat of dirty water and boiled the mixture for three days under the full moon. It was all Coal could do to sip it all down, but the bread was good enough that he saved a chunk to erase the taste of the Lakota "coffee".

Maybelle didn't talk too much. Maura did most of the talking, and sometimes Coal. Even the boys pitched in now and then. Maybelle would nod here and there and smile with her eyes. There were a few topics, however, where her speech was very animated, and one of those was the surprising subject of hunting.

She took the conversation in the new direction, then proceeded to enlighten Maura and Coal with the tale of how she and her eighty-one year-old hands (it was the first time Coal had heard an exact age) had gone out hunting with some of the local men the fall before. She had gotten (in his mind Coal inserted the word "wobbled") to a cluster of boulders along a trail, then lain in wait with a .30-30 Winchester until a herd of elk wandered by, where-upon she dropped the gigantic herd bull with a shot through the spine of the neck, gutted it, and sat down on it for a soft chair while she waited for the warriors' return.

Telling this story brought the most animation to Maybelle's face Coal had yet to see, and then, off and on throughout the rest of the visit, if things got quiet she would suddenly bring up that rifle shot again, every time bringing her hands up to demonstrate how she had held that rifle. "If you was stayin' longer, I'd cook you up some elk meat. Then you'd see what Lakota cookin' means."

Coal pictured her hunkered over a little fire, somewhere out on the plains, with a tepee behind her sheltering her from the wind. *That* was how he imagined Lakota cooking.

It took quite a while for Maura to work up enough courage to start asking her old protector the real questions he knew had been burning in her heart since their arrival. He knew when she started to grow quiet, and the conversation altogether lulled, that she was building herself up.

Finally, she tried to get Maybelle to meet her gaze. "Unci . . . Do you know of my mother and father? My sisters and my brother?"

Maybelle stared at the floor for a few seconds, her brow knit-ted. She appeared to be concentrating, as if trying to understand the question, and Coal watched in fascination as this frowny look turned her wrinkles into furrows and her cracks into fathomless canyons. Her silence went on so long even the boys started taking notice, looking up at her, then at each other, as if the old "unci's" mind had left the party.

"Listen to me, Peta. I'm thinkin' maybe it would be not so good for you t' see your fam'ly."

Coal had instinctively kept his eyes on Maura as Maybelle spoke. He saw her use all her strength to hold a calm expression on her face and not show the fear already in her eyes that started to grow much deeper.

"Unci . . . I have to know about them, even if I don't see them."

Maybelle nodded her understanding. Her eyes swung past Coal, although she didn't make eye contact with him. She had yet to do so.

"Okay. Well, your *ate*—your father—he still lives, but I believe he has the bad liver. The whisky . . . Ahhh . . ." She made an angry face and tossed her hand. "I always knew it'd git him, but I never thought it would take so long."

Maura nodded, her face grave but otherwise expressionless. Coal saw no sadness there for her father.

"But your *ina*—your mother . . . Ah, your ina. She is hangin' onto her breath. I don't know why. I never knew why. She is . . ." Maybelle ran her eyes past Coal again, perhaps wondering how much he knew of Maura's past. "She is weak, but about the same person she was. Not a good woman. I'm sorry." She stared at the floor, shaking her head.

Maura seemed unable to stop nodding, as if the tendons had popped loose in her neck. "I know, Unci. It's okay for you to say it. I know."

Maybelle let out a long sigh, folding her hands together and scrubbing them as if right then realizing they were filthy, and as if she had any water and soap to do the job.

"Your *misu*—your brother, *Hoka*, he works in Wounded Knee. He is often not here. Which is good. Hoka—I call him Edward now—is a bad one, Peta. Bad. He an' . . . the name I will not speak . . . they are friends together. It is very bad. Bad people." Then her face grew soft and sad, almost wistful, and she put a hand up on her cheek. "Oh, an' he was such a sweet baby boy, Peta. I wanted t' keep him, if only he woulda come here too."

Maura tried to smile. She was holding up well. "I know, Unci. I wish he would have."

"I don't know very much about Ile—Nora Sue. She found a man. No—*two men.* I think maybe she married the first one. The other she shared a tepee with." Her eyes crinkled up when she thought about that. " 'Cept it wasn't no tepee—it was a little eight-sided house he made from cinder blocks, but he didn't put no cement 'tween them, just plain clay mud, an' when a big cow went t' scratchin' on a corner one day, all that house come down." She slapped her knees with both hands and laughed, making her eyes close all the way over. It was the first time Coal had seen her break out in real laughter. Maybe she was growing used to the presence of a white man in her dwelling—her *tepee.*

Maura sat up straighter and stared at Maybelle. "Was anyone hurt?"

"No. Oh, no." Maybelle shook her head exaggeratedly and slapped her leg again. "Nobody got hurt. Weren't nobody home. Then I guess Ile she decided livin' with that fool was too dangerous, an' she went an' made a house out of boards like mine. She lived there for a while, but I guess it got burnt up one night. I think from that no good man she found. Now I got no idea where she's gone. She still perty too—like you. No figurin' why that girl got no man. Maybe just can't find no good one left."

Maybelle stopped talking, and Coal saw Maura grow nervous. She started rolling her coffee mug back and forth between her hands. Finally, she took a big breath. "What about Cordelia? What do you know of my baby sister, Unci?"

At this question, Maybelle's eyes fell. She pressed the palms of her hands together and knifed them down into the fabric of her skirt, between her knees. She began to shake her head, first a faint motion, but slowly becoming larger, and faster. She sighed, and Coal thought she would start to talk again, but she didn't.

Maura reached over and took two fingers of her own left hand in the grip of her right. She squeezed hard enough it looked like it might hurt. "Unci?" Coal watched a spark of hope burning out in her eyes.

Still shaking her head, and with her gaze concentrated on her hands, Maybelle said, "Peta. Some things you gotta leave be. You understand that, don't you?"

"What happened to Cordelia?" Maura's voice was more forceful now.

Maybelle shook her head harder. "I don't like t' tell you."

"I have to know, Unci. Please."

"Little Wowahwa . . . She is gone. Just . . . gone."

Tears dimmed Maura's eyes. "Unci . . . gone where?"

Maybelle raised a hand, lazily waving toward the ceiling. "Gone. To the spirit place."

Maura steeled herself, squeezing her fingers ever harder and sitting up straight, pulling in a huge breath. "How?"

"She was little, Peta. She . . . Girl—*wicicala*—you need t' go an' forget your fam'ly. Let your heart heal an' be happy you gone outta here."

Maura lurched to her feet, taking a step closer to the old woman, who dropped her head even more, a turtle trying to hide in its shell. Coal stood up beside her. "Tell me, Unci. I am a grown woman now. I have to know what happened to Cordelia."

"She . . . She left when she had only eleven winters."

"To the home for girls in Rapid City?"

Maybelle shook her head. "No, not to the home."

"Then where?"

Maybelle looked up and made fleeting eye contact with Maura. The closest thing Coal could imagine to pleading was the emotion he read in her eyes. Her chin had begun to quiver.

"She went with that man whose name I won't have in my house. He just took 'er, an' didn't nobody stop 'im."

"When she was *eleven?*"

Maybelle nodded fervently, looking down at the floor again. "Peta, you need t' go. Go home."

"Not until I know all about Cordelia."

The old woman raised her chin of a sudden, stood up and took a step forward, leaning down and grabbing both of Maura's wrists in the fierce grip of her tiny, gnarled hands. She stared at Maura's chin.

"Yes. She had eleven winters, an' he came t' your folks' home. He gave some money for whisky t' that old fool who was your *ate,* an' . . . Then your ate, he said t' take the girl but bring her back when he didn't want her no more. Only he never brung her back."

"Where did he take her?"

"Nobody knows, Peta. Somewhere. But she is gone. Her body. It's gone. I have felt her spirit come to me. She is gone to the land of spirits, an' I hope *Wankan Tanka,* the Great Spirit, has give her plenty o' peace."

Doing her best to hold back her tears, Maura looked up at Coal, and on some hidden signal they moved together toward the door. Once there, they hesitated to open it up again to the wind and the cold. They turned to look down for what Coal hoped would be the last time at Maybelle Littlebrave, and it was at that moment that something happened. The diminutive woman raised her eyes far up, as if taking a chance on looking at the strange white man who had come to her home.

For what Coal was certain was the first time, Maybelle saw his face. Her eyes widened, and her mouth dropped open. As both hands came slowly up to her mouth, she lost her balance and almost fell over backward. Coal stepped forward and caught her with both hands behind her back, bringing her back up straight as she continued to stare up at him, making a kind of eye contact he had yet to experience on this reservation. She was staring at him as if watching the moon split in two.

"Are you all right, Unci?" asked Maura.

The old woman, not taking her eyes from Coal, said, "It is him. It is him."

Confused, Coal glanced at Maura. Old Maybelle was losing her mind. That was his big thought. Flat-out going crazy. She thought he was someone else. Maura only shrugged.

When Coal knew Maybelle had regained her balance, he drew his hands away from her back and stood there feeling—and most likely looking—uncomfortable. Maybelle's hands were trembling as she reached out and fumbled them around Coal's, which made hers look like those of a child who had spent too long in the bathtub. She squeezed his hands, now looking at his midriff, not his face. The tremor in the old woman's grip seemed to go all the way to Coal's shoulders.

"You are him," she said again.

"I'm sorry, ma'am. I'm who?"

Maybelle gave a tiny wobble of her head, and a smile came to the corners of her mouth, but still she didn't meet his eyes again as she gave his hands another squeeze and a shake. "You are him."

"It's all right, Unci. It's just my friend Coal," said Maura. Another glance at her told Coal she must be thinking the same thing he was—that Maybelle's mind had gone out to lunch.

Maybelle only smiled bigger.

CHAPTER THIRTEEN

Maura embraced Maybelle, the woman she claimed had saved her life, with all the warmth and love he knew was in this woman. They left Maybelle, Joseph, and Billy, but somehow Coal's guts told him they would see them again before this trip was over. He didn't like it, but he couldn't deny it.

They sat down in the car, happy to get back out of the howling January wind. Coal looked at Maura. "Well, that was interesting."

She gave him a sad smile. "I'm sorry. I don't know what was going through her mind. You must have reminded her of someone."

He chuckled. "Well, at least I think it was someone she liked." He drew a deep breath and started the car. The breath seeped back out of him.

"So what was all the rest of that mumbo jumbo in there, anyway? All those Lakota words. I thought you said your sister was named Nora Sue."

"She is. But Maybelle usually called us by the Lakota names she gave all of us. I told you I was Peta, for Fire. Edward was Hoka, which means badger—and if you knew him when he was little you would see why." She smiled with some memory she was keeping to herself. "Nora Sue was called Light-on-the-Mountain, but for short she was just *Ile,* which means light. And my little Cordelia—" Maura's voice broke on her youngest sister's name, but she steeled herself and went on. "She was *Wowahwa.* It means 'Peace'—for Child-of-Peace."

Coal sat there for a second using his old knack for languages and running over all the names in his head, then pronounced each of them back carefully to Maura. She listened with obvious intent to correct him on the instant if he messed up.

"Nice! I'm very impressed."

"So I get points?"

Maura laughed, driving out of her expression the pain of learning about little Cordelia's fate, if only for the moment.

Coal had learned enough about Maura PlentyWounds on this trip to have guessed already where their next stop was going to be. He would gladly have heard her prove him wrong, gotten on the road, and headed back home, but he knew she wouldn't. And there was a part of him that was beaming with pride for her, although going with her to her family reunion was pretty much next in line in his choices of things to do after hitting a wolverine on the butt with a stick.

He tapped the steering wheel with his fingers for maybe ten seconds, then gave Maura a sideways cast of his eye. "Okay. Where do they live?"

Maura had been looking out her window. When she heard his words, she let out a laugh. But it held little humor. "I'm sorry, Coal. But thank you for being with me. And for making me do this."

"Whoa. *Whoa.* Don't even include me in this one. I made a little comment. If I could go back in time I don't know if I would have said it."

"You said the right thing. I've needed to do this for a decade. Without you, I would never have been strong enough."

Coal nodded. "Where to?"

"Back toward town."

He pulled the car out of the pathetic dirt yard and turned right at the highway, going past the outlet to the lake the locals called a swimming pool. Once they got past there, they came to a left-turn-ing road with a sign that said GOVERNORS DRIVE. For obvious reasons, thought Coal, they didn't turn there. The houses along that way weren't anything a millionaire would live in, but they cer-tainly seemed too nice and well-kept for what he expected out of the kind of people he was understanding Maura's folks to be.

As he approached the next road, Maura touched his sleeve. He glanced over at her, and once again she was shivering, and tears pooled along her lower eyelids.

"Here, I guess."

She answered him only with a nod.

He turned on this nameless road into a wasteland of multi-col-ored trailer houses and decrepit shacks that leaned away from the wind to seek protection from whatever lay on their leeward side. He soon found to his surprise that this area was at least laid out in nice, straight streets, with possibly ten houses or so to the lane. That wouldn't have made living there any easier for him, but at least it showed some kind of foresight had gone into the planning of parts of this community.

In this trailer village, like most of its kind anywhere across the country, there was no upscale neighborhood—no one place where the houses seemed better kept than anywhere else, with nicer lawns. No, in this little Indian village, like he imagined the tepee cities of old, the more well-off mingled with the poor, and those who cared about their property with those who allowed tumble-weeds to insulate the bottoms of their houses as often as they did bales of straw.

They had almost reached the end of the line, with one street left to turn on, when Maura said, "It's this last one. Turn there."

Seeing as there was nowhere else to go but back the way they had come in, he turned.

"Stop."

He stopped. In the middle of the road. With several of the homeliest properties he had yet to see in this park running along ahead of them on both sides of the street.

She pointed two houses ahead on their left, to one of the strangest and ugliest residences he had ever beheld, a place bordering the back of the park, where grassy prairie began again, and ran off into the near distance—a place he imagined he would have loved to run, as a boy, but where, if the wind decided to come in from that way, he could envision the clouds of dust and debris that must cover this trailer house haven. The only thing that broke the horizon were the tiny lumps of something one might refer to as hills, but which to Coal would hardly have been worth the three- or four-mile walk to reach them.

"Why'd we stop here?"

"Please wait." She was trying to breathe deep, and she had shoved her hands underneath her thighs. So he waited.

Finally, she took a particularly large breath. "Okay. I'm ready."

Coal eased on up and pulled in at the left road edge, facing the wrong way into traffic he was certain would never notice or care. His eyes slowly swept this place which he had to admit was nothing short of a conversation piece—sort of a masterpiece of its kind.

To start with the yard, it was possibly the most wonderful, amazing, and varied garden of weeds he had ever witnessed, all of them now brown, yellow, or a dozen shades of gray, being battered and bending before today's gusty wind. A perfect row of discarded tires of various sizes, buried halfway down in the dirt, created a sort of fence around the place—a fence Coal couldn't guess the purpose of, since any animal alive could either jump it or cross from one side or the other through one of the holes. Some of these tires lent the wonderful effect of color to an otherwise fairly colorless property, apparently having been spray-painted in greens, blues, yellows—even some in pink. Others, for no apparent reason, were left black.

The house, however, was the true pièce de résistance here. It presented itself in three sections, the middle one being sided in brown wood, with a low gable roof, a place that appeared at one time to have been an entire home unto itself. But apparently as the family's needs grew, someone had come up with the wonderful touch of attaching a small trailer house to the left side of the original house, a trailer house with tan siding on the bottom—apparently intended to be a somehow flashy wainscot, and white on top, with the mostly flat roof typical of its kind. To finish it off in all its imaginative glory, the right side of the brown house had another trailer house sewn on, but this one really only a chunk—perhaps a fifth or sixth—of a hideous yellow-on-bottom, white-on-top trailer that if Coal had to guess he would say a fire had probably destroyed the rest of, and some whisky-swilling home-grown engineer had decided to chainsaw this portion off and make good use of—the way any good old mix-and-matcher worth his salt would do.

Incredulous, without even taking his eyes off the magnificent home to look at Maura, Coal said, "You grew up in this place?" He was starting to understand why she thought life in a single-wide trailer was acceptable—at least hers came in just the two nicely-matched greens and had always been intended as one piece.

Maura caught the disdain in his voice that he hadn't been smart enough to hide. "Not everybody is a rich white man, Coal." Her voice was sharp, and it cut deep. "And no—that right side wasn't attached when I lived here. It was only the other two."

He thought about apologizing, but if he did it would have to be later. Right then he was too embarrassed and offended to tell her he was sorry.

Without saying anything else, Maura slid all the way over to her own side and popped open the door. As she got out, Coal did too, because even if he was a little unrighteously miffed at her for the moment, he would be hung and smoked before he allowed her to go into that place by herself. Their doors slammed as one, and the sound seemed to call up a big, howling gust of wind that pelted them with dirt and rattled a piece of loose tin on someone's roof. Among this army of single-wides, it was hard to see which one it was. A dog came and poked its head out from under the next trailer over, leering at them for a moment, deciding barking wasn't worth the trouble, and then going back into its hole.

Maura started walking. Coal tried to catch up and get beside her, but this woman was *motating*. She got to the rickety obligatory set of two-by-four railing, plank stairs, and plywood landing that all downtrodden people with trailer houses seemed to have the same plans for—except that this one had no green indoor-outdoor carpet—and before Coal could hit the first stair she was pounding on the door with the side of her fist, rattling it. Coal could have opened it with a boot in a few tries—and the door was supposed to swing *out*ward.

The face that appeared as the door swung open was none of the faces Coal was prepared for. By the way Maura reacted, nearly falling back into him, he was sure it wasn't a face she had expected either.

The person at the door was a woman who might have been the same age as Maura, or a few years to either side of her. Like Maura, she had the perfect rounded eyebrows, pronounced nose, and full, dark lips of a woman who might be called beautifully handsome, or handsomely beautiful, but seldom "cute." Unlike Maura, her hair was deep brown, nearly black, but her skin tone wasn't much darker than Maura's. Also like Maura, she was tall and well-built, and she shared Maura's sense of style, dressing in a blue and black plaid Western shirt, boots, and tight-legged jeans, a dark brown suede leather jacket with garish fringes on it concealing most of the shirt. The jeans were tattered and faded, apparently from old age and her own hard use.

The woman stared at Maura for several seconds before her jaw dropped. Maura had the same reaction. When she recovered, she didn't leap forward for the embrace Coal thought long-lost sisters might share. And the other woman didn't make that move either.

"Hello, Nora Sue," Maura said, as if she saw this woman every day of her life—and didn't care much for her.

"I wondered if you'd ever be back."

"I . . ." Maura stared at her sister, looking confused. Finally, her face seemed to settle as she digested the fact that her sister was not elated to see her. "Well, I'm here."

Nora Sue PlentyWounds raised one eyebrow. "I guess you want to come in." As Maura was giving her a shrug, Nora Sue's attention had already swiveled over to Coal, and she swept him with blue eyes only a touch darker than Maura's.

"Coal Savage." He thought he should offer the woman a name, but he didn't offer his hand.

The eyebrow had gone back to normal, but it came up again— a natural occurrence, Coal guessed, rather than something she did on purpose. "That's a funny name. Should be a Rez name."

"It's French and English," Coal offered.

Nora Sue's reply was a nod. "Well, come in."

The two of them stepped into the house. The fire in the stove was well-aged and dying, and there was no fresh firewood close by, the resulting cool atmosphere explaining Nora Sue's wearing the leather jacket inside. The interior of the masterpiece trailer house mirrored the exterior.

"Your house is going to get cold," Coal remarked.

"My lazy father didn't cut wood."

Coal wanted to ask Nora Sue if she had ever learned to do that for herself, but he refrained.

"So you forgot how to keep yourself warm?" That was Maura.

Nora Sue smirked at her as she turned and went toward a cupboard. "I hope you don't want anything to drink. Unless you want horse pee, as usual." As she said that, she jerked open the cupboard, which resembled a shelf at the five and dime winery. "The old man has some Ripple, some Mad Dog, some Night Train Express—and oh, yes—how could I forget his favorite? Thunderbird. If you wanna rot out your guts pretty much just to get stupid, name your poison."

"No thanks," Coal spoke to the back of her head the moment he could get in a word. "And no thanks for her too."

Nora Sue then executed the nearest thing to a whirl or about-face, crossing her arms over her chest. "Why did you come back here, Maura?"

Maura stared at her. "Nora, I . . . What did they tell you about me to make you hate me so much?"

Nora Sue laughed. As she did, she unfurled her arms and stuffed her hands deep in her pants pockets, having to work them back and forth to find room. "Hate you? I don't even know you, Maura. You left here when I was just a kid, remember? You left me here to fend for myself with Rotten Guts and his white squaw and to try to keep Cordelia from harm. I don't hate you—no. I despise you. And yes, I've wanted to tell you that for years."

Maura whirled away, but not before Coal caught the tears in her eyes.

CHAPTER FOURTEEN

Maura started for the front door, but Coal grabbed her arm. Still more than a little gun-shy, he half-expected her to come around swinging, but she didn't. She stopped, leaving her back to the two of them, and turned only her head to the side, trying to see him apparently without her sister seeing her face.

Coal turned and leveled a glance at Nora Sue. "Why don't you find a hole for a minute? Looks like there are plenty of them in this place. I need to talk to your sister."

He didn't often feel an urge to speak so bluntly to anyone he had just met, especially a woman. But Nora Sue PlentyWounds—or whatever last name she was going by—had earned the right to be spoken to like that.

A look of solid despite crested over Nora Sue's face. "She ain't *my* sister. Go ahead. I'm goin' to the bathroom. Maybe I can throw up in there." She started down a dark corridor that had to pass for a hallway, then whirled back. "Oh! And don't drink all the wine."

When they heard the bathroom door shut, Maura turned around. Coal was pretty sure she was going to step into his arms. He was going to be called on to be her protector. But she didn't. Regrouping, he said, "Hey. Don't let her get to you. Your folks obviously lied to her. That's not her fault, right?"

Maura stared at the floor until finally she swallowed, clenched her jaw, then looked up at him. "Maybe at first. But she's believing all that on her own now."

"So make her see the light. Your parents aren't here. Talk to her. At least you should try, after coming all this way. I'm guessing she's really the one you came here to see."

Maura nodded, and it made Coal almost smile to see how her eyebrow came up, the same eyebrow that liked to rise to the occasion for her sister. "You're right. It was her. Those people aren't even my parents. They gave up that right a long time ago. Now it looks like I came here for nothing."

Reaching into his pocket, Coal jerked out the keys. "See this?"

Maura frowned at the keys. "Sure."

"I'm still driving that car out there. I came a long way down here for you to take care of some things, so we're not leaving until you tie it all up. Got it?"

It took some time, but a smile finally tried to battle off the frown she was affecting for him. Somehow, the frown won, but not before Coal knew she had softened.

She folded her arms—as Nora Sue had done—and looked along the darkness of the hall. "So . . . What do I do, go knock on the door? What if she isn't coming back out?"

"She'll come back. Give her a minute. If she doesn't, I'll go roust her out of there."

This time he garnered a grin and a soundless laugh. "Yeah, you'd like to go catch her in there, huh?"

He reached up and tapped her on the tip of the nose. "Funny. No, not particularly."

No sooner had he spoken than they heard the sound of the toilet flushing. Water ran, and the door came open. As Nora Sue walked toward them, she was wiping her hands on her jeans, and when she saw Coal watching she laughed. "Yeah. We use our towels for pants here too. It's a lot cheaper."

Maura jumped in with both feet, making Coal proud. "Nora. I need to talk to you."

The brunette turned her jaded eyes on the blonde, both of them bearing a quarter Lakota blood, but both of their skin paler than Coal's. "Isn't it a little late?"

Maura looked aggressive as she stepped toward Nora Sue, and Nora Sue actually took a couple of steps back, almost putting up a hand. "What are you doing?"

"Nora Sue. Please listen to me. They've all been lying to you about what happened. I would never have left you on purpose. Ever."

Nora Sue stared at her. Doubt moved back and forth in her eyes. Years of lies were battling with a truth Coal believed she was trying to see in her sister. Her face hardened. "I don't believe you."

"If you'll just listen, you will."

Nora Sue's eyes remained doubtful. "Why would I?"

The words had just left her mouth when something out the window drew her attention. Her face filled up with fear, and she swore. "Oh no."

Not liking the look in her eyes because he expected the parents were home, Coal took a step to the window in the door and pushed the little curtain away with the tip of his finger. Stopped in front was a beauty of a car, a shiny, deep green late sixties Ford Thunderbird with a matching vinyl top and suicide doors in the rear.

"Is that your folks?"

"No," said Nora Sue, and before Coal could ask more, she said, "You gotta get outta here. Out the back."

Coal looked at Maura, who went to peek out the window in the door as well. She let the curtain fall back without any look of recognition in her face. "Who is it?" she asked her sister.

"You don't want to know."

"I think I do."

"It's Asa Iron Rope. Leland's son."

Maura froze. The most powerful look of fear he thought he had ever seen in her face leaped there like a flash of lightning. Maura whirled and looked back out the window, where Coal was still watching. Altogether, five Indian men ranging from perhaps their late teens to their mid-twenties had disembarked from the Thunderbird, all smoking cigarettes. One of them was large and well-built—not a match for Coal, but certainly a bad one to fight if all five of them came at him together.

"Please go." Nora Sue stepped close and grabbed Maura by the upper arm. *"Please.* I'll meet you somewhere—anywhere. Just go. Now."

Coal's revolver was under the seat of the LTD, which the five Lakota were walking around now, studying it like they had an interest in buying. One of them actually kicked a tire. Coal had weapons on him, but all of them were the ones he had been born with. And there were five men out there much younger than he was who looked like they might enjoy a fight.

"Out the back," Nora Sue pled. "I'll meet you at the mercantile later."

"When?" asked Maura.

"I don't know. In an hour or so? Two o'clock. Please *go!"*

Coal never liked to run from a confrontation. But at the moment he had more than himself to think about. He had these two women, and he had the fact that he was a stranger on this reservation, which was considered a sovereign nation. Any fight he got in here, his status as a white man's sheriff wasn't going to do him one bit of good.

"The mercantile. Two o'clock," he said to Nora. "If you're not there, we're coming back."

With that, he and Maura stepped to the back door and slipped out. As the rear door was clicking shut, they heard a loud pounding at the front.

Creeping around to the end of the house, Coal peeked past the corner to make sure all five of the men had stepped inside. Then he grabbed Maura by the hand, and they hot-footed it across the weeds and scrambled into the LTD. Just as Coal's door was shutting, he heard a man yell, and he turned to see two of them coming down off the porch into the yard.

From the corner of his eye, he saw the others boil out of the house as he fired up the engine, threw it in drive, and roared down the street.

When he looked in the rearview mirror before making the next corner, he saw the five men standing in the front yard, this time with Nora Sue. None of them made a move toward the Thunderbird.

Coal slowed down, and when they reached Highway 18, he stopped. "Well? Now what?"

Maura was trying to calm herself back down. She gave a little shake of her head, obviously not yet ready to speak.

"All right. Who were they?"

"I know only one. And only because of his last name."

"And that would be?"

"The one Nora named: Asa Iron Rope. He's Leland Iron Rope's son."

Coal stared at Maura and felt like a complete fool. Only now, with the full name spoken once more, did he remember that unique name he never would have believed he could forget. *The man who hurt me,* Maura had said.

What had this fiend done to this girl who meant so much to him to turn her entire life upside down? There were all of a sudden two Coals in the car with Maura, and he couldn't even tell her: One of them wanted to keep her safe and beg her to leave with him now and go back to Salmon. The other one—the blood-stained warrior—wanted to find Leland Iron Rope and have a come to Jesus meeting.

And that was the man Coal had to get a rope on and tie down, before it became too late.

"Why're they at your parents' house? And what about your sister? Why's she there?"

"How would I know?" Maura shot back. "You know everything I do."

Without any good suggestions from the woman, Coal ignored the bite of her tone, turned left, and headed up the highway. They had an hour to kill, and even then there was no guarantee Nora Sue could get rid of the five young Lakotas and be waiting at the mercantile for them at two.

The mercantile in question appeared to the left not long after Coal got on the highway. He looked over at Maura, but she was staring out her window, one hand up over the lower part of her face. She had lately started getting back into the habit of sitting all the way over by her door again, and he didn't like it. But this wasn't the time to address childish things like that.

It didn't take very long driving west for him to realize that this road would lead back to 385, the highway they had traveled heading up to Mount Rushmore, and once they hit that one, if they wanted to turn left, to the south, it was only a short drive to the Nebraska line. They had nothing behind them. Everything they had brought was on them, under the seat, or in the trunk of this car.

Coal took in a deep breath and thought about a battle plan. Not a battle plan for the Iron Ropes, but one for talking to Maura. Sometimes, that felt more like a fight than a real fight.

He decided to jump in with both feet.

"You know what highway we're coming up to, don't you?"

Maura looked ahead. "I'm not positive. But I think probably the one where . . ." Her eyes hooded over. "Yeah. The one where I first found out you were driving up into South Dakota."

He nodded. So far, so good. "I don't know if you've given it any thought, but it goes the opposite way too, you know? If I turn left when we hit it, we'll go back to Nebraska. And then we can start heading home."

Maura leaned against the seat back. He looked at her, and she appeared ostensibly to be in a daze. But he could see something different behind her eyes. She was really deep in thought. He wondered if she might actually be considering what he had said. And in a flash he wondered how he would feel if she really did up and decide it was time to leave. It seemed she had come so far trying to heal from her past. If they headed home now, were they leaving undone some important task God had given her? Or even one she had given herself?

In the end, it didn't matter. They hit the big highway, Coal stopped at the stop sign and looked over at her, the question implicit in his glance.

She turned to meet his gaze, her eyes unfaltering. "Okay. Turn around and go back."

Coal smiled, almost to himself. He did know Maura after all.

He swung the car around, and the three of them, Coal, Maura, and the beautiful blue Ford LTD, headed east. Had Coal only known what fate awaited them, he would have fought the girl, but had she known, he would not have had much of a fight.

CHAPTER FIFTEEN

Out in the front lot at the mercantile in Oglala towered a red and white gas pump Coal was pretty sure he had once seen Fred Flintstone pumping "fossil fuel" out of. There was a newer red Dodge pickup stopped at it, and a man, apparently the driver, was deep in conversation with the middle-aged attendant, who looked a little light-skinned to be full-blood Lakota.

Coal pulled around to the side of the mercantile, hoping to keep the car out of public view as much as possible. He and Maura glanced around at a handful of vehicles, most of them obvious reservation run-arounds, and none worth a second look.

They stepped inside a replica of a general store from a John Wayne movie—belied only by the thirty-year-old gas pump in front. The place had a time-darkened barrel with crackers for sale, and on the counter a jar of pickled pigs' feet—a delicacy Coal had never quite picked up on. Every wall was lined with some kind of merchandise, even the wall behind the fifteen-foot-long mahogany sales counter, where two copper-skinned clerks, a mid-twenties young man and an emaciated woman with large cheekbones, who might have been the sister of the other clerk, stared openly at Coal and Maura. They had apparently been doing that since seeing them pull up in the only nice car in the lot, besides the pickup being fueled.

To the left, in front, were two rows of booths with benches on either side of them, and several older men and two old women were scattered through the smoky room, drinking coffee and smoking cigarettes. They might also have been involved in conversations moments earlier, but with the entrance of the two blue-eyed white people, evidently as rare a sight as scarlet ibises, all talk had ceased.

Coal looked at an operable cuckoo clock that was also for sale on the wall behind the sales counter. It said two-oh-five. He looked at Maura. She didn't seem bothered by her sister's tardiness, and she had been watching the clock too.

"Want to sit and order something?" she asked.

"You're actually hungry?"

"My stomach's upset. But I think food might help it."

"You choose."

"Let's sit. I know the Rez. When someone says two o'clock, that could mean anywhere between one-thirty and three."

Coal nodded, a little disgusted to think of a possible hour or more sitting here. "All right. They're your people."

"Not anymore."

They sat down at a booth near the window, trying to ignore the open stares of the other patrons. The young woman from behind the counter came and took their orders, a tar-black coffee for Coal and a hamburger and Pepsi Cola for Maura. She abruptly swapped the Pepsi for water when she saw the look in Coal's eyes, and after the waitress left, he couldn't help but laugh, and she stuck her tongue out at him. For a moment, he was able to pretend all was like in the old days.

Catching a movement out on the road, Coal glanced over, wondering what Nora Sue PlentyWounds would be driving, since he hadn't seen any vehicles at the house, or if she would have to walk here.

Maura swore. Good and hard. The dark green Thunderbird was pulling into the parking lot. Coal swore too, and it might have sounded like an echo except he chose to string several together, and Maura hadn't been imaginative enough for more than the one.

Coal was cursing because once again he had left the Smith and Wesson out under his seat. Up to this point, the car was out of sight of the men in the Thunderbird, but the revolver was far out of reach as well.

The Thunderbird slowed at the gas pump as the pickup driver was paying the serviceman, and one of the Indians flew out of each back door before it even had the chance to stop all the way. Another man piled out of the front passenger seat, and the last one came out of the back, where he had been stuck in the middle. The driver then rolled on and stopped a couple of vehicle lengths away.

Coal watched warily as two of the young men engaged the owner of the red pickup in what appeared to be friendly conversation. The main thing that alerted him was the look on the face of the pickup owner. He didn't seem to believe the four men accosting him were friendly.

One of the young men started working his way around to the far side of the pickup as Coal watched two of the others artfully keep the pickup owner talking and worked him around so his back was to his pickup. Then, without seeming to bat an eye, the third one stepped over to the truck and ducked inside. The driver must have left his keys in the ignition, because it now lurched forward, apparently died, and as its owner spun toward it, the thief got it started again and squealed the tires out of the parking lot, loud enough to hear through the windows of the mercantile. He was the only one now in the vehicle, as his partner in crime who had gone to the other side was standing with two young boys whom he had by their coat collars and was raising up onto their tiptoes. Coal was pretty sure he recognized them as the two boys from Maybelle's house, Joseph Afraid and Billy Pierre.

The truck owner started to run after it, but it took him seconds to see that race was futile. The pickup was already a hundred yards away. Besides, the two boys he had brought here, and who were obviously in his care at least for the moment, were being held by one of the accomplices in the theft of his truck.

By now, the Thunderbird had parked, and the driver got out and swaggered toward the growing crowd around the gas pump. It was of course the same man who had pulled the Thunderbird up in front of the PlentyWounds home, and Coal hadn't realized quite how big he was before. Not only was he big, but there was a mean look to his hooded eyes and the downward cast of his wide, thick lips. His long hair swept back from his face, and was held there both by the stiff wind and a black stocking cap. As he walked toward the pickup owner and the two boys, he was making gestures with his hands that Coal classified as aggressive, mostly jabbing a forefinger toward the man and the boys, and waving his arms around as if telling them to vamoose.

Coal swore again and thought of his revolver. He threw a look at Maura. "What kind of law enforcement do they have around here?"

"Ha! Last I knew? Nothing. A tribal policeman or two in Wounded Knee and maybe two more in Pine Ridge. I don't know who else. But I've never seen one come here unless there was a big crash."

The driver of the Thunderbird—Asa Iron Rope—stopped in front of the pickup owner. Then with no obvious warning he struck out and hit the man square in the mouth, knocking him on his back, where dust flew away from the downed man's coat. Coal could tell Iron Rope found the blow, and the fall, hilarious.

Taking his cue from Iron Rope, the man holding the boys by their coat collars suddenly kicked the feet out from under the scared one—Joseph—and let him fall hard on his backside. He turned and practically threw the other one, Billy, toward the third man as Coal saw the red pickup come racing back and spin in a fast circle just off the street, raising a cloud of dust off the asphalt.

From the corner of his eye, Coal saw one of the old people across from him and Maura struggle up out of his booth. He started fiddling with a cane. "I ain't gonna just sit here an' let 'em hurt Paul an' them boys. Come on, somebody. Come help me talk to 'em." Nobody moved. But the old man had played his hand, and he knew he couldn't back down. As fast as he could walk with an obvious bad leg and the help of the cane, he headed for the front door. Coal heard him yelling something as the door was swinging shut behind him.

The scene outside was going from bad to worse. And still no Nora Sue anywhere in sight.

As the voice of the old man yelling at Asa Iron Rope registered on his ears, he slewed around, saw him, and cut loose with something he must have thought was funny, for he followed it with a bellowing laugh. Then he started toward the old man, and Coal swore again.

His Smith and Wesson was a long ways off, but his other weapons—his head, hands, and feet—weren't.

"Coal! No! They'll kill you!"

Coal was pretty sure those were the words he heard behind him, which he figured must have come out of Maura's mouth. The silly girl was concerned for him. And he should have been concerned as well. He hadn't even realized until that moment that he was up and headed for the door.

Coal the warrior, the man he had sworn to rope, was on the loose, and there was no tying him now. As he was shucking his coat, throwing it on the floor inside the entry door, he saw little Billy go down on his face, right on the asphalt, and then big Iron Rope kicked the old man's cane out from under him, and he fell too, first to a knee, and then onto his back—with the help of the bottom of Iron Rope's boot.

Coal let the door swing shut behind him and walked away from every last common sense thing he could have thought to do.

Images from Korea and Nam flashed through his mind. But they weren't visions from actual fighting in the wars. They were scenes of foolish fights in bars and clubs, in back alleys. The same kind of stupid fights he had gotten involved in in California as well, when he was stationed there trying to train troops in the use of firearms in combat.

Without exception, in every fight he had felt he was right. Some injustice had been done, or more frequently was being done right at that moment. And the mighty Coal Savage was coming to the rescue. Because he could.

The stupid part of his fights was not the fact that he got involved, that he wanted to help some underdog in need. It was the glaring fact that no man can ever know if he is going up against someone better, or faster, or stronger. Or, a bigger danger—a man who is armed, in one way or another. Yet none of that ever stopped him, and God had to keep proving that "the good Lord takes care of children and . . . Coal Savages."

Coal heard the door open behind him, and he had to glance that way to make sure that somebody else wasn't on the way to help his enemies. It was Maura, and after her, the male clerk. Nobody else from inside the store set a foot outside.

Iron Rope looked up, laughing, from where the old man with the cane was sprawled on his back. He kicked the cane flying across the parking lot, yelling, "Jeez, old man, you never learn!"

And then he saw Coal. And Coal had the eye of a wolf intent on the kill. He knew it, and it couldn't be helped.

Straight toward Iron Rope he walked, watching his hands, his eyes, his feet, listening for his voice. "What the hell you think *you're* doin', white man?" Iron Rope roared, then laughed raucously. Coal kept walking. He hadn't come here to talk.

A cautious look swept over Iron Rope's face, but he laughed it away. "Who are you, pale face? Go on, get out o' here!" His voice was a loud roar, meant to intimidate. Attacking warriors of many armies, particularly those of the North American Indians, had used the same strategy for centuries. Scare them with noise. Confuse them. And win. It was all a part of posturing.

Coal had almost reached Iron Rope, and he sensed the others were beginning to take notice. Somewhere in the back of his mind, he realized the red truck had come speeding back into the parking lot, and he knew its driver had climbed out, and that he had left the truck in neutral, and it was rolling across the lot.

"Hey, you better—"

Coal had turned to the right, as if he meant to throw a haymaker at Iron Rope. But he didn't. With seemingly no effort at all, it was with the edge of his left hand that he struck out, knifing into the side of Iron Rope's neck, just below his jaw. Coal's all-time favorite target.

Apparently, Iron Rope's rope was the only thing about him made of iron. Or at least his carotid artery wasn't. His knees went out from under him like jelly fish as Coal struck, and he went down hard—not unlike his victims. For now, and probably for some time, he was out of the fight.

He headed for those who had hurt Billy and Joseph. None of them were small men, in particular, although none was the size of Coal, even Mr. Iron Rope. But there were four of them now that the driver of the stolen truck had returned to the fray, and Coal expected at least something of a challenge.

Perhaps it was the look in his eyes. Coal would never know. What he did know was that as he approached the cluster of Lakotas, all standing there yelling obscenities at him and ready for a brawl, they waited until he was six feet away, and then they scattered in every direction like so many quail.

Before he knew it, however, they had come back in, probably afraid of what Iron Rope would do when he was able to regain control of his body and pound on them. They started to surround him, once more screaming taunts.

He didn't expect to talk, but he heard himself say, "Who goes next?"

And then, with a hop and a side kick to the underside of the man's ribcage who had knocked Joseph down, he saw him fly backward and slam his back against the gas pump.

He turned with hands up and ready to take out the next contender.

That was when he heard the shotgun rack.

CHAPTER SIXTEEN

Coal had seen men hit with shotgun blasts. Even the smallest gauge shotgun was a deadly affair at close range, and the weapon he had heard being racked could not have been much closer. If the wielder of the gun wanted him and was unafraid of the consequences, he had him.

Coal had to fall back on his knowledge that most men are afraid to kill, and pulling the trigger on someone at close range is something very few people can do—that is, unless they had gone through the type of training they were using on the troops going to Vietnam.

The other truth is that even if a person can convince him or herself to pull a trigger, it often takes time to decide on that course, and time is to a defender's advantage.

Coal moved into the man who had thrown Billy Pierre on his face, and abandoning his karate, he went into judo form, using a single back throw to lay the man hard on the asphalt. He hit with such force it almost hurt Coal to hear the sound, and with a *whoosh* of air out of his lungs, he lay still.

Dropping to a knee near the downed man, Coal grabbed one wrist and made to bring him up for a human shield between himself and the man with the shotgun. Then he stopped.

The man holding the shotgun didn't have it aimed at him, but at Iron Rope's two last remaining cohorts. It was the owner of the pickup.

The man scanned the other two, swiveling his head to look over at Iron Rope, who was struggling to rise on legs made of cooked noodles. No one was around who felt like assisting him.

"You trouble makers wanna steal a man's truck an' play with his livelihood? Just one o' you make a move. I'm tired of all the games." The man's jaw was set, and his finger was inside the trigger guard. At a glance, Coal guessed this man had been dealing with thugs for some time, and he had made up his mind. He was ready to end the harassment, the only way he could.

Slowly, hands in the air, Coal got to his feet. He made eye contact with the shotgun bearer, needing to make sure he knew he was on his side, for the man looked a little wild-eyed.

The other man nodded at him. "Hey, I got you covered. I don't know your business on the Rez, but you might wanna get in your car an' get outta here. This could get really ugly—'specially for somebody with your skin color."

Coal blinked away the fury still surging through his blood. He shook his head and looked around, then sucked in a deep breath of ice-cold air. The first two upright Lakotas from the Thunderbird stood by the gas pumps, and Iron Rope had come fully to his feet, although a glance at him told Coal he hadn't yet gained the confidence to try walking. That chop to his neck was something most men took a while getting over, and Iron Rope had done well simply getting up without help.

"I understand what you're saying, but I'm pretty hesitant to leave you here by yourself," Coal said.

The man nodded. "Well, thanks. You wanna go look in my pickup and see if my keys are still in there? If they are, we'll leave here together. That suit you?"

"I'd prefer it," Coal said, and walked over to the pickup, where it had rolled to a stop and the owner, apparently while retrieving his shotgun, had taken time to set the brake. Coal glanced at the ignition, turned and spoke to the owner. "Keys are here."

The man nodded. As Maura walked over from the front of the store, he turned and looked at her. "You must be with him." She nodded, and he went on. "Go get your car then. We're all goin' out of here together before these punks get nervy."

Maura looked at Coal, who tossed her his keys. She caught them out of the air, turned and hurried to the end of the store. In half a minute, she pulled the LTD around front and stopped near Coal, getting back out.

The pickup owner looked at Iron Rope. "Can you walk yet?"

Iron Rope stared at him balefully.

"I asked if you c'n walk."

Iron Rope, seeing the man's anger, nodded.

"Then get over here with these others. An' hurry up."

Iron Rope started walking, with a bit of a wobble. When he got to his standing accomplices, he looked down at the other two, who were trying to get back up, among their groans of pain. He returned his eyes to the man with the shotgun.

"You might as well move off the Rez now, Paul. If you think this is over, you don't know the Iron Ropes very well."

The shotgun-wielder, Paul, grunted. "I know you people too damn well, Asa. So well I oughtta shoot you now."

"Then do it."

Iron Rope didn't believe Paul would do it. That was plain by the look in his eyes. He was talking big for his friends. His eyes widened as Paul brought the shotgun to his shoulder and leveled its barrels at his head. He jerked his hands up and made a scared yelp. Paul laughed.

"You're a damn fool," Iron Rope growled.

Paul's only reply was to walk over and lower the shotgun so its bore was too close to the left front tire of the Thunderbird to miss. Iron Rope jumped toward his car and yelled out a protest, but the sound of his voice was lost in the roar of the twelve-gauge. In not much more time than it took for Paul to recover from the shotgun's kick, the tire was flat on the ground, a cloud of mist and dust dissipating around it.

Iron Rope started into a fine-tuned stream of curses aimed at Paul the shotgun-wielder, everything he ever had been or ever would be, along with all his ancestry and descendants.

Paul turned to Billy and Joseph and jerked his head toward the pickup. As the two boys ran toward the open driver's door, Paul backed away.

Maura was climbing into her own side of the LTD, and the two boys into the pickup as if synchronized, and then Paul and Coal did the same. The vehicles wheeled out of the now-quiet parking lot of the mercantile and drove away in the direction of the trailer park.

As Coal followed the red pickup, Maura sat next to her door, speechless. Coal drove the same way. It seemed like there was nothing to say. Finally, Maura found her voice.

"I don't think I'll see my sister again."

Coal nodded. "I'm sorry. I really am. I just couldn't let those guys . . ." His voice trailed off.

"You did the right thing. It's not your fault." Another long moment of silence as they continued trailing the pickup, which seemed to be traveling with exaggerated lethargy, as if its driver was contemplating how his life was about to change forever. "I feel bad for that man, though," she echoed Coal's own thoughts.

"Yeah. He should have stayed out of it."

She smirked. "Apparently, he didn't know Coal Savage."

Coal looked over at her to see if she was being facetious. She wasn't looking at him. Rather, she had her head leaned back against the seat now and was staring at the back of the red pickup. "What does that mean?"

She rolled her head over to look at him, her face so relaxed she looked like she could fade off to sleep. "If he had stayed out of it everything would have been fine for him. There were only two more of those guys."

They drove past the slapdash home of Maura's one-time savior, Maybelle Littlebrave, and within a quarter of a mile afterward pulled up in front of another driveway. But after sitting in front of this much better-kept place than Maybelle's, the pickup drove on past, stopping next in front of a beaten down white trailer house whose skirt was lined with straw bales, with one cluster of them serving as an apparent cave for a couple of dogs that hung around on the ends of chains outside of it barking.

After a second, the pickup pulled in here and drove all the way around back, well past the dogs. Coal followed, and when the pickup came around the far end of the house and stopped, Coal was forced to stop exactly at the end of the house.

Paul got out of the pickup as the boys piled out the passenger side. He looked back at Coal and Maura, questioning why they didn't get out. Answering his look, Coal and Maura got out as well, and Coal stood behind his door, looking his own question toward Paul the Lakota.

"I'm gonna have you park that car here," the man said. "I can't think of no other place for it to be safe this close to town, unless you two plan to head out of this country, and fast."

Coal looked over at Maura. She only shrugged. She didn't offer an opinion either way on the question of whether they were leaving.

Coal's and Maura's doors slammed shut at the same time, and they walked to Paul. He looked them both over more closely than he had at the mercantile. Finally, he held out his hand, and Coal took it.

"Paul Wolf Guts."

Coal was about to introduce himself as well, but his mouth clamped shut and for a moment he stared, trying to decide if the man was pulling his leg.

Paul gave a little shrug and half a smile. "Sorry. That's the real name. I know it sounds funny to you white eyes."

Coal shrugged. "I'm getting used to it. Coal Savage."

The side of Paul's mouth curled up even farther as he looked back and forth between Coal and the woman. "Now you see, to me, that name sounds strange."

Coal grinned. "I'm sure." He jerked a thumb at Maura and introduced her, making Paul Wolf Guts's eyes narrow as he gave her a closer scrutiny.

"PlentyWounds. Okay, things are comin' t'gether. Back when I moved in here there was talk about this little blond girl who used t' live around these parts. Fire-in-her-Eyes, they called her. Fire for short—Peta. Yellow hair, blue eyes. Not hard to figure out that little girl come home."

Maura nodded. "Yes. I'm that little girl come home."

"And Eddy's your brother," said Paul Wolf Guts flatly.

"Yes."

"I'm sorry t' hear that."

Maura gave him a shrug in reply. "It's really that bad, huh?"

Paul answered her shrug. "I hope you weren't close to him. That's one boy I wouldn't mind seein' dead. An' I'm not the only one thinks that."

Maura swallowed hard and looked over at Coal.

Paul turned and clapped Joseph Afraid on the shoulder. "Well, come on. I need t' introduce you t' the friend o' mine that lives here. Yer gonna laugh at his name, but it ain't spelled like the girl's name. It's spelled like white man's name for our people."

With only that explanation, Paul walked up the wooden stairs and knocked, and within ten seconds the door opened, and a man of unknown age peered out. By the world's standards, he looked to be in his sixties, but Coal had stopped guessing, because on the reservation it seemed some folks aged double hard.

The man stood around five-foot-eight and wore pants made of buckskin and what was known in the Indian powwow world as a "ribbon shirt," this one in faded red, with black, white, and red ribbons streaming down from the yoke.

"Hau, Paul." He looked past his friend, and his eyes narrowed on Coal and Maura. "What's goin' on?"

"Sioux, this here is a couple of folks I met at the mercantile. We had kind of a melee down there, an' I need a place t' hide their car out for a little bit."

The man named Sioux, a phrase which made Coal have to hold back a laugh just as Paul had warned him, looked the two of them over a little more closely but spoke to Paul. "You vouch for 'em?"

"You bet. This guy stepped in an' helped me out when Asa Iron Rope an' his punks was messin' with my truck an' roughin' up the boys. They're good folks."

"Iron Rope, eh? Now I see why you're wantin' t' hide the car."

Paul nodded and turned to Coal and Maura. "Coal. Maura. This is my friend Sioux Returns from Scout." He looked back and forth between them, seeming to expect to see them looking doubtful of the old man's name. When neither of them made a comment, Paul decided to make it himself. "I know you thought Johnny Cash was singin' about some made-up guy, didn't you? This Sioux is the real deal: Only like I told you his name is spelled like the name they call us Lakota: S-i-o-u-x. Bet Johnny Cash stole it from him."

At this obvious invitation, Coal laughed. "Well, it's good to meet you, Mr. Returns from Scout."

The old man's eye corners crinkled up, although his mouth didn't appear to be laughing. "Rather you just call me Sioux."

Coal offered his hand, and he was impressed with the man's grip. That made him look him over a little more carefully, gauging the breadth of his shoulders and the depth of his chest, along with his big, work-hardened hands. Whatever this Sioux Returns from Scout had been in his younger days, Coal guessed he still would not be a man to trifle with.

After a quick visit inside the old man's well-kept trailer house, Paul led the others outside into the cold wind once more. He looked down at Joseph and Billy. "Hey, boys—I'm sorry but you gonna have t' ride in back 'til we get t' my house. I'm gonna have Coal an' Maura ride up front."

Coal jumped in. "That's all right, Paul. We can handle the cold."

"Or the boys can sit on our laps," Maura cut in.

Paul looked back and forth between them. "You don't mind?"

Maura smiled. "Of course not."

Neither of the boys argued about not having to ride in the icy wind. They simply climbed dutifully up onto Coal's and Maura's laps, and they drove back to the first trailer house Paul had stopped in front of, where he pulled in and parked around back.

"This is me," he said, and although he didn't come across as proud about it, he might well have been, for his property shone above most of the others Coal had been close to so far. This one was tan, with a dark green roof, and a chocolate-brown wainscot, all in good condition. Handmade wooden flower planters lined his front windows, although with winter they were empty of anything other than soil. Whatever had filled them had been carefully cleaned out to wait for spring. The grass immediately around the house had been cut short, and what lay beyond it was native blue grama, with a scattering of less prevalent species, and the dried stems and pods of wildflowers. There was a little shed to one side, made of wood and neatly painted.

He led them all into a house that was chilly but still smelled of the pine he had been burning in a small stove that sat in the center of his living room, where the two sofas were the same sand-tan, and the shag carpet bright blue.

"It ain't all that much," Paul Wolf Guts said, "but it's home."

"It's nice," said Maura.

"Says Peta," Paul said, directing his gaze to Maura's eyes. "So do you mind if I ask why you come back here? Most folks, they get away from the Rez, they don't bother comin' back."

Maura glanced over at Coal, knowing he must be asking the same thing. She shrugged. "I had to see my family. Especially my sister. And I wanted to know what happened to Maybelle Little-brave."

At mention of that name, Paul's eyes crinkled up. A look of fondness came over his face. "That's some woman. The boys said you went t' visit her already."

Maura nodded.

"She keeps on goin', that woman. I think she might live longer than all the rest of us."

Maura smiled. "She deserves to live forever."

Paul grunted. "You sure don't mean that. Wishin' her a life forever on this piece o' land, with what she has. Naw, she needs t' be up in the good spirit land, that woman. She done whatever the Great Spirit asked her t' do. You should know that—you, of all people."

Maura shrugged. "I know you're right. But it will be a sad world without her."

"It will that. It sure will that."

They all heard a vehicle pull up outside, and Paul bent over to peer between slats in the blinds. "Well, speakin' o' Maybelle. Here she is. Her an' Chessie Bad Milk, that old goat." He chuckled, going to the front door. In spite of the cold and the wind outside, he opened the door and stood there waiting for the two anything-but-spry Indians to climb out of Chessie's low-riding brown Dodge pickup.

"Hau, Maybelle," greeted Paul. "Chessie, what you doin' in this wind?"

"Survivin' is all," replied old Chessie. "Saw what happened with your truck. I tried t' help ya."

Paul shook his head. "Yeah, I saw that. Them young fools. An' Chessie, you're an old one. What were you thinkin'? Hey, you all right? Looked like you fell pretty hard."

Chessie nodded, raising his cane above his head and giving it a shake. "Sure am, you bet. I got my cane Maybelle give me."

Paul grinned, then on a last-minute thought went down the stairs to help both of them up. As Maybelle was easing up his stairs, his hand holding her elbow, he said, "So you two come t' see the crazy hero?"

Maybelle almost met his eyes, and she almost smiled. "I come see if he is so brave or if he jus' got no brain. An' maybe I come t' give him a Injun name."

With another grin, bigger than the first, Paul said, "Well, I bin tryin' t' figger it out myself—if he's got a brain."

He came up the steps behind Maybelle, acting as her herder and standing right behind her in case she should try to fall.

When Maybelle and Chessie were standing in the living room, both leaning on their canes, their eyes shifted back and forth between Coal and Maura.

"Young white man's makin' big talk happen down at the mercantile," said Maybelle, her eye corners wrinkling up but still not using up one of her hard-to-find smiles.

Coal smiled at the thought of being called young. Maybelle could get away with that, he guessed. "I didn't mean to, ma'am."

"Well, you did good. You did good." She shook her cane, then hurriedly put the end of it back on the floor so she could lean on it. "But them boys, they will be comin' after you. All o' you." She turned and skewered Paul Wolf Guts's chin with her eyes. "You know that, don't you?"

Paul's jaw flexed. He knew it, and so did Coal. And Coal knew that he could disappear, but Paul was stuck here.

Maybelle hobbled over to where Coal and Maura had sat down on one of the sofas and looked down at him. She glanced over at Maura and motioned toward Coal with an upward wave of her hand. "Tell him to stand up."

Maura gave her a big smile. "I guess you'd better stand up, Coal."

Coal rose from the couch, towering over Maybelle and making her look like one of J. R. R. Tolkien's Hobbits, or a wizened dwarf.

Maybelle fumbled a hand out and clutched Coal's hand by the fingers, raising it up and giving it a little shake. "You a good white man."

He said, "Thanks," not knowing how else to reply.

"No. I mean what I'm sayin'. You good. I come here because we figgered this is where you'd go. An' I wanna tell you a story."

"Okay." Coal glanced over at Maura, who smiled.

"We gon' to sit down. Paul?" She turned and sought out the homeowner. "You make up the fire."

Paul grinned. "Yes, Grandmother." And he set about his duty. While he was stoking the fire back up, he sent the boys running to bring in more wood, and to chop some kindling.

While this was ongoing, Maybelle motioned for Coal to sit back down on the sofa, and then she went and dragged a brown chair over from the table, refusing help. When she had it in place in front of Coal, she eased down on it, facing him, and reached down, her arm shaking, to take his left hand once more. Only then did she say, "I'm gon' hold on your hand, while I tell an old story. Very old—older than me."

Coal nodded, embarrassed now that everyone had their eyes on him, including the boys, who had just come back in with their first loads of wood.

"I bin known long time here at Pine Ridge as a giver-of-names. Not the normal names, but real names—names that mean some-thin'. The names of the old ways."

Again, Coal nodded, unsure of what he was supposed to say, so deciding to say nothing.

The old woman shook his hand up and down. "I drove me down t' the mercantile store, an' ever'body down there talkin'. Talkin' 'bout this great big white man that come an' challenged five big Lakota boys all by hisself. Chessie already done told me about him, but I had t' be sure it was you." Again, she shook his hand, this time letting go of her cane and reaching over to put her left hand with her right, holding onto his hand as if she were afraid he might get away.

"Two things happen here t'day. My little yellow-hair girl, she come home. Fire-in-her-Eyes. I saw her return in a dream, an' I knew it was real. An' then there she was. An' I dreamed she come with *Wakinyan Tanka*—you would say 'Thunderbird'. But then when she come it was with you, an' I laughed at myself. No Wakinyan Tanka—only a fool white man don't know where his place is. That's what I said then. That's what I said 'til I looked in your face."

Coal was straining hard to make sure he understood everything she was saying. In her broken, toothless voice and imperfect accent it was difficult, but he was pretty sure he had caught everything so far.

"Then I hear about the mercantile," she went on, "an' me and Chessie, we went down there. Sure enough, it really was you. An' the stories they're tellin'. They would put your face red like ours, if you heard 'em.

"I'm gon' tell you the old, old story about the Return of the Thunder Beings—in our language, Wakinyan. An' the Great Thunderbird, who is called Wakinyan Tanka. In our *Paha Sapa*—the Black Hills—our season of celebrations begins with the Return of the Thunder Beings, the Wakinyan. We know they are comin' back, in the season of planting, because we see lightning, we hear thunder—which is called also by the name o' wakinyan—an' then the big rains come. This is the way we know the Thunder Beings are comin' back again.

"The Wakinyan, they live out there—in the West. When they come, t' tell us it's the season of plantin', the birds come back, an' the animals come across the prairie, goin' to the Black Hills, an' before *wasichu* come—the white man—the buffalo herds also would return t' give us of themselfs. It was a good time. A time of plenty. Animals that sleep in the ground get up, an' the plants grow, an' pretty flowers come out.

"But like the thunder you hear, an' the lightnin' flashes from the sky, bad things can come with Wakinyan too, an' destruction. Storms come t' the land. The Wakinyan have power t' give life, but they also have power t' take it away. With the wind, they blow things down—sometime even houses. With the rain, they can make great waters carry away things: children, animals—even the cars the people drive. Or maybe so they don't send no rain at all, an' then things die, with no rain. But if the people are good, Wakinyan is good, an' with the thunder beings come the good rains, an' all life comes back again. The people become happy.

"The real old-time Wakinyan was a big bird—big as this house. So strong. So full of power." She reached way over and thumped Coal on his right biceps with her left hand. "Like this. *Strong.* An' they make the rain an' wind an' the sun do whatever they like. Their voice is the thunder, an' they shoot the lightning out o' their eyes. Their wings are like great trees, an' their claws—" she raised both of her hands, formed like talons "—they are like swords. They can protect, an' at the same time they also can destroy.

"Wakinyan is good. A friend to good people. Good spirits. They are keepers of the truth an' protectors of good people. Like my boys." She looked toward Billy and Joseph and almost smiled.

The old woman squeezed Coal's hand even tighter, and for the second time she let her eyes meet his, although she pulled them quickly away. "When I first heard your story, I wanted t' call you: *Nanwica Kciji*. It means Stands-up-for-Them. But Wakinyan Tanka, he speaks t' me when I was drivin' here, an' he tells me. It was you that come in my dream with Peta. There is a reason you come here, Savage. You come as a protector an' a destroyer. Both the same now. An' the Great Spirit, it tells me that your name is a name that is maybe almost never give t' no one—maybe ever.

"Your name for us here at Pine Ridge is a sacred name, the name all good, true Lakota will know you by, because you will save us from an evil that has been with us for many years, since before Peta was come down t' the earth.

"Savage? You will take on you the name of Wakinyan Tanka—Thunderbird."

CHAPTER SEVENTEEN

After Maybelle Littlebrave had finished pronouncing Coal the man from her dream, the savior of Oglala, the protector of all that was good, and the destroyer of all evil, he couldn't even think of how to reply. To call himself overwhelmed was certainly an understatement.

He knew what his heart said about all this malarkey, however, and a part of him was glad Maybelle Littlebrave didn't know the same thing. Yet another part of him knew he should tell her. In the end, he didn't. He simply didn't have the heart. The fact was, Coal Savage was no *Wakinyan Tanka*. He was no great champion of anyone in this place, other than perhaps Maura. Although it was true that his sheepdog nature had come to the momentary rescue of old Chessie Bad Milk, Paul Wolf Guts, and the two boys, it pretty much stopped there. He had every intention of taking Maura and getting off the Pine Ridge Reservation as fast as his LTD could carry them.

Before the two of them departed, Maybelle stopped in front of Billy and Joseph. "You two stayin' here?"

"Just for a while, Grandmother," replied Joseph. "We'll come home soon."

She tried to smile. Coal deduced that perhaps her smiler was faulty. He had seen her make several attempts, but little ever got past her eyes and all the way to her lips.

Chessie Bad Milk hobbled over to Coal, following Maybelle toward the door. He shuffled his feet for a moment, then brought his eyes all the way up to Coal's throat, where they stopped. "Glad you come here, Savage. This place bin needin' someone like you a long time."

Coal nodded. He was going to shake the old man's hand, but Chessie turned away before he could make that move and followed Maybelle out.

After they were gone, Paul Wolf Guts brought coffee he had been brewing and poured cups for Coal and Maura without asking if they wanted any. Coal looked down at it and cringed, although he tried not to let on. He was tired of drinking what other people referred to in their sick way as coffee. Paul caught the look that slid across Coal's face before he could hide it, and he grinned and nodded, blowing across his own cup and taking a tentative sip. He let out a sigh of contentment.

"This ain't like other people's coffee—Wakinyan. You'll like Wolf Guts java."

Coal had to laugh. "I see you're a mind reader, among other things."

Paul shrugged and gave Coal a mild smile. "Wasn't hard to read you. An' I guess we're alike that way. I hate me some bad coffee."

Coal had little choice but to test out Paul's claim, and when the near-boiling liquid touched his taste buds, he smiled. "Huh. You're right."

"Told you."

They sat there for a few minutes without speaking, Maura pressed against Coal on the couch. Apparently, although she had taken to sitting near her door in the car again, it was all right to be close to him in other circumstances. The boys were watching some show through an ugly snow storm on Paul's black and white television.

"You ain't stayin'. Are you." Paul Wolf Guts's words should have been a question, but the intonation of them made them a statement. He already knew.

"No."

Paul nodded. "Can't blame you."

"What about you? You've got some trouble coming."

A shrug from Paul was what Coal had expected. "Yeah. Sure do. I been in trouble before. You know, I fought over in Nam."

For some reason he didn't have time to analyze, that revelation surprised Coal. "Really? Where?"

"Place called Quang Tri."

"Who with?"

"Marines—of course. The Fourth. Company E of the Second Battalion."

"Well, Semper fi," said Coal.

"You too?"

"I was Marines during Korea. In Nam I was Army."

Paul gave a little grin. "Couldn't hack the rough stuff no more, huh?"

"I kind of wish I'd stayed in the Corps," said Coal with a laugh. "Being in the Army as an MP put me right in the middle of the Long Binh riot."

Paul whistled through his teeth. "Oh, I take it back. Bad medicine there, man. My hat's off to you. Or my warbonnet, at least," he said with a grin.

"We could talk about Nam all day," Coal said. "But the real subject isn't Nam. It's right here at Oglala. You've got trouble coming, and I can't help you. That idiot has four friends that I can't imagine are just going to brush off that fight any more than he will."

Paul laughed without humor. "Four? Hell, I wish. His little war gang he drags around with him is more like seven or eight, last I knew. Some o' the others actually have real jobs, believe it or not. But nights an' weekends, that bunch is hell around here."

"Why aren't the police doing anything?"

"Ha! Police. We got almost thirty-five hundred square miles here, Savage. And less than ten cops for all of it—*scared* cops, mostly. They got families to think about too, you know. Asa Iron Rope and his turds, they ain't the only game out here. There's bigger fish other places. The whole Rez is a war zone. Nam on a smaller scale."

This revelation made Coal feel almost ill. Paul Wolf Guts was acting the tough Marine, an image Coal knew all too well. But inside he had to be scrambling to figure out what he was going to do.

"Anyway, yeah. I don't blame you for goin'. You should wait until it's dark, then go. That's what I'd do. You know, just like the Old West—safer to travel at night."

Coal nodded. "That's the plan. I wish I could help you."

"Maybelle's sure gonna wish that too. But she's grabbin' at old dreams. Hopin' for old ways. These punks on the Rez now, they got no respect for how things used t' be. They're bootleggin' alcohol, makin' money like there's no tomorrow off these poor folks in here, the ones that can't even afford gas t' drive off the Rez for hooch. It's sick, Savage. If I could get out I would too."

"That's what this is all about? Bootlegging?"

"Yep."

"How big is it?"

"Big. Huge. The old man? Leland Iron Rope? He's been like a gang lord for a couple decades, what they tell me. For the Rez, he's a rich man. All them punks at the Merc? Those are his gang. Yeah. Hell, sometimes I think maybe the police are part of it too."

Coal's heart had started pounding harder than he liked at the mere mention of the name Leland Iron Rope. *The man who hurt me.* Maura's words kept echoing through his head. By now, Coal had surmised most of the rest. The name seemed to make his blood pressure climb to new heights.

The more Coal heard about the situation on the reservation, the sicker he felt for Paul and the others. He could see no legal solution for something like this, especially if the local law enforcement was involved in it, or, at the very best, turning their heads the other way.

"What would you do if you left here?" asked Coal.

"Fix cars, just like I'm doin' now. My daddy got me into it— when he wasn't drownin' out his own life with Thunderbird." Paul suddenly thought of the connection to Coal's new name and grinned. "An' I ain't talkin' about the *Wakinyan* kind o' Thunderbird."

It seemed funny to Coal how the smallest things came together in one's mind in the strangest of ways. That was how it happened right then for Coal, who now remembered Nora Sue Plenty-Wounds talking about Thunderbird wine, and shortly after that the Lakota hardcases showed up in a Ford Thunderbird, followed by Coal himself being dubbed "Thunderbird" in the Lakota tongue. A superstitious man might think there really was something other-worldly about it all.

"I wonder if you know what that name even means, Savage," said Paul, shaking Coal from his thoughts.

"What's that?"

"The name Maybelle give you: Wakinyan Tanka. Thunderbird. I ain't sure, but I don't think any Lakota has ever had that name. *Ever.* Leastways not that I ever heard of. We got a lotta great names on the Rez. A lot o' names that make them that's wearin' 'em sound perty big an' bad. Take me, for instance. Wolf Guts. Now there's a name. The original Wolf Guts was at the Bighorn. Then we got names like PlentyWolf, Big Bear, Fasthorse. But Wakinyan Tanka, now—Thunderbird. If you don't understand that whole story, and who he is, you should read about it. He's a god, Savage.

No different from your Zeus. Who uses the name of a god t' give to a regular Joe? Nobody, that's who. The closest I ever heard is an old guy over around Pine Ridge name o' Danny Thunderhawk.

"But no, she didn't give you any Thunderhawk. Or Thunder Eagle. Thunder Horse, Thunder Bear. None o' that. Even though them are all names off this Rez. Maybelle was inspired t' give you the name of a mythical god. I gotta say she's gonna be perty shocked when she finds out her god cut an' run."

"I thought you *said* I should go."

"I did. An' I still do say it. But I sure don't think Maybelle ever expected it. She's thinkin' she had some deep revelation 'bout you, an' she's about t' find out you're no different than any other man."

A strange sensation suddenly came over Coal. Not a good one. But it was nothing to do with Paul Wolf Guts's speech. He got up without saying anything and went over to the door, pushing it open a few inches to look out toward the highway. There, exactly as he had feared, sat the dark green Thunderbird, idling in the road.

Paul must have caught the change in the air, and he walked over as well, looking out past Coal's shoulder. "How'd you know they was there?"

"Those old senses don't ever go away, Paul."

Paul grunted. "Yeah. But maybe mine are rusty."

A few seconds later, the Thunderbird sped off down the highway. Coal knew they'd be back.

Maura had come to the door with Coal and Paul, and she was in time to see the Thunderbird driving away. Coal looked at her, hiding his real thoughts. "I don't know if I should be flattered at all that your friend would give me a name that's the same as what those wild boys are driving around."

Maura frowned. "Hey, can I talk to you alone for a minute?"

Coal glanced over at Paul, then back at her. "Sure."

He followed her down the hall a ways, where she stopped and turned to him, leaning in close. "You know they'll be coming here for him tonight."

"Probably."

"You're not just going to leave when it gets dark, are you?"

"He said to."

Again, she gave him a frown, and speared him with her eyes. Maybelle had said the Thunderbird had eyes that shot lightning from them, and that was certainly impressive. But Maura's, true to her Indian name, shot fire.

"I know what he said. He's trying to look tough."

"Yep."

"Yep? That's all you can say? Coal, if you leave him here, I'm staying."

"What the hell are you talking about?"

"I'm staying. He helped you. You can't desert him. Especially if there's more of those men coming tonight."

"One of them might be your brother," Coal pointed out. "What about that? Do you really want to stay and see what happens to him?"

"If he's with an Iron Rope, he's no brother of mine."

For a few moments, Coal looked at her, eyes noncommittal. Finally, he turned to go back down the hall, but she grabbed him by the arm.

"Coal."

"What?"

"You can't just leave."

"I know. Because we're damn fools, and we're staying."

Coal didn't see which came fastest, the tears into Maura's eyes or the smile to her lips.

CHAPTER EIGHTEEN

An hour before sunset, the hard, dusty wind that had been howling all day seemed simply to run itself out of energy, and the world turned eerie with its stillness. Coal could hear the steady *tick, tick* of the clock hanging on the backside of the kitchen cupboard. In his mind, he could hear each *tick* speaking to him: *Just—wait—they—will—be—here.* And they would. He felt a little more like Davy Crockett at the Alamo than George Custer against the rush of two thousand blood-thirsty Sioux, Cheyenne, and Arapaho warriors screaming up the foothills out of the valley of the Little Bighorn, but the concept was the same: Hell had been unleashed, and it was coming.

Coal and Maura were still on the couch finishing up plates of fry bread, beans, and diced fried venison. Paul Wolf Guts broke the quiet of the contemplative dining to break out his supply of Diet Pepsi and Tab, Coca Cola's answer to sugar-free Pepsi. He held a can of Diet Pepsi in his left hand, Tab in his right. "Which one you want?"

Coal's eyes shifted between the two. "You're kidding me, right? Neither. Thanks anyway."

Paul looked hurt. "What? You don't like pop?"

"If I did it wouldn't be that nasty stuff."

His face relaxing, the Lakota chuckled. "Yeah, it don't taste all that good. But at least it's got no sugar."

Coal chuckled. "Right. How's the water?"

"You don't want any o' this water."

"Well." Coal swore and finally reached for the Diet Pepsi. "I guess I'm probably going to be up all night anyway."

Grinning, Paul said, "Yeah, it's a long way back t' town. An' by the way . . ." He glanced out the window. "It's gettin' perty late. Be dark soon. We better get you back over t' Sioux's house so you c'n get your car."

"No, leave it."

Paul stared at him. "What're you talkin' about?"

"Leave it. That's plain enough, right?"

"You gonna walk t' Rapid City?"

"Not until after the fireworks."

Paul broke the apparent taboo of looking into someone's eyes, and he broke it in a big way, staring Coal down for no less than ten full seconds.

"I thought we decided you was leavin' for Rapid City at dark."

"That was back when we both still thought I was smart."

A knowing look came over the man's face, and his eyes slid over to Maura. It was pretty obvious he was thinking back on the private little confab she and Coal had held in the hallway earlier. He looked back at Coal and bunched his lips.

"Well, you ain't all that smart—Wakinyan."

Coal grunted. "You don't have to tell me."

*   *   *

The pale sun melted beyond the western mountains—supposedly right past the home of the real Wakinyan Tanka—the giant Thunderbird. For a while, a greenish sky lingered over the horizon, and then it turned to a sick kind of orange-brown. Coal and Maura were sitting in the Wolf Guts trailer house, not in Rapid City, where they should have been.

The lights in the house were off now. The boys were safely back home with Maybelle Littlebrave, although Billy had fought having to leave. There were only two lights burning in the house, and one was the tip of Paul Wolf Guts's cigarette. He tried to blow every lungful of smoke up and away from Coal and Maura, but the stifling stench of it was filling up the trailer, regardless.

Coal's Smith and Wesson sat beside him, along with a box of cartridges they had gone over to Sioux Returns from Scout's house to retrieve. They had also retrieved the man himself—Returns from Scout. He had refused to be left out of tonight's party, and his cigarette was the second source of light.

"Big doin's tonight," breathed out Returns from Scout with his latest breath of smoke. "Can't believe you'd try t' cut me out."

"Can't believe you're so anxious t' lose yer house," replied Paul wryly.

Returns from Scout shrugged. "Ah, I c'n make me another one. Can't make me no other friend, though." In the eerie glow of his cigarette, the old man's face crinkled into a smile of wisdom and friendship. His face could not have appeared any calmer.

The darkness in the house meant it was safe for tough men to say mushy things. There was no reply from Paul Wolf Guts.

"They're here."

Maura's voice broke several minutes of thoughtful quiet, and Coal jerked his eyes over to her. There was a question in his eyes, but if she saw it her only answer was to squeeze his knee.

Pushing up off the couch with his .44 magnum in hand, Coal walked over and pushed down a slat of the blinds, peeking out. Maura was right, and this time he hadn't even felt it. He couldn't make out the vehicles, but in the road were now three sets of head-lights, stopped with maybe three or four feet between each car.

The others came over, and while Maura looked past Coal's shoulder through the window in the door, Paul and Sioux went down a ways to the window in the hall. Coal saw a shadow pass in front of the headlights of the front car, and then another. He could make out those two, and within moments perhaps five or six oth-ers, and maybe more. But it was too dark to see what they were doing. It almost looked like some of them were carrying something.

A match flared up, surprisingly bright in the darkness, and a huge pile of something exploded into fire. All three vehicles were lit up now, the green Thunderbird in front, then a tall pickup, and some other long car Coal couldn't make out in the back. Instead of eight people, in this new spotlight of the bonfire, burning in what appeared to be a pile of pallets, Coal counted ten. Firelight flickered off long guns, either shotguns or rifles, that several of them were carrying around.

Through the walls and windows of the poorly insulated trailer, an unearthly wail rose in the night. Maura clutched Coal's arm, squeezing with surprising strength. He didn't think to tell her it kind of hurt.

"What the hell?" Paul Wolf Guts's voice came in a whisper.

Silence answered him, until half a minute later, over the sounds of frightening moans, howls, and outright squalls, Sioux Returns from Scout said, "They're chantin' war songs. Doin' a war dance."

The fire-lit shapes of Asa Iron Rope's gang contorted, pranced, and leaped up and down on the edge of the highway, some of them raising their guns in the air and shaking them. A hundred scenes from old Westerns couldn't help but flash across Coal's mind, although it was hard for them to find room among the beautiful array of curse words bouncing around in there. He shouldn't have stayed. But he couldn't leave Paul Wolf Guts alone. What was going to happen to Maura now?

It was as if Paul Wolf Guts read Coal's mind, and he padded over, making no sound on the carpet. "Hey. I got a back door, an' out behind my biggest shed there's a trail—okay? It goes way up, maybe a quarter mile, then starts into some chalky hills. I've been huntin' up in there, an' I seen animals hidin' almost in plain sight."

After a moment of silence, Coal shrugged. "Okay?"

"Okay. When this starts, you gotta git her packin'. Understand, Miss?" He turned to Maura, the cigarette glowing between his lips.

"I can shoot as good as anybody."

Silence. One, five, ten seconds' worth. The tip of Paul's cigarette turned at last to point at Coal. "You gotta choose, not me. But if this goes real bad . . ."

"I'll make her go," said Coal.

"So I can go up there and freeze to death?" Maura interjected. "I'm not leaving you. Do you have another gun?"

After a thoughtful moment, Paul laughed. "Yer spunky, Miss. I like spunky. Do I have another gun, you ask?" He laughed again, this time a more drawn-out sound. "Does a bear crap in the woods? What do you want?"

"What do you have?"

"Get her a shotgun," Coal cut in.

"I'll get you a shotgun."

"Why don't you get me a shotgun?"

Chuckling, Paul whispered away down the hall and came back a minute later. Coal could hear the clatter of gun metal as the Lakota laid his arsenal out on the couch. He left again, and when he came back he nudged Coal with a box, to draw his attention.

"I got two shotguns and three rifles over there. Two pistols. You want anything else?"

"A grenade launcher?"

"Damn, I left that in Nam."

"Then we're good."

"Of course we are. Yer the Thunderbird, ain't you?"

Coal grunted. To have lightning flare out of his eyes, yes, now that would be a gift.

"Hey! Hey in there!"

The lone voice rang across a now-quiet yard. The bonfire still reared up high, some six feet above the ground, lighting up all the fools who now stood restless around it. Coal wondered how much rotgut they already had in them.

"Should I answer?" asked Paul.

"It's your party," Coal replied.

Paul inched the door open. "Hey out there."

"So we burnin' this place down with you in it, or out?"

"Maybe neither, thanks."

Some of the figures out there roared with laughter once they all understood what Paul had said.

"Then we have t' choose."

"I'll choose for you," replied Paul. "The first man brings a can o' gas or a light over here, I shoot him."

The speaker from the road, who was big enough he could only have been Iron Rope, roared with laughter. It took a moment, but some of his cohorts finally joined him.

"You gonna kill us all?"

"You never watched no Westerns when you was growin' up, did ya?" Paul called back.

"What the hell you talkin' about?"

"They always tried t' kill the chief first. An' I know yer just a little piss ant, Iron Rope, but t'night I figger all these other winos are lookin' at you as their chief. Guess what that means."

Iron Rope laughed, but this one sounded a little more forced. "Ha! You ain't got the guts—Wolf Guts!" He roared with delight at his own pun.

"I'm done talkin', bad boy," Paul said, and he shut the door.

The riotous dancing and singing had ceased, and the crackle of the flames could not be heard inside the house. Soon, Coal saw the Lakotas gather up in a cluster, and there was a lot of animated movement, stomping and waving of arms.

Soon, figures started marching toward the vehicles. Coal breathed a sigh of relief. Were they leaving? Had Paul's hard stand worked?

One by one, the vehicles began to move forward. But they weren't leaving. The Thunderbird rolled first into Paul's yard, with bodies hanging out the windows. The first flash of orange was accompanied instantly by the *boom* of a shotgun. The yelling began again, in earnest, sounds Coal had listened to for years as a boy, every time he went to a so-called "cowboy and Indian" movie. Guns were flashing, and the din of them filled the night.

Paul swore, running over to the dining room window on the opposite side of the house to see the Thunderbird careening through that side of his yard. The front seat passenger fired out the window, and this time the flame was going sideways rather than up. But of course there was no way to see where.

Paul swore again. "I'm goin' out."

"No! They think you're by yourself, Paul. You go out there an' they just might shoot you."

"What am I supposed t' do?" Paul yelled back, sounding angry.

"Wait. Just wait. You were in the war. Come on. You remember what it's like to kill somebody. And that's just the start of your trouble."

Simultaneous with the next flash of light and thunder of a shotgun, a window down the hall shattered, and glass sprayed nearly to the entryway.

Paul yelled something inarticulate and threw the door open, leveling his shotgun.

CHAPTER NINETEEN

The blast of Paul Wolf Guts's shotgun shook the inside of the house. He racked in a new round and fired again, the spent shell flinging across in front of Coal's eyes.

Paul racked another one in, swinging with the suddenly accelerated pace of the car, a dark blue Pontiac Grand Prix of mid-sixties vintage. By now, the Thunderbird had hit the pavement of the highway and fishtailed as its driver gunned it. As its tires grabbed traction, it sped away toward town. The pickup wasn't far behind it, but its over-excited and likely intoxicated driver over-shot the asphalt and spun off into the grass on the other side, kicking up dust as they strove to get back out on the road. With a jolt, it hit the asphalt, and the engine roared, sending it hot after the Thunderbird.

The Grand Prix's driver didn't even appear to make an attempt at turning with the highway. The car flew straight across the road, and on the other side of the highway there must have been a drop, because the undercarriage made a loud crunching noise as it bottomed out. The taillights vanished, and then only the right one appeared again as the driver tried to get the vehicle back up on the road and follow the fleeing Thunderbird and pickup.

Amid a swirling dust cloud that appeared like dirty fog in the head- and taillights of the Grand Prix, movement ceased. The car's motor revved to a high RPM, billowing up an even larger storm of dust behind the car. This went on for fifteen or twenty seconds before doors started flying open, vomiting shapes that were dim and gray in the darkness and dust. Voices yelled back and forth, and then Coal saw one or two of the shapes take off through the prairie grass at a clumsy run.

"They're stuck good," Coal said.

"I'm goin' over there."

"Like hell you are! Stay in here!" Coal wasn't in the habit of barking commands at people he hardly knew, but he fell back on his former rank now.

Paul whirled on him, staring even though they could barely see each other in the dark. "Why?"

"You've got who knows how many guys over there, man? Scared, drunk, and their car stuck in the dark—and they all have guns. You just put three loads of buckshot in the side of their car, and they're probably thinking you plan to finish the job. You really want to walk into that?"

Paul kept staring. Coal wished he could see him better, but he wasn't about to flip on a light for the privilege. When Paul didn't answer, he followed up with, "Think about it. You got 'em on the run. Leave well enough alone."

Beside Coal, Maura spoke: "They shut off the lights now."

He looked back to see full darkness across the highway. Clouds had come in to seal over the sky, so not even a star could be seen, and the driver of the Grand Prix had given up and shut everything off. He must have headed out on foot following the others.

The wind had picked up again, and a bad chill rode the air. Unfortunately, the same chill, thanks to the hallway window being shot out, was now in the house.

Paul swore helplessly. After a moment, Coal heard him say, "Here." Instinctively, he reached out and felt the Lakota's shotgun being pressed toward him, and he took it. "Cover me, will you? I need to go out and get some boards to put over the window hole. I can feel snow comin'. Do we dare turn on a light?"

"Aw, hell. Yeah, I guess we'll have to. Or maybe use a lighter?"

Paul made no reply, but Coal could hear him digging in a pocket, and a few seconds later a lighter sparked and spouted a tiny flame. Coal could see Paul's face in its dim light. "All right. Well, I'm headed out to the shed. I'll be back."

While Coal, Maura, and Sioux Returns from Scout waited inside the trailer in full darkness, Paul traipsed off to his big shed. He returned a few minutes later with half a sheet of plywood, a drill, and screws. Within minutes, he had the board secured over the broken window, working by the light of his Bic, which Coal held up for him.

"Now what?" asked Paul. "We gonna be in the dark all night?"

"You plan on throwing a party?" Coal countered.

"Huh?"

"Do you need light? Maybe some of us ought to try and sleep."

Coal continued allowing the lighter to burn, because he hated holding conversations in the absolute dark. Paul nodded. "Yeah, you're right. So here's what I was thinkin' when I was out in my shed: Those pukes have no idea I wasn't in here by myself. You two and Sioux are still safe. Am I thinkin' right?"

After a moment's thought, Coal nodded. "Yeah, I guess that's right. So?"

"Okay. So I know I did some serious damage to that Pontiac. I can't imagine a bunch o' drunk Injuns are gonna let that be. You three need t' get out o' here."

Coal shook his head. "Maybe tomorrow. I'm not leaving tonight while they're still full of piss and vinegar. That is if you have some place we can roll out a blanket."

Paul gave a nod. "Fine. Well, like they say, it's yer funeral. Come on. I'll show you a room."

*   *   *

Throughout the first part of the night, the four of them each took turns watching outside for a half hour at a time. That was about all their eyes could take of straining into the dark with only the pathetic porch light to illuminate anything.

Around half past midnight, the sky lightened a little, and shortly after that snow began to fall, driven ahead of a stiff wind. Coal was watching the window when it came. Although in the dirty-looking night, and being shot like bullets before the wind, he might not have called it pretty, it certainly was welcome. Those drunk Lakotas would lose interest now in coming back around. The first time he had been on watch, he had seen one of the cars come down the road from the direction of town and stop, perhaps a half-mile off. He figured they must be picking up their lost gang members, because after a few minutes they backed around in the road and headed back the other way.

With the snow falling, and all their gang rounded up, Coal made an educated guess: The rest of the night would be uneventful.

Saturday, January 27

Maura had insisted on being with Coal all night. Even when he went on watch she got up and tried to doze on the sofa. Those Iron Ropes had her scared of her own shadow, it seemed. It was past time to get her out of this place and head home.

Coal woke up in bed in spoon formation behind Maura, his left arm draped across her. The sound of her gentle snoring wasn't annoying. It was rather peaceful, and he lay and listened to it for some time before a smile came to his face. He still didn't know everything that had happened to this girl out here when she was a child, and maybe he never would. He didn't know if coming here had brought her any peace, or maybe made things worse. He only knew it was his duty to get her away.

A light tap came at the door. Coal pushed away from the woman and went to open it, finding Paul Wolf Guts there.

"Snowed almost half an inch last night. I think it chased those thugs off."

"Good. I thought it might."

"It looks like the sun's gonna be out t'day, too. So good travelin' weather."

"What are you trying to say, Paul?"

"That I want you gone." He gave a half-grin.

"That's not very neighborly."

"Aw come on, Savage—Thunderbird. This ain't yer fight, man. Just go on. Take that girl outta here. You're just gonna get her hurt, an' nothin' she c'n find here is gonna be somethin' she needs t' find."

"I'll tell her that."

"Do. So hey—why don't you two get a little more rest, huh? I'm gonna chase us up some breakfast, an' then we'll head over t' Sioux's place and get yer car. Good?"

Coal sighed and gave him a nod. "Good. I guess."

Paul shut the door, and Coal went back and snuggled up against Maura, closing his eyes. But it didn't last.

"I need to see Nora Sue."

Coal swore silently. "Good morning."

"I need to see her, Coal. Do you understand?"

"Can't you write her a letter? Maura, this isn't a game. Those boys are going to be out for blood."

"It was Paul that shot the tire. And shot their car."

"And it was me that humiliated them in front of everyone at the mercantile. And I'm white. That's unforgivable. I know guys like this."

Maura lay there breathing. After a few minutes mulling over her situation, she said, "A letter wouldn't be the same."

"But you'll say what you need to say. She'll listen or she won't. And in the meantime, you don't get hurt. Come on. Let's be smart. You tried. That's all anyone could do."

*   *   *

They left the settlement of Oglala without saying goodbye to anyone but Paul and Sioux, two men they hadn't even known a day earlier yet were now comrades in arms.

Coal had done some fast talking. He didn't want to be the reason Maura always claimed she was never able to find closure. But at the same time he knew the dangers of staying on the Pine Ridge Reservation. In the end, of her own accord as Coal had hoped it would be, she decided to go. She didn't want to face Maybelle again because she didn't want to see her old friend disappointed in Coal for leaving when she had been so sure the Great Spirit had sent him here to be their savior. And she didn't go to Nora Sue again, in large part because she had no desire to see the people who claimed to be her parents. She would write her a letter, like Coal suggested. Maybe it wouldn't mean much, but it would have to be enough. As for her little lost sister, Cordelia, wherever her body was would be a mystery no one ever solved.

So they brushed the light snow off the LTD and climbed in. It fired up, and soon the heater was blowing hot air. Coal got out on the highway, and they drove past the disabled Grand Prix stuck in the grassy field, then all the way through Oglala without seeing the Thunderbird or the pickup from the night before.

It was a quiet drive out to the main highway, where Coal turned south toward Nebraska at Maura's request. She was happy to have seen the last of Rapid City, and to leave her bad memories—along with the good ones—far behind.

It was a tad over an hour on the icy road to the little town of Chadron, Nebraska. Because they had slept so poorly the night before, they decided to get a room early and recuperate. Coal found a nice big hotel called the Blaine, one street over from Main, at

159 Bordeaux, and the slow time of year gifted them with a parking space directly in front.

Inside, the desk clerk decided since it was the off season to allow them an early check-in, on top of the low rate of ten dollars. After putting their bags on the bureau by the huge Zenith color TV, they took off their boots and propped themselves up on the bed to numb their minds for a while with some network programming.

In spite of all she had said about making up her mind, Maura seemed despondent. The movie on the television, *The War Between Men and Women,* starred Jack Lemmon, and would normally have struck Coal as pretty humorous, but none of it seemed to strike Maura's normally good sense of humor. She sat there toying with her black marble and the broken piece of plate from the girls' home. After a while, Coal lost interest as well. The enjoyment of laughing alone never lasted very long.

They napped off and on through the day, and once they even braved the cold and the wind and strolled around the quaint little town. The long rows of interconnected, varicolored brick and rock buildings were the epitome of picturesque small-town America, the sky was beautiful, and the air crisp and clear.

In the early evening, Coal decided to take a shower. Maura was still sitting on the bed. They hadn't spoken to each other in over two hours. She was in her own head, and he had given up trying to carry on a conversation with some kind of zombie.

He paused at the entry to the bath area and looked back at Maura, who stared, apparently transfixed, at the TV screen. "I'm getting in the shower. Don't do anything I wouldn't do while I'm gone. Okay?"

She looked up at him and forced a little smile. When she dropped her head back against the headboard it made a soft *clunk*. With a sigh, Coal stepped into the bathroom and started getting undressed. He had been looking forward to a nice hot shower all day. And it sure beat sitting out there with Maura PlentyWounds.

When he got out, he took his time drying off, looking at his overgrown hair in the mirror and making himself grin at how it looked when he pushed it all straight up. It was definitely time for a haircut. He took a razor to his scruffy face, careful with his now overly-large, sculpted sideburns, combed his hair back down so he might resemble a human, and splashed a little Brut aftershave on. Maybe if nothing else he could entertain Maura making her try to guess the brand.

He got back into his jeans, mostly because he hadn't brought any sweat pants or pajamas, and because he had no intention of getting into bed in his underwear with Maura there. For the past five minutes he had wracked his brain trying to think of some way he could liven the woman up, some way he could get her mind off Oglala and her ugly past. But he was drained. It was time to drift into his own mind like she had and either sit there staring at the pointless entertainment playing on CBS or try to get some much-needed real sleep.

Stepping out, he looked over at the bed. It was empty. Confused, he scanned the room. Unless Maura was hiding by lying on the floor on the opposite side of the bed, he was alone. He checked, and she wasn't.

Thinking she must have gone after something in the car, he started to turn toward the bed, then saw the piece of notebook paper by the TV. On top of it, as if being used for a paper weight, was the broken piece of plate from the girls' home. Going over to the note, he took up the piece of plate and held it in his hand while he read her scrawled message.

Hey, Coal, I really need to go for a walk and sort some things out in my head, okay? This little thing is pretty sharp in my pocket. Will you hold it for me? Don't worry about me. I'll be back in a while. Maura

He sighed again, and he startled himself with the sound of his own voice: "Huh." Apparently, after all the hours of silence other than the TV, he wasn't used to the sound of a real voice. He gave himself a lopsided grin and went over to settle onto the bed.

He held the chip of porcelain between thumb and finger, turning it over and over. Anyone watching would have thought he was studying it for some tiny detail, but really he was only trying to feel Maura PlentyWounds's presence in it. Somehow, he knew that was really how she had meant it, and why she had left it behind.

Well, there wouldn't be any sleeping now—not until Maura came back. He hoped she found whatever answers she was searching for.

An hour passed, seeing Coal all the way through Roger Mudd's CBS news commentary and then *Hee Haw. All in the Family* came on next, and he wanted to get up and change the channel, but it was so far away. He marveled at his own laziness and wondered how he called himself a bodybuilder if he couldn't even summon the energy to cross a space the size of this hotel room and change a channel.

The show, although only half an hour, seemed to go on and on. A couple of times he nodded off, but he snapped awake again to the bright sound of the opening of the *Mary Tyler Moore Show*. He looked around disconcertedly. Still no Maura. He checked his watch. She had been gone five minutes shy of two hours.

Now what the hell. *Two hours?* He knew the woman had a lot to sort out, but it was eight-thirty at night, and it was cold out! This was ridiculous. Maybe she was sitting down in the lobby. Maybe she didn't need to be someplace private and quiet. Maybe she only needed to be away from him. Well, he wasn't going to be the meddler. If she had that much to sort out, then let her do it. It was time for some sleep. She knew the way back to the hotel.

It wasn't until then that he noticed the little cut in the palm of his hand. He had been gripping the porcelain chip so hard that it broke his skin.

Getting his energy up enough to walk to the TV and turn it way down, for background noise, he got back in bed, rolling over to face away from Maura's pillow but holding her bit of plate in his hand like a lifeline.

It felt good to lie there. The mattress was nice and solid, the way he liked them. It felt brand-new. He imagined himself sinking deeper and deeper into his pillow, and into the mattress. All his cares were floating away from him. Sleep was claiming him. He was dead to the world.

Only none of that was true.

No, he lay there with his attention going back and forth between the broken piece of plate and the drapes a few feet away from his face, wondering what was taking Maura so long. Did she really need to be away from him so bad? If he had known, maybe he would have volunteered to leave himself, and she could at least have had the warm room in which to do her soul-searching.

He finally started to doze. He was so tired . . .

He jerked awake and looked around. Maura must have woke him coming back in. He closed his eyes, to feign sleep. He waited. And waited. No sound.

At last, he couldn't take the stress. He rolled the other way and searched about, in the room lit only by the TV. Still empty.

With a sigh of frustration, he sat up, swinging his feet to the carpeted floor. He rubbed his eyes and scratched his head. His yawn was a fake one. He was such an idiot he was even trying to fool himself into thinking this whole thing didn't bother him.

He hated doing it, but he looked at his watch. Maura had been gone over three and a half hours! It had been fully dark for hours out the window beyond the drapes. Chadron wasn't a particularly dangerous-looking place, and Maura was tough enough to handle herself, but still, why would a good-looking woman like her go wandering around in some strange town at night?

One last thought made him get up and go peek around the corner at the bathroom door. It was open, and the light was off.

He loosed out loud the handful of choice phrases he had been so proud of himself for keeping in since finding Maura gone. With a long sigh, he leaned down and got his boots, drawing them on and tying them. He had wanted to wait the woman out, but he had lost. It was time to go find her. She at least needed to give him some good reason she had decided to leave him alone. Nobody needed three and a half hours to sort their thoughts.

Putting on his last clean shirt and thinking they would soon need to find a laundromat, he stepped out in the hall. There was only one room key, and Maura had taken it, but he didn't want anyone messing around in the room, so he locked the door. The desk clerk would just have to let him back in later or grant him another key.

He didn't make it far down the hall before remembering that he had left the piece of Maura's favorite plate on the bed. It was silly to want it on him, but he did. Just not bad enough to go get the clerk to open his door.

He went downstairs and stepped down the hallway to the clerk's desk. No one was in sight there, only a little silver bell to call for service. Frowning, he turned away. He scanned the lobby, but it was a small room, and there wasn't much to scan.

He went up and down every hall in the building, getting more impatient with Maura by the minute. He couldn't think of any time she had been more inconsiderate. This was going to take him a while to forgive her for.

Finally, he went outside and checked the car. It was empty. He walked along the entire front of the building, thinking maybe she had found a chair somewhere. Then he went all the way around and ended up back at the main entrance, where he had come out.

He swore again. It tasted good, too, but he wished Maura were here in front of him right now. He wanted to try a few of his words out on her ears.

Chadron wasn't a huge town, but he pictured their little tour of it and thought how futile it could be wandering the streets in hopes of finding someone who wished to remain lost. His guts were starting to hurt now. His anger and irritation were slowly working themselves up into something a little more . . . Worry?

Taking a deep breath, he stepped back inside and slammed his hand down on the bell on the desk, making it ring way longer than it probably did normally.

The clerk appeared, a different one from the woman who had checked them in. This was a middle-aged man with a big round head nearly vacant of irritating hair to comb. He had an old-fashioned pencil mustache that failed miserably to make him resemble Clark Gable.

"Yes sir. Can I help you?"

"Yeah, sorry to bother you. I know you're not the one that checked us in, but . . . The lady I was with in room 214—she went for a walk, and it's been over three and a half hours."

The man shook his head, his eyes saying he didn't know what he could do to help.

"Well, she's blond. Beautiful girl. Handsome, I guess you'd say. Wearing a slick dark green coat with a fur collar? Blue eyes?"

"Oh, shoot! Yeah, I did see her. And you're right: It was about when I first came on shift, so that's been about three and a half, maybe four hours."

"And you haven't seen her since?"

"Nope." Coal could guess by the man's eyes what he was thinking, that he and Maura had argued, and that she had left in a huff. Maybe he even thought it was a really bad fight, and she had decided to take off for parts unknown.

It was right at that moment that a kick-in-the-guts thought struck him: What if she had decided to head back to Oglala?

He swore. Profoundly. Profusely. The clerk got nervous and apologized to Coal—for what, Coal couldn't figure out. *He* was the one with the foul mouth.

"No, *I'm* sorry. Well, if you see her, her name's Maura. Could you call me in 214? And I guess I'll need another key."

The clerk handed Coal the requested key to slip into his pocket. "Sure, I'll call you if I see her. I hope everything's all right."

Coal hoped so too. He wanted to go back up and go to bed, but he couldn't. It was going to be a long, long night. He would be cruising the streets of Chadron so calling him in 214, he realized, would be just about impossible.

CHAPTER TWENTY

The sign at the Chadron city limits said: POP: 5921. That was some two thousand people less than the entirety of Lemhi County, so on the surface it seemed like a simple job to drive the streets looking for a wandering female. Then again, Salmon itself was home to just under three thousand people as of the 1970 census, and there had been plenty of times Coal had driven its streets looking for someone without seeing a sign of them.

With that sobering thought in mind, he drove only until he located the police station, which was part of the municipal building on Main, just around the corner from the hotel. Of course the imposing brick structure was closed for business that time of day, but

ringing a bell brought to the door a fine-haired blond man in a uni-
form who looked to be near high school graduation age and introduced himself in turn as Officer Whelan. He took Coal back into
the police offices, where he sat behind a desk with a pile of paper-
work near as tall as he was when he sat down behind it. Coal told
him about Maura.

"I'm glad you came in, Sheriff Savage. I'm not sure we can do
a lot for you, but I'll have dispatch put an APB out. We have four
guys on the street tonight. Yeah, it's a pretty quiet place," he said
in an apologetic tone. "I'll get them looking."

As Coal pulled away from the curb, he was hoping he had just
narrowed his hunt down by four-fifths. At least in Salmon he knew
they would have made this a priority, especially on a slow night.

He had been cruising the streets for over an hour, and he
couldn't imagine there was any area left he hadn't covered. By
now, he was feeling more than sick to his stomach. Had he done
something to make Maura do this? He almost wished they had
stayed in Oglala and taken their chances. He hadn't dreamed she
was this upset.

It hit him that she was probably back at the hotel room by now,
so he drove back, parked and went upstairs. The room was cold
and lonely and empty.

Taking off his hat, Coal ran his fingers back through his hair
and walked to the window. He pushed the drapes aside and stared
down at the dark street. The thought crossed his mind of calling
home to check on things there and to cry on his mother's shoulder
about the current situation. But he dismissed it almost as it came
to him. It wasn't fair to keep Connie up all night with worry just
because he would be.

He paced the room for a while, trying to think of any place
Maura could be. She wouldn't have found some total stranger and
gone home with him. Would she? What about businesses? Local
restaurants that stayed open late. Bars. *Bars!* Of course. He hadn't

thought of that earlier simply because he had never known Maura as a carouser. But judging by how she had been acting all day, why not? Nothing else about her was normal today either. He could see her going to some local club to drown her sorrows, then losing track of the time.

A huge, but slightly forced feeling of relief flooded through him. The answer seemed so obvious. Going back to the car, he started on a tour of Chadron's alcoholic dives, first stopping at the Legion Club, simply because it was the first place he came across as he drove down Bordeaux away from the hotel. Then, on the other side of Main, on the block between First and Second, he hit the jackpot. This was apparently Chadron's designated alcoholic block, where he explored The Cave, The Favorite, and then a third one on the same stretch along Main with the colorful name of Hermann the German. He almost wished Maura had been in that one, because the food they were cooking in back smelled nothing short of fantastic.

The fifth club he came to was the 120 Bar, off West Second. Apparently, this town was into numbering their drinking establishments, for right next to it stood the 77. For some reason he had a feeling about this particular place, the 120. As he walked into the fog of cigarette smoke inside, the first sound to greet him was the *clack* of someone breaking the balls at a billiard table, and then a good-natured roar he guessed came from a crowd of spectators.

Scanning the room, it took all of five seconds to spot her, on a stool at the bar. She had her back to him and had just raised a glass to her lips. Seated on the stool next to her was a brawny, good-looking man with a well-trimmed beard and obvious good taste in women. He was laughing at something Maura had just said, and for some reason that set Coal off instantly. She certainly hadn't been in any kind of mood to joke around earlier.

Taking a deep breath to calm himself did the opposite, choking him with the smoke of probably every brand of cigarette known to man. After a brief bout of coughing, his mood turned even darker. He thought about turning around and leaving, going back to the room and letting Maura find her own way whenever she felt like it or became sober enough to. He didn't need her company. Then again, with the way she and this bearded man seemed to be hitting it off, maybe she wouldn't come back that night at all.

This was a case of taking the bull by the horns. If he didn't accost her now and get this straightened out, he wasn't going to get a wink of sleep all night. And maybe he wouldn't anyway, but at least he would know he had tried.

He stalked through the haze to Maura and stopped behind her. "Hey!" Her companion, even amid the din in the crowded bar, realized this newcomer was addressing his female companion, and his eyes glancing back and forth between her and Coal must have alerted her to that fact as well. As she started to turn, Coal said, "You could at least have told me where you were—"

Coal froze. This blond woman who looked so much like Maura from behind had the face either of a clown or of someone who had been hired by several makeup companies at once and had put on a pound of each of their products to use as a demonstration before going out on the town. Either way, clown or makeup mockery, it wasn't Maura.

As Coal tried to find his voice, the bearded companion was stepping off his stool, measuring himself against Coal—and coming out with the short stick. The woman's eyebrow had come up the way Maura's often did, and she glanced Coal up and down, trying to think of something to say.

"Who the hell is this?" the other man said. He appeared to have enough alcohol in him not to notice the size difference between himself and Coal. He certainly had Coal in the department of looks, but Coal had him in size by four inches and an easy forty pounds. Not to mention maybe twenty years, but of course that was no plus.

Coal cut off the woman's reply. "Hey, I'm sorry. I thought you were somebody else."

The bearded man was somewhat slow on the uptake. "Listen, I'm with the girl, buddy. You need t' move along."

"I said I thought she was somebody else," Coal repeated.

The bearded man must have taken Coal's explanation as a sign of weakness. He took a step closer, and his right fist balled up at his side. "If you're lookin' for trouble, mister, you found it."

The blonde jumped up, putting up a hand to stay the other man. "Jeez, Sam, take it easy. Didn't you hear him? He thought I was somebody else."

"Well, I don't—" Sam had taken another step. He stopped, and his eyes shifted around. Was he looking for a weapon, or was the real situation only then beginning to register on him?

The woman turned fully and put her hand on Sam's chest, easing him backward. "Come on. Come on. He made a mistake, that's all. Besides, he looks pretty tough to me, hon. This isn't worth it. Let's go dance."

Sam raised a hand and jabbed his finger at Coal's face. "You better back off, buddy." For the first time, Coal noticed him swaying as he spoke.

Gritting his teeth, he turned away. From behind the bar, he heard a voice that, although gruff, was very female. "Hey! Mister."

He turned to see a hard-looking but still attractive brunette who, like the blonde, could have used a scraper for her makeup but filled out a plaid shirt nicely yet modestly. "Yes?"

Before she could say another word, her dark eyes skipped to her right, and in his peripheral vision Coal saw Sam lurch close to him, and his clutching hand reach out.

Coal had little patience already, and Sam had stepped on his final nerve. Side-stepping past the grasping fingers, then right within his clutches, he stomped down hard on Sam's instep, and as he growled in pain Coal swiveled and drove his right fist upward into his solar plexus, a move that would even have worked wonders on a Tyrannosaurus rex if any man had been around then to try it. The wide-eyed, wide-mouthed look on Sam's face was instant gratification, and he stumbled backward sucking for air, with the blonde following him, trying to get her arm around him.

Coal watched the blonde wrestle Sam down to a sitting position on the floor, and finally he rolled over onto his side and threw up, making the blonde lunge up away from him and stand there looking down in disgust. She obviously either didn't know what to do or was deciding if she should do anything at all.

Coal turned back to the brunette, who had her hands on the bar and was obviously up on her tiptoes, peering over the bar to observe the results of Coal's temper.

"Sorry about that."

The dark eyes slid back to him, and one side of her mouth came up in a dry smile. "Ah, don't worry about it. It really didn't look like you had much choice. And I knew Sam was drinkin' too much anyway, but he's always on the lookout for trouble. Idiots." She shook her head in disgust. Then she smiled again. "Hey, I couldn't help hearin' you earlier. You know, there *was* another girl in here, by herself. She had hair about the same color and style as Barbara there. I'd never seen her around here before."

Coal perked up, still keeping an eye on Sam and hoping he was smart enough to know when he had lost. "Did she leave?"

"Yeah, a long time ago. Hours. I sent her out the back way because she said she thought someone was following her."

Coal cocked his head against the loud music that seemed even to be making the smoke clouds in the room shiver. "Now what's that? Following her?" A feeling of dark foreboding came over him.

"That's what she said."

"What does the back way go out to?"

"Just kind of an alley."

"And you said she's been gone for hours?"

"Right. Maybe three. So . . . she's with you?"

"Yeah. Supposed to be. Hey, do me a favor, will you? Call the police if she comes back in here. They know about her, and they're looking too. I appreciate it."

"Sure."

"Thanks. Can I use the back way out too?"

"You bet." She lifted her arm out straight to point the way. "Hey." Her voice stopped him, and he turned back to her. "If you get bored and you don't find her, I get off work at two."

Stunned, for a moment he only stared at her, the smoke writhing around between them. "Thanks. I'm going to have to keep looking."

Before she could reply, he turned and walked past Sam, who was sitting up again with Barbara's support. He hoped they were planning to clean up the floor before they left.

Coal almost had to fight his way through the revelers in the back of the bar, watching two or three games of pool in progress. One man with a load too many in him was waving his arms around like a windmill, telling some story, and his audience broke into laughter as Coal went by.

He spotted the back door and made for it, but before he got there he noticed three women sitting at a table by the wall. He stopped. "Excuse me. Have you been here long?"

The trio, two blondes and a brunette, looked him up and down, and one of the blondes looked over at the other two and said something too quiet for him to hear. They all laughed and looked back up at him.

"Have we been here long?" repeated blonde number one. "Are *you* long?" She and her friends giggled like junior high girls.

Coal didn't even crack a smile. Every time he had to deal with stupid drunks he was reminded why he hated them. He took one more chance. "There was a blond woman a few hours ago that came back here and went out this door. Any of you see her?"

The three women stared at him with a glassy look in their eyes, either miffed that he didn't appreciate their ribald humor or too far gone to instantly catch what he had said. As Coal was about to give up and turn away from them, the brunette, who seemed the most sober of them, said, "Yeah, I think I saw her. Cute little thing? Cowboy boots and a coat with a fur collar?"

Coal squared himself to them again. "Yeah. Yeah, that's her."

"Yeah. Quite a while ago. She looked kinda scared."

He was scrambling to think of any questions he could ask that would help his cause. "So she came past, looking scared . . . And then . . . What, she just left?"

"Yeah, yeah. And a guy followed."

Coal straightened up. "A guy? Who was he?"

"Just a guy, I don't know." Waving around a glass of some amber liquid that sloshed precariously, she looked about at her friends. "Right? You girls saw him too, didn't you?"

Blonde number one nodded. "Yeah."

"So he followed her and you never saw them again?"

"Oh no!" said blonde number two, the only one who hadn't addressed him yet. "No, sugar, the fella came back, but the girl didn't."

"He did? Where'd he go?"

She waved an arm toward the pool playing crowd. "I think he's in the middle of all that mess."

Coal turned and swept the boisterous crowd with his eyes, feeling sick. He turned back to the table. "Can you remember who he was? Do you mind showing me?"

"What're *you* gonna show *us,* honey?" blonde number one countered.

Coal held himself back. He wanted to reach out and slap a little soberness into all three of them.

"Hey, ladies, this woman that walked past you might be in big trouble. The cops are looking for her." His intention was to make them see how serious the situation was in hopes they would stop messing around with him. He should have known better. The mention of cops only made them clam up.

"Well, we don't know her," said the brunette. "Or him."

"Come on. I need help."

"Not if you're gonna get her busted," said the brunette.

"I'm not trying to get her busted. I'm trying to help her. The cops are looking for her because I reported her as a missing person."

"Oh! *Oh!*" That revelation seemed to change everything. The half-sober woman, whose hair only came to light as being auburn as she lurched up from the table, scanned the crowd of pool players and onlookers.

She stumbled around the table, spilling some of her drink on blonde number two and putting her hand over her mouth. "I'm sorry, Jeannie! Crap! I'm so sorry."

Jeannie laughed. "Well, it ain't like I don't already smell like a brewery, right?"

"Come on, sweetheart. Let's find this guy," said the brunette.

Coal steeled himself and followed her closer to the crowd. She started searching, then stopped, turned to him, and knifed her hand straight out between them. "Hey. I'm Melinda, by the way."

Reluctant, he took her hand. "Coal."

She gave him a broad smile and a hard pump of his hand, and he thought how as a sober woman she was probably decent looking. "Good ta meet ya, Coal. Now let's see . . ."

Her eyes picked through the group, and after a moment they widened, and an even bigger smile came over her face. "Hey, that's him! Yeah! Right there—the guy with the green ball cap."

Following the invisible trail made by her pointing finger, he saw a lean, dark-haired man in a John Deere cap and plaid shirt. "That guy in the plaid?" he said.

"Yeah, him. Want me ta go innerduce ya?"

"You know him?"

"Well . . . no."

"Then I can introduce myself, thanks."

"Okay." She gave him an exaggerated shrug. "Just tryin' ta help."

"You've been a big help. Thanks, Melinda."

"When you get done, you wanna dance or somethin'?" she asked.

"Maybe later," he said to placate her.

She smiled and put out her hand again, forgetting they had just shaken. He shook her hand, then turned to leave while she was still talking to him.

Weaving through the crowd, he got to John Deere. The young man, perhaps twenty-two, was turning toward a coat rack.

"Hey, excuse me." Coal had to yell because Creedence Clearwater Revival singing "Have You Ever Seen the Rain" was reverberating through the smoky room at a ridiculous volume. After the way the past week or two had been, it was an ironic song indeed to have blasting in Coal's eardrums right now. The guy grabbed a coat off the rack and started to turn, so Coal tapped his arm. "Excuse me!"

The guy turned to see who had touched him. He scanned around with eyes Coal was relieved to see looked more or less sober.

"What's up?"

"Can I talk to you where it's not so loud?"

John Deere made Coal repeat his words twice, then raised his eyebrows in understanding. He yelled back, "Yeah, man! Maybe out the back."

They headed for the back door and stepped out into a freezing cold night that smelled like rancid grease, booze, and vomit. Even after the door shut, Creedence was playing at about the volume Coal would have had it if he actually wanted to enjoy it.

The other man shook his head. "Jeez, man, you're right! My head's ringin'. So what'd you need? I ain't got nothin' to loan you, if you're after money," he said, holding his hands up in front of him.

"No, nothing like that. Some girls in there said you followed a blond woman out here earlier in the evening."

The man's eyes narrowed. "Okay." He wasn't committing to anything.

"I'm looking for her. She's with me."

"Oh! Okay." His face relaxed. "Well, I wouldn't have known that."

"Did you see where she went?"

"Sure. You know, she was by herself, so I was thinkin' maybe I could get her t' dance, but . . ."

"But what?"

"Well, when she came out, she started walkin' too fast, an' I took off after her down that way, toward Chadron"—he pointed left— "to try and talk to her. She got to the street, and some car pulled up. These five or six guys got out, an' they looked like they meant business. So I just kinda backed on out of there."

"You came back here?"

"Yeah, man. I'm not here for a fight. I just wanted t' dance."

"You didn't see what happened after those guys got out of the car then?" Coal's heart was pounding. He tried everything to hold his emotions inside and not let this man see the fear creeping up on his face.

"No, bro. Not a clue."

"Did you see what kind of car it was?"

"Jeez. Uhh . . . I'm not sure. A dark one? Long. Man, I don't really know."

"What did the men look like?"

"Man! Uh, just mean—I don't know. It was dark—like now—and I didn't hang around to talk to 'em." This guy was getting flustered as he realized how little help his observations truly were. "I wish I could help you more."

As he started to turn back to the barroom door, Coal caught his arm and eased him back around. "That woman could be in big trouble, kid. I need your help. You can't remember anything else?"

The young man started to shake his head, but then he stopped. "Hey, you know what? There was one other thing I noticed because I always thought it was cool. When those guys were gettin' outta that car, I saw the back doors opened the wrong way—you know, those suicide doors."

The sick feeling that had been growing in the pit of Coal's stomach exploded like an ink bomb. He was certain his face went white. "Suicide doors? Could that car have been a dark green Thunderbird?"

"Oh, yeah! Yeah, that's probably it. Right! One of them late sixties T-Birds. Great car, man!"

Coal could not have felt more terror flood through him if the afore-mentioned Tyrannosaurus rex had fallen out of the sky and landed on its feet in front of him. He had been unable to locate Maura PlentyWounds because she was not in Chadron, Nebraska.

She was well on her way back to Oglala, South Dakota, and he could only pray she was still alive.

CHAPTER TWENTY-ONE

Driving back to the police station, Coal found the door locked again, and ringing the bell didn't raise anyone. He drove up and down Main Street a few times hoping to see a police car somewhere, but with no luck.

He didn't realize until most of the way to the hotel how slow he was driving. It was as if he was in a trance. His head was whirling, and his stomach hadn't felt this way since finding out that Hague Freeman had Katie, and, before that, his race home after getting the call about Laura.

Parking in the check-in area of the hotel, he stepped through the front door to an empty lobby. He walked with leaden feet and thumped on the bell button and made it chime. He heard it like something coming from a distant building.

After twenty seconds that seemed like minutes, the desk clerk managed to find his way in. Coal's shock was still too deep even to berate him for taking so long.

"Any luck?"

Coal blinked his eyes and swallowed, shaking his head. "I have to check out."

"What?"

"I'm checking out," he said softly.

The man stared at him, and Coal could see all the jumbled thoughts whirling around in his head. He must be thinking Coal and Maura had really had a serious falling out.

"Uh . . . any reason?"

Coal had to tell someone. Until he did, none of this seemed real. "Yeah. The woman I'm traveling with was kidnapped."

Shock came over the clerk's face. *"How's that?"*

"She was kidnapped. I'm sorry, I need my receipts and . . . Well, anyway, I just need to go." In the back of his mind he realized he must appear to be drunk. He was having a hard time collecting his thoughts. He felt drugged.

"Hey, mister, I'm really sorry. Here." He slid a paper across the counter. "Just sign that, all right?" Reaching into a drawer, he pulled out some cash and counted Coal's room fee back out to him. "I'm not gonna charge you. Man, good luck with this. I wish . . ." His voice trailed off. There was nothing more to say.

Coal nodded at him as he pocketed the cash. "I appreciate it. Can I make a phone call from my room? To the state police?"

"Of course! You bet. Anything else we can do, you just let me know."

Coal went upstairs. His senses were starting to clear. Questions raged through his head, wondering how the Lakotas had known where they were, and how they had caught Maura alone. Or had they come here planning to catch them both together and only lucked into a better opportunity? It didn't matter. Either way, they had her, and Coal had already heard all he needed to know about how things were when he was in Oglala. If he didn't get her back soon, there would be nothing left to take home.

The race to Oglala was painful. Coal was glad it was a straight road, and even more glad that the game kept off it that night. He was traveling at times over a hundred miles an hour, and far outdistancing the reach and usefulness of his headlights. He knew how dangerous it was, and how foolish, and yet he couldn't slow down.

As the horses under the hood thundered him up the highway, he tossed around all the things he needed to do when he reached Oglala, and he tried to sort them into some kind of order. He had contacted the state police, and they had taken a report. But nothing they told him sounded promising. He would contact the FBI to-morrow, because kidnapping someone and traveling across state lines turned it into a federal offense, and because hopefully he still had connections with the FBI that could grant him some kind of pull.

His fear was that Asa Iron Rope, who he was sure was the instigator of this, would plan on moving fast, then getting rid of the body before anyone could even start an investigation.

It shocked Coal into stillness even to think of the word "body." This was Maura! The woman he— A great friend. He had to do something, and he had to do it fast, so there never would be a "body."

He drove into and through Oglala without stopping, going straight to Paul Wolf Guts's house. He was relieved to see it still standing, and Paul's red pickup parked in front, to all appearances unharmed. Sitting out on the highway, he tried to decide his next move. In Paul's place, someone banging on his door at one in the morning right after last night's incident would make him roll out of bed with a shotgun in his hands. But he couldn't simply walk in and wake him up either.

He chose the knock and yell method, praying in advance for Paul's forgiveness. This was not a way anyone would choose to wake up in the middle of the night.

Parking the LTD on the far side of Paul's pickup, blocked from the line of fire, he went up on the porch. He hesitated with his hand in the air, then steeled himself and started knocking. After four knocks, he yelled Paul's name. He made up his mind and contin-ued yelling it. He wasn't about to stop until Paul opened his door.

An inside light blinked on after half a minute and ten or more yelled "Pauls". Soon, Coal could hear the deadbolt clicking, and Paul opened the door and peeked out. "What the hell? *Savage?*"

Coal nodded vigorously. "I've got to come in, Paul."

"Sure! Sure, brother. Come on." Paul pushed the door open wider and stepped back, allowing Coal's entrance, then looking out past him. "Where you parked?"

"On the other side of you. I didn't want to get shot."

Paul chuckled and glanced over at his clock. "Sit down, man. Or whatever. Where's the woman? What the hell you doin' back here? What's—"

"They got her, Paul." His words cut the Lakota mechanic short.

A long pause. "Now *what's that?*"

"Paul. They followed us to Chadron. Maura went for a walk, and they got her."

"There's no way! Are you sure?"

"Of course I'm sure. Five or six guys in a dark car with suicide doors. I'm as sure as I've ever been of anything."

Paul swore and reached out to grab Coal's arm without seeming to think about it. He gave it a hard squeeze, then dropped his hand away. "I'm real sorry, Savage. Sit down. Sit down, man. You want some coffee or somethin'?"

Coal took off his hat and threw it over on the couch, running his hands through his hair. "Uhh . . . Yeah, sure, if you have some."

"I'll have to heat it back up, but it's still good." Paul was moving to the stove even as he spoke. He turned the propane on to one of the burners and struck a match, and the flames leaped up high, making him swear again. Like Coal, tonight that kind of language was probably waiting very close to the surface. "And that right there's why Injuns ain't got no hair on their face," he said with a chuckle. "Always gettin' too close t' the fire."

Coal couldn't laugh. The humor didn't even register on him.

While the pan of coffee was making its little pinging noises of expansion, Paul turned and rubbed his face vigorously, then worked his eyes, trying to drive all sleep from them. "What're we gonna do?"

"Damnit, Paul," Coal replied on the instant. "That's what I don't know. I don't even want you involved, except . . . Hell, I don't know what to do. I don't know where to start."

"You wanna sleep here?"

Coal chuckled. "Huh! That's what I almost asked, but then I realized there's no way I'm going to sleep."

A sheepish look came over Paul Wolf Guts's face. "Yeah, sure. Me either. Um, well, we c'd drive by the Iron Rope place an' see if that car's there mebbe? Huh?"

"You know where it is?"

Paul frowned. "You're funny, white man. You seen the size o' this village?"

Coal's turn to feel sheepish. "Right."

Paul turned and sloshed the coffee around in the pan, then poked a finger in it. He looked around at Coal. "How warm you like it?"

"If it'll boil my tongue it's hot enough."

Paul grinned. "Okay. Still a minute. I'm gonna go get my guns ready."

"Damnit, Paul," Coal caught him turning toward the hall. "I told you I don't want you in this. There's going to be enough trouble for ten men, but you've got to live here."

"Savage." Paul stared Coal down. He seemed to be the only Lakota on the Rez that Coal had become friendly with who was in the habit of looking in someone's eyes. "You're loco if you think I ain't in this already. I pulled a gun on 'em, brother. I shot their friggin' car. I'm in it. Like it or not. Semper fi."

Coal nodded. Of course the Lakota was right. But he hated to think what was going to happen to him. This man didn't owe him a thing, and yet here they found themselves, a white man and a pure-blood Lakota, standing back to back against other members of the tribe. Fate was a funny thing.

Coal stared at the floor and boiled his tongue sipping coffee. What was he supposed to do? Other than Paul, he had nobody he could rely on. At least no one who could be here in time.

He tried to calm his nerves, thinking perhaps an overload of caffeine wasn't the best way to do it. Maybe he could go to the Iron Ropes' and buy some of their bootleg whisky.

He sipped the last of the coffee. Paul looked at his hands, perhaps to see if they were shaking. He knew they weren't. He prided himself in that. "More?"

"No. I need to go."

Paul came up as if spring-loaded. "Then let's go. Better park your car around back first, though. In fact, let's put it all the way back around that big shed. I think that'll cover it from the highway."

He held out a Winchester carbine. "Here. I'm sure you didn't bring no big guns."

"Thanks."

"No problem. You gotta watch my back with somethin'. That gun's good luck. My daddy killed two moose with it in two shots, back in twenty-two."

After moving the LTD into concealment, Coal went back around and got in the pickup where Paul was idling it in the dark yard. Paul looked over at him. "I kinda like that yellow-haired woman o' yours, Savage. We'll get her back safe for you. Got it?"

Coal nodded, his throat too tight to speak.

"Hey, brother." Paul gave his leg a light punch. "Semper fi. Always faithful. We're Marines, remember?"

Coal found his voice. "Sure. Semper fi. Hey, what do you think about calling the police?"

"The *Rez* poe-lice? Ha! What for?"

"Are they that bad?"

"Worthless, man. I already told you. Brother, this is the Old West out here on the Rez. An' 'specially for you an' that pale-skinned girl. You want anything done, you want any chance o' get-tin' that girl back alive, you're gonna have t' do it yourself. I wish it was different."

When Paul pulled the pickup out of the yard, he turned left, rather than back toward town. They drove the speed limit for a while, until well past Oglala Lake, that sparkled out there in the darkness. Paul slowed down and puttered along for several more miles. Coal was starting to wonder how far out the Iron Ropes lived when Paul began to ease way down on the brake.

"Comin' up here, Savage. Another two hundred yards mebbe." He seemed to be reading Coal's mind.

Coal's heart started to thunder. Maybe old Maybelle should have chosen him the name of Thunder*heart*.

Paul eventually stopped where a dirt road cut to the left. "This is their driveway. Last time I knew, they had dogs in here. Some big mean ones—you know, keepin' the fire water safe."

"What do we do?"

"Hell, Savage, I ain't thought that far ahead. You?"

Coal shook his head. It made him almost physically ill to think what might be happening to Maura right now. At least there was some sort of twisted honor to Hague Freeman when he had Katie. With the Iron Ropes, it was doubtful they even knew what honor meant.

"Who all lives here?"

"The son, Asa. And his old man."

"Leland." Coal felt darkness close over him just saying the name.

"Yeah. Leland."

"So it's just the two of them?"

"That's all that lives here. The other ones hang out here a lot, though, but I doubt they'd be here this time o' night."

"Tell me about this Leland." Coal wanted to add to the end of that sentence, *the man I'm going to have to kill,* but he kept that part to himself.

"Leland? All right. Well, I call him the old man, but he ain't terribly old. Leland sells a lot of bad booze on the Rez—mostly vodka—but he was never much of a drinker. Guess he'd rather ruin everyone else's life. So his liver's prob'ly healthy. He could live t' be eighty."

But he won't, thought Coal. On the Pine Ridge Reservation, the life expectancy for males was supposed to be around forty-seven. But Asa was never going to reach it, and Leland had already used up all his extra years. At least that was true if he found they had hurt Maura.

Coal took a big breath. "Well, I've got to go in there, Paul."

"I know you do. What you want me t' do?"

"Stay out here, I guess. At least be here with the truck in case I come back."

Paul chuckled. "Savage, you're the Thunderbird—a god. Maybelle says you come t' save us all, an' Maybelle ain't never been wrong yet. You gotta do it, an' you can't do it if you're dead."

Coal's feet crunched in the snowy grass. He could only take a slow step at a time. A gusty wind was in his favor, howling into his face. Any other night he would have cursed it, but tonight he praised it, because it carried his scent away from the house. He had to parallel the dirt road, which bent off to his right, because he still couldn't make out the house from the darkness.

Paul had told him there must be three hundred feet of driveway, and he had nothing else to go on. So he took a gentle step at a time, counting each one, holding the Winchester carbine in half frozen, gloveless hands.

Finally, the silhouette of a house came into view. One light-colored house, nestled among trees. This house appeared to be stick-built, not a trailer. Apparently the firewater kingpins of the Pine Ridge Reservation had it all.

Scanning his surroundings, Coal could see the silhouette of a large bluff directly behind the house. There was no way to see vegetation, but if there was a mountain, that meant rocks, and where there were rocks there would be places to hide. If things went to hell, and he couldn't get back to Paul, he would head for the hills. If there was any place he felt at home, it was there, and Indian or no Indian, he doubted the Iron Ropes could best him at a game of cat and mouse in the bad country.

He took a step. Then another. The snow crunched under his boots, and he had to lean his weight slowly onto each foot to make the crunching blend in with the whipping of the wind.

His face felt raw now, like his hands. The wind had even started cutting through his coat. He didn't like it, but maybe the cold had forced all the Iron Rope dogs inside as well. If he did nothing else tonight, he at least had to see if the Thunderbird was here. He had no other lead.

Without warning, a dog with a voice the size of thunder began barking. Coal froze. That dog was close. It was big. And it might as well have been a piece of the night, because Coal couldn't see it.

There is one thing worse than a dog: two dogs. Or three.

But Coal, frozen in place in the snowy grass, could now make out the barking of possibly four. They were coming his way out of the dark jaws of hell.

And Paul Wolf Guts's pickup was about four dogs too far away.

CHAPTER TWENTY-TWO

The four dogs suddenly began snarling, and another horrendous sound split the night. If Coal had already cocked the rifle he might have fired off a round on reflex. Whatever mix-up was happening couldn't have been much more than twenty yards in front of him, and it sounded like wild demons snarling and raging over the prairie snow.

It took several more seconds for Coal to recognize what was going on. This was a nasty fight with a feline—most likely a bobcat. Those dogs didn't likely have a clue there was another human within miles of the house!

He began stepping backward, almost inching along. The fierce battle was raging so hard in front of him that none of the animals involved would likely catch any other scent or sound, but he couldn't take a chance.

He had made it fifty steps when lights came on in the house, and soon after that the front door opened to allow a rectangle of light to stream across the yard. "Hey!" The voice flung hard across the prairie toward Coal from a man standing in the doorway. Coal jerked when the man raised a rifle and fired it into the air.

The explosion sent the cat scrambling, and the dogs as well.

It took about three seconds for Coal to realize the cat was headed right for him, and all four dogs were yelping behind.

The cat flew past on Coal's left as he was deciding to drop to his belly in the snow. He didn't have time. Two dogs surged by on his left, but another went right through him. With his legs shot backwards, Coal went down hard on his face, losing the carbine as the fourth dog went right over the top of him.

Coal rolled over and dug in the snow for the Winchester, picking it up. A glance toward the door of the house showed two men there now, and both of them with rifles. He could hear one of them shouting angrily at the other, and then one of them started across the yard. He was quickly lost in the darkness of the yard and the trees.

Turning, Coal took off running for the highway. He could hear the dogs some three hundred yards away now, well across the other side of the highway. He was still a ways out from the road when he heard Paul's truck speed off down the road, its headlights off.

With a sick feeling in the pit of his stomach, he whirled back toward the house to see another pickup with its lights on driving his way up the driveway. Praying they hadn't already spotted him, he dropped into the grass, pressing his face against the icy grit. He breathed shallowly as the pickup came on, seeing the lights reach out over his hiding place.

He was going to jump up. He had to get up and fight! They had found him! But something bade him stay.

Soon, the headlights swept around as the pickup made the straightaway to the highway, then stopped. They were idling some forty feet away from him now. He heard the opening of one door, then the other.

"Well, you're the one that let 'em out!" That was the voice of a somewhat older man.

"I was lettin' 'em pee. I told you!"

"Well now look. Hell, if those dogs get hurt . . ."

"They're not gonna get hurt. It was a bobcat, I'm tellin' you!"

"That wasn't no bobcat, you dumb turd. That was a panther!" countered the older voice.

The younger man Coal was certain was Asa mumbled something he couldn't make out.

After a minute or so, the older voice sounded again. "Well, I can't even hear the dogs anymore at all. You got any idea which way they went?"

His question was punctuated by one, then two, then three evenly spaced rifle shots, far along the highway away from town.

Asa Iron Rope swore. "What was that?"

His cussing didn't come close to matching that of the older man. "What do you think it was! Somebody's shootin' my dogs. I'm gonna bust you, boy. So help me, if I gotta retrain some dogs . . ."

"Sorry!" Asa's voice was a growl. "Come on, let's drive down there an' see."

The doors both slammed seconds later, and the truck spun out of the gravel, hit the pavement, and sped off in the same direction Paul Wolf Guts had gone.

Coal got up. He knew he had to make tracks out of here. He had to get as far away from the Iron Ropes' place as he could before they came back. He had—

Wait. Paul had said only the two Iron Ropes lived at this house. And they were both gone!

He looked along the highway at the Iron Ropes' quickly fading taillights. He looked toward the house. He glanced in the direction the dogs had gone.

Then, gripping the Winchester tight, he started at a jog toward the house.

The front yard light was still on. Coal crept all the way around the house. When he got back around to the front, he swore bitterly. There had been no sign of the Thunderbird. Where could it be! His heart was pounding so hard he thought he was going to throw up. He looked back toward the front door. He had to know what was in there. He *had* to!

Going to the door, he put his hand in his coat pocket and used it to turn the knob. He stepped into the realm of the enemy, like walking into a modern-day tepee camp. As fast as he could without missing anything, he went through every room. He left nothing unturned, yet he found less than nothing, other than one room containing probably what amounted to more than one or two thousand dollars' worth of bad booze. "Maura!" he yelled. "Maura, are you in here? It's Coal."

Silence greeted him. Nothing but sheer dead silence. Helplessness swept over him, engulfed him, threatened to destroy him. He had no idea where else to turn. What if the younger man out there in the truck wasn't even Asa Iron Rope? What if there was a third person here Paul didn't know about?

Going to the front door, which he had left standing open, he went out, once again using his coat to shut the door behind him.

As he was stepping off the concrete stoop, a shadow made him jump. Before he could even react, a second one ran up beside it, and both of them scrambled to a stop some twenty feet away across the lawn.

It was two Rottweilers, both breathing hard, with their tongues lolled out. All four of their eyes were hard upon some looming shape in front of the house that didn't look or smell like their masters.

The first dog recovered from his surprise and confusion, and a low growl rumbled out of his throat as he took three quick steps forward. The second followed, stopping a few steps closer.

They were fifteen feet away . . .

Slowly, Coal raised the carbine, which he had jacked a round into the chamber of earlier. As he brought it up, he drew back the hammer. He had no choice what to do now, and no time to think. From his hip, the carbine exploded upward, sending a flash of orange out the muzzle. The closest dog went down writhing. The other one turned and looked at it, and Coal saw indecision cross its face as he was jacking the lever of the carbine again.

The dog growled louder, baring its teeth, and took two steps closer . . .

Coal ran across the snowy grass as hard as he could, the sound of the two shots still echoing over the prairie and off the bluff behind the house. A glance to his left showed headlights approaching, but they were far enough away that he couldn't tell the speed of the vehicle.

He got up to the highway, crossed it, and trotted along on the opposite side, heading toward Oglala. He kept looking back, keeping his eye on the oncoming vehicle. If that was the Iron Ropes, he was sure they would pull into their yard before doing anything else. If they had been driving when he fired the two rounds, they probably had not have even heard. And they might not find the dead dogs right away, because he had dragged them out of the gleam of the yard light, toward the far side of the yard. Maybe they would go in and go to bed.

He kept running, and sure enough, the headlights veered off. By now, he was three-quarters of a mile away. He continued jogging along, hoping to see Paul eventually. It couldn't be much more than fifteen degrees above zero now, and his lungs and throat were starting to freeze, along with his hands.

Suddenly, another vehicle was almost on top of him, moving slow. He turned around and leveled the Winchester, but the vehicle lurched to a stop, and the driver's door flew open. "Savage! Is that you?"

"Of course it's me!"

"Get in here," Paul said, swearing. "Let's go!"

He ran around and jumped into the cab of the pickup, which felt like an oven compared to the outside. He leaned back against the seat, fumbling the full cartridge out of the carbine's chamber, then leaning the weapon against the seat beside him. As Paul fired questions at him, he sat there with his eyes shut and pretended he was deaf.

Finally, the truck slammed to a stop again, still in full darkness. "Talk to me, Savage! What the hell happened back there?"

Coal sighed deeply and shook his head. He looked over at Paul, but it was too dark to see anything but a silhouette. "Dogs."

"Yeah! I know, man, I saw a whole pack of 'em come racin' across the road."

"They were chasing a bobcat."

"Oh! Well then what?"

"Then two guys came out yelling at each other and got in a pickup and drove off."

"No kiddin'! I left right before they did an' had t' hide out down there."

"I'm glad you did."

"So where you bin since? You shoulda been halfway back t' my house by now."

"I've been through that whole house."

"You *what?*"

Coal told him about his search, and about the empty house. "And there was no T-Bird there, either."

"Except you," quipped Paul. When his lame attempt at humor was met with silence, he said quietly, "Sorry."

"And now we're in some big trouble," Coal went on.

"What're you talkin' about? Bigger than we already were?"

"I'm talking about two of the dogs came back—before I could get out of there."

"Ah hell." Paul had long since started driving again, headlights still off, but he flopped his head back against the seat now. "Ah hell," he repeated. "You killed 'em, didn't you?"

"Well? They didn't kill me."

"Yeah, you look perty healthy—for now."

Reaching out, Paul turned the headlights on and hit the gas. They sped down the road, trying to get as much distance between themselves and the Iron Ropes as they could.

CHAPTER TWENTY-THREE

The rag in her mouth tasted bitter. Since it smelled like old gasoline, she assumed that was the taste in her mouth as well. Maura PlentyWounds lay in pitch blackness, her eyes blindfolded, the wadded-up rag in her mouth tied there with another rag around her head. Her hands were lashed too tightly behind her back, but for the moment they had removed the rope from around her ankles. It didn't matter, though. She had managed to stand up once, but there was nothing worth standing up for. Wherever this dark, dank, moldy-smelling place was, it had no furniture in it, and nothing else, either. If she was going to rest, she was going to do it on a damp floor, which felt hard enough to be concrete but smelled like dirt.

Maura was still in shock, but her tears had long since dried. Probably because there were simply none left in her. Strangely, the biggest thing on her mind was Coal. Other than her note, he wouldn't have any idea where she was, and by now he must long since have decided she had gone crazy. *Oh, Coal.* How could she have done this to him? How could she have dragged him into this? She knew that man too well. Until the day he died, he would always believe her disappearance was his fault. And chances were good the kidnaping would never be solved. Nobody knew who had taken her, so no one could know where she had gone.

This was a Leland Iron Rope thing. She had seen only Asa and his friends, but there was no doubt in her mind Leland was behind it. That meant that she, like Cordelia, was going to die. And her body would molder away somewhere in the hills where no one would ever find even her bones.

A sick emptiness filled the pit of her stomach. She thought of Coal and his family. She thought of her boys. She thought of Nora Sue, and her little Emmy Lee. She wondered how long the people who cared about her would mourn her, and if in time they would find some kind of closure of their own.

Her head throbbed, a dull ache. Asa had struck her on the side of the skull, but she wasn't even sure this ache came from that. It could have been from her bitter weeping. It was so cold in here, and she couldn't stop shaking. She would not have made a very good old-time Lakota, traveling across the barren winter plains with no home but a tepee.

How was she going to die? That thought plagued her mind. Would it be by the knife, by a gun, by fire? Would Leland rape her again, as he had so many times all those years ago when she was so young and innocent? She had to pee. She had had to for hours. But her captors were obviously not worried about it. She finally went and squatted in a corner, with her pants still on, because her hands weren't free to do anything else. Most of it would drip away from her, but it would still be so cold anyway, and in time it would be ice.

She walked back to the farthest corner, hoping she would remember which was which. She guessed the smell would probably tell her if she guessed wrong. She lay back down on her side, her head tilted unnaturally far over because there was nothing for a pillow, and she obviously couldn't lie on her back, for her hands would be beneath her.

She wondered if there really was a God who cared about her. She had been wondering that for much of her life.

*   *   *

"If we are out drivin' when the Iron Ropes come into town tonight, they will have no question who was in their house. An' who done the killin' of their dogs."

Paul Wolf Guts sat in the cab of his pickup with the engine idling and stared solemnly at Coal, who was trying to argue with him about ceasing their search for the Thunderbird this early in the night.

"If they come to town for what?"

"Come on, Savage. You killed those dogs. They'll be comin'. As sure as the sun's gonna come up in the east tomorrow. They'll be comin'. They're gonna come drivin' around, just t' see what they c'n see, if nothin' else. They'll be drivin' this whole part of the Rez, tryin' t' find some sign who was at their house."

"Then I'm ready. Let's bring it on."

"Bring what on? A war? Let's say you meet 'em, an' you start a fight. An' then what if you kill both of 'em? An' what if they're the only two who know where that yellow-haired girl is?"

Coal could only stare. He had no answer for that. The fact was, he hadn't been thinking clearly enough for it even to cross his mind. Tonight, he was in the mood for one thing, and one thing only: killing.

"Another thing, Savage: I've had me a lotta time t' think about killin' since what happened last night. Remember what you said t' me 'bout killin'? You said somethin' like 'that's just the start o' your trouble'. Well, you were right. But now everything's changed. They took your friend, an' now it's you that wants t' go killin'. A time might come for that, Savage. But it sure ain't right now. You wanna save that girl, you gotta think smart."

"So what do I do?"

Paul shook his head. "No, brother, it's still *we,* not *I.* I ain't desertin' you."

Coal sighed. "All right. *We.* What do *we* do?"

"We're goin' over to the place of a medicine man."

"Judas, are you kidding me?"

"I ain't Judas, an' no, I ain't kiddin' you." Paul smiled, but Coal couldn't. "Sorry. Dumb humor. We're goin' over to a man who might be able t' help us. Right now he's the only hope I c'n think of. But you gotta put all your white man so-called intelligence in a hole for a while an' do whatever I tell you to. Or whatever he tells you to. Got it?"

Coal stared at him, feeling helpless. He guessed he didn't have much choice. He was far out of his element here. Any step he took could mean his death. And if he died, so did Maura. Whatever they had done with her, they couldn't afford to let her go. Coal Savage was in a race against time.

"Got it," he finally agreed.

"There's just one bad thing."

"What's that?"

"We gotta drive right past the Iron Ropes' place t' get there."

Coal swore. "Great. So what do we do?"

"We gotta wait."

Sunday, January 28

Coal wasn't able to sleep that night, but Paul Wolf Guts did. Paul stayed up, sitting in one of his two easy chairs, but he had his bare feet kicked up, and he was snoring like not a thing in the world was wrong.

Coal had stayed awake all night, sitting on the couch drinking coffee, pacing, looking out the window. He happened to be at the door when the Iron Ropes' pickup cruised slowly past the driveway, stopping only a little farther on. Paul had been right. It was only two in the morning, and they were patrolling their domain, searching for anyone who might still be awake at this hour. Like Paul had said, that would have been their first clue as to who had been on their property, and who had killed their guard dogs.

At the tail end of a full pot of coffee, Coal stood at the window behind Paul Wolf Guts, peering out at a silvery blue sky, where the sun was getting ready to chin up into a new day. Venus and Jupiter had both come up and hung bold and beautiful in the sky, and a deep blue lighting filtered over the snowy fields, but to Coal right then, nothing seemed beautiful. An icy wind was battering the grass around and rattling the trailer house.

Coal threw etiquette to the wind and shook Paul's shoulder. His friend came up out of his chair like any good Marine.

"What's goin' on?"

"Nothing. I just thought we should get moving."

"What time is it?"

"I think around six-thirty."

"Shoulda woke me sooner. You c'n bet them Iron Ropes were gone t' bed a few hours back."

"I guess I should have."

"You make me any coffee?"

"Yeah."

"Great."

"And then I drank it all."

Paul frowned. "Are you kiddin'?"

"No, sorry."

"Well, thanks. Okay, we don't have time t' wait around here for a new pot. Let's go."

Getting their coats on and grabbing the rifles and their handguns, they went out where the wind was hammering at them and the temperature was in the single digits, and Paul got the truck going after a few tries.

"That big engine don't like bein' awake in this cold any more than this little Injun does," said Paul with a grin.

The pun got a laugh out of Coal. "Always trying to lighten the mood, aren't you?"

"I try."

They headed off down the road after the engine was warm. After a while, Coal recognized the bluff behind the Iron Ropes', even though he had only ever seen it in the dark, and just as Paul raised his hand to point at the house, Coal said, "I know. Iron Ropes."

"You're perty good, Savage."

Coal only nodded.

Not much farther down the highway, they pulled off on a little-traveled road. They drove a good eighth of a mile of ruts and frozen mud before a little hovel came into sight in a cluster of wind-blown trees. An old, poorly kept barbwire fence surrounded the place, with half the juniper posts leaning away from the wind and the wire in disarray. Out a ways from the house, in an area of swaying bunch grass, hunched a tepee, and as they pulled close to the house Coal could see a well-worn trail from the front door of the house to this ancient-looking traditional Lakota dwelling.

"No tellin' where old Emery is," said Paul. "Knowin' him, he mighta slept in that tepee. Else he got up to smoke in there."

"Emery?"

"Emery Afraid of Lightning. The medicine man."

Paul stopped the pickup a little ways out from the house. The whole time, Coal was wondering what they were doing here, but he couldn't afford to offend the only real friend on the reservation by asking too many questions. If Paul thought it so important that they consult this so-called medicine man, then Coal wasn't going to say anything about it. He only prayed it wouldn't take too long.

Getting out into the icy breath of the wind was a slap in the face. With the howling wind, it felt like twenty below zero. Coal had started walking toward the house before he realized Paul had gone the other way, toward the tepee.

"Emery? You out here?"

Coal heard a muffled voice from the tepee, and he felt his eyebrows raise. Paul motioned him over.

They got fifteen feet from the tepee before Paul spoke to the smoky canvas: "Emery, it's me, Paul Wolf Guts."

"Come in, Paul. Just gettin' a fire lit."

Paul turned to Coal. "Follow me. An' I mean *follow* me. Turn left when you go inside. You always gotta go clockwise when you enter a tepee."

Coal nodded.

Pushing the door flap aside, Paul went in and took a few steps to his left. Coal followed. Inside, smoke was just starting to curl out of a pile of sticks and brush and wadded paper in a fire hole in the exact center of the floor. Nothing inside these deep shadows could be seen clearly, but a man who appeared much younger than Coal was expecting looked up from his work, where he was squatted on his heels on the far side of the fire. He was dressed in full plains Indian attire, the general look Coal would have expected from some old Western.

"Hau, Paul." Emery slowly stood up, without using his hands. Unlike Coal, his joints didn't make a single crackling noise. On his feet, he was some eight inches shorter than Coal, and his face was more lined than it had seemed at first glance in the half-dark of the tepee. Yet his hair appeared black except for a few silver strands. The medicine man looked Coal up and down. His next words shook him. "Is this the Wakinyan they're talkin' about?"

Paul looked over at Coal, but it still took a moment for the words to register on him. This man was talking about *him!*

"Yeah, Emery, this is him. Coal Savage."

Coal could smell the rising scent of juniper smoke now. It was a comforting odor, in spite of the dire circumstances.

"Coal, this is Emery Afraid of Lightning," Paul introduced. "He can help you."

"I knew you would come," said Emery Afraid of Lightning, ignoring Paul's words and looking at Coal's chest.

"What's going on here? How could you know *anything?* I was already gone—heading home."

"I knew you would come."

Coal went silent, his chest filled with anguish, for he couldn't get Maura out of his mind. He guessed Emery would tell him in time what had brought him to his conclusion that he would come.

"Sit." Emery waved toward the wall behind them. "Please."

Paul turned around and picked up what appeared to be a mat of smooth, blond sticks, laid out side by side and somehow connected to each other. It turned out to be two of the same, and he handed one to Coal. "Willow backrest. Sit on it."

The backrest was attached to two crossed sticks at its back, which held the largest portion of it vertical, leaving only a foot or so to sit on. Following Paul's lead, Coal propped it up and sat down with his legs crossed. Emery Afraid of Lightning took his own backrest and sat down on it across the fire from them. The backrests were surprisingly comfortable.

From a dark, smoky leather bag, Emery drew out a long pipe, with a bowl made of red stone. Two stretches of beading decorated its two feet of length, and a cluster of six red-tailed hawk feathers, tied behind the bowl, dangled from it. He took out a little pouch of tobacco, and with a number of small pinches he painstakingly filled it.

Finally, he took a brand from the fire and held it to the bowl of the pipe, puffing until the tobacco glowed red. "We will smoke," he said.

He began to pull deeply at the stem of the pipe, then to blow in the four directions, then once up toward the smoke hole, and once at the ground. He held the pipe horizontally out to Coal in both hands. "Now you. Smoke."

Trying not to think of Maura, Coal took the pipe and mimicked what he had seen Emery do. It was the first he had tasted tobacco smoke in quite some time. He finished, and Emery motioned toward Paul, so he passed the pipe on to him.

When all three of them had smoked, Emery took out two tied bundles, one of them appearing to be grass, and the other some kind of grayish plant. He held them both to the flames long enough for the ends to glow red and start smoking, and then he used each, in turn, to pull smoke from and draw it toward himself.

Coal and Paul were directed to do the same. All the while, Coal tried to hide his impatience. He only wanted this ritual to be over. If Emery had something to tell him about Maura's whereabouts, let him come out with it! This was taking too much precious time. He knew nothing about Indian magic, or whatever they called it. But he needed to be trying to find out where Maura was, not sitting here in the tepee of some strange Lakota "medicine man" pulling smoke onto himself.

"You are cleansing," Emery explained finally. "With white sage, and sweetgrass. It will purify you, an' it will make it so you can understand what I say."

He studied Coal's face for a long time after that, until it began to be uncomfortable. Emery slowly began to nod.

"You do not believe."

Emery Afraid of Lightning's sudden statement was fact, but hearing it spoken took Coal very much by surprise.

"What was that?"

"You do not believe."

Now that the truth was out, Coal's impatience came out with it. "I'm sorry. There's a woman depending on me to save her life. I don't understand why we're sitting around here smoking."

"Would you believe me if I told you that Leland Iron Rope also came to me to cleanse him?"

"What? Why? When?"

Emery almost smiled. "Slow. One question at a time. When? Only two suns back. Why? He has bad dreams of a girl from his past comin' back to kill him."

Coal could only stare. Could this be true? That girl would have to be Maura!

"What happened?"

"I turned him away."

Emery Afraid of Lightning shrugged. He pulled more smoke to himself and breathed deeply, finally opening his eyes when Coal was at his most impatient.

"I could sense that he was here for a bad purpose. He wanted this girl's spirit banished from the earth. What I do is not for those with evil intentions, but for pure people. Leland Iron Rope is not pure."

Coal stared at the medicine man. He had no idea how to reply, especially when the man was right about him: He *didn't* believe. But then, neither was he a "pure" person. So would he refuse to help him too? The medicine man went on, and his words began to claw at Coal's heart.

"You seek the girl, Fire-in-her-Eyes, Peta, who is gone from you. She has been taken by Iron Rope. Before another three suns pass, she will lie asleep forever in the Paha Sapa—the Black Hills—where her young sister has long since gone to rest. Unless you are willin' to do what you must, as the spirit of Wakinyan here on earth that you are appointed to be, you will not see the yellow-haired girl again."

Emery Afraid of Lightning stared at Coal's chin, the closest he would come to looking into his eyes.

"Now do you believe?"

Coal nearly choked on a reply. His heart was pounding so hard it almost hurt. He looked over at Paul, knowing the pleading in his eyes, and unable to stop it.

Coal lurched to his feet, pointing down at Emery. "What's going on here? Do you have something to do with what happened?"

Emery remained calm. Of course he wouldn't meet Coal's glare, but he raised his face toward him, although his eyes were closed, and fanned more smoke his way.

"Paul, you need t' tell your friend t' be seated. Please."

"Coal." Paul looked up. "Come on, man. Hear 'im out."

Coal stared down at Paul. "I don't like this. I've got to go find her, Paul."

Paul eased to his feet and put a hand on Coal's shoulder, speaking softly. "Listen, buddy. You ain't thinkin' straight. This ain't black magic, man. Emery's one o' the good guys. Just hear 'im out."

Coal forced himself to take a deep breath, blinking back tears. Finally, he sat back down and faced Emery Afraid of Lightning.

He would have suspected Emery had been speaking with Maybelle Littlebrave, yet there were things Maybelle could not have known, most importantly of Maura's disappearance. And yet Emery did.

Coal drew another deep breath. "At least tell me how you know. How do you know they took the girl? What do I have to do?"

Emery nodded knowingly. His eyes sliced over to Paul, and then back to Coal's chin. "Let me speak free, Wakinyan. You have come with thunder and destruction. This much I have come t' know from Maybelle Littlebrave. You have come, as she said, with fire in your eyes as the lightning, an' thunder in your hands. There are people in Oglala that you must destroy, as the lightning and the flood would destroy. These are the men who bring the alcohol from outside Pine Ridge to sell to our people, to bring them to the earth in bondage."

He held up a finger for each name he spoke: "Levi Weaselbear, Norbert Sam, Pat Highhorse, Jimmy LeBeau, Isaac Lefthand; and then Leland and Asa Iron Rope. Until these are gone, this people is not safe, an' you will not be allowed to leave Oglala."

Coal stared at Emery Afraid of Lightning. "There's a name you left out."

"I did not leave any name out."

"What about Edward PlentyWounds, the girl's brother?"

"PlentyWounds is not yours t' destroy, Wakinyan. Forget him. He is the blood kin of the woman you seek. Let him be."

Coal took off his hat and scratched the back of his head, then put it back on and forced a few more deep breaths into himself.

"I can't do this thing by myself, this thing you're asking me to do. Hell, I can't do it at all! This is Indian land. Do you know what would happen to me if I killed seven Lakotas—on the reservation?"

"Do you know what will happen to Peta if you do not?"

Lunging suddenly up from the ground once more, Coal stood looking from Emery to Paul. He couldn't even find the words to speak. It felt like he had been thrust suddenly back into the war. But this wasn't war. The law was going to look at this differently. What Emery Afraid of Lightning was speaking of, in the eyes of the law, was murder.

CHAPTER TWENTY-FOUR

Coal stared down at the medicine man, Emery Afraid of Lightning.

"Can you at least tell me what's happening to her right now? And where she is?" He wasn't sure he wanted the answer to the first question. But maybe if he had it it would fuel his ability to go through with what Emery Afraid of Lightning was suggesting— that he take up vigilante law.

Emery's eyes swung up, and in the dim light it almost looked as if they made contact with his own. He brought his hand up and made a motion as if he were patting a child softly on the head. "Sit back down, white man—wasichu. Sit."

Coal had to comply.

"Do you have anything that belongs t' the woman?"

"Like what?"

"Anything only she would have. Somethin' personal."

Feeling embarrassed, Coal leaned to the side and dug in his right front pocket, the pocket away from his keys. From out of it, he pulled the shard of porcelain. He felt stupid about having this, but he handed it to Emery.

The medicine man seemed to read his thoughts. "Wakinyan. You feel shame because you keep somethin' you find t' be silly. But this is somethin' our people would do—a bit of medicine." His words made Coal instantly feel better.

Emery held the memento sandwiched between the palms of his hands, running them several times through the juniper smoke. He then pulled them in close to his abdomen, bowed his head, and closed his eyes.

For a long, excruciating moment, the medicine man held still. Coal could neither see nor hear him breathe. After a moment, he realized even he had been holding his breath.

When the silence had almost become too much, Paul sensed it, and he reached over and gripped Coal's arm. Coal looked at him, and his comrade shook his head, bidding him remain silent.

At last, Emery opened his eyes, and his face came up. "I can tell you this, Wakinyan: Your woman is alive."

Coal stared at him, wanting to believe. "How do you know?"

"Because I saw. I saw her someplace dark an' alone."

Coal thought he might be pushing his luck, like in some way Emery would feel his power and his very abilities as a medicine man were being questioned, but he couldn't stop himself. It was in his nature to get facts.

"I'm sorry, but I'm having trouble understanding why you would have a vision about her. What is she to you?"

"She is only a trigger, Wakinyan. She is what the Great Spirit brought to Oglala to be sure you would return."

That thought made Coal sick—if he believed it, that is. So Maura was suffering right now because of him?

Coal felt his impatience and his ire growing stronger by the minute. He fought the urge to jump up and leave. For what if this man really knew something? What if his crazy visions really were true, and Coal ignored them?

"You still aren't telling me—why *you?* Why didn't any visions come to *me?"*

"Because you were not ready, Savage. You were not ready to act in the place of Wakinyan. What did you think was gonna happen when you gave me this thing that is close t' your woman? It is all within the heart of this little thing. You only need t' be able t' hear.

"Come with me, Wakinyan," said Emery Afraid of Lightning suddenly. Coal fought the urge to yell at him to stop calling him that, but as Emery stood, so did he and Paul. "Come." Emery motioned to them, and Paul grabbed Coal's arm to make him follow him all the way around the fire, behind the medicine man.

With the bitter wind hammering at them outside, Coal's eyes got moist. He had to wipe at them to be able to see, before the tears could turn to ice.

Emery pointed toward some distant mountains behind his house. "Look. In the mountains, do you see the sleeping horse?"

Coal peered at the place Emery was pointing. "Sleeping horse? No."

"Keep watchin'. Look close."

Coal studied the mountains, fighting at his impatience, his desire to curse Emery Afraid of Lightning and his stupid game.

"Do you see it?"

Coal shook his head. He was growing too angry to trust himself to speak.

"Here. Put your hands this way." The old man raised his hands up in front of him, thumbs pointed down and touching together, index fingers together at the top.

Coal gritted his teeth and did the same. Then Emery came to the side, turning Coal until his hands were just right. "Now. Look."

Coal peered through the hole created by his hands, and as if by magic the form of what appeared to be a horse made of stone appeared in the mountains, with two sharp ears, a nostril, an eye and all.

"You see," said Emery Afraid of Lightning. "Now do not move your hands. Look at them."

It hit Coal suddenly that with his hands he had formed the shape of a heart. He dropped his hands and stared at the medicine man.

"You cannot always trust what your normal eyes will tell you. You cannot always trust what you have heard. What unbelievers have said. Sometimes, Coal Savage, you must see things through the eyes of your heart. Listen with this." He thumped his chest. Then, he held his closed fist out to Coal, upside down, and Coal let the porcelain chip tumble into his palm.

"I guess . . . I don't know how."

"Yes. You do. You did not, but now you do. That is why you came t' me. Paul Wolf Guts has saved you, Wakinyan. You were not ready t' follow your path."

A chill ran from the back of Coal's head and passed all the way down his body. There was too much to all this. Emery Afraid of Lightning was right. He had come here blind, and he had intended to leave the same way. But he couldn't go. There was too much to all Maybelle and Emery had seen in their dreams.

Down deep, somehow Coal knew that in spite of all this hocus pocus, Emery Afraid of Lightning had seen something. Maybelle had seen something. Whether it was God talking to him, or the Holy Ghost, or some dark magic, *something* had spoken. Maura was alive, and for some reason only Coal could save her. He was suddenly back in Korea. Back in Nam. Back in the Lemhi Range seeking to kill the man who had stolen his daughter.

"This is finished," said Emery, looking between Coal and Paul, carefully avoiding their eyes. "It is time for you t' act. I feel that you wanted t' run. You wanted t' bring other forces here. Bigger forces than only you. You are afraid to go against your laws. But no matter what you try, it will keep on comin' back to this one truth, Wakinyan: You must fight this evil that has brought you here. And you must choose t' fight now."

Part of Coal caved in to the madness. "Did you see anything else? What is going to happen to the woman if I try to bring in the state police? Or the FBI? Even the reservation police?"

"Too much time will be wasted. Perhaps after it is finished, these bad ones will be taken away and locked up. An' that is good for Oglala. But your woman—she will be no more."

"Why? What are they doing?"

The Lakota drew a big breath. There seemed to be a part of him that was loath to speak. But he did. "I know Leland Iron Rope, Wakinyan. He came t' me wantin' me t' perform a ceremony for him that would cause this girl t' die, or t' make her spirit go away if she was already gone. I told you he has dreams. Bad visions that wake him in the night. He believes if the woman is gone, an' this earth is cleansed of her body an' her ghost, he will be free at last. An' now he knows she is still alive, an' he cannot let her stay. He will seek out a man on the reservation who works in bad magic."

For the first time, Coal realized how fast his heart was beating. He was thinking of Tony Nwanzée, Sam Browning, Alex Martinez—all of his old comrades at the FBI, the men who should be here beside him in this fight, except that Browning and Martinez had walked away from the Bureau some time back, in frustration. But Emery was right: If they came, they would be too late.

"What will they do?"

Looking helpless, Emery glanced over at Paul. He cleared his throat. "They will take her t' the sacred Black Hills and sacrifice her."

Reading the shock in Coal's face, Emery put his right hand on his shoulder and made a broad motion with his left, seeming to indicate all that surrounded them, the ground, the sky, the mountains.

"This is the time the Lakota call 'the moon when the sun is scarce'. Some call it the 'hard moon'. In Lakota—Wióthehika Wí. You whites call it January. An' according t' your times there is only a few days left.

"The moon that follows is Chaŋnápȟopa Wí, or 'the moon of poppin' trees'. 'The moon when the trees crack'. The white man calls it February.

"Wakinyan, this is what you must know: On the last day of the hard moon, your yellow-haired woman will die."

*   *   *

As Paul drove away from the medicine man's place, and slowly past the Iron Ropes', Coal studied their yard. Of course the Thunderbird wasn't there. It would have been too easy.

"What do we do now, Paul?"

"Hell, man, I don't know. I thought you'd have an idea. Remember what Emery said: You gotta follow the eyes of your heart."

Coal closed his eyes and rubbed them. He looked back at the Iron Ropes' as it faded away behind them, then returned his eyes to Paul. "Judas priest. Paul, give me some time to get used to all this. This isn't my world, buddy."

Paul nodded. "I understand. It ain't no easy thing. I guess the only thing I can think to do is drive."

"Drive?"

"Yeah. This whole place might have a hundred fifty people. I guess there could be two hundred, countin' everybody scattered out in the boondocks. How hard can it be to find a car like that?"

Coal shrugged, not feeling any hope. "I guess. But then we could find the car and still not find Maura."

Paul nodded and kept driving. When they got close to Sioux Returns from Scout's place, he slowed way down. "Hey. I'm gonna stop here."

Coal shrugged again, hardly listening. His mind was awhirl with trying to come up with some better plan than simply driving around.

Paul pulled into Sioux's yard and shut off the truck, throwing his door open. When Coal didn't move, he jerked his door back open wide. "Hey. You comin'?"

Without responding, Coal got out, the wind battering his face and pulling so hard at his hat he had to reach up and put his hand on it to make sure it didn't blow away.

Paul went up and knocked on the door, then entered without waiting for permission. Sioux Returns from Scout was getting off a kitchen chair. He wore a dark gray wool shirt, buttoned to the neck and cuffs, and his steel-gray braids hung down the front of it, clear to the bottom of the pockets. His pants were green jeans, and his shoes moccasins.

"Hau, Paul. Savage. You two want somethin' t' eat?"

Paul looked at Coal, letting him choose. Coal's first choice was to say no, but then he realized he might need all the strength he could muster in the next few days.

"You have meat?"

"Do I have meat! I'm a Injun, Savage. I got meat. Elk good enough?"

"Perfect."

Later, they sat down to plates of elk steak and brown gravy. Paul cut off a bite that was way too big for anyone but a wolf, making Coal wonder if his eating habit was a family tradition and perhaps was how his forbear had come by the name of Wolf Guts.

"Hey, Sioux, we need your help," said Paul when he had chewed off enough venison and swallowed it to find some empty space in his mouth.

"Shoot."

"If you get around town, be lookin' for Asa Iron Rope's T-Bird, all right?"

"All right. Any reason?"

Paul told the older man a brief version of the story. Coal was watching the old Lakota when it all began to come out, and he

wondered how many people Sioux Returns from Scout had frightened with the hot, angry look that flashed in his eyes.

"That man needs t' die."

Paul looked up, pausing in mid-chew. Coal saw him trying to
digest Sioux's words—and his anger. "That would be good. But
don't you get involved, old friend. Leave this kinda crap t' the
young bucks."

"I ain't so old."

Paul stared the older man down while several seconds passed.
He must have seen the iron in Sioux that Coal had read. "No. No,
I guess you ain't. Anyway, we'll be out drivin' the area. Lookin'.
You happen t' see that T-Bird . . . Well, maybe give a call down t'
the mercantile. Talk t' Bonnie. An' we'll check in there now an'
then."

"Okay. I'll be lookin'. I'll make a point of it."

The thought of having another person to search the reservation
gave Coal an idea as they were driving away. Before they could go
past Paul's place, Coal told him to pull in.

"Why? You hungry again?"

Coal didn't crack a smile, although he knew Paul was trying to
lighten the mood as usual. "I got thinking it would be nice to have
a third car looking."

"You an' the Ford?"

"Yeah."

"You sure that's a good idea? You all alone? Bein' . . . Well,
you don't exactly fit in around here."

"Paul, that Emery already knew all about me, didn't he?"

"Sure, why?"

"Because that means somebody's talking. If he knows, maybe
the word about me is spreading. Maybe any people out here who
could help us already know what I'm supposed to be."

Paul nodded, making the turn into his driveway. "You
know . . . Maybe. *May*be. All right, you get your car. I'll make sure

it'll start before I take off. Then let's figure out a search pattern—just like in the war, huh? An' we'll keep checkin' back in at the Merc."

"Merc?"

"Mercantile."

Coal soon found himself driving alone, the Smith and Wesson strapped to his hip, Paul's .30-30 leaning against the passenger seat. Every time he drove past a place that had a garage or barn, his heart ached. Any one of those places could contain the Thunderbird. But how could they check them all?

He had been driving around for over an hour when he pulled into the parking lot at the mercantile and got out. He went in, and a big-boned woman who looked to be close to Coal's age but could have been ten years either side of it looked him up and down.

"You Wakinyan?"

Coal had been about to address her, but he clamped his mouth shut. Then he chuckled. "I guess Paul's already been in."

The woman stared at him, her face blank. "No, no Paul. But old Maybelle, she's bin talkin'. She says you come here t' set this place free."

"I don't know what I'm here for," said Coal with a sigh. "I'm just looking for a friend."

"We heard about that too."

"You heard about what?"

"Your friend. They took her?"

Coal's mind spun in circles a few times in quick succession. Each time, it came back to the same place: Only he and Paul and old Emery knew about Maura. And now Sioux Returns from Scout.

"Where did you hear that?"

"People."

"Can I ask what people? Nobody should have known."

The woman stood still, her eyes shifting around.

"Are you Bonnie?" he guessed.

"I am Bonnie."

"Paul told me about you."

"Paul. Wolf Guts? Is he with you?"

"Yes."

Bonnie scanned the store, which appeared empty at the moment. Her eyes returned to him. "There's a man named Isaac Lefthand. A friend of Asa Iron Rope. But . . . Hey, I won't talk about nothin' unless you give me your word you'll never say nothin' t' nobody about how you heard."

"I won't tell a soul, Bonnie."

The woman scoffed. "Like I should ever trust a white man."

Coal couldn't say anything to that. He could understand where the comment came from. The Lakota and white men had a long history.

"I like your eyes, Wakinyan," Bonnie finally said. "You didn't hear this in here, but Isaac Lefthand, he likes t' drink a lot o' what the Iron Ropes an' them others bring back to the Rez t' sell. An' then he talks."

Coal's heart had begun to beat faster. He felt like he was holding his breath, but he couldn't stop.

"He come in this mornin' an' told me Asa Iron Rope got your woman in Chadron. Maybelle calls her Peta, right?"

"Yeah. Peta."

"They're gonna have a fire. An' a cleansing. Then—"

Bonnie stopped suddenly, and Coal waited. "What?"

It was then he noticed that her eyes were looking past him, and they were filled with fear. She swore. He turned around in time to see three vehicles rolling slowly into the parking lot, almost side by side: a pickup, a mid-sixties Pontiac Grand Prix . . .

And the dark green Thunderbird.

CHAPTER TWENTY-FIVE

Doors began to swing open, and some fifteen hundred pounds of Lakota trouble started unfolding out of every one of them. Their eyes shuttled back and forth between Coal's beautiful dark blue LTD and the windows of the store.

Bonnie swore again. "Wakinyan, I'm beggin' you please. They can't know I ever told you nothin'."

"I promise you're safe, Bonnie. You're safe . . . I'm not."

The first wave of Lakota came through the door in the form of a tall, broad-shouldered man wearing what was most likely a cast-off green army jacket from the surplus store, the sleeves two inches too short for him. His hair hung loose, conspicuous by being medium brown in color and having a bit of wave to its lower six inches, which came to about the level of the bottom of his breastbone. A fuzzy caterpillar rode his upper lip, and the grip of a revolver peeked out from behind his belt.

As the others came in, Coal saw with a jolt that some of them already had pistols in their hands. He, meanwhile, did not.

The second-to-last man through the door stood almost eye to eye with the first one. Asa Iron Rope.

Coal tried to look calm as the Lakotas slowly circled him. He had his back up against the store's counter or they would have completely closed him in.

Asa Iron Rope stopped four feet in front of Coal, hooking his thumbs behind his belt. Like the one with the lighter hair, he had a not-so-well concealed pistol behind his belt, this one an auto, a Colt 1911 or clone of one.

He ran his eyes up and down Coal's length with an ugly sneer on his face that made a sunken scar above his right lip look even deeper. He seemed oblivious to the two inches and twenty or thirty pounds of muscle Coal had over him, and for good reason. One man against seven was suicide, and every person in the room knew it.

"The big, macho *wasichu*," said Asa Iron Rope. "White man! You remember what happened last time I saw you, wasichu?"

Coal stared him in the eyes, noticing that unlike so many others Asa had no problem keeping eye contact with him. The strange thought crossed his mind that if he survived the next five minutes he should ask Paul Wolf Guts about this.

"Not speakin', huh? Hey, wasichu—you don't know anything about some dogs that got killed, do you?"

"I don't."

"You don't. Ha." Asa forced a laugh. Some of the others aped him. Coal noticed the lighter-haired one's conspicuous silence.

"This guy botherin' you, squaw?" asked Asa, sharing his ugly sneer with Bonnie, who stood somewhere behind Coal.

"No. He's fine."

"He's fine. She says he's fine." Laughing with glee, Asa looked around at the others, again prompting a laugh out of three or four, not including the lighter-haired one.

Coal took a chance at freedom. "Well, I'd like to stay and visit, but I need to get going." He didn't follow his words up with any move to walk away. He first needed to see Asa's reaction.

Asa raised his eyebrows, pursing his lips. "Oh. You gotta go, uh?" To Coal's surprise, he moved his right foot back, making him cant away like an opening door. But Coal still didn't move. Nothing could be so easy.

Asa waited. Everyone watched. "I thought you had t' go, wasi-chu. So go."

"I changed my mind. So what year's your T-bird?"

After a moment to grasp the turn in the conversation, Asa Iron Rope laughed, shifting his foot back to square himself with Coal again. "My T-bird? Nice car, uh? It's a sixty-eight. What's yours?"

"Seventy-one."

"Uh. Seventy-one." The Lakota swiveled his head to look out at the LTD, then returned his almost-black eyes to Coal. "Funny, it looks all burnt-out."

This time all the others laughed—except for the lighter haired one.

"You know my name, wasichu?"

Coal nodded. "Yeah, I think so. Asa Iron Rope."

Asa pursed his lips again, nodding. He seemed impressed. "Good. You ain't quite so dumb, I guess. You want me t' show you why I'm called Iron Rope?" He reached for his pants zipper, and his gang roared with laughter, except for the one who never laughed.

Coal let one side of his mouth come up, his only acknowledg-ment that he caught Asa's twisted humor. He had a dozen things he wanted to say, but probably not a single one that wouldn't gar-ner him a kick in the crotch from Asa's worn-out suede "waffle stompers."

"Well, hey, white man—wasichu. It's kinda windy outside. Cold as a frozen gun barrel too. But I want you t' see somethin', an' you couldn't watch it from here. Plus, the squaw's keepin' this place so nice an' neat, an' I wouldn't wanna change all that."

Here it came. Coal could read the future pretty plainly, and his view of it said he was about to get some teeth loosened, and prob-ably much worse. He didn't move.

Then the lighter haired Lakota took a couple of steps back, and Coal, still watching Asa, from the corner of his eye saw the other man draw the revolver from behind his belt and level it at Coal's midsection.

"I don't wanna get the Merc all messy, wasichu," said Asa. "You get it? Just go outside."

Coal couldn't keep the hateful look out of his eyes. "Well, since you put it so nicely."

Asa laughed, but his eyes remained as hard as ever, matching Coal's, hate for hate. Again, Asa turned to the side, and Coal took a deep breath, ever-conscious of the revolver in the other Lakota's hand, and walked stiffly toward the door. He wondered just how alive or dead he was going to be when the next five minutes were over.

Two of the other Lakotas raised their pistols to point at him as he came by. Apparently, they had at least learned something from his first encounter with them. He noticed with faint amusement that one of them had a large bruise on one side of his face and recognized him as one of the two he had thrown down on the asphalt during their first enjoyable go-around.

Once outside, Coal was completely surrounded. Asa hadn't drawn his pistol, but all the others who had weapons had them trained on him—a fact that necessarily put their own gang members in the line of fire across from them as well. Apparently they hadn't thought of that or maybe didn't care.

"You got the keys t' that car, wasichu?" asked Asa in a voice as politely conversational as if they were friendly acquaintances.

Feeling sick and knowing any fast move—or perhaps any move at all—would find him lying mortally wounded on the ice-cold asphalt, Coal dug into his pocket and produced the keys. Inside, he was praying for the appearance of Paul Wolf Guts, or maybe even a reservation cop. U. S. Marshal Matt Dillon riding in in the nick of time on his big buckskin was probably a little too much to ask for.

Coal tossed the keys to Asa, who unhooked the thumb of his left hand at the last second in time for them to jingle into his palm. He grinned at Coal and sauntered toward the back of the LTD. When he was halfway there, he turned back. "Turn around, wasichu. Don't want you t' miss nothin'."

Coal turned. Bitter hate and anger surged through his veins. There was nothing he could do at this point to save himself or even to put up a fight. He knew the gut-wrenching feelings that must have gone through Lieutenant Colonel George Custer's soul as he saw two thousand battle-hungry warriors racing up the slope out of the valley of the Little Bighorn.

"Damn, it's cold out here," said Asa as he leaned down to fit the key into its hole in the trunk, then popped it up. With both hands on the trunk lid, he peered down for a moment, then pulled out Maura's bag, setting it on the edge of the trunk. He unzipped it and laughed with delight, pulling out a black, lacy pair of Maura's underwear. "Nice! I bet you look good in them, uh, wasichu? Don't know if I wanna see it, though. Maybe some other time."

All but the one laughed at his great sense of humor. Then he turned over the bag, flinging its contents around the parking lot. Socks, underwear, shirts, pants—all Maura's things lay like forsaken rags. Coal's bag was next, and Asa plucked out a pair of Coal's underwear, holding them up by the waistband with his thumb and forefinger. "I wonder who might wear these. They don't look nothin' like them others you have." Another round of laughter. Coal wondered if Asa had to pay his friends to laugh at his jokes, and if he just hadn't paid the big, lighter-haired one enough.

Leaning down, Asa looked into the depths of the trunk, then grunted and pulled out a tire iron. He stood up and slapped it against the palm of his hand a couple of times. He turned and looked at the lighter-haired Lakota.

"Hey, Eddy. Why don't you hop in an' back this ugly car over there about fifteen feet? Away from the gas pumps."

Eddy! Was this Maura's brother Edward? Coal turned and looked closer at the big Lakota. The lighter hair and skin, the curl to the hair . . . Yes, there was no doubt who this Lakota was.

Eddy caught the keys out of the air with his left hand, then stuffed his short-barreled revolver back behind his belt. Without a word, he got in and fired up the LTD, putting it where Asa had requested.

Asa motioned to Coal with a broad sweep of his arm. "Come on, wasichu. Don't get left behind." He walked over to where Eddy was standing outside the car now. The others waited until Coal followed him, and then they resumed their places around him, obviously hungry to be the first to pull a trigger when the moment came.

Asa turned and skewered Coal with his eyes. Was Coal watching him? Of course he was. He swiveled back at the waist, and swinging hard, he put the wrench end of the tire iron through the back window. The sudden move made Coal jump, and his heart fall. Glass shattered and flew around. Asa hit the window in a few other strategic places to knock most of what remained of the tempered glass inside. He gave Coal a big grin, and the wrench end of the iron an impressed look.

He walked slowly behind the trunk, relishing every step, every moment of time. On the far side of the car, he put the wrench through the rear passenger window, licking his lips with open enjoyment, then did the same with the front one. The passenger side of the windshield fell next, and then, for good measure, he turned and took off the rearview mirror. That must have reminded him that he had missed a few breakable things in back, because as he stalked around the front, he took out the side reflectors and the headlights and turn signals.

Now back on Coal's side of the LTD, he shattered that side of the windshield, struggled a bit to get the wrench back out, then used his embarrassed energy to hit it three more times. Coal's window was next, then the back window, the last survivor for glass.

Coal figured he would put a few dents in it now, for the sheer hell of it, but apparently Asa Iron Rope was done wasting time with petty vandalism. A careless toss left the tire iron in the back seat, and then he walked back to the front of the passenger side. He reached in and came back up holding Coal's eight-track Marty Robbins tape.

"What the hell is this? Some wasichu bull crap?" He let out a boisterous laugh. Then digging his fingers down into one of the holes where the tape was exposed, he grabbed it and started pulling it out. He pulled and pulled until a long brown ribbon was being batted around on the parking lot by the angry wind. "Guess you won't be listenin' t' no more *gunfighter ballads,* uh, wasichu?"

He got two more tapes out and turned them over a couple of times. "Merle Haggard? An' Waylon Jennings? Funny names." He must have been bored of pulling tape, for he threw those back on the seat. Reaching in one last time, he drew out Paul Wolf Guts's .30-30, which was still leaning up against the seat. "Wouldn't wanna waste a nice piece like that," he said. Then he motioned to one of the Lakotas Coal had thrown down on the asphalt at their first meeting. "Go on, Pat. Get me the stuff, uh?"

With a grin, Pat hustled over to the Thunderbird, and he reached inside and came back out with a gallon gas can. Turning, he looked at Coal and sloshed the can around for effect. It sounded half full or better.

Swaggering back to Asa, Pat looked a question at his fearless leader. Asa nodded toward the car, motioning Pat on with a flick of his fingers. Pat's grin grew even bigger as he unscrewed the cap of the gas can and started dumping gas inside the car. By now, Coal's heart was down in his boots. There was no saving the LTD.

Probably no saving him, either, so perhaps it really didn't matter. His biggest concern now was for Maura. And oh, how he hoped Paul Wolf Guts could somehow save her, against all odds.

When the gas was only trickling out of the can, Asa Iron Rope growled, "That's plenty."

Pat backed away, and that was the signal for the others to do the same, including Coal. It took zero imagination to see what lay in the LTD's future.

Asa threw the .30-30 to one of his cohorts who didn't have anything in his hands. Then he pulled out a pack of cigarettes, shook one loose, and drew a lighter from his pants pocket. Putting the butt end of the cigarette between his lips, he sheltered the tip and the lighter against the battering wind, then puffed a few times to make certain the cigarette was lit.

Putting the lighter back in his pocket, Asa drew deep on the smoke, letting it flow out his nostrils. He sucked down on it again, this time forcing the smoke out his nose like an angry cartoon bull.

He wasn't looking at anyone in particular now, just standing there knowing every eye was on him, and to all appearances simply enjoying the daylights out of that smoke, as if it were the last one he would ever experience.

He turned at last to look at Coal, tugging the cigarette, half-smoked, out from between his lips. With a little smile, he held it out to Coal. "You wanna do the honors? Before all them fumes go away?"

Coal stared darts of hate into Asa's face. He didn't speak. That was the wrong thing to do, apparently, because Asa walked near him and held the cigarette closer. When Coal still didn't move, Asa turned and sank a fist into his midsection, doubling him over. Coal had been prepared, hardening up his abdominals, but it wasn't enough. It hurt anyway.

When he recovered and came up, pulling fresh air into his lungs, Asa held the cigarette out to him again. "Now you ready?"

Coal didn't move. From his peripheral vision, he saw gun barrels pivot back onto him. All of a sudden, Asa let out a laugh of glee. "Oh, well, I don't care. I'd rather do this myself."

Taking a step closer to the LTD, he leaned down and to one side, then flung the glowing butt through the driver's window. The car exploded in flames, much like in the movies, the heat driving Asa Iron Rope back.

"Whoo-hoo! Damn!" Asa started laughing and batted at the side of his face, as if trying to put out a fire in his hair. "I think that singed me."

The car was already crackling and popping, and a noxious cloud of black smoke billowed out of every opening.

"Hey," the light-haired Lakota named Eddy spoke suddenly, "I noticed the gas gauge was half up. We might wanna move away."

That warning was no sooner spoken than the others started to back off. The car kept popping, and remainders of the windows falling into it, for another five or more minutes, and the paint was mostly gone, before a tremendous explosion rocked the parking lot.

The force, or some piece of debris flying away from the car, shattered the glass in the store's front door and littered the sidewalk and just inside the store with chips of glass. It drove the Lakotas even farther away from the now tremendous heat emanating from the LTD. Some of them were laughing, but it was a nervous sound—the sound made by men who realized things had been too close for comfort.

Asa stared at the front door of the store, laughing. "Poor squaw's gonna freeze in there now. Guess we shoulda pulled it farther away from the Merc." He shrugged, to demonstrate his apathy about whatever happened to the mercantile.

"Now I guess it's time for you t' remember what you did t' me an' my friends last time we seen you, wasichu."

Asa turned fully toward Coal and grabbed the butt of the pistol behind his belt. Everyone seemed so intent on Coal that no one heard the screech of tires as a vehicle slid to a stop at the edge of the parking lot.

"Asa Iron Rope!" a yell came to Coal's ears. "I'm gonna shoot somebody if you chickens don't scatter outta here."

Coal didn't move his head, but his eyes flickered toward the sound of the voice.

It wasn't Paul Wolf Guts standing there, but old Sioux Returns from Scout. Coal had never been so glad to see a man live up to his name.

CHAPTER TWENTY-SIX

The tough-looking old man, Sioux Returns from Scout, stood next to an early fifties Chevy pickup that to judge by the occasional swatch of remaining paint had once pretended to be dark green. Now its hood, roof, and everything back of the left front fender were a mélange of that green with a lot of browns, some maroons, and grays, while the fender stood out like a dune of tan sand. Irony of ironies, Coal was pretty sure at a glance there was a faded, multi-colored thunderbird painted on the now-open door. All in all, in that moment, it was one of the most beautiful pickups Coal had ever laid eyes on—and tough old, gnarled Sioux Returns from Scout perhaps one of the prettiest men.

Sioux stood there by the pickup, his iron gray hair in perfect braids, as well-kept as his trailer house. They hung down the front of another green army coat. Coal guessed they must have a surplus store in some nearby town. In spite of only being five-eight or so, Sioux's broad shoulders, large, leathery hands, and the determined look around his eyes and mouth made him look ready to take on Asa Iron Rope and all his thugs—alone, if need be. He held a twelve-gauge pump shotgun leveled at Asa to back that up.

Coal's eyes slid back to Asa, who had a look on his face that made him arguably the ugliest man he had seen in some time, as if his scarred, arrogant face and heavy-lidded eyes didn't accomplish that already.

Asa stared Sioux down, while the others seemed to hover, awaiting some move or word from him.

"You damn crazy old man. You don't wanna mix up in this. What the hell you doin'?"

"Gettin' ready t' send you t' the spirit world, Asa Iron Rope."

"For a damn wasichu? You better start usin' your head, you crazy bastard."

"I'm usin' it. An' you punks better start usin' your feet."

Asa slowly brought up his hands in a placating manner. His eyes seemed to tell the story that he was starting to understand old Sioux Returns from Scout not only would shoot him if he was forced to, but perhaps he actually *wanted* to. For the first time, a hint of uncertainty, maybe even fear, crept into Asa's eyes.

"Uncle, you better remember somethin'. This wasichu won't always be around here. An' you can't stay awake forever. Sometime you gotta sleep. You better start thinkin' ahead t' when this is all over. 'Cause no Iron Rope or any of our friends are ever gonna forget what you're doin'."

"You young *gnaye*. I think there is an awakening happenin' here on the Rez. The Lakota are gettin' tired o' you an' your kind."

"Be careful who you call a fool, old man."

Sioux Returns from Scout's eyes hardened like obsidian. "Iron Rope, you see that perty green Thunderbird? I'm sorry it's got such a good name, an' I'm sorry it's in the hands of a gnaye like you.

But if I see it sittin' there twenty seconds from now, it's gonna have a big ol' hole in the side of it."

Asa raised his hand and jutted his finger out at Sioux. "You don't touch that car! We got guns everywhere. You crazy?"

"Yeah. Yeah, I s'pose I am."

"You're dead, old man. You might as well go home an' kill yourself. 'Cause it's comin', an' you might not like how it happens if you wait for us t' take care of it."

As calm as a cobblestone in the rain, Sioux Returns from Scout raised the barrel of his shotgun and fired into the sky, racking another shell into the chamber and leveling it on the Thunderbird. But Asa didn't see it. He was scrambling for his car.

With Asa Iron Rope's quick exit, there was soon no one left who had arrived in the Thunderbird or the Grand Prix. But the pickup remained standing, with two frightened Lakotas who had both shoved their handguns into whatever hiding place they had come from—and Eddy, the unsmiling, light-haired Lakota in the army jacket.

Holding the shotgun like a man very familiar with firearms and what they could do in the right—or wrong—hands, Sioux Returns from Scout took ten or so slow, even paces toward Eddy.

"You damn fool, Eddy. What the hell you doin' with these punks? You know what they're doin'?"

Eddy stared the old man down, his pistol hanging at his side. Nothing when it comes to violence is ever a sure thing, but Coal, with his vast training at reading people, saw no sign in Eddy that he meant to use the gun. Just the same, thanks to Sioux, he now had the upper hand, so he drew his .44 magnum and made ready.

"Asa's gonna kill you, Uncle. You're as good as dead. You know that?"

"Then let 'im kill me, Eddy. Let 'im kill me. You're the brother o' that *wicicala*. You're on the wrong side."

Eddy stared Sioux down, his eyes like flint. Finally, a little confusion seeped into them. "I don't speak that Lakota talk much, Uncle. I don't even know what you said."

"Wicicala? That girl. You're the brother o' that yellow hair girl."

Eddy's eyes narrowed. "That yellow hair girl don't mean a thing t' me no more. She's dead t' my family. She's the one that left here t' live with white people."

"So you are Eddy PlentyWounds?"

Eddy slowly turned his eyes on Coal. As hard as they had looked on Sioux Returns from Scout, they glittered as hard and unyielding as diamonds on Coal. "What do you know about my name?"

"A hell of a lot more than you do, I think."

"Go t' hell, white man. If you're still hangin' out on the Rez by t'night, Asa Iron Rope's gonna have your hair—just like in the old days."

"Before you go, Eddy, let me tell you something about your sister. She was forced away from here against her will to live in a girls' home in Rapid City. Leland Iron Rope made her leave because he got her pregnant. You'd better think about that before you make any other decisions."

Eddy stared at Coal. A hint of doubt crossed his face, but he forced it away. Without another word, he and his cohorts got in the pickup. As they were pulling out of the lot, away from the burned-out remains of Coal's LTD, where fingers of flame still jumped up now and then and noxious puffs of black smoke rose randomly away from the wind, Paul Wolf Guts's pickup came driving in. He drove close, staring at Coal's car, and Coal could see the sick look on his face.

Paul stopped and got out, unable to take his eyes off the LTD. He swore quietly, shaking his head.

"About time you got here," Coal said. He too felt sick to his stomach, but he wanted to lighten the mood as Paul was always trying to do.

Paul pried his eyes away from the wreckage, shaking his head. His face was like a stone. "That beautiful car."

"Cars are a dime a dozen," Coal lied, broken-hearted at seeing his beautiful LTD that way. "What makes me want to kill them is what they did to my Marty Robbins tape."

This comment finally got a laugh out of Paul, who shook his head again at Coal. "You're somethin', man. They destroyed your car, an' all you c'n do is make jokes?"

Coal shrugged. "It's gone now, buddy. I guess I'm just glad Sioux came along when he did. I might look just like that car by now."

Paul nodded, his face sober. He looked over at Sioux. "Glad you come, old friend. But now you're marked too—just like us."

"I bin marked before, Paul. They can't do nothin' t' me like they done at Omaha Beach."

Coal's eyes flew to Sioux, where they riveted. "Omaha Beach! Sioux—you were at Normandy?"

Sioux Returns from Scout's face took on a faraway look. He seemed to be staring right through Coal's face to another land, another world, very far away and filled with pain. "Hundred and sixteenth Infantry, twenty-ninth Division. I was with Company B." The old Lakota's voice had gone awfully quiet. The little smile that found the corners of his lips had no humor in it. "They made me sign on with a made-up white man's name. Funny, huh? They called me John R. Scout—but Scout, for short."

Coal was overcome with a feeling of reverence. He had known a few other veterans of the D-Day invasion of the beaches of Normandy, but Sioux was the first one he had met who was Indian. He wondered if Sioux had volunteered or been drafted—but that was something a military man of honor would never ask.

This new revelation explained a lot to Coal about Sioux Returns from Scout's proud, self-confident, and calm demeanor. That was something displayed in so many veterans of that "war to end all wars."

Paul Wolf Guts looked around the parking lot. "We should git."

Coal shook his head. "I need to pick up all the clothes I can, and I need to say something to Bonnie. I can't just leave my car here like that and not say anything."

Paul nodded. "Sure. Well, let's do it together."

The three of them went around gathering clothing and stuffed it in the cab of Paul's pickup.

As Coal was leaning in, Paul said, "I'm surprised they left you with your gun."

Coal grinned. "They had me surrounded. It didn't seem to cross their minds. But I'm sure it would have in time, if Sioux hadn't shown up when he did."

Paul grunted in reply. "Well, let's go inside. Too damn cold out here in this wind."

They went into the store. Coal had been distracted every other time he came in, but this time he noticed that instead of bells, when one entered the Merc the sound set up to greet them was that of tom toms. Looking up, he saw two small drums swinging above the door on a string, and attached above them to a stick was a handful of fat steel bearings. When the door opened, it caused the bearings to swing out, then come back and beat the drums. Cute.

Bonnie stared at Coal and the others, sucking on a Coke.

"Bonnie, I'm really sorry about the window."

Bonnie tried to smile and gave a shrug. "My boss is comin' t' put up a board. He said it's gonna be a while before it c'n be fixed."

"Well, I'm sorry," Coal repeated, feeling awkward. "And about the car. I don't know how to move it."

"I know you didn't ask t' have them *wicasa sica* come burn your nice car. Oh, sorry—that means 'evil men'."

"Evil men, huh? You're right about that, on both counts. They are evil. And I would just as soon still have that car."

"I think old grandmother Maybelle may be right," Bonnie volunteered. "Maybe you really are the Wakinyan come now t' free our people from them bad men."

"Huh. Well, I started out on a bad foot then."

"Your good luck saved you," said Bonnie. "For a reason."

"We'll see." Coal turned and looked at the other two. Unlike Bonnie, they both met his eyes. "We're going to go now. If anyone gives you any trouble, you call Paul's number, all right?"

Bonnie nodded. "I will. Thank you, Wakinyan."

Coal smiled, although he knew she wouldn't see it since she wouldn't look at him. "You're welcome, Bonnie."

As they walked out into the parking lot, a car came into sight from the direction of Oglala Lake. Paul Wolf Guts swore. "Well, here they come. Adam 12 to the rescue."

The car was a brown four door Dodge Polara from the mid-sixties, and dead-center on the roof was mounted a red dome. The driver was alone, and a glance confirmed him to be Lakota, a gray-haired man of middle age with sagging cheeks and a white cowboy hat.

He stopped near the burned out LTD and got slowly out, glancing around the lot before his eyes settled on Coal. He came closer with a swagger, his right hand near the butt of a Colt revolver on his hip. Finally, he turned his gaze to Paul Wolf Guts, only favoring Sioux with a glance.

"What's happenin', Paul?"

"Not much now."

The officer, whose badge read WHITE CLOUD, turned to look again at the LTD, this time only for emphasis. He looked back at Paul and hooked both thumbs behind his belt.

"Not much, huh? I never seen that car before."

"It was never there before."

"Why's it there now?"

"Its owner had a little incident with Asa Iron Rope."

Officer White Cloud nodded slowly. For the first time, Coal noticed he had a wad of tobacco in his lip, and he spat on the ground, too near Coal's boot.

"Oh yeah?"

"Yeah. You wanna take a report?"

White Cloud shrugged, raising one hand to wipe at something that pretended to be a mustache on his lip. "What happened?"

"Maybe you should ask Coal here. He's the owner of the car."

The man's eyes passed over Coal, having to raise up several inches to meet his glance. He returned his attention to Paul. "I'm askin' you."

"But I wasn't there."

"You know that car can't stay there, right?"

Paul stared at the officer, and Coal could feel his ire rise. Coal's had already risen. "I don't think we planned on leavin' it, Dave. But we didn't really plan on havin' it get burned out either."

"Okay. So I'll give you twenty-four hours to move it," said Officer White Cloud, and he turned back toward his Dodge.

Coal assumed he was going to get a notebook so he could take a report. He opened his door and sat down, then reached over and picked up a pair of sunglasses, settling them on his nose. And then he threw his car into drive, wheeled it around, and left the parking lot.

Paul stared after him for a moment. "Son of a bitch. An' now you know why we don't call the cops around here."

Coal was still trying to grasp what had happened. "Is he coming back?"

"No, he won't be back. I don't expect so, anyway."

"He didn't even take down any information."

Paul looked up at Coal. "Listen. He knows one thing: Asa Iron Rope was on the other side. That's all he needs t' know. Just be glad he don't throw you in jail for litterin'."

Coal nodded. A chill ran up his spine. So he really was alone out here. No matter what happened, he would not be able to expect any help from the police.

"Where is the police headquarters?"

"Down the road past the lake. In Pine Ridge. It's about fifteen miles."

Again, Coal nodded. His mind was racing, and it took him a few steps ahead of his last conclusion. Not only would he not be able to expect any help from the police, but they might come into any altercation on the other side. It was a sobering thought.

"Paul, I need to go back in and use the phone."

"Why can't you use mine?"

Coal sighed. "I guess I can."

Coal went and got in Paul's truck with him, and Sioux started following them home. They only got to the forlorn trailer park, however, before Coal said, "Turn in here."

Paul slowed way down but didn't turn. "Why?"

"We're going to the PlentyWounds' house."

Paul slammed on his brakes and brought the truck to a dead stop in the road. Luckily, Sioux was paying enough attention not to run into the back of them.

"What the hell? You tryin' t' get killed?"

"Why?"

"Because. That's like walkin' right into the middle of the enemy camp."

"Isn't that how you stay safe with Indians?"

"Damn, Savage, you bin watchin' too many old Westerns. It ain't like that no more."

"Paul, I'm out of options. I've got a woman I think the world of that I brought to this country against her wishes. She's being held prisoner somewhere, she's probably cold, and lonely, and scared. And she has no idea what's going to happen to her. Or maybe she does. Maybe she already knows they're going to kill her. What do you want me to do?"

Paul stared at Coal, and Coal saw the change in his friend's face when he realized the truth. They were out of choices. Spinning the steering wheel, he made the turn into the trailer park.

Coal started to tell him where to go, but Paul held up a hand to shut him down. "I know every house in this place."

He drove right to the PlentyWounds residence and stopped in front. Sioux Returns from Scout pulled up behind them. "You want me to go in with you, white man?"

One side of Coal's mouth came up. "No, red skin. You stay here."

Paul grinned.

"On second thought, maybe you should. Sioux can watch the trucks. Maybe you can get more out of these people than I could."

"Maybe. Or maybe . . . Ah hell. Let's go."

Paul threw open his door and got out into the bitter wind. Coal followed suit, holding onto his hat until they got to the front door and were somewhat sheltered by the house. Paul knocked, and heavy footsteps sounded inside.

Soon, a once heavy-set but now shrinking man with a yellowish tinge to his skin and the whites of his eyes opened the door. It was obvious the man had Indian blood, but he certainly wasn't full-blooded Lakota.

"Hello, Weldon," said Paul with no emotion. "I need t' come talk t' you."

"About what?"

Paul made the little step up into the house and eased Weldon PlentyWounds out of the way with the palm of his hand. "That's what we'll be talkin' about. This is my friend Coal Savage. Maybelle Littlebrave calls him Wakinyan."

Weldon's startled eyes jumped to Coal's face, then immediately away. "You shouldn't be here, Paul. You gotta go."

"We're not goin' nowhere."

"Where's Nora Sue?" Coal cut in.

"You don't got no reason t' talk t' her. Why you comin' here?"

Paul put his hand on Weldon's shoulder, steering him toward the living room. "Come on, old friend. Let's go have a seat."

Weldon PlentyWounds didn't seem to have any strength to fight Paul, so he went with him, breathing heavy by the time he reached a chair and Paul pushed him down into it.

A wizened, pale-skinned woman with blue eyes and stringy gray hair with some residual blond in it came down the hallway, her face filled with concern. "Old man, what's happening? What're they doin' here?" She looked right past Paul and Coal.

Weldon sighed. "These men come in. They . . . Woman, get me a drink."

"You don't need no drink, old man. You're sick enough already."

"Give me a drink!" It seemed to take Weldon PlentyWounds all the strength he could muster to yell at his wife.

Paul took a seat on the couch, so Coal sat next to him, although he felt the urge to be moving, to be doing something—*anything.* Yet there was nothing he could do, and perhaps whatever he could get out of these people would change that.

The old woman went to a cupboard and brought back a whole bottle of Thunderbird and no glass. She dumped the bottle without ceremony in her husband's lap and turned away.

"Darlene, you stay in here too," Paul said sharply. "We need t' talk t' you both."

Darlene turned back. A haunted fear filled her eyes as they stared at Paul. "What you doin' here, Paul? Please leave us be. Can't you see Weldon ain't doin' so good? Go away."

"They're gonna kill your daughter, Darlene. Sit your butt down here an' listen." Coal sensed that Paul was holding part of his anger back. It was obvious that he had come to care about Maura, and the old soldier in him was coming to the fore. *"Sit down."*

The old woman grabbed a chair from the table and pulled it over. "They find you in here, they're gonna kill you."

Paul shrugged. "They're gonna try an' kill us anyway, woman. It's too late t' worry about that."

"Why're you doin' all this?" asked Darlene, while Weldon stared at the floor.

"Doin' what? Darlene, they brought this t' us. Don't you know about your daughter?"

"Nora Sue?"

"No, damnit all! Not Nora Sue. Peta—Maura."

Darlene's face hardened, and her eyes flitted away from Paul's face. "I don't have no daughter by that name."

Coal jumped off the couch and advanced on the old woman. He wanted to grab her by the arms and jerk her off her chair. He wanted to shake her like a rag doll. "Why are you doing this? Where do they have Maura?"

Darlene stared at the floor. Finally, she managed, "I don't know nobody named that."

Coal's string broke. Reaching down, he grabbed the old woman's emaciated arms and jerked her up, shaking her. "What are you doing? They're going to kill her!"

"Leave me alone," Darlene cried.

Coal felt a touch on his arm, and he started to whirl around, in war mode. Paul's face was there. "Savage. Come on. This ain't the way, brother."

Coal turned to Weldon. "You bastards. They're going to kill your daughter, and all you can do is sit here. What kind of animals are you?"

Hearing sudden footsteps in the hall, Coal looked up. He could see by the silhouette, and the bouncing hair, who was coming along the unlit hallway.

Nora Sue PlentyWounds exploded into the light. "You get out of here! You're not gonna do nobody no good. Just go!"

"We're not going!" Coal growled. "Not until we get some answers. They're going to kill your sister, Nora Sue. Do you know that?"

"You heard my mother. I got no sister." Nora Sue folded her arms across her chest.

Coal felt Paul try to grab his arm as he stalked across the living room toward Nora Sue, but the Lakota missed. Coal stopped in front of Nora Sue. He had seldom wanted to slap a woman, but he wanted to now. Nora Sue made it easy for him.

With what felt like all her strength, the brunette version of Maura struck out, the palm of her hand landing hot and sharp on Coal's cheek. Before she could even have sensed it coming, he returned the favor, throwing her face to the side. Coal heard Paul Wolf Guts swear.

Nora Sue turned shocked eyes up to Coal. She stopped herself short of slapping him again. Maybe she was having visions of such contests with the men in her past life and remembering how those had ended.

"You're bringin' nothin' but pain in this house, white man!"

"No, you people brought the pain here."

"Why don't you go? Leave us alone! This ain't your world. You don't know nothin' about life on the Rez."

"Where's your brother?" asked Coal.

"I'm not tellin' you."

Coal had to stop himself from raising his hand again. Returning blow for blow was one thing. Striking first was simply not in him.

"Why would you hate that girl so bad?" Coal said, unable to hide the bitterness and the desperation in his voice.

"She left me. *Us!*" Coal suddenly realized that Nora Sue's eyes were filled with tears.

"She never wanted to leave here."

Nora Sue raised her hand to hit him again, but with the tears in her eyes, he couldn't let her, because he wouldn't have the heart to hit her back. He caught her wrist midway to his face and jerked it back down.

"Ask your parents where Maura went. Ask them why."

Nora Sue's tears burst over and ran down her cheeks. "I *know* why!" She screamed the words like a wild animal. "Everybody knows! She hated the Rez, and she didn't care about any of her family. She ran an' left us all alone—to be with white people!" A sob broke from Nora Sue, and Coal caught her other hand just in time.

"Don't hit me again, woman. I'm trying to save you from yourself. You've been hiding from something all these years. Do you really want to know what happened back then?"

"Yes! Yes! But you can't tell me!"

"No, you're right. Get your coat and shoes. We're going to Maybelle Littlebrave's house."

"I won't go with you!"

"Then I'll drag you out. It's time for you to see past your parents' lies."

Darlene came over and grabbed Coal's arm from behind. "You leave her alone. You've brought enough pain here."

Coal whirled back on her, conscious of Paul Wolf Guts, who now stood there silent, letting Coal run with this. "You people are the ones who brought the pain. Your disgusting habits, and your filthy weaknesses. Your husband would rather die than not have his fire water—and you didn't give a damn what he did to your daughters."

Darlene tried to shake Coal's arm. He jerked free and shoved her backward. She fell to the floor, struggling to get back up.

"Paul," Coal said without looking back. "Keep her off me." He looked again at Nora Sue. "You going to get your shoes, or do I take you out like this?"

The girl deflated. Suddenly. Her cheeks streaked with tears, he saw all the will and the fire go out of her. "I'll go. But there ain't nothin' for me t' hear that can make no difference."

"There's a part of me that almost wishes you were right," Coal said. He didn't intend for his own voice to be so soft.

Thinking better of allowing the girl to go down the hall by herself, for fear of her coming back with some weapon, Coal followed her. She went into a back bedroom that was littered with garbage, and whose bed was a shambles. She gave out an annoyed grunt when she realized he had followed her. "It ain't always like this in here."

"Yeah, I'm sure." Coal stood and watched her sit down on the disheveled bed and tug on her cowboy boots. She got up slowly and glanced around the room. She appeared to be dazed.

"Looking for your coat?"

She nodded.

"Is that it on the floor?"

She looked over and stared at the place he indicated, then made her way over and reached down to pick up the bundle he had spotted, the dirty brown suede leather coat he had seen on her before, the one with all the long fringe. Putting it on, she stuck her hands in the pockets, shrugging her shoulders up tight around her neck. She couldn't even meet his eyes.

"Nora Sue."

She stood there, and he repeated her name. She forced herself to look up at him.

"I think you've known for a long time you didn't have all the truth. You owe it to yourself to listen."

She gave him a defeated nod. Turning back toward the door, he took her elbow, and he was surprised she allowed it. They walked down the hall together to the deadly stillness in the front room.

Paul Wolf Guts was standing by the coffee table, while Darlene PlentyWounds sat like a statue on her hard chair, and what was left of her husband Weldon had melted down into his easy chair. Both of them stared at the floor. The pieces of their world were unraveling before their eyes.

Coal and Nora Sue stepped out onto the porch without either of them looking at her parents, and Paul followed.

A big, ugly pickup made the corner at the same time as Coal's feet hit the yard, and he swore with a lot of feeling.

The nightmare was never going to end.

It took less than two seconds to recognize the rig Eddy PlentyWounds had traveled away from the mercantile in, and now it stopped parallel to Paul's pickup, in the center of the narrow lane.

Three Lakotas stepped out of it, and Coal let go of Nora Sue's arm and reached for his gun.

It was time for this to come to a head.

CHAPTER TWENTY-SEVEN

Big Eddy PlentyWounds saw Coal drawing his pistol, and yet his eyes showed no fear. "Hey, dumb white man. You know we got way more people comin'. You stepped in a trap you can't get out of."

Coal stared Eddy down, wondering if there were any truth to what he was saying and if he was really as fearless as he appeared.

Eddy looked at Coal's Smith and Wesson, his own gun behind his belt. Neither of the others had drawn their weapons either, nor had Paul Wolf Guts. Coal alone was brandishing a gun.

Eddy came closer. He truly seemed to have no fear of dying. And maybe that was true. Maybe dying was preferable to living this sad, hopeless, helpless life on the Pine Ridge Reservation.

He stopped ten feet away. Coal had only to pull the trigger to blow an unhealable hole through his middle.

"You sure look real brave with that gun," said Eddy, staring Coal down. "I bet you ain't so tough without it."

"I bet you're not going to find out."

"Damn coward. Well, you know what then? We'll all just stand here an' wait 'til Asa an' the others get here, 'cause I know you ain't got what it takes t' pull the trigger. Or else . . ."

"Or else what?"

"Or else you fight me like a man."

Coal almost laughed. "You're a bigger fool than I thought, Eddy."

"Because you think you can take me?"

"Because I know I can."

"With knives?"

Coal grunted. "Only a fool gets in a knife fight. That's a sure recipe for both sides to bleed. Why would I put down my gun for that?"

"Okay, fine. How about hand-to-hand?"

This time Coal couldn't hold back a laugh. "How about you're a fool? What do I win?"

"You drive outta here. Do whatever you was gonna do. Be gone."

"How do you guarantee Asa Iron Rope will agree?"

"Because I can kick his butt too."

"Why are you with him then? You know they plan to kill your sister, Eddy. Right away. That's if she's not already dead." It hurt Coal even to say those words, but he felt the truth in them.

Eddy stared, his eyes hardening. Maybe Coal was searching too hard, but some of the hardness in Eddy seemed put on.

"She ain't my sister. I only got one sister, an' you got her right there."

"Everybody sure is ready to hang Maura from a tree."

"She hung us from a tree," countered Eddy, and spat to the side.

The Smith and Wesson was growing bitter cold in Coal's hand between the single digit temperature and the biting wind.

"You never gave her a chance," said Coal.

"She's the one that left."

"She didn't leave. She was sent away."

Eddy swore. "You come in here thinkin' you know so much. You don't know nothin' that goes on on the Rez."

"Yeah, that's what Nora Sue keeps telling me. We're killing time," Coal said. "I'm walking out of here, and she's going with me."

"Like hell."

"What's going to stop me?"

"I am."

"I'm going to blow a hole through you big enough to fit your fist."

"Go ahead. I see your gun, but I don't see no guts. Come on, white man. Shoot me."

Coal knew at that moment that Eddy wasn't bluffing. He would have to kill him to leave. Eddy didn't care. He had made up his mind to prevail or die. Life really must be hell on this reservation.

Coal spoke out the corner of his mouth. "Paul? If I give you this gun, will you shoot Eddy and his friends if things get squirrely?"

"What's squirrely?"

"If it turns into anything but just me and Eddy." This was an unfair gamble for Eddy, because Coal had no question he could beat him. But if he was willing to make the offer, then who was Coal to question it?

"You'd better be careful, Savage," Paul said. "This might not go the way you're thinkin' it will."

"Shut up!" growled Eddy, then turned his attention back to Coal. "If you lose, Paul takes you off the Rez an' turns you loose. No more pryin' into our lives. Is that the deal?"

"That's the deal."

Eddy raised his hands to the sides. "All right. I'm gonna reach and get my gun. Okay? I'm just handin' it t' Ike."

Coal glanced at the scrawny kid over Eddy's right shoulder who took a tentative step toward Eddy. "Go ahead. If you feel like trying to shoot me, I'll welcome that too." For emphasis, he cocked the revolver.

Slowly, using his thumb and forefinger, Eddy lifted the pistol from behind his belt and held it out to the side for the kid called Ike to take it. He accepted it with a trembling hand and put it in his coat pocket.

Coal let the hammer down on the Smith and Wesson. "Paul?"

His friend stepped close and took the revolver. "I got you."

"Watch 'em, buddy."

"I got you, Savage. This is my Rez, remember? I got less reason t' trust these fools than you do."

Big Eddy PlentyWounds went into a partial crouch, twisting his right side away from Coal, his hands up, palm open. The stance took Coal by surprise. He let his eyes scan Eddy carefully. Six-foot-one, one hundred and ninety pounds, lithe and lean. Coal had him by a few inches and around fifty pounds. But he also had years on him. Looking Eddy over, the first hint of doubt crossed Coal's mind. Eddy wasn't approaching this fight like very many people he had taken on before, like a backstreet brawler.

Eddy came in and powered out with a side kick. It would have driven Coal back into the steps if he hadn't managed to side-step it. So far, Eddy was nothing Coal had expected.

Coal tried a side kick of his own to Eddy's knee. But the knee was gone as Eddy bounced away. In his head, Coal swore, but outwardly he tried to look confident. Were Asa Iron Rope and his friends really coming? This could be a long, strenuous fight.

Eddy shook Coal with a strike to the ribs he didn't even see coming, and he cringed and leaped back and away. Made confident, Eddy stepped in, and Coal feinted with his right but came in with a short strike to Eddy's breastbone that Eddy failed to avoid. His reflexes brought a hard hand around, and the back of it struck Coal a grazing blow across the top of his head as he ducked away.

Coal tried for a kick to the outside seam of Eddy's pants, where a good blow would take him to the ground, but to no surprise of Coal's the leg bounded upward, and the strike was ineffectual. While Coal was recovering, Eddy came in and struck him in the ribs, then in the mid-abdomen. Somehow, Coal managed to bring the palm of his hand up under Eddy's chin, and Eddy wasn't fast enough to block it.

The blow shook Eddy, making him reel back. Coal came in hard, but Eddy had taken hard blows before, and he made his recovery while Coal was still planning the next move.

Back and forth the fight went. Adrenalin was high. Coal's heart was pounding, furious. He felt the pressure of successful strikes on different parts of his body. He felt pressure to the side of his head, and he went to a knee. He rolled away and came up in time to block an incoming strike to his throat that might have ended the fight. It might have ended Coal altogether. He countered with a strike that glanced off Eddy's head.

Eddy PlentyWounds was one tough, seasoned fighter, the hardest man Coal had fought in some time—since contests he had entered in Vietnam, in fact. He could taste blood but didn't remember the blows that caused it to flow. Blood ran down Eddy's forehead into his left eye, and Coal had no recollection of doing the damage. They were machines, employing every fighting method either of them knew, but wearing down fast.

If Asa Iron Rope was really on his way, Coal would have nothing left when he arrived.

The blow that turned the fight—in fact, ended it—was sheer luck. Eddy had struck Coal hard in the left side, a blow that sickened him, but he reacted on instinct, driving the knife edge of his hand at the side of Eddy's neck. It hit directly home.

Stunned, with eyes wide, Eddy crumpled to his knees. He tried to bring himself up, but Coal didn't believe in letting opponents up. This was no friendly competition.

He came in with a downward-sweeping ram's horn strike with his right fist above Eddy's left temple. Eddy stiffened up like a head-shot snake. His eyes grew even wider, and then rolled back in his head. He pitched over onto his side, and his friends stared in shock. Coal guessed they had never seen Eddy go down.

Sucking for air, and pulling in much that was far too icy, Coal hacked and coughed, fighting to keep alert to what the other two men were doing.

In the back of his mind, he heard Paul's voice: "Isaac and Norbert. You both saw the fight. Wakinyan won it fair and square. Your boy lost. I call it good."

Norbert and Isaac kept swinging their eyes back and forth between Paul, Coal, and their defeated friend. Coal tasted blood. He almost liked it. The blood of victory.

"Nobody can give a man the name o' Wakinyan," said the one called Norbert. "There ain't no Wakinyan."

Paul growled against the wind: "There sure is now."

Coal lowered himself to help Norbert and Isaac drag their defeated hunk of flesh to the bed of the pickup and lay him in, Paul watching the proceedings with Coal's Smith and Wesson in hand, and Sioux Returns from Scout standing in front of his pickup grill with his shotgun leveled.

The Lakotas' rig drove meekly away into the afternoon, and Paul got in his pickup. Coal opened his door and motioned Nora Sue in ahead of him. As he shut the door she let her head plop back against the seat.

She breathed the words, "Nobody ever beat Eddy in a fight."

Paul chuckled and swore. "I don't think Eddy ever saw a fight like that. Nora Sue, I think this really is Wakinyan. Maybelle was right."

Nora Sue scoffed. Other than that, and a long exhalation, she made no sound.

They pulled up a few minutes later in front of Maybelle Littlebrave's hovel. "I really would rather not be here," said Nora Sue, her voice subdued.

Coal, sitting next to her, had started feeling every place Eddy PlentyWounds had hit him. By tomorrow, he would probably be able to count his unbruised places on one hand. He licked his split lip. "You need to hear what this old woman has to say, Nora Sue. Your parents have lied to you your whole life, and you and Eddy and Maura paid the price."

Maybelle let them in quietly at Paul's knock. The only person whose gaze she would meet was Nora Sue.

"I want to go," Nora Sue said to Coal. He looked at her and saw something in her face he had yet to see. She looked vulnerable. Her tough woman exterior had melted away, and she appeared as a child wanting to hide in the protection of its mother's arms.

"Sit down, Nora Sue," Coal told her. This time when he took her arm it was gently, and he eased her down into one of the ragged pieces of furniture he guessed Maybelle called a sofa. Coal and the other men stayed standing.

Maybelle stopped staring at Nora Sue and walked to the stove. She started fussing around there while Coal, Paul, Nora Sue, and Sioux waited. In time, it became apparent that she was only fidgeting. She had no aim at the stove whatsoever. At last, she turned back around, looking at the filthy rug on the floor. "You wan' me t' make some coffee?"

Coal had already prepared himself for the strain of understanding the old woman, so her words came with surprising ease this time. "No, ma'am, I think we'll be fine. We only want to talk."

Maybelle turned back to the stove and crossed her hands in front of her. From behind, the tiny woman looked like something almost other-worldly, a being from the land of the little people, dressed in ancient traditional Lakota clothing that swallowed her whole, and lost in the wrong time. She began to nod as if to herself, then took a huge breath and turned, eyes zeroing in on Nora Sue again.

"I've asked the spirits for this for long time, Ile. Long time. Finally, you come t' me."

Nora Sue avoided her eyes. "I wish you wouldn't call me that, Unci. I'm not anything like a light on a mountain. I didn't even want to come. You don't have anything t' tell me."

"But I do," countered little Maybelle. "Girl, I got lots t' tell you. But you need t' be ready t' hear."

"Miss Maybelle?" Coal cut in. "Please tell her whether she's ready or not. This might be our last chance for this."

Maybelle's eyes came past Coal's face. She looked like she wanted to run away, and he didn't blame her. At last, she gave an exaggerated nod. "You are right. I reckon it's time."

The old woman tottered over in front of Nora Sue.

"Ile, you gon' look up at me?"

Nora Sue's eyes came up furtively, then flitted away.

"Then I guess I just gotta talk. Girl, no person likes t' know they bin lied to. An' no person likes t' learn that the people they trust has gone down a dark path."

Without looking up, Nora Sue said, "I don't trust anybody."

"Well then maybe this will be easier. Your daddy and mama, they bin lyin' t' you, girl. All these years. Your sister Peta, she never runned off. They took 'er an' give 'er up."

Nora Sue boiled up off the couch. "I'm gonna go."

Coal grabbed her arm. "No you aren't. Sit down."

"You can't make me!" she almost screamed.

"Listen." Coal's voice was hard. "I don't know if you're ever going to get a chance to tell Maura you're sorry. I don't know if we're going to see that girl again." His voice caught, and for a second he wondered if he could go on. He took a calming breath. "But if you do see her again, and *when* you do, you're going to know the real story—as hard as it is to hear." Coal himself didn't even know all of it. He wondered if Maybelle knew that or if she assumed Maura had told him all. He wondered if he would be ready for Maybelle's words any more than Nora Sue was.

Coal's tone softened, and he pushed Nora Sue back toward the couch. "Come on. I'll sit here with you."

She scoffed but plopped back down, making it plain she wasn't interested in the proceedings. Coal sank down beside her.

"Your daddy an' mama called a man. A man nobody on the Rez ever seen before. He come an' took Peta one day an' drove her to a home in Rapid City, an' that's where he left her, in a home with a lot o' other Injun girls nobody wanted. They never did give 'er no choice."

Nora Sue's lip began to quiver. "I really want to go."

"You're not going," said Coal. "If you want to go after Maybelle tells you everything, I'll take you home. But not until she's done."

Nora Sue folded her arms tight across the chest of her buckskin coat.

"I wish your brother was here," said Maybelle. "This needs t' be complete. Everybody needs t' know."

"You'll never get him here." Nora Sue's voice was sullen.

"No. No, I reckon I won't. Listen t' me, girl: They took Peta away because she was gonna have a little baby. You understan' me? A little baby girl. She done had that baby, an' she give it the name o' Emmie Lee. Then they come an' took it away. Sold it off or done somethin' else. I guess nobody's ever gonna know what come o' that baby."

Sometime during Maybelle's revelation, Nora Sue had raised her eyes. She seemed to be searching for truth in the old woman's craggy face. "How would my sister have a baby? She was only thirteen."

"An' twelve when she got in the family way. Yes."

"But . . . *how?*"

"How? I'll tell you if you'll sit quiet an' listen. Your daddy, he was tradin' Peta t' Leland Iron Rope for his wine an' whisky."

Nora Sue jumped up again and snarled down into Maybelle's face. *"That isn't true! It's not!"*

Coal was up and standing beside Nora Sue, and he didn't try to push her back down. He put a calming hand on her arm, but she jerked away from him. "Why are you tellin' me these lies?"

"They ain't lies, little girl," said Maybelle softly. "They's all truth. When Leland Iron Rope didn't want nobody knowin' what he done, an' he didn't want no baby comin' that was his, he give your daddy two cases o' Thunderbird wine t' send 'er away an' hide 'er."

"Why wouldn't my mother stop it?" Nora Sue practically screamed, tears running down her cheeks.

"Because your mama made the choice too, girl. She knowed all of it. Your mama didn't care no more'n your daddy did."

Nora Sue turned around, desperately searching the room. There were the two boys, Joseph Afraid and Billy Pierre, Paul, Sioux, and Coal. She was seeking someone to comfort her, and there was no one.

Blindly, she tried to get to the door. The rug tripped her, and she fell to her hands and knees. She started sobbing, and everyone else froze. Finally, Coal knelt down by her and spoke as quietly as he could. "Hey. Come on, Nora Sue. Try to be strong. These boys are scared."

Nora Sue sat back on her lower legs, burying her face in her hands. Then, because he was the only human close to her, she turned and fell against Coal, sobbing into his coat. She kept saying something he finally made out as, "You've gotta tell me this ain't true. Please. *Please.*" But Coal couldn't tell her that.

Nora Sue finally staggered to her feet, and before anyone could stop her she got to the front door and ran out into the wind. She took off out to the road, and then started running along it, and Coal watched her for a moment, thinking she might stop. Finally, he swore. She wasn't going to stop.

"Catch up to us, Paul," he said, and then he too ran outside and started down the road.

He caught Nora Sue PlentyWounds a few hundred yards away and grabbed her around the midsection, drawing her up short. She fought him ineffectively for a while, all the time saying something unintelligible through her tears.

"I can't understand anything you're saying! You've got to calm down."

Nora Sue finally sagged into his arms, her energy spent. The wind kept battering their hair around, and Coal could feel his cheeks beginning to freeze.

Looking to his left, he saw Paul Wolf Guts sitting beside them in his pickup, and for all Coal knew he might have been there a while, for he hadn't heard him drive up.

Coal carefully turned Nora Sue to him and dried off her tears with his thumbs before the cold and wind could turn them into chips of ice. "Talk to me, Nora Sue. Where are you going?"

"We've gotta tell my brother! We've gotta stop Asa Iron Rope and his father from what they're gonna do!"

CHAPTER TWENTY-EIGHT

Later, they sat quiet on Maybelle Littlebrave's salvaged furniture while Maybelle emptied her soul to those who were listening. She didn't try to protect Joseph and Billy from the truths she was revealing, and Coal thought that was the right thing to do. The boys might as well understand how life was—on the reservation and elsewhere. They might as well know now, and perhaps they could make decisions at this age that would set them on a path of protecting others, rather than hurting people like the Iron Ropes and their ilk.

When there was nothing left to tell, and too much minute detail for Nora Sue ever to doubt what Maybelle had said, the young woman turned again to Coal. Her eyes were pleading.

"Can we save my sister?"

"I'm praying we can."

"Then we have to find my brother."

"Where would he be now?"

"There's no way to know. Are you even sure you didn't kill him?"

Coal smiled. "I'm sure. That's one tough kid, Nora Sue. I wish somebody had told me that sooner."

She laughed. "I'm sorry. But you probably wouldn't have believed me. Eddy travels all around the whole reservation and fights for money. Sometimes he even goes to Rapid City and into Nebraska. He's pretty well-known around this area."

"I don't doubt it," Coal said. "But back to finding him . . . Isn't there someplace we could start?"

"Sure. At Norbert Sam's place or Isaac Lefthand's. Those are the other two guys you saw 'im with at my parents' house. After that, there are three other friends of his besides Asa: Levi Weaselbear, Pat Highhorse, and Jimmy LeBeau. But if you look long enough, you're going to run into Asa and his father."

"What if I do?"

"What if you do? Savage, those guys have killed people! Nobody can prove it, but we all know. They'll kill you too."

"And Maura."

"Please don't say that."

"I'm sorry. But we know they're going to try."

"I know. We have t' get t' my brother."

Paul Wolf Guts spoke up: "How about we go back t' your folks' place, Nora Sue? You could start makin' some calls around t' see what you c'n find out without havin' t' drive anywhere."

"Yeah, I guess we could do that."

They went outside and headed for the trucks. Sioux Returns from Scout swearing stopped them, and they all turned back to him. They didn't even need to ask him what the problem was. As soon as they saw his face, they followed the line of his eyes, and everyone saw the same sight. In the east, two large columns of heavy, black, sooty gray smoke curled up into the sky, fighting the wind.

Paul Wolf Guts stood still. A Lakota statue. He didn't say a word, not even to curse. There was nothing to say.

A gust of wind came out of Coal's mouth, and an ache fell over him. His immediate response to the smoke clouds was to think he was the cause of them. If he had never suggested that Maura come back here, none of this would ever have happened, and life on the Rez would have gone forth the same as always.

"They got my damn dogs," said Sioux Returns from Scout, his voice quiet. "Man, my dogs." A cloud of emotion engulfed the old man's face.

"You sure, Sioux?" asked Paul. "Maybe we should go look."

Sioux nodded. "Maybe in a while. But I sure can't imagine they'd bother t' turn 'em loose."

Paul nodded soberly. "Sorry, brother."

"Where we stay now?" asked Sioux, turning to look at Coal and Paul.

Coal clenched his jaw. "At the Iron Ropes' house."

*   *   *

When the two pickups rolled up in front of Leland and Asa Iron Ropes' property, there was smoke curling out of the chimney, whipped into oblivion by the wind.

Down the road the way they had come remained two piles of black rubble where homes once stood, and the bales of straw Sioux Returns from Scout's dogs had been using as a home had gone up as well. Both dogs lay as far toward the ends of their ropes as they could reach, but it hadn't been enough. Every sign of life or property at both places was gone, except for the land itself. Only smoke and cinders remained, and the piles of ash and coals that were still hot, and would be for a day or so.

They had gone first to the PlentyWounds residence, knowing there would be nothing left to save at their own, and sat drinking coffee, ignoring Weldon and Darlene while Nora Sue called around looking for her brother, with no luck.

Finally, they left Nora Sue there, locked in the bedroom she was using because she couldn't bear the thought of staying out in the main part of the house with the parents who had been lying to her for so many years and who had basically sold her sister into sexual slavery. It didn't take long to figure out that was the same kind of thing that had happened to their baby sister, Cordelia— only she wasn't left to tell the grisly tale.

Coal looked at Paul. Paul looked back. "You sure this is what you want?" the Lakota asked.

"I'm sure."

"An' you don't think it will make things more dangerous for your woman?"

Coal flinched and swallowed hard. His heart was sick, and every part of him mourned for Maura. But nothing he could do would make her situation worse. The Iron Ropes already planned the worst for her.

There was hardly a way for Coal to reply. "Let's go."

Paul turned the wheel, and the pickup rolled slowly up the dirt road, Sioux Returns from Scout trailing along.

The Iron Rope dogs were nowhere to be seen, probably inside the house because of the cold and the hard wind. Paul pulled past the spruce trees. Sioux followed. Where they parked, no one could see the vehicles. If they hadn't already spotted them, they might not know they even had visitors. But Coal knew dogs, and he would bet those Rottweilers were raising the roof from inside.

Coal looked at Paul and Sioux as they converged by Paul's truck. Since the Lakotas had taken Paul's .30-30, Coal was down to only his revolver, while Sioux had his pump twelve gauge, and Paul his rifle.

"You've got the shotgun," Coal said to Sioux. "The dogs are yours. Paul? I guess you can mind the old man. I'll take Asa."

Paul and Sioux nodded. Reverting to long-ago days in the military, both said, "Yes sir," and for some reason that made Coal smile, but his thoughts were grim.

They moved toward the side of the house. There could be no prolonged stand-off allowed here. The pickup Coal had seen the other night was parked in the yard, and this time so was the Thunderbird. They were on the offensive, and immediacy was their friend.

Coal kicked the front door as hard as he could, and on the very first try it splintered open. Two cannonballs of black and tan fury streaked outside snarling, where Sioux Returns from Scout was standing in wait with his twelve gauge.

Stepping over the now very docile dogs, Coal moved in with the magnum up and ready, and Paul came behind him and peeled the opposite way. Asa Iron Rope ran around the corner from the hallway with a rifle in his hands, but Coal brought him teetering to a stop with the barrel of the revolver against one nostril. Asa didn't need to be told anything. His rifle clattered to the floor.

"Where's your old man?" Paul demanded as he picked up the rifle—his own .30-30—from the floor.

"In the john," said Asa, his eyes as wide as they could be given their heavy, hooded lids. "Man, take it easy."

"Take it easy, my butt," Coal said. "You get the old man out here. Now!"

"Hey! Dad! You gotta come out. An' don't bring your gun."

There was a muffled banging around in another part of the house, and soon a heavy-set, shirtless man with Asa's ugly, hooded eyes and another twenty or twenty-five years of age appeared, buttoning his pants. He stopped and stared, his hands lifting to the sides.

"Paul! What the hell?"

"What the hell yourself, you old bastard. You seen my house?"

"What're you talkin' about? I ain't seen it."

"Yeah. Me either."

"Where are your truck keys?" asked Coal through clenched teeth.

"Why?"

"Where are they!" As he spoke, he shoved harder with the revolver, making Asa's nose push up and to the side, and making him start backing up as tears of pain flooded his eyes. He moved until he came up hard against the wall, and a little trickle of blood started down his upper lip.

"They're in my pants. Back in my room!" said the older man. "Where are my dogs? What'd you do with my dogs?"

Coal, Paul, and Sioux ignored him. What did the old man think the two shots from the shotgun signified?

Paul and Sioux practically dragged Leland Iron Rope down the hall to his room while Coal tried to get Asa's nose to bleed some more down the barrel of his gun.

A minute later, the old man came stumbling back in from the hallway, Sioux's shotgun prodding into his back.

Coal looked over from where his gun sight up Asa's nose had made the Lakota's eyes water to the point that tears were running down his cheeks. "Now guess what, Iron Rope? You and your son are taking a drive in your pickup. Understand?" He would have made them walk, but he reasoned that they needed a vehicle to track them by, hoping they would drive to wherever Maura was being hidden.

"What do you mean? What are you doin'? Where we s'posed t' go?"

"I don't care where you go. Find some place. You've got friends. Since Paul and Sioux don't have homes now, we're taking over yours."

"Hey, you can't do that!"

"We just did."

"Where are the keys to the Thunderbird?" asked Coal.

"In my pocket, man," Asa managed to sputter.

"Get 'em out."

Asa did, and he fumbled them so hard that instead of handing them to Coal they fell on the floor at his feet.

"Do you own that thing? Where's the title?"

"Huh?"

Coal jammed the gun barrel up harder, making Asa cry out. "The title! Do you even know what that is? A little piece of paper that says you own that car?"

"I don't know."

Coal stepped back, putting his left hand on Asa's throat and pressing forward, the gun barrel still going up his nose.

"They call me Savage. You want to see why?" As scared as Asa looked, Coal wondered if he even realized his own words were being tauntingly thrown back at him.

"Huh?" he said again.

With his hand still on the man's throat, Coal took a step back and slammed the barrel of his pistol down as hard as he could on the point of Asa's shoulder. The Lakota cried out louder than the first time.

"Where's the title?"

"I told you, man—I don't know!"

Coal cracked the cylinder of the pistol into the side of Asa's face, breaking the skin. A gush of blood seemed to wait for a few seconds, then flooded down from the gash in his cheek.

"Now do you know where the title is? Because I still have a lot of places left on you that my gun wants to explore."

"It's in the drawer in the kitchen," said Asa, his voice the epitome of defeat.

Coal let go of his throat and grabbed his shirt by the collar, shoving him toward the kitchen. "Show me."

Asa stopped near one of the drawers. "Right there. I'll get it."

Coal jerked him back. "Hey, Paul. You want to look in there?"

Paul obliged, walking over and pulling the drawer open. Coal saw him raise a .380 auto from the drawer.

"Is that the title?" Coal said, and he slammed the barrel of his gun down against the point of Asa's other shoulder, where collar bone joined humerus. The pain tore a piteous moan from the

Lakota, and he collapsed to the floor. "Now where is the real title? The one made out of paper."

"I got it in a safe," Leland jumped in. "With my truck papers."

"Paul, why don't you take the nice s.o.b. to get the titles? Might as well get both of them."

The three men again went down the hall, and by the time they came back, Coal had Asa up and sitting on a stool at a bar that ran up to the edge of their kitchen. He had seen a notebook under the .380 in the drawer, and he pulled it out and threw it in front of Asa with a pen.

"You know how to write?"

Asa shook his head.

"You're joking."

"You try goin' t' school on the Rez, man," Asa said sullenly, wiping at the blood running down his jaw.

"All right. Watch him, Sioux."

While Sioux held the shotgun on Asa, Coal scratched a few quick sentences on a blank piece of paper, then slid it out to Asa, setting the pen on top of it. "Make your mark where I drew that line at the bottom."

"What does it say?"

"It says you just sold me a dark green 1968 Thunderbird. I'll add the VIN in a minute and have you sign the title over too."

"You ain't gettin' away with this!" old Leland growled. "We got laws."

Coal laughed as he watched the barrel of Paul Wolf Guts's rifle crash down in the middle of the back of Leland Iron Ropes' head, and he dropped to his knees on the floor.

"You hear that, Sioux? They got laws."

Sioux smiled with one side of his mouth. "Yeah, I hear. Too bad he didn't know that sooner."

CHAPTER TWENTY-NINE

After the Iron Ropes drove off down the road in Leland's pickup—more correctly the pickup Paul Wolf Guts was loaning him, since he, like his son, had signed over his title—Coal went out to inspect his new Thunderbird. It seemed only fitting that he own this car, considering his Lakota name.

He carefully looked the body of the car over for as long as he could stand being out in the wind and found it nearly impeccable, other than a little dent just in front of the rear part of the left side passenger door. The inside was another issue, as it reeked of cigarettes and alcohol, but nothing that couldn't be made like new with a good detailing. It certainly wasn't his LTD, but under the hood it bragged the famed 429 Thunderjet engine and 360 powerful horses, so all in all it seemed a fair trade—and certainly much less burned-out than his last ride.

Coal's vehicle inspection had to be cut short, because he needed to get on the phone with Nora Sue PlentyWounds. He dialed the number, and it seemed to jump off the hook without completing a full ring.

Hello? The greeting, almost yelled into the phone, made Coal jerk his head away.

"Take it easy, Nora Sue. It's me."

Sorry. What happened?

"They're on the run. I'll give you the details later, but for now I need to let you know they headed for town about five minutes ago in the old man's tan Ford pickup."

Was the T-Bird out there?

"Yep. And it still is. Asa decided he wanted to give it to me to make up for burning down my car."

There was a drawn-out moment of silence. *Say that again?*

"I'm joking. I'll explain everything later. So do you have a car you can borrow, or somebody you trust to take you around? We need to see where the Iron Ropes went."

Savage? My brother is here.

Now it was Coal's turn for a moment of silence. His profanity remained in his head. "That doesn't sound good."

He's pretty beat up.

"I'm sure he is. He probably feels about like I do. What's he saying?"

I'm havin' a hard time. Do you think I should take him over t' Maybelle's? He's . . . he's like I was. She sounded deeply ashamed.

"Well, don't blame him. You do what you think is best. If he'll go to Maybelle's, maybe that's the thing to do."

Okay. Are you going to stay there at the Iron Ropes'? Can I call you there if I find out anything?

"Yes. We'll be waiting for your call."

Okay. Bye. Coal started to set the phone back on the base but heard her yell. *Hey! Savage?*

"I'm still here."

You be careful, okay?

"Yes, ma'am." He hung up with a mixed bag of emotions inside: fear for Maura, hatred for the Iron Ropes and their breed, and a new and surprising feeling of warmth toward Nora Sue PlentyWounds. Maybe between God and Maybelle Littlebrave, *anyone* could be turned around.

Sioux Returns from Scout rummaged around in the cupboards and found a carton of Adam's brand brown cigarettes with only one pack gone. "Hey. Looks like I hit the jackpot."

He offered one to Coal, shared one with Paul, and the two of them started fumigating the entire house. With smoke soon clogging the room, Coal began to think being out in the wind wasn't such a bad option after all.

"We gonna make 'em sign the deed t' the house over to us too?" Paul asked Coal. "I could easy live in this place."

Coal chuckled. "That might be a little trickier than the cars."

"Then where're me an' Sioux gonna live after you're gone?"

"I don't know, my friend. I'm sure sorry about that."

"Ah, hell. That ain't nothin', Savage. We used t' live in tepees, right? And tents, in Nam."

A cuckoo clock on the wall that seemed to fit the Iron Ropes' personality about like ballet slippers would fit Coal, kept the time. The seconds seemed to drag. Coal sat in a well-smoked brown chair and stared out at the white butte half a mile or so behind the house. He had pulled the phone in from the kitchen, and it sat on his lap. But the darned thing didn't want to ring.

Sioux Returns from Scout blew a remarkable smoke ring. Boredom and too much practice bred skill at trivial things.

"Sioux, you ever do any talking about the War?"

Sioux looked at Coal, then away, blowing smoke out of fish lips toward the ceiling. "Not much."

Not much. That was Coal's cue not to pry. He knew how it was. Some things were best left buried.

Sioux smoked the brown cigarette down to a nub and snubbed it out on the sole of his boot. He flipped another one out and lit it, staring at the floor. Paul, sitting across from him, had laid his head back against the chair, and he seemed miraculously to have fallen asleep. Coal envied him for that. Sioux's surprising voice broke five minutes of quiet, contemplative smoking. He was looking out at the same butte Coal had been studying, which directed his eyes away so Coal would not see them.

"They called me Private John R. Scout," the old man repeated the only thing Coal already knew. The voice was soft, smooth, monotone in the way of a wise, thoughtful old Lakota. "I was thirty-two years old. I was a good shot with my rifle. Best in the whole company.

"We was Baker Company. We was second in t' land. Loaded in them big boats, you know. Dozens of us, I guess. Americans, and English guys too. I was at the back. Ya know, when I started trainin', them guys all hated me. 'Damn redskin,' they called me. Blanket ass. Other stuff like that. Then they seen me shoot. An' some o' them seen me fight too, with my hands an' feet. In a way they didn't want. I won, an' they lost. An' then my boys, they started t' change. They wanted me t' teach them t' shoot like me. Ha!

"So even bein' with a bunch o' white guys, I had me a lot o' friends, Savage. A whole lot. Good guys. Penny Bruce. Dal Bottoms. Lynn Hardwood. Pappy Whitewater. Ha! That little guy was a firecracker. Yeah . . .

"It was cold out there. Them waves . . . Man, they was big and gray at first. An' the wind. All of our boats a-movin' on in. No stoppin'. It was too late. We was scared. Can't pretend we wasn't. Smoke everywhere. Guns goin' off. The water . . ." He raised a hand and rubbed vigorously at his mouth. "The water . . . Savage, it was . . . It was gray, an' then, all of a sudden, it was all red. Red like paint. Helmets floatin'. Some with heads still in 'em, an' the bodies hangin' down in the water. Drowned guys. An' shot ones. Everywhere. Floatin'."

A long moment of silence passed. Coal couldn't speak, although part of him wanted to tell Sioux he could stop. But he knew a flood gate was opened. Sioux needed to go on. By the time he did, Coal had looked over at Paul and noticed that even though his head was still leaned back, he had opened his eyes and was listening with rapt attention.

Sioux ran a hand back over his head and grabbed one of his braids, pulling down on it. But that was not where his mind lay.

"We couldn't see nothin' up there, ya know? On the land. Up on them ridges. Clouds o' smoke. Dust. Couldn't see Able Company's boats at all. They was first in t' land, ahead of us. The Great Spirit, he forgot those guys. Let 'em go. Yep." He blew out a cloud of smoke, looking anguished yet serene, a combination Coal thought of but could never have explained. He could only think that the 'serene' part was a mask.

"A bunch of the English tried t' make 'em turn our boat back. 'Cause ya know, it was suicide t' keep goin'. But I heard the captain's voice yellin'. He yells, 'No, by God, you're goin' in.' So ya know, they did. We went on, and then he yells t' drop the ramp. He had t' choke out one o' the guys who wouldn't help drop it. Then they dropped it. Yep. They dropped it, all right." A deep sigh seeped out of him here. "Machine guns . . . They had them great big guns up there on the hill. Couldn't hear 'em—not till it was too late. Everybody's fallin', tryin' t' get out in the water. An' it's too deep. My friends . . . Well, damn. Everybody's dyin'. Shot. Drownin'. No gettin' on that beach, Savage.

"But then I remember I was crawlin', all wet. I was crawlin' in that red paint. Up over the sand. There was pieces o' guys—good soldiers. Guys everywhere. Dead ones. Guys with their arms an' legs gone. Some of 'em's cryin', t' their mothers, t' God. Some . . . just cryin'. I grabbed a dead guy's rifle—ya know, I had t' drop mine when I got outta the boat. Maybe that's how I swum t' shore. I crawled up the beach. Nobody I know out there now. It's all mixed up. Couldn't hear nothin' no more. My ears was ringin'. I think they're still ringin' t'day. Well, bullets are hittin' the dead guys all around me, an' I'm . . . Well, I'm covered in blood, ya know—an' other stuff. Pieces of guys.

"I never killed nobody on that hill, Savage. Not one. They's mostly all gone 'fore I got up there. But I . . . I . . ." The old man's voice broke. "I found some o' them Krauts, an' I shot 'em. Not live men, ya know. Not live ones. Dead guys. I shot 'em. I hated 'em. They killed all my friends. Every one. I shot one guy till my gun was empty.

"Finally, I found one alive. I was by myself. Lookin' t' kill. An' I seen this guy. This kid. Young. Maybe not eighteen yet. He was cryin'. Beggin' me not t' kill 'im . . . I tried t' shoot 'im anyhow—just because. But I couldn't pull the trigger. After all that time, all that wantin' t' kill some German, I couldn't even pull the trigger. All my boys, dead. An' I couldn't even make one shot t' revenge for 'em."

Sioux Returns from Scout clenched his jaws, and Coal saw him raise a hand and wipe it over his eyes. He could barely breathe. The cuckoo clock ticked on as if nothing had happened, but Coal Savage had listened to a story about hell, and he could never be the same.

CHAPTER THIRTY

The last white slice of sun lay flat on the horizon by the time the phone rang in Coal's lap, almost half an hour after Sioux Returns from Scout went silent and left Coal contemplating the tragedy of his story.

When he jerked the phone off the base and answered it, he heard Nora Sue's almost hopeful voice. *Savage? It's Nora Sue.*

"Hi."

Hi. I got Eddy to Maybelle's.

She stopped there, leaving him breathless. "And?"

Well, now he's in the same place I was. An' he doesn't know what to do.

Coal's heart leaped. "He's in the same place you were? You mean he believes the truth about Maura?"

Yes, but . . . Leland Iron Rope is really powerful, Savage. He ain't nobody t' mess around with. If Eddy goes against him . . .

She left her thought unfinished, but Coal knew what she meant. "Do you think he'd talk to me?" He doubted Eddy would want to speak with him after their epic fight, but he had to take the chance.

I'll see, replied Nora. *Hold on, okay?*

While Coal was waiting with his heart pounding, and both Paul and Sioux watching him, cold purple shadow fell over the house. The sound of the wind batting at the eaves had slowed way down. In fact, it could seldom be detected at all. But it was a sure bet the temperature had plummeted as well.

The sound of Nora's voice startled him again after an excruciating five minutes. *Savage? He said he'll talk to you.*

Now came the big moment. Coal had been trying to come up with something to say to Eddy if he had the chance to speak with him. Suddenly, everything he had been thinking of went away.

Hello. This is Edward. Eddy's words were slurred. He had obviously taken a blow or two on the mouth, which Coal didn't even remember doing.

Coal hated how his heart felt at the moment. And he hated his inability to find meaningful words.

"Hi, Edward. Coal Savage."

I know.

The sullen sound of Eddy PlentyWounds' voice hit Coal hard. He suddenly knew whatever they had to say must be in person.

"Edward, will you meet with me somewhere so we can talk?" He had almost no hope for this, but it was worth a shot.

Sure, I guess. Where?

Caught off-guard, Coal didn't reply for a few seconds. "Uh . . . Maybe you should come out here to the Iron Rope place. There'd be less chance of them finding out we talked than if we met somewhere in town."

Long silence. Then Eddy cleared his throat. *Yeah. That sounds all right. I'm gonna have Nora Sue bring me out there so my truck can stay here at Mom . . . At my parents' house.*

Twenty minutes later, a late fifties Ford Country Squire station wagon pulled into the glow of the yard light at the Iron Ropes'. It had once been white with full-length wood panels down the middle, but like many of the vehicles Coal had witnessed out here on the Rez it now had the appearance of having been rolled down a rust-colored mountain. One headlight was out, and the front bumper was missing in action. If the vehicle's death rattle hadn't announced its arrival, the noxious cloud of blue smoke might have.

Coal walked outside as the car stopped in front, leaving Paul and Sioux in the house. They had decided amongst themselves it might be best for Eddy's pride for him to meet Coal alone.

Eddy stripped his big, rangy frame out of the passenger side of the station wagon and eased his hands up to flip the collar of his green army jacket up around his ears. He threw both braids over his shoulders, then stuffed his hands deep in the pockets of his jacket.

Seeing Eddy's face gave Coal a moment of guilt, but then he realized he must look much the same—bruised all over any exposed skin and scabbed up like he had recently been through a major prize fight.

Eddy's left eye was half swollen shut, and it seemed to cause him pain to look at Coal through both eyes but didn't stop him from trying. He stepped toward the house, and Coal met him halfway, noticing a big drop in the temperature, from an earlier rise to just over thirty to what now couldn't be fifteen degrees and was probably less.

Coal wasn't sure how to start a conversation with this man who had recently fought him so hard, both bravely and viciously. He decided to go the route of diplomacy, and he needn't even lie.

"You fought a damn good fight, Edward."

Caught off-guard, Eddy looked at him for a moment, his head turned a little so he could view him mostly through his right eye. "Yeah, man. You too."

With one success under his belt, Coal took a chance on another and put out his hand. Eddy looked down at it for a few seconds. When Coal was starting to feel uncomfortable and think he had made a miscalculation, Eddy dragged his hand out of his pocket, and they met in the middle. The big Lakota's grip was warm and strong and not in the least overbearing.

"Where'd you learn t' fight like that?" Eddy asked as his hand fell away and disappeared into his pocket again.

"A lot of years in training, from high school on."

Eddy nodded. "Well. You're pretty good. I never expected that."

Coal was surprised by the grin that came to his own face, and he ignored the pain of it. "That makes two of us. I'm not used to having a real challenge."

The big Lakota nodded again. "So . . . I listened t' that old Maybelle."

Coal waited.

"I wish I woulda known that stuff before."

"Me too."

Eddy shrugged. "So now I don't know what t' do."

"Help me save your sister."

"Man, you don't got any idea what happens t' me if I do that. You don't gotta live out here."

"What if we get the FBI involved?"

Eddy scoffed. "Ha! That ain't gonna matter. This bootleg mafia out here . . . Man, they're gonna bury me."

"So what about Maura? She's been sold out and abused by everyone who should have been a hero to her since she was just a little girl. And what, now we just let Iron Rope kill her?"

"I don't even know if I c'n help, Savage. I don't have a clue where they took 'er after we brought 'er back here. Leland paid us two hundred bucks each t' go get 'er, we dropped her off here, an' that was that. He has some big plan for her."

"We already know. He's gonna sacrifice her. To the spirits in the Black Hills. I think that's where he buried your other sister, Cordelia."

All this time, Nora Sue had been sitting behind the steering wheel of the station wagon, watching them. Finally, with the engine still running and its blue smoke fumigating the yard, she got out and came over.

"Hey, Savage."

"Hi, Nora Sue."

Her glance flitted back and forth between them. "So you two okay?"

They both nodded, and Coal said, "Yeah, we're good. But Maura's not."

Nora Sue looked at her brother. "Hey. You know what you gotta do."

Eddy avoided looking at her. "No, I don't. Not really."

"We gotta help her if it ain't too late."

"Come on. Let's get outta here."

Saying that, Eddy went back to the car and got in. Coal and Nora Sue watched him sitting in there, but he wouldn't look over and acknowledge them. When Nora Sue looked back at Coal, she had tears in her eyes.

"Please don't give up, Savage. I wanna see my sister again, alive."

"I'll never give up."

Nora Sue studied the middle of Coal's coat for a moment. Then, without warning or saying a word, she walked over and softly put her arms around him. Surprised, he gave her a squeeze. "I'll die if I have to trying to save your sister, Nora Sue." He meant to say more, but he found himself unable to speak.

Nora Sue told him goodbye after a final, hard bear hug, then walked toward her side of the car. Before she got there, Eddy's door opened, and he stepped out but kept the door between him and Coal, like a shield.

"Hey. Savage."

"Yeah?"

"I think Leland Iron Rope must be meetin' with a old Injun that lives up past Highway Eighteen, on the next road goin' north."

"Forty-one?"

"Yeah, I think it's the first turn-off on the right."

"Meeting with him why?"

"Because he tried t' get one of our local medicine men t' help 'im do some ritual with Maura, an' he told 'im no."

"That was Emery Afraid of Lightning," said Coal.

Eddy looked at him with some surprise. "Man, you get around, don't you?"

Coal smiled. "I try. So who's this other guy?"

"Well, he's sort of like Emery, but on the other side. Emery's a healer. The other guy's into stuff more like black magic. Witchcraft stuff. He's a bad old man, Savage. Real bad. He calls hisself Wamblee Sota. I think it means something like Smoking Eagle."

"What does he do?"

"He's the guy Leland woulda gone to if he was wantin' t' do some kinda bad spell on our sister, or some kinda sacrifice—somethin' like what you're talkin' about. Nobody else around here woulda helped, but I think he would, if Leland paid him good. That's not what he went to Emery for. That was just for a cleansing. And it was before he had Maura."

Coal nodded. "So you say his name's Wamblee Sota?"

"Yeah. Or he might just call himself Sota, which means Smoke. But you go up there, man . . . I'd rather you not tell 'em how you found out about 'im."

"I won't tell." Coal started to turn back to the house.

"Hey. Savage."

He turned back around.

"I wish I could help you, man. I hope you understand."

Coal nodded. He guessed he would never understand, but he could only ask so much.

After Nora Sue and Eddy drove away, Coal went in and told Paul and Sioux about Wamblee Sota. Sioux nodded knowingly as he spoke.

"That don't suh-prise me none. Old bastard. We shoulda run him off the Rez years ago. He's brought a lotta dark spirits here. He's bad medicine all the way around."

"What do we do?"

Paul shrugged. "Well, we don't have much t' go on. I say we go out to his place t'morrow an' have a talk with 'im. If he don't know where the girl is, maybe we can at least get *somethin'* from him."

Now the only question was how did Coal sleep that night, wondering where Maura was and how she was surviving her ordeal. And wondering if she were even still alive . . .

*   *   *

Coal . . . Where are you? Maura lay still. Her pants were cold, especially where she had urinated and they were still wet. There was no drying out in this environment. She was lucky to be alive.

A sob escaped her, a sob which seemed to come out of nowhere, for she had thought herself drained of any ability to cry. They had not fed her. They had barely even given her anything to drink. Maybe a full cup of water, and nothing more. She could feel herself slowly slipping into death. At times, she found herself welcoming the thought—a release from all her cares of the world, and especially from this cold, empty darkness.

Coal . . . Did he even know what had happened to her? Did he realize they had taken her, and that she didn't simply walk away from him? Had he given up and headed home? She could only imagine what must be going through his head. No matter what it was, she couldn't blame him. For any of it. She was a tortured soul, so much more than she had realized. The Rez had brought all that pain and hopelessness back to the front of her thoughts. The helplessness. How could any man with normal tastes, needs, and desires agree knowingly to take on a woman like her? The answer was plain: They couldn't. They wouldn't. A normal man like Coal, even as much as he wanted to help people who had been plowed under by life, would never subject himself to the pain and sorrow that a life with her would have brought him.

Her left shoulder was asleep, so like some strange moth, still inside its cocoon, she struggled until she was able to roll over to the other side. As frozen and dehydrated as she was, and with the dearth of energy because of the nourishment she lacked, that seemingly simple movement left her drained and out of breath. She tried to bring tears, thinking maybe it would help her if she could empty out some of the helpless heartache that filled her to the brim. But nothing came. No tears. She had nothing left to cry.

The only thing she could find to be grateful for had come in an unexpected way. When they took her, five big, strong Lakota men, she had assumed they would take her into the middle of nowhere, rape her, and kill her, maybe even after torturing her. After bringing her back to the reservation, and after she found out they were delivering her to Leland Iron Rope, who had turned out still to be plenty strong, and seemed almost even young, she was sure that he would do what the other five had not.

But it didn't happen. It didn't happen, and no one explained it to her, at least not on purpose. Instead, here where she lay in the cold dampness, a strange voice had come to her ears from upstairs, a voice she had never heard. She had no idea even how long ago that had been, for down here in the darkness the hours all ran together. All she knew was what she had heard. This man, whoever he was, had given Leland Iron Rope strict instructions, leaving her to wonder if this thing was even bigger than the Iron Ropes. If she held some huge significance in the grand scheme of things that she didn't understand and likely never would.

She remembered the voice, as clear as a bell. She was pretty sure she even recalled his exact words . . . *Leave her down there, tied tight. But do not harm her. Do not touch her. Do not take her as a bull takes a cow. If you wish to cleanse yourself, and you wish your bad dreams gone, this is the most important thing you will have to remember. If you touch her, and I learn of it, then this is finished. You will have to find a way without any ceremony of mine. My hands are tied.*

She lay for hours afterward, trying to digest the words, trying to memorize the strange voice. And praying. Praying that by some miracle Coal would find her. Or that she would die, and soon.

She fell asleep from sheer exhaustion, and sometime later she awoke to the sound of voices. It was the strange voice of the man she had heard before, speaking with Leland Iron Rope, the man she hated with every part of her soul.

Go get her, came the man's voice. *You know we gotta do this, now.*

Monday, January 29

Coal surprised himself the five or six times during the night when he woke up in his easy chair realizing he had actually fallen asleep. It shouldn't have, for he couldn't have slept a decent five hours in the past three nights. But surprise him it did.

He made himself coffee while Paul slept on the couch and Sioux Returns from Scout stood at the rear living room window watching the pale eastern sky, puffing on more of the brown Adam cigarettes—"getting back to natural taste", or so their ad claimed.

This time Coal had made what almost amounted to a whole vat of coffee, for he was loath to be accused again by Paul of not making him any.

Paul woke up to the smell of the coffee and grinned when he saw the size of pot Coal had used. "You learn good, Savage."

Coal matched his friend's grin. "I'm hoping to keep you awake today."

"I'll be awake. So what do we do with your new car if we're goin' t' Wamblee Sota's place?"

"I'd like to leave it here, but I guess I'd better take it. Otherwise, it might disappear."

"I know a guy that raises cows on the way up there t' this place we're headed. We c'd drop it off there."

So it was decided. And after polishing off some two pounds of bacon and twelve eggs between the three of them, they piled into the three vehicles and headed out, stopping on the way to park Coal and Sioux's rides on the property of Paul's friend, Dennis Yellowhand, then going on up to Wamblee Sota's place in Paul's pickup.

After the turn-off to Eighteen, they watched close, and the drive that was supposed to be Wamblee Sota's was only a bit farther on the right. The property around the house was completely treeless, a wind-swept looking little shack covered mostly in tattered tar paper, sitting in the middle of the grass prairie, with rambling canyons and rocky escarpments not far beyond it to the east, where a smattering of cottonwood trees announced the presence of water not too far beneath the surface.

Paul drove up to the front door, and they all climbed out wearing grim faces. They walked to the front door, and Paul hammered on it with the side of his fist.

A man perhaps in his mid-fifties opened the door wearing what appeared to be an old-time Lakota medicine shirt, made of two pieces of leather cut out to match the shape of a man's torso with the arms extended to the sides, then sewn together, with the arms and bottom then cut to make fringes. All over the shirt were carefully painted Indian symbols Coal recognized from a hundred old Western movies. The man was wearing a black strip of cloth that appeared to be silk around his silver-laced black hair, and braids wrapped in otter fur plummeted down almost to his waist. His forehead was almost the widest thing about him, as his face appeared to have been caved in with a vise, and his body seemed to be constructed around the skeleton of a snake.

"Hau. C'n I he'p you?" the man spoke in a strange voice that was deep and gravelly but at the same time sounded somewhat feminine, something Coal couldn't explain even to himself.

"You Wamblee Sota?"

"Who's askin'?"

"Paul Wolf Guts."

"Okay." Wamblee Sota's mouth widened in thought. He seemed to be trying to decide if he knew anything about the name. "What c'n I do for you?"

"You bin helpin' Leland Iron Rope with anything?"

Wamblee Sota's eyes narrowed. "Hey, what is this all about?"

"So the answer's yes."

"No answer," corrected Sota, his eyes sullen. "I don't talk about my clients."

"What if I wanna be a client?"

"You speak too late," said Sota. "I already see you're up t' no good if you're askin' about other clients. You better git. If Iron Rope sees you out here, there's gonna be hell t' pay."

There was going to be hell to pay anyway, thought Coal. They had tipped their hand, and this idiot would be on the phone with Iron Rope the second they were gone. Or at least he would have had he known where Iron Rope was staying.

"Hey! You the guys that kicked Iron Rope outta his house?"

Inside, Coal swore. Iron Rope had already reached him.

Paul turned to Coal and Sioux. "We might as well git goin'. We ain't gonna find out nothin' here."

"Yeah, that's right. You go on." Wamblee Sota's strangely feminine voice was only short of a growl. "Git, an' don't come back."

Paul, Sioux, and Coal got back out in Paul's pickup and pulled out onto the highway. Coal turned to Paul. "You know he's going to call Iron Rope right now and tell him we were here."

Paul looked over at Coal. The look on his face was milder than Coal had expected. "He is?"

"Well of course. He must know where he is, or he wouldn't have known we took over the house."

Paul pulled his pickup over on the side of the road only a hundred feet farther along and jerked a lasso from where it hung in front of the back window. Going out to the low-flying telephone wire that hung down loosely from a too-short pole, he found a branch of sagebrush and jerked it free of its mother plant, then fitted it into the loop of the lasso. One throw upward made the rope flip around the phone wire with enough momentum to swing back around itself and tie itself in a hitch. Looking over at Coal, Paul said, "Well, come on."

Between the two of them bearing down on the end of the rope, the phone line soon snapped free of the pole, severing everyone down the line from phone service.

Paul retrieved the loop of his lasso and proceeded calmly to coil it back up. "Well, Wamblee Sota ain't callin' nobody now."

"That was good thinking," Coal said as they climbed back into the pickup. "Except he might already have been on the phone with him."

Sure enough, on the way back to town they saw a vehicle racing toward them, and when it passed they recognized Leland Iron Rope's pickup, with Leland behind the wheel and one other person in the passenger side, assumedly Asa.

Paul swore. Coal and Sioux remained silent.

A hundred yards down the road, Paul began to slow down as a second vehicle approached from town.

"What're you gonna do?" asked Coal.

"I think we oughtta go back."

Coal was about to agree until the car flew past them. It was an all too familiar Pontiac Grand Prix, and it appeared to be packed full of people.

Paul swore again.

Coal sighed and looked at him. "Now what?"

Paul had stopped in the road. "Do we still go back? There's a lot o' firepower headed that way."

Coal thought of Eddy PlentyWounds and Nora Sue. He tried to think of anyone else who could be of help. There was no one.

"If we go back there you know there's going to be big trouble," he finally said.

Paul nodded. "Yeah. Pretty big trouble."

"Do you think that old shaman was right about the time period for Maura? Do we still have a couple days?"

"I wouldn't bet anything on that, Savage. I think he was just saying Iron Rope would do something *before* February. It could be today—an' especially now, if we're makin' 'em nervous."

It was finally Coal's turn to swear. *Maura!* In his mind he cried out her name. *Where are you?* Was she even alive? They could have killed her the first day they brought her here. But Coal was counting on Lakota superstition, praying it would keep Maura alive until Wamblee Sota was able to do whatever magic ceremony he planned to do to ensure that Maura never haunted Leland Iron Rope's dreams again.

He was in a state of near-panic. If they went back to Wamblee Sota's place now and gunfire erupted, he was fairly confident that he, Paul, and Sioux could prevail, all of them being veterans of war. But what if they ended up killing everyone there, and there was no one left who knew where Maura was being kept?

There was the other option of confronting one of Iron Rope's flunkies without a fight. But if they couldn't get Maura's own brother to say anything, he doubted any of the others would dare volunteer anything with Leland Iron Rope still alive. From what Coal had gathered, he seemed to be more or less the head of the whole bootlegging operation, which was how all those thugs were making a living. They weren't going to help Coal cook their golden goose. And they certainly wouldn't put their own lives knowingly in jeopardy.

"Let's go back," Coal said suddenly. He didn't even know why. He only knew they had to do *something*.

So Paul backed the truck up a little, started a turn, backed it up again, and on the second try they were flying back up the highway toward Wamblee Sota's place.

They hadn't driven two minutes before Leland Iron Rope's pickup, and shortly after it the Pontiac Grand Prix, drove sedately past them. Out the passenger window of the Grand Prix came a hand, and it didn't take much of a glance to see that it was displaying something besides the peace sign.

Paul stopped again and looked over at Coal. "Now what?"

"Go back to Iron Rope's place, I guess."

"You think we can? He knows we're not there now. I bet he's goin' back t' repossess it as we speak."

Coal swore. "Yeah, you're right."

Paul turned the pickup around and started to drive back toward town without asking for permission. After a minute, he said, "Good thing we parked your rigs at Yellowhand's place."

Coal grunted agreement.

They pulled into the property of Paul's friend Dennis Yellowhand and got the Thunderbird and Sioux's pickup, then continued on toward town. Paul slowed down when they started passing residences, then stopped and waited for Coal to pull up beside him, motioning for him to roll down his window. "The PlentyWounds place?"

Coal thought for a moment. "Yeah, I guess we don't have a lot of choice."

They drove to the PlentyWounds', parked, and knocked on the door. Nora Sue must have been watching out the window. She jerked the door open so fast it startled Coal. Her eyes were red and swollen. She reached out and grabbed the sleeve of Coal's coat.

"Eddy left!" she said, almost sobbing.

"What? Where?"

"Some of the guys came and got him, and he took off with them."

"Some of the guys? What are you talking about?"

"Levi Weaselbear came in his Grand Prix, and Eddy left with him. I'm pretty sure he had all the others with him: Norbert Sam, Pat Highhorse, Jimmy LeBeau, and Isaac Lefthand."

The news hit Coal like a kick to the stomach—a bitter pill to swallow. He didn't swear out loud, but he swore plenty inside. Eddy! He really had allowed himself to believe they would yet win Maura's younger brother over. Now it was plain that all was lost. Eddy was too afraid of Leland Iron Rope to go against him.

"Well, we passed the Iron Ropes a bit ago on the highway, so I'm sure they went back out to their house," Coal said. "And I'm sure we couldn't kick them out so easy the second time. They'll be waiting for us—probably the whole bunch of them."

Nora Sue nodded, wiping at her eyes. "Come in then. You can stay here."

Paul and Coal looked at each other, and Paul returned his eyes to Nora Sue. "What about your mom and dad?"

"I don't care what they say. They've lost any rights they had. After what they did to Maura, they can lock themselves in their room for all I care."

Nora Sue backed out of the doorway, and Coal and Paul stepped inside. Before Sioux Returns from Scout could get all the way in, Coal heard his voice outside the door.

"Oh, here we go."

He looked out in time to see the Grand Prix puttering down the street.

It stopped in the middle of the road, and six people climbed out. Every one of them, including Eddy, were brandishing rifles.

CHAPTER THIRTY-ONE

Coal, Paul, and Sioux all had their handguns, but none of them carried any bigger weapon. Still standing inside the house, but able to look over the top of Paul and Sioux thanks to his height, Coal saw the Lakota bootleggers coming, and he nudged Paul in the back with his thumb.

"Come on. Let's take this outside and leave Nora Sue out of the line of fire."

Sioux heard him and started down the steps with exaggerated slowness. Paul and Coal drew their pistols and came behind him, spreading out at the base of the stairs. Coal heard Nora Sue come to the door, and he spoke over his shoulder. "Nora Sue, get back inside." He wasn't able to watch and see if she obeyed. He couldn't take his eyes off Eddy PlentyWounds, who he guessed in Asa's absence would be the one everybody looked to.

Eddy stopped on the edge of the property, his rifle held down low across the fronts of his legs. One of his friends stopped to his right, while the others hung back.

Eddy's eyes were noncommittal. "You might as well go, Savage. They already did it."

Coal stared at him. "Did what?"

"She's gone. Maura's gone. They took her this morning."

Coal continued staring. His chest felt hollow. He wanted to speak, but no words would come.

"How do you know?" Paul Wolf Guts cut in.

Eddy looked over at his friend Isaac Lefthand and motioned him closer with a jerk of his chin. "Ike?"

Isaac Lefthand was trembling. He seemed hardly able to walk. He came near Eddy, unwittingly lining up with the bore of his rifle.

"Come on, Ike. Tell 'em."

In a trembling voice, Isaac said, "Yeah. The Iron Ropes was stayin' at my house because . . ." His eyes flickered with the sudden realization that Coal and the others already knew why the Iron Ropes hadn't been at their own house. "Well, they was stayin' at my house, an' . . ."

"Go on, Ike," Eddy insisted. "Tell 'em."

"I didn't have nothin' t' do with it," Isaac said. "Honest."

"Shut up, man! Just shut up about that an' tell 'em what you gotta say."

"They said they was goin' t' do it, an' then they got 'er an' left, real early. I heard 'em go."

Coal tried to remain calm. He could hear Nora Sue inside the house crying out loud, so she had stayed long enough to hear the news. What did this mean? Was there any reason to stay now? Did he stay and take revenge on Leland Iron Rope and Asa? Take a chance on losing his freedom, not to mention his life? Or did he take everything he had to the FBI and the reservation police and pray it was enough?

Maura! She was gone. His knees felt suddenly weak. He steeled himself. These men would never see his weakness. They would never see his pain.

"Now what?" Coal heard himself ask. He didn't know why. There really was no question. The Lakotas expected him to leave now. But what about Paul Wolf Guts and Sioux Returns from Scout? The moment he was gone, they would be the Iron Ropes' targets, and they would never rest until both of them were dead.

"Now you go," said Eddy. "Get off Injun land an' don't come back." Eddy's face looked as hard as ever—maybe even more so, beneath all the bruises and broken skin.

Coal heard another vehicle coming up the road. He didn't want to take his eyes off Eddy, but he had to. When he looked over, he saw Leland Iron Rope's pickup, with just one person inside.

It stopped a couple of vehicle lengths away, and a tall Lakota stepped out. It wasn't Leland, but Asa Iron Rope. He had his Colt auto in his hand.

Letting his eyes take in the situation before him, Asa grinned. He looked his smugness toward Coal, Paul, and Sioux. "Looks like we got 'em surrounded."

Eddy sliced his eyes toward Asa. "Yeah, I already told 'im t' clear out."

Asa raised his eyebrows a little, which made them barely lift off the tops of his narrow-set eyes. "Clear out? Ha! He ain't goin' nowhere."

"Why?"

"He just ain't." Asa turned to Coal, bringing his pistol up a little. "You ain't goin' nowhere, are you . . . Wakinyan?"

Coal didn't see a reason to reply. Asa had his pistol partway up, and so did Coal. It was a stand-off, and Coal was going to win. Then fate would see how brave the rest of them were.

"The cat got your tongue, white man? I thought you were s'posed t' be this great big savior of the people. Now look at you—caught with your pants down."

"Just let 'im get outta here," Eddy cut in. "We don't need 'im."

"Need him?" Asa looked over at Eddy, incredulous. "Ha! No, we don't *need* him. You're right about that. But he's gonna pay for what he did t' me an' my dad. An' he's gonna sign my car back over t' me too."

Coal's mind raced. He thought about trying to get back inside the house, for shelter. But inside the paper-thin walls of the trailer,

Nora Sue was in danger of getting hurt in a fire fight. And that young woman had been through enough.

Thinking of the girl seemed to call her up, and before Coal knew what was happening, an angry, snarling mountain lion surged out of the house and down the steps, stalking out toward Asa. While everyone else stood spellbound, she went right up to Asa and screamed something unintelligible into his face, then brought up her hands and raked her fingernails down his cheeks before he could fall back away from her. Enraged, Asa drove his fist into her cheek, knocking her backward and to the ground.

Asa put his free hand to his face, and it came back smeared with blood. He stared at it in shock, then looked at the woman on the ground. "You stupid bitch!" he screamed, and he brought his pistol to bear on her.

"Asa!" Eddy PlentyWounds's voice cracked like a bullwhip.

Asa whirled. "You shut up! She's dead."

Eddy had already made his way close to Asa. "You leave 'er alone. You've already done enough around here."

"Like hell!"

Asa raised his pistol again. The barrel of Eddy's rifle was a rattlesnake, striking out so fast no one even saw the blur. Asa's pistol went off into the ground, then fell from his limp grip, and he grabbed at his wrist, where the barrel of Eddy's rifle had struck him.

"What the hell you think you're doin'?"

"You're not hurtin' my sister. She's the only one I got left."

Still holding his wrist, Asa scanned the others. He took strength from knowing they were all armed, and that they would be on his side. "Hurtin' your sister! Ha! I *am* gonna hurt your sister—just like the other one. You know, she begged for mercy. *Begged!"*

Eddy raised his rifle to his shoulder, aimed at Asa's chest. As Asa flinched and brought his hand up, like he could protect himself from a rifle bullet, Nora Sue screamed. *"Eddy, no!"*

She clambered up off the ground while all the others stood frozen. "Don't do it, Eddy. He ain't worth it."

Eddy stared at her. There was real pain etched all over his contorted face. His rifle fell suddenly from his trembling hands, and he advanced on Asa.

Asa struck out hard with his left hand, catching Eddy by surprise and snapping his head backward. He struck again, this time with the right, and it connected with Eddy's cheek, driving him to a knee.

Coal started toward them, but from the corner of his eye he saw rifle barrels bristle upward. The other Lakotas had aimed their weapons at him—all but Isaac Lefthand, who stood to one side and looked as if he were about to take off running. He had dropped his rifle in the yard.

Eddy PlentyWounds came suddenly off the ground with a beast-like snarl, driving Asa backward in a very unprofessional fighting move, but in this case an effective one. His pistoning legs drove Asa up off his feet, and Asa hit the asphalt hard, his head snapping back with an ugly thud.

Eddy staggered up, in a position to the end the fight. But foolishly, he didn't. He allowed Asa to get back to his feet.

The combat that ensued was bloody and brutal. It was like Eddy was a completely different person from the man Coal had fought. This Eddy, like Asa Iron Rope, fought using every dirty street-fighting technique Coal had ever seen—kicking, gouging, yanking hair. It was as if he knew he could defeat Asa too easily, and he wanted to toy with him.

Yet in this fight Asa more than held his own. For every blow Eddy delivered, he got one back, and although Eddy was the aggressor, none of this fight came easy. Both men were rasping, sucking for air, wiping at the blood that ran into their eyes. Then, at last, Eddy went into a karate pose, and his foot sliced between Asa's upraised hands and into his chest. He kicked again, with the other foot, and that one took Asa under the left arm, staggering him sideways.

Eddy came up to full height and brought the ram's horns of his right fist down in a short but brutal strike above Asa's left temple, and Asa folded motionless to the icy asphalt.

The other Lakotas stared at their fallen leader, then began to look around at each other. The group fell into sheer confusion until Eddy whirled on them.

"Anybody else wanna hurt my sister? *Come on!*"

"We're not hurtin' nobody," said one of them, the one Coal thought he remembered as Norbert Sam, the other one who had been here with Isaac Lefthand for Coal's fight with Eddy.

The other three also lowered their rifles. These would be Pat Highhorse, Jimmy LeBeau, and Levi Weaselbear. They stared at Eddy, and he stared back. There was no small challenge in his eyes.

Levi's eyes dared shift over to Asa Iron Rope, where he lay on the street, and then he looked at his cohorts. "Hey, guys, we gotta get Asa outta here. He'll freeze if we leave 'im on the road."

Eddy, his eyes crazed, backed over closer to Nora Sue and took her by the elbow. Reaching down, he eased a Colt Python out from behind his waistband. He didn't point it at anyone, but the promise was there. "I'm stayin' here," Eddy said.

The others stared at him. Their eyes flickered over to Coal. Finally, Levi Weaselbear, the owner of the Pontiac Grand Prix, dared voice what the others must be thinking: "With *him?*"

Eddy glanced over at Coal, blinking wild-looking eyes. "I guess."

"What about Leland?" asked Levi. "He's gonna go wild, man."

"Then let 'im."

"Are you . . ." Weaselbear paused. "You ain't gonna fight on *his* side, are you?"

"I ain't fightin' on nobody's side no more," said Eddy. "I got one sister left alive, an' I'm leavin' this Rez. An' takin' my sister with me."

CHAPTER THIRTY-TWO

Pat Highhorse and Jimmy LeBeau left with Levi Weaselbear in his Grand Prix, Norbert Sam and Isaac Lefthand in Asa Iron Rope's pickup, once they roused him and got him inside—not an easy chore. Scrawny Isaac Lefthand had been inclined to stay, but Eddy PlentyWounds, who now closely fit his last name, wasn't in the mood for company. Isaac did his best in helping wake Asa Iron Rope, and hoisted him to his feet as well. Then, reluctantly, he got in, with Norbert Sam at the wheel, and they followed the Grand Prix quietly away.

Nora Sue turned with her bloodied brother, and they made their way back to the house, neither of them looking at Coal or the others. Without any better idea where to go, Coal followed them up into the trailer house, and Paul and Sioux Returns from Scout came up behind him.

The woman seemed to be in shock. She moved like a robot, making Eddy sit on one of the hard chairs while she went in the kitchen and got a dishrag wet and filled a bowl with warm water, then came back to start dabbing at the sores on his face.

Coal and the others sank into the living room furniture. Like Nora Sue, Coal felt like he was in shock. Completely numb. He looked around at the others, but he could think of nothing to say.

He closed his eyes, but when he did Maura came to him, and he jerked them back open. Now she was going to haunt his dreams too.

With all the death Coal had experienced lately, it was almost as if he were back in Korea or Nam. Only all of the recent deaths were so personal. Maura! Maura . . . In his head, he spoke her name. How could he have known the day he was planning this trip how it would end? He would have driven any other way had he known what ghosts haunted Maura here. Maura . . .

What was he going to tell his mother? And the children? What was he going to tell Maura's boys?

Coal jerked at the sound of a gunshot and grabbed for his revolver, rolling over to his left. He heard Paul Wolf Guts and Eddy swear in unison. Another gunshot followed, and Coal was off the couch, kneeling on the floor, looking around. Where had the shots come from? They seemed almost as if they had come from this very room!

The living room had fallen into deathly silence. Suddenly, it hit Coal like a mule kick to the guts where the shots had come from. And he knew the danger, if there ever was any danger, was passed. He fumbled his Smith and Wesson back into its holster as he stood up woodenly to see Eddy PlentyWounds moving past him, down the long hall to Eldon and Darlene PlentyWounds' bedroom.

Half a minute later, Eddy stepped out of his parents' bedroom and eased the door shut behind him. He cat-footed straight to Nora Sue, who stood at the edge of the kitchen awaiting him. The scene was surprisingly calm. Eddy took his sister in his arms and pulled her close, and there they stayed for the next five minutes or more while Paul and Coal stood in the living room waiting.

Sioux was puffing furiously at one of his brown Adam cigarettes, standing in front of the door to the outside.

Eddy made the call to the reservation police in a subdued voice and told them to send the coroner as well. And then they waited.

*   *   *

It was hours before all the legal I's were dotted and T's crossed, before the reservation police finished taking photos of the Plenty-Wounds in their bedroom, where Eldon had apparently been shot in the chest with a .30-30 by Darlene, his wife of thirty-eight years, who then took a .45 Colt revolver to her own chest.

Coal tried to broach the subject of Maura's kidnapping and apparent murder to the officers, but to no surprise nothing they told him sounded promising. They took his report and told him they would "let him know if anything turned up." Then they simply left. There was no doubt how the two Lakota officers felt about a white man trying to take part in reservation affairs.

Nobody in the PlentyWounds home seemed too superstitious about sleeping in a house where two people had taken their lives the same day. Nora Sue wept off and on throughout the day, wept the tears of a woman whose entire life had changed, almost overnight. The only thing she wanted was for Eddy to stay close by her that night, so he slept in a chair beside her bed.

Nobody was interested in sleeping in Eldon and Darlene's room, and the third bedroom was such a cluttered disaster that it was easier for Coal, Paul, and Sioux to stay out on the living room furniture, sitting up all night.

But there would be no "all night" slumber for any of them.

Coal sat there still as a stone, his mind on Maura, and how his whole world, not unlike Nora Sue's, had once again changed. With his heart throbbing, full of pain, Coal made his decision. As badly as he wanted to stay here and help put Leland Iron Rope away, he was going to have to leave it to the FBI. Having worked for them, he knew how professional they were, and he knew they would do everything they could. Coal would never have been able to do a good investigation with things as they were out here. He would be thwarted at every turn, simply because of the color of his skin. Besides, he had no jurisdiction here, and no court that would listen to anything he had to say, even the plainest truth.

It was time to go. He had to return to his own family and let the law take its course here in Oglala.

It felt to Coal like he had barely drifted into deep sleep when he awoke to the sound of a crash. In spite of being completely disoriented, he was up out of his chair, grabbing for his Smith and Wesson, when he realized the room was on fire.

Coal turned to yell at Paul and Sioux, but both of them were already awake. He whirled and ran down the hall to Eldon and Darlene's bedroom, flipping on the light. The bed covers were in disarray. He grabbed as many as he could gather and ran back out into the living room.

The flames seemed already uncontrollable, but he had to try. He threw some of the blankets to Paul and Sioux, yelling at them, "Use these!" and then he went to work on the burning carpet, throwing down the two blankets he had and stomping all over them.

Eddy and Nora Sue had tried to run down the hall, but the flame wall was too big by the front door, and it drove them back toward her room. Soon, however, Eddy was back, and he flung something at the fire, something that looked like a small blanket. When he did it a second time, both of them good shots, the flames backed way off, and Nora Sue came running again from the area of the bathroom, handing something to Eddy. Again, Eddy threw it, and again the flames banked down.

And then, between Coal's blankets and whatever Eddy was doing, the flames were gone.

Trying to guard his face with his forearm, Coal ran coughing and threw open the front door. A gunshot split the night, and he stumbled backward, tripping over the fire blankets and going down on his butt. More shots came from the dark, and then he heard cars speeding down the street.

Jerking out his Smith and Wesson, he crawled to the closest window at the back of the house and threw it up, feeling an instant rush of cold air. He fumbled through the house doing the same everywhere he could find more windows, while the others did the same.

"They're gone," he heard Sioux Returns from Scout say, and he looked over to see the old man standing by the front door with his shotgun. "All gone. Your T-Bird's gone too, Savage."

Coal swore. Keeping his pistol in hand, he walked to the front door and scanned the street. Sure enough, Paul's and Sioux's pickups were there, but the Thunderbird was gone.

And both hoods were up on the pickups. To think either of them was going to start would be the most optimistic thought in history.

They were all standing at the front door looking out when Eddy said, "Looks like I'm marked now too." And they all noticed then that his hood was up as well.

Although it was too dark to do anything, they walked out to their rigs. All the wires on their distributor caps had been cut, and every tire, even the spares, was flat.

"I guess none of us are leavin' the Rez," said Paul.

His comment was punctuated by an engine turning over, and in a moment, it fired. They all looked over to see Nora Sue stepping out of her ugly old Country Squire. "Well, we still have *one* car," she said.

Eddy PlentyWounds called the police to report the arson and vandalism. They took his report and said they would send someone. Then five minutes later the phone rang. Everyone stared at it. It was three in the morning!

Eddy walked over and answered it. "Yeah… Right—Plenty-Wounds. Yes… Sure. Doesn't surprise me." He hung up the phone.

"That was the dispatcher again. He said they'll have t' send someone over tomorrow."

"What the hell's going on?" Coal growled.

"Leland Iron Rope. That's what's goin' on," replied Nora Sue. "Him an' his damn alcohol run this Rez, an' everybody's scared of him."

"He's payin' somebody off," said Paul.

The silence in the room spoke nothing but agreement.

The whole house stank, but the smoke itself had been cleared out after twenty or thirty minutes, and they were able to shut all the windows. They would have gone somewhere else to sleep, but there was nowhere to go. Besides, none of them dared leave.

Everyone was sitting in silence in the living room when Sioux Returns from Scout said quietly, "Hey, PlentyWounds—you got any gas?"

"For what?"

"Whatever. Chainsaw?"

"Oh. Sure. Out in the shed."

"I need some."

Eddy stared at the old man. In fact, everyone stared at him. But apparently nobody had the energy to interrogate him.

"Help yourself. Just make sure you shut the door when you're done."

After Sioux left, Coal sat thinking how foolish that last order sounded. The way things were going, it wasn't going to matter. It wasn't going to be long before the Iron Ropes had this whole place burned to the ground anyway.

When Sioux came back in half an hour later, he shut the door without comment, then went over to the half-burned blankets on the floor. Taking out a jackknife, he began cutting shreds off them and stuffing them in his pockets. Coal watched him, wondering what he was up to but figuring he would volunteer the information if he felt like it.

Sioux came and sat down, his pockets bulging with rags from the blankets. "Boy, Weldon sure did drink a lot o' wine."

With that cryptic statement, Sioux closed his eyes. The others all looked at each other, eyebrows raised. Paul shrugged. Coal smiled.

Within fifteen minutes, the room was silent, except for Sioux's snoring. They sat there in the dark, with the overpowering stench of wet ash and smoke from burned carpet in their nostrils and tried to rest and wait for sunup.

Coal kept pushing thoughts of Maura out of his head. It made him want to cry when he thought of her last hours of life, how desperate and frightening they must have been, and how he hadn't been able to save her.

He wondered idly if the police really would come in the morning to investigate the night's crimes.

Coal woke with a start.

CHAPTER THIRTY-THREE

Tuesday, January 30

Disconcerted, Coal moved his eyes around the room. It took a while to realize where he was and that he had actually, by some miracle, gone to sleep, when all around outside the trailer house wolves were prowling, waiting . . .

The dark room reeked of burned carpet and blankets. Paul Wolf Guts was asleep in his chair nearby. But Sioux Returns from Scout, otherwise known as army Private John R. Scout, stood in the kitchen lit only by the glow of the electric unit of the stove. He was making today's coffee.

Coal sat still, listening to the pinging sound of the pan heating up under the coffee and contemplating Maura PlentyWounds, and all that had happened in the night. Like his entire misadventure on the Pine Ridge Reservation, it all seemed very surreal.

When the smell of the coffee began to permeate the room, Paul stirred. From that point, it took him only a few seconds to rouse himself and look around, feeling for his rifle, which leaned against the chair near his leg.

No one spoke. They were soldiers in a besieged camp. This earliest part of the day was a time for soul-searching, not talking. When the sky began to grow light, however, and everyone sat in the living room sipping coffee, including Eddy PlentyWounds, Paul cleared his throat.

"Hey, Savage?"

"Yeah?"

"I'm sure sorry about how your time on the Rez went. This place sure ain't been hospitable to you."

Coal shrugged. "I guess I've seen two less hospitable places."

Paul grunted. "Yeah. Korea and Nam. But that was war."

"So is this."

"Good point. Anyway, I'm really sorry about your friend too." Coal couldn't find any words to reply. His pain ran too deep. "Soon as it gets light, we'll get Nora Sue t' take us down t' Chadron. We'll get some tires an' whatever else we need for under the hood down there, an' maybe you c'n rent a car t' get you home."

Coal frowned. "Like hell."

"Huh?"

"I'm not going back home."

"Don't you be a fool, man. Like you said, this is war. But it ain't yours."

"You couldn't be any more wrong. Paul, you and Sioux have stood by me ever since I got here. It's pretty obvious after last night those guys aren't going to rest until both of you are dead, or until you leave the reservation. Do you plan on coming with me? Getting out of here? Running away?"

Paul's glance bounced over to Sioux, then back to Coal. "This is our home."

"Yeah. That's what I thought. Listen. They've already taken your houses, and I'm surprised they didn't set your trucks on fire too, while they had the chance last night. This is never going to go away. You defied the Iron Ropes. You're done here."

"Like hell," Sioux mimicked Coal. "We ain't done, not by a damn sight."

"Then I'm not either."

Sioux stared at Coal, then tipped his cup up and drained the last of his coffee. "All right, white man—Wakinyan. Then you better buckle up."

"Hey."

Coal's voice stopped Sioux as he was starting to stand out of his chair, and he sank back down. "What?"

"I have a question for you, something I've been wondering about since I got on the reservation. Why do most people avoid eye contact with me? Are they scared? Or do they just not like me?"

Sioux chuckled. "No, man. Nothin' like that. You know, Savage, to a Injun, it's a sign of respect if you don't look somebody in the eyes."

Coal mulled that over for a moment, feeling guilty that in all the years the Shoshone village had existed right there on the Challis Highway at the edge of Salmon he had never taken the time to question this and learn. "So what about you two? Guess you don't respect me much, huh?" he said with a grin.

Paul answered with a grin of his own. "For me, it was the Marines. For Sioux, the Army. They took that part of our culture away like they took a lotta other stuff."

Coal nodded. "So when Asa Iron Rope and his father were staring me down, it was a challenge."

"You got it. Welcome to the Injun world, *khola*."

With a laugh, Coal said, "I've never heard that one. Cola? Is that my new nickname?"

"It ain't the kind o' cola you're thinkin', Savage," cut in Sioux Returns from Scout. "In Lakota, that means 'friend', usually spelt with a k an' a h . . . *khola.*"

"Wow. All right, then it sure fits—khola."

Coal beat Sioux to his feet, and Paul and Eddy followed suit.

"I'm goin' with you guys," Eddy announced.

"To Chadron?" asked Paul.

"Not t' Chadron. To the Iron Ropes'."

"Eddy, you need to get Nora Sue out of here to safety," Coal corrected. "This isn't your fight."

Eddy's eyes pierced Coal's right into his brain. "The hell it isn't. It's more my fight than it is yours."

The question was on the tip of Coal's tongue: What had changed Eddy's mind in the night? But that was a question one warrior didn't ask another.

"What about Nora Sue?"

"We'll take her t' hide out at Maybelle Littlebrave's," replied Eddy. "We'll keep those guys too busy t' come here after her."

"Bull."

Everyone whirled to see Nora Sue PlentyWounds standing in the hall with her coat and a ball cap on, her dark braids hanging down her chest. "I got one family member left, an' he's not leavin' here without me."

Eddy started to say something, probably a rebuttal. Then he must have read the fire in Nora Sue's eyes. She was truly the little sister of Peta: Fire in her Eyes.

"That's my dump of a car out there, and you guys ain't goin' anywhere in it unless I'm drivin'."

The others could only look at each other and shrug. A woman had spoken her mind, and there would be no changing it.

The warriors loaded up grimly. No one spoke. Every weapon in the PlentyWounds house came with them, and Sioux carefully loaded some of his own implements of war into a box in the back of the station wagon without saying anything about them.

They drove to the Iron Ropes' house and stopped out on the highway. The first thing they noticed was that Leland's pickup wasn't there, and neither was the Thunderbird. Coal's heart fell.

"Pull on in," ordered Paul Wolf Guts. "There's one car there, anyway."

Nora Sue drove in and parked near what appeared to be a 1950 Custom Ford sedan with a remarkable amount of its original cream paint still intact. For a twenty-three year-old vehicle on this reservation, that was some amazing coup.

Disembarking with weapons a-bristle, they started toward the house. The front door cracked open before they reached it, and a trembling voice slid out into the cold morning air.

"Hey! Hey, guys, don't shoot! It's just me, Isaac Lefthand. Don't let 'em kill me, Eddy. Please!"

"You by yourself, Ike?" Eddy shot back.

"No. I got Norbert an' Jimmy."

"All three o' you get out here," Eddy ordered. *"Now!"*

Compliance was immediate. Already wearing coats, the three Lakotas scrambled outside with their arms as straight up as they could manage. Scrawny Isaac Lefthand was in the lead.

"Don't shoot! Please don't shoot!"

"Get down!" Paul ordered. "On your faces!"

The three dropped down. "What're you guys doin' here?" asked Eddy. "Where're the rest of 'em?"

"They're gone, man. Gone! They left us here t' guard the house."

"Where's my Thunderbird?" asked Coal.

The three men kept eating on the dead grass in the lawn, apparently too busy chewing to speak.

"You heard 'im!" yelled Eddy, shoving his rifle barrel into the back of Jimmy LeBeau's neck, because he was closest to him. "Where's the T-Bird?"

"In back! Eddy! Man, it's in back!" Jimmy sounded like he was on the verge of tears. "But please don't take it. They'll kill us."

"Why's it here?"

"I don't know," Jimmy shot back. "They just left it. We were s'posed t' keep you guys from gettin' it."

That gave Coal his first smirk of the day. Isaac and his cronies weren't too trustworthy as guards, but for him that was good. "I'm going to get the car," he said. "I'll be right back."

When he came back around the house a few minutes later, once again the proud owner of a repossessed dark green sixty-eight Thunderbird, Paul and the others had the three Iron Rope flunkies lined up against the front wall of the house.

"Isaac says Leland's goin' back t' Wamblee Sota's place," Paul told Coal.

"Why?"

"Don't know. They got Leland's pickup an' Levi's Grand Prix with 'em."

"Who's they?"

"The Iron Ropes, Levi Weaselbear, and Pat Highhorse."

"All right. Then let's go," said Coal.

"Not so fast," replied Sioux Returns from Scout. "This soldier's been wantin' t' watch somethin' since I saw my dead dogs the other day."

Without any explanation, he went to the back of the station wagon and swung the door open. Coal glanced over in time to see the old man smiling grimly as he unthreaded the lid off a bottle of Thunderbird—only the amber liquid inside it didn't look like any kind of wine Coal had ever seen.

Sioux tossed the lid away and dug into his pocket to pull out one of the rags he had cut from the blankets the night before. He poked it two thirds of the way down into the bottle.

As he walked back to them, he pulled a Bic lighter out of his coat pocket, still unable to wipe the little grin off his face. "You boys got anything in the house worth dyin' for?"

The Iron Rope trio stared at the bottle. It was obvious they had seen one of these makeshift fire bombs before. Isaac Lefthand's eyes got big, and he swore. "No, man. Nothin' worth dyin' for."

"You know Leland'll kill all of us for this, don't you?" Norbert Sam cut in, staring at Eddy.

"Sorry, man," Sioux cut in. "That's part o' war. Besides," he added, looking at Norbert, "who says Leland's gonna be able t' kill you or anybody else after t'day?" Saying that, he thumbed the lighter's little wheel, and the flame leaped up. One touch to the protruding rag, and it exploded in flame. Sioux looked over at his friends, grinning big enough to reveal his missing eyetooth. "Well, here's to christening a house."

With all his strength, he hurled the bottle through the front bedroom window, and with the shattering of the glass the bedroom burst into flame.

Sioux grinned without humor. "I wonder if this is how Iron Rope felt the other day."

"Maybe. But the difference is this is justice," Paul said. "His was out o' pure meanness."

Everyone stared in awe as the gasoline spread the flame quickly through the home's interior.

"Better move your car over there," Eddy told Isaac, pointing to a spot away from the house. With that permission, Isaac scrambled for his car and pulled it out of the way, as did Nora Sue.

Sioux sighed. "Never seen a fire go so fast. Wish we c'd stay an' make use o' this nice heat a bit longer."

Coal laughed, but he was sure it sounded grim, more than joyful. "This smoke's going to be visible a long ways off. We'd better get moving."

Motioning Eddy to follow him, Coal walked over to where Isaac and the others sat in the idling Ford and indicated for Isaac to roll down his window.

"We can't have you boys getting on the phone with Iron Rope, so you're coming with us. Eddy will drive your car."

"No, man!" Isaac pled. "Don't make us go out there."

Without missing a beat, Eddy said, "He's right, Ike. Scoot over." Dropping his head in defeat, Isaac slid over to the middle of the seat, next to Jimmy LeBeau, and Eddy climbed in. Looking up at Coal, he dropped his left arm out the window and slapped the side of the door. "We're ready."

"All right. Then follow the Thunderbird."

When Coal got in the Thunderbird, Paul climbed in the passenger side. "Always liked these rides," he said, rolling down the window to sniff the black smoke rolling away from the Iron Ropes' house. "Nothin' like the smell o' Napalm in the mornin'—right?"

Seeing the seating arrangement, Sioux Returns from Scout got out of Nora Sue's back seat and took up his position as shotgun rider. This time with Coal in the lead, the three cars wheeled out on the highway, headed for Wamblee Sota's den of misguided magic.

When they reached the little ranch of Paul's friend Dennis Yellowhand, Coal pulled off, giving the other cars enough room to stop behind him. Paul looked over. "What's up?"

"I have a bad feeling about where we're going."

"No kiddin'."

Coal chuckled. "Don't worry. We're still going. I just want to leave the Bird here."

"That's thinkin': Sacrifice Nora Sue's and Isaac's."

"No, not Nora Sue's. We'll park it when we get close and go in with Isaac's."

"All right. Now I see why you moved up the ranks," said Paul with a grin.

Taking their weapons with them, Coal and Paul switched vehicles, Coal getting in with Eddy and the thugs, and Paul riding with Nora Sue and Sioux Returns from Scout.

Coal carefully checked the loads in his weapons, again. He took a big, calming breath. He thought of battles gone by that were much more dangerous than what they were headed for today. But those battles in foreign lands hadn't carried the legal consequences this one was going to. He wondered how this morning would alter the course of his future.

And he knew because of Paul, and Sioux, and the Plenty-Wounds, he had no choice.

CHAPTER THIRTY-FOUR

Coal had his window rolled down. He couldn't believe the rise in temperature from the day before. Not even ten o'clock, and it was already over forty degrees, with less than a five mile an hour wind. As an Oglala chief by the name of Low Dog supposedly said on the day the Sioux and Cheyenne laid Custer's men low, it was a "good day to die."

A quarter mile out from Wamblee Sota's, Coal told Eddy to pull over. The car rocked to a stop at the roadside, and Nora Sue pulled up in the grass behind them.

Coal turned around in his seat. "Isaac, I guess Eddy knows where you live, right?"

"Yeah, man." Confusion filled Isaac's face. "Why?"

"Because this is where you three get out. Start walking back to Oglala. We'll bring your car back when it's all over."

"Eddy?" Isaac's voice was pleading. "Don't take my car, man. Come on."

Eddy copied Coal and cranked himself around in his seat. "We'll bring it back."

"Yeah, what if you don't make it?"

"That's not much faith, is it?"

"Well . . . But what if you don't?"

"Listen, Ike—the car's goin' in one way or the other. Get it? If you're stayin' with the car, then you're goin' t' the fight. At least if you walk home an' somethin' goes wrong, you, Jimmy, and

Norbert might have a chance t' get t' Nebraska before Leland finds you."

Isaac swallowed hard. Finally, he blinked rapidly a few times and nodded. He, Norbert, and Jimmy opened their doors and stepped out on the highway. As the two cars pulled away, Coal looked back. The three Lakotas hadn't moved. They stood on the side of the road staring after them.

A hundred yards away from the house, Coal had Eddy stop again, and he ran back to Nora Sue's car, leaning down with his hand on the door. Everyone could see Leland's pickup in Sota's front yard, with the nose of the Grand Prix peeking out from the far side.

"Change of plans. We'll take both cars. Let's roll in fast. Take them by surprise if we can. And at this point, I guess I don't care who you shoot. We'll have to deal with it all later. This is war—don't forget it."

"Hoka hey!" said Sioux Returns from Scout.

"It's a good day to die?"

"Sure. It is that, but that's not what that means. It's more like what you just said: 'Let's roll in fast.' 'Let's get goin'. 'Let's do it'."

"Damn Hollywood. Well, you learn something new every day," Coal said. He grinned, and it surprised him. He didn't think he had any real smiles left.

The two Fords flew into the yard, Coal thinking they would catch the Iron Ropes and the others inside the house. He was wrong.

The Grand Prix shot out from behind the pickup, headed for the highway. The driver jerked his head to the side, and his eyes flew open in surprise as he saw the Fords pulling up. He opened his mouth, and even through closed windows it didn't take a lip reader to know the kind of language that was coming out.

"Ram him!" Coal yelled.

Eddy was already on it. He stomped on the gas and veered to the left. The two vehicles met where Wamblee Sota's drive touched the highway. The impact slammed Coal and Eddy forward and whipped the head of the Grand Prix's driver over to smash through the window, exploding glass everywhere.

"Back up! Back up!" yelled Coal. Eddy threw it into reverse and once more put the gas to the floor, peeling back some fifty feet.

Luckily, Nora Sue had gone to the right when Eddy took off after the Grand Prix; Eddy missed her car by mere inches.

The front door flew open on the other side of the Grand Prix, and as Coal rolled out his side of the car a rifle shot broke the now still morning. Coal heard it impact Isaac's car as he scrambled on hands and knees for shelter behind the trunk. He heard another shot, and the round pinged off the ground near him, whining away.

He managed to get behind the car, joined soon by Eddy. A jolt ran through him when he saw Eddy's empty hands. In the fury of the moment, neither of them had had time to grab their rifles.

A shot rang out from the direction of Nora Sue's car moments after Coal heard the sounds of men yelling over near Wamblee Sota's house. The sound of the bullet's impact rang off the Grand Prix. A man leaped up from behind the Grand Prix and fired toward Nora Sue's car, and the shot hit its target, if its target was Nora Sue's car.

Coal heard a door open, and he looked around the underside of the Grand Prix to see a man take off running. A shotgun blast from the direction of Nora Sue's vehicle made Coal jerk, and the running man pitched forward, screaming.

The man at the Grand Prix came up again in a blur, hesitated, and his rifle roared. Coal heard somebody groan by Nora Sue's car, and the woman screamed.

Coal came up firing with his .44, not bothering to aim as he tried to lay down a covering fire, raking the side of the Grand Prix.

His third shot hit with a strange *thunk*. In a moment, he saw fluid pouring out from under the car. He had struck the gas tank!

"Sioux's hit!" Nora Sue's panicked voice came. "Savage! He's hit bad!"

Coal looked over at Eddy. He meant to ask him to run to Sioux while he covered him. But he couldn't. That was Coal's place to do. Where was Paul? He realized one of the voices near the house had to be his. He must have caught the others there.

"Can you handle one of these?" Coal held the magnum up to Eddy.

Eddy gave him a curt nod. "I can handle anything, white man."

"All right." Clenching his jaw, Coal dug cartridges out of his pants pocket and replaced the empties, then handed it to Eddy. "Prove your stuff—*red man*. I'm going after Sioux."

Eddy smiled with one side of his mouth. "Go get 'im."

Coal started up just as he heard a struggle and an ensuing argument behind Nora Sue's car. The woman's voice rose. "You can't do that! Sioux, stay here!"

Sioux Returns from Scout growled something Coal didn't understand, and Coal scanned the area around the car, trying to decide what the old man was up to. He wasn't going to make this deadly run to Nora Sue's car if he didn't have to.

Seemingly from out of nowhere, the old Lakota exploded from behind Nora Sue's car, a Molotov cocktail in his throwing hand. Blood streamed down the front of both his pant legs from several inches above his groin area. A disastrous place to take a bullet!

"Get down, Sioux! Get *down!*" Coal heard himself scream the warning.

Three thunderous, close-spaced shots came from Coal's Smith and Wesson. Another sounded from behind the Grand Prix, and Sioux Returns from Scout jerked and clutched at his chest. The old man grimaced in pain as another shot exploded from the Grand

Prix, and another bullet pierced him. Coal heard Eddy shoot his magnum, and the man behind the Grand Prix let out a yelp of pain.

Sioux Returns from Scout—Private John R. Scout, of the United States Army—gritted his teeth and fired his lighter, put its flame to a dangling rag, and as it caught fire another bullet from the Grand Prix struck him in the middle, and another bullet from Coal's Smith and Wesson tore a second groan from the other shooter.

With the last of his strength, Sioux flung his bottle at the Grand Prix, and his true aim shattered the back window. The entire back seat blossomed flame. Almost simultaneously, the underside of the Grand Prix burst into orange, and flame curled everywhere. Screaming, the man behind the car staggered away from the squatty inferno with his feet and legs on fire and fell in the grass writhing.

Coal turned and threw a handful of shells out of his pocket at Eddy. "Cover me!" He ran for the Grand Prix, where the driver still leaned unconscious against the window.

Jerking at the door, he realized it was locked. In a panic, he turned and yelled at Eddy. "Eddy! Shoot out this damn window!"

He ducked out of the way, and the Lakota's bullet hit the window up high and shattered it into a thousand sparkling cubes of tempered glass. Freed from the confining window glass, the driver's head fell sideways as Coal jerked up the lock and tried to yank the door open. It wouldn't come. The impact with Isaac's car had damaged it too much. With an oath, Coal reached down into the car and grabbed the man by the belt and by his far arm. He dragged him up out of the seat and onto the ground, needing all the strength he could muster, and scrambled backward with him until they were well out of the blistering heat. Then he batted out the smoldering pieces of the unconscious man's coat that had already caught on fire in the car.

Eddy PlentyWounds was up and running toward the far side of the Pontiac before Coal could warn him away.

"Hey! Hey!" Coal heard a man's weak voice, and he whirled, dropping into a crouch.

"Hey, you gotta . . . help."

The voice came from Wamblee Sota, who lay on the ground in a pool of blood where Sioux Returns from Scout's shotgun had cut him down, halfway between the Pontiac and his house.

Coal swung his eyes over the carnage in the yard, seeing Nora Sue on her knees beside Sioux Returns from Scout. Paul Wolf Guts was holding a kneeling man at gunpoint near the house.

Still unsure of other gunmen, Coal made a low run over to Wamblee Sota, scanning him for weapons. When he made sure the man appeared to be free of guns, he looked down at his shattered legs. Sioux's shotgun blast had likely crippled Sota for life.

"I can't do anything for you right now," said Coal, standing back up.

"No! No, not for me," the man's weak, pathetic voice drew Coal's attention back. "That girl! You gotta . . . She's . . ." His hand came up and waved weakly toward the Pontiac, and then Sota slumped back onto the ground.

Coal whirled and stared at the Pontiac. His mind raced. *The girl . . . The girl?* What girl was he talking about?

And then it hit Coal in the guts like a cannonball. The girl! Maura! *MAURA!*

In a state of panic, he raced to the Pontiac, trying to look inside for the keys. Everything was in flames. There was no reaching inside, for keys or anything else. He ran back to Nora's car, where its back door still stood open. Looking past Sioux Returns from Scout's cardboard box of Molotov cocktails, he saw a rusted tire iron lying there in the open, glaring up at him—a dark, final hope.

Coal snatched it up and ran back to the Pontiac. He was praying out loud, and he didn't even realize it. He was no longer aware of anyone, or anything happening around him. He only knew he had to get the trunk open!

He jammed the sharp end of the tire iron through the lock, then again. One more time, for good measure. Ripping the iron loose, he fired it between the lip of the trunk and the lid, right beneath the lock, then bore down on it. On his second try, the trunk lid broke free. As the almost unbearable heat from the back window of the car tried to drive him back, he grasped the trunk lid and threw it upward.

He felt himself almost break into tears as the opening trunk lid let loose a billow of heat and revealed its precious lone cargo. Maura was bound at the feet, her hands tied behind her, with a rag stuffed in her mouth and fastened there. But her eyes were open wide.

She was looking at him!

Coal grabbed Maura's arms and jerked her upper body up. He muscled her out onto the ground, losing his footing and falling backward. Maura landed on top of him. Recovering, he rolled her off to one side, came up and went into a crouch, cradling her and standing with her to run over by Nora Sue's car.

"Maura? *Maura!*" Coal heard Nora Sue's scream behind him.

But like a good nurse, she tried to stay with Sioux Returns from Scout, until Coal heard the old man's weak voice. "You git over there, girl. Get away from me an' go see your sister."

As Coal sliced through the ropes around Maura's ankles, and then her wrists, she tore at the cloth tie over her mouth, jerking it down by her throat. Tears streamed down her face, and Coal realized he had plenty of those himself.

Maura came up off the ground and nearly knocked Coal backwards throwing her arms around him before he even had time to stand all the way back up. Pent up anguish and fear exploded out of her in loud weeping and crying out Coal's name, over and over.

Unable to hold herself back, Nora Sue wrapped her arms around her sister from behind, and they stood there in the yard that way, a cluster of love and long-held emotions.

CHAPTER THIRTY-FIVE

Coal heard a choking sound behind Maura and Nora Sue. He pushed Maura away from him to see Sioux Returns from Scout struggling to rise. The pool of blood around him now, and the trail that led from the car to where he lay, were astonishing.

Coal hurried to him. "Hey, old man, stay down, damn it. Stay down!"

He scanned old Sioux's body and cringed. Blood had soaked the upper part of his pants. It had even started to soak into his coat. He put his hand on the old man's shoulder. "Easy does it, partner. We'll get some help for you."

Coal looked up at Nora Sue. "Run in the house and call the ambulance. You'd better call the cops too." The thought of them showing up here made him cringe. There was going to be hell to pay.

He returned his eyes to Sioux as Paul came up herding Levi Weaselbear and Pat Highhorse. "Hang in there. Help's coming."

"They killed my dogs, Savage. Burned 'em up."

"Hey. Hey. Don't worry about what happened today, Sioux. They sure had it coming. You hear me?"

The old man smiled. It was weak, but it was a smile. "We give 'em hell, didn't we?" His voice was so quiet Coal almost had to ask him to repeat. After a moment's thought, he deciphered what he had said.

"Yeah, we did. We sure gave 'em hell—khola."

The old man smiled again. "Yeah . . . khola. Wakinyan."

Coal reached down and gripped the old warrior's hand, giving it a squeeze. "Come on, Sioux. Hang tough, all right? That ambulance will be here in no time."

"Yeah. No time," rasped Sioux Returns from Scout. "Hey! Savage, you know what?"

Coal leaned closer. "What's that?"

"I think I finally made up for Omaha, didn't I?"

Coal smiled as Sioux's face disappeared behind the film of tears in his eyes. "Yeah, you did. You sure did that, old friend."

And then Sioux Returns from Scout's hand went limp.

*   *   *

Nora Sue and Eddy PlentyWounds vanished before the reservation police arrived, taking her car. They took Levi Weaselbear and Pat Highhorse with them, in exchange for the two thugs keeping their mouths shut about what happened in Wamblee Sota's yard that morning.

Paul sat near Isaac Lefthand's car and watched their prisoners, while Coal, nearby, held Maura PlentyWounds to his heart. Like a little girl, he stroked her hair and patted her back and whispered in her ear that everything would be all right. She was safe now. Only the scars in her heart would remain.

Coal had bandaged the shotgun wounds in Wamblee Sota's lower legs the best he could, and he sat in the cab of the pickup now. They covered Leland Iron Rope's legs as well, and brought a pillow from the house to put under his head, along with five thick blankets. But he had suffered severe burns all the way from his feet to his crotch, and that was too much for any man.

Pushing away from Coal, Maura walked over and looked down at Leland Iron Rope, who had been so strong, so invincible, and so cruel. He looked up into her eyes, and one corner of his lip curled up. "You . . . shoulda died. You're a little devil."

Maura stared fire darts down at the dying man. "Rot in hell, you filth." Strangely, a tear ran down each cheek as she clenched her jaws. This part of her life was closing fast, leaving open wounds that time alone could mend.

As Maura stared down at him, refusing to turn away her gaze, Leland Iron Rope's life ebbed away minutes before the police arrived, and the ambulance still wasn't in sight. Coal put his arm around Maura and squeezed. Her body shuddered and a sob escaped her as she turned and fell back into Coal's arms. He held onto her while he looked down at the dead gang leader, feeling no compunction for any part he had played in Iron Rope's death.

As for Asa Iron Rope, in spite of Coal's effort to save his life, he had at the very least suffered a massive concussion, the left side of his skull was swollen and spongy-feeling, and only time would tell if, and how well, he recovered. Perhaps, if fate was not kind to him, he would live the rest of his life wishing he had gone out in the way of his father and old Sioux Returns from Scout.

On a whim, Paul put on gloves and went and took out the makeshift fire bombs, emptying the fuel into Isaac's tank, then throwing the bottles in a burn barrel beside Wamblee Sota's house. There was no reason the police should know they had come here looking for a war.

*   *   *

After the ambulance arrived to take Wamblee Sota and Asa Iron Rope away to the hospital in Chadron, and the undertaker carted off the bodies of Leland Iron Rope and Sioux Returns from Scout—in the same compartment, much to Coal and Paul's disgust—the reservation police started in on Coal and Paul. They seemed particularly hard on Coal, which was no surprise. After all, he was only a *wasichu*—an outsider and a white man.

In the end, it was all rough questioning, but it was only questioning. The two officers drove away with a notebook full of notes and drawings, and a camera full of photos that would do them little good.

The police had left things to Coal, Paul, and Sioux, and the three of them had done what warriors always do in times of trouble. They took care of their own.

*   *   *

Nora Sue's car was sitting back at the PlentyWounds trailer when Paul and Coal pulled quietly in. The door flew open, and Nora Sue came onto the porch, saw Maura, and instantly fell apart.

By some miracle, the brunette made it down the steps to her sister and embraced her, while Coal and Paul stood there, embarrassed, and wondered just how long a hug could last.

Eddy came down the steps with an affected look of toughness about him. He pretended hardly to notice his sister, the one called Peta. After all, she was just another girl.

"There's Isaac's car," said Coal, tossing Eddy the keys. "It looks a lot tougher than it used to," he said with a grin.

"Yeah," said Eddy. "Guess that's what you gotta expect when you choose t' live like a felon, huh?"

That sounded pretty hypocritical coming from a man like Eddy PlentyWounds, but Coal understood. He had a feeling if the vehicle was Eddy's he would have said the same thing.

When Maura finally broke away from Nora Sue, she turned her eyes to her brother. "Hi, Eddy."

"Hi. I'm glad you finally made it home."

She smiled, and tears broke out and ran free down her cheeks. "I never wanted to leave you," she said, sounding broken.

And big, tough Eddy took her in his arms. Apparently, he didn't care anymore who saw.

Wednesday, January 31

The Thunderbird was warm. The cigarette smell remained, but now it melded with a jasmine-scented cake of sawdust that Coal had bought in the Oglala mercantile and set underneath the front seat.

There was something Coal had found that he didn't like about his dark green Thunderbird, and he might have to get it changed. A console sat in the middle of it, between the seats, and Maura couldn't sit next to him. That was a travesty he couldn't abide by.

They had had to change their travel plans after saying goodbye to all of Maura's people in Oglala. It was Isaac Lefthand, in fact, who changed them. He came to Eddy PlentyWounds with a secret that had long been held among the bootleggers, all but Eddy, for obvious reasons.

It had always been rumored that Leland Iron Rope's uncontrolled lust had been the death of young Cordelia PlentyWounds, the youngest child in the family, and that Iron Rope had buried her somewhere in the sacred Black Hills. It wasn't true.

There was a lonely, chalky white butte thirty-five miles north of Oglala known only as Hawk Butte. At its base, in a rocky crevice where boulders had been gathered and laid, lay the bones of Cordelia PlentyWounds, who had died at fourteen years of age, at the hands of a monster.

Isaac Lefthand drove his car through the barren country and finally pulled over to the roadside. Coal stopped the Thunderbird in the dead brown grass behind him. He looked over at Maura, and she was staring at a white bluff to their right. As Coal stepped out his side of the car, Nora Sue's station wagon came up and parked behind them.

Isaac got out and walked slowly back to them. He pointed out across the barren land. "That's Hawk Butte."

Eddy and Nora Sue had walked up, and Maura came over by Coal. He put his arm around her shoulders.

"Why did Leland tell anyone?" Coal asked.

Isaac shrugged. "You know, I think because he wanted us all t' know what would happen if we ever crossed him."

"Didn't he ever think one of you could turn him in?"

"Ha. Nobody ever dared. An' he knew it. He owned the cops out here, white man. He always did. Just like Asa will now."

"No he won't," said Eddy with gritted teeth. "That's all over. Anybody wants booze out here now, they're gonna have t' find a way t' get t' Nebraska on their own."

Isaac nodded. "Well . . . I guess you don't need me no more, right?"

"No, Isaac," said Coal. "You can head back to town. Hey." The word stopped Isaac as he was turning away, and he looked back at Coal. "Thanks for coming clean. These people needed some peace."

Embarrassed, Isaac nodded again. "I know, man. I'm sorry I didn't do it sooner." Before anyone else could say anything, he turned and went back to his car, started it up and turned around, heading back toward Oglala, and whatever pathetic life awaited.

Coal looked down at Maura, who had tears streaming down her face. She wiped at her eyes. "It's a long ways out there."

"We've got a few hours," said Coal.

Everyone stood together. No one spoke. Overhead, a red-tailed hawk cried, and Nora Sue looked up. Then she looked over at Maura and reached out and gave her arm a squeeze. "Maybe that's Cordy," she said, and as she did tears filled her eyes.

Maura raised her glance to seek out the hawk, drifting lazily on the breeze far overhead. "Do you think she's found any peace?"

"She got off the Rez," offered Eddy. "That's a pretty good start."

"I guess I'd like to just sit here for a while," said Maura. "Just me and Coal."

Eddy glanced from her to Coal, then back. "All right, Maura. I guess I'll take Nora Sue back t' town then. Will you be okay?"

Maura nodded, whipping a sleeve across her eyes. "Eddy?"

He didn't reply, but his eyes watched her.

"Can I have a hug?"

He smiled. "Sure. You don't have t' ask." He stepped closer and took her in his arms. "It's all over now. He's gone. You don't ever have t' worry about Leland Iron Rope again."

Maura could only nod. After Eddy, she turned to Nora Sue. She tried to speak and couldn't. Nora Sue hugged her fiercely. They both wept.

Five minutes later, Coal and Maura—Fire in her Eyes— watched Nora Sue's station wagon disappear in the distance, back toward Oglala. "Do you think they'll make it?" Maura managed to ask.

"I think so. They've got each other. And you set them free."

Maura leaned over into Coal. "No, I didn't. You did, Coal. You set all of Oglala free."

He swallowed a big lump in his throat. "That wasn't me. That was Sioux Returns from Scout."

She nodded. She didn't look up at him as he stood there with his arm around her shoulders and they stared out at lonely, barren Hawk Butte.

"Do you think we'll ever be the same?" Maura asked.

Coal thought about that for a long time. He drew in a deep, lung-filling breath, and his eyes scanned the treeless horizon all around. "I don't think so. I know I won't be. And I don't think we should be. This trip should drive everything we do for the rest of time. Don't you think?"

"Yeah. Yeah, I guess it should."

"I'm sorry, Maura."

She sniffled and still didn't raise her eyes. "For what?"

"For bringing you here."

She shook her head. "I could never have rested if you hadn't. Someday maybe you'll see that."

And maybe he already did. But he could never forget the torture Maura had passed through, body and soul, in Oglala, South Dakota.

The red-tailed hawk called again and came down low and fast, landing hard out in the grass, where it must have caught a ground squirrel. It turned intense eyes on them, and their gazes locked.

Tears rolled again down Maura's face. "Maybe it is Cordy," she said, her voice very quiet.

"Maybe it is," Coal agreed.

They drove away from Hawk Butte half an hour later, got on Riverside Road, and drove over the Cheyenne River. At last, they came to the big highway junction, and Coal pulled over so they could gaze at the Black Hills together, where the timber stood straight and tall and proud. Neither of them spoke. Maura's hand was over the console, holding Coal's, and every time emotions overcame her he knew it because her grip tightened.

He wondered how long it would take to know if Maura was recovered from her trauma in Oglala. He wondered if she would ever come to blame him for suggesting that she go back there and face her fears. He wondered if things could ever be the same between them, or if they had crossed their own "Great Divide," a point from which they could never return.

They continued north, and in time passed quietly through Rapid City, lost in their own thoughts and knowing there was no need for words.

At the far edge of the city, a shudder passed over Maura, and she leaned back in her seat. Coal glanced over, and there were silent tears streaking her face. She had made it. She had survived.

Coal squeezed her hand. "I'll always be here if you need to talk, Maura. I hope you know that. Thank you for trusting me."

She wiped her eyes, looked over, and smiled, adding her other hand to the pile and squeezing his with both of hers. "No. Thank you, Coal. Thank you for staying when you could have run."

In truth, she had to know that wasn't true. He could never have run. He would rather have died.

He continued driving, feeling peace in his heart, and they crossed into Montana on a wonderfully sunny afternoon.

Whatever had been born or died between Coal and Maura on this long, long trip back to her homeland, and into her tragic childhood, one fact stood out above all the others:

Coal had found Maura, he had saved her life, and now he was bringing her home to the Lemhi Valley to stay. In the end, that was all that really mattered.

THE END

Look next for *BOOK 6: SAVAGE ALLIANCE*

Author's note

A hearty thanks must go out to Terry Sandstrom and to the other citizens of Chadron, Nebraska, for their help in recreating the town as it existed in the 1970's. Another big thank you to Ashley Bullock, as always, for her lovely portrayal of Maura PlentyWounds, on the cover, and this time to her little sister Annie Shockley, who looks so perfect as Maura's sister Nora Sue.

A nod doesn't seem like enough to those authors who have taken their time creating maps of the Pine Ridge Reservation, along with those who have compiled all the information I could ever need about Lakota spiritual ceremonies and medicine men, those who have put together dictionaries of the Lakota language, and those who have photographed the almost third-world conditions of life on the Rez, which my imagination fed off in a big way. Many of the sights you have seen within the pages of this book are real scenes from Lakota existence in that corner of South Dakota.

As always, the country in the book, all the way from Salmon to Oglala, South Dakota, was carefully re-created and brought to life from firsthand research. The 1968 Ford Thunderbird, I might add, is mine, a car I purchased specifically for Coal Savage to adopt with this book, and it will roll forever in glory, in its place of honor in the barn behind our home, or on the open road.

About the Author

Kirby Frank Jonas was born in 1965 in Bozeman, Montana. His earliest memories are of living seven miles outside of town in a wide crack in the mountains known as Bear Canyon. At that time it was a remote and lonely place, but a place where a boy with an imagination could grow and nurture his mind, body and soul.

From Montana, the Jonas family moved almost as far across the country as they could go, to Broad Run, Virginia, to a place that, although not as deep in the timbered mountains as Bear Canyon was every bit as remote—Roland Farm. Once again, young Jonas spent his time mostly alone, or with his older brother, if he was not in school. Jonas learned to hike with his mother, fish with his father, and to dodge an unruly horse.

Jonas moved to Shelley, Idaho, in 1971, and from that time forth, with the exception of a few sojourns elsewhere, he became an Idahoan. Jonas attended all twelve years of school in Shelley, graduating in 1983. In the sixth grade, he penned his first novel, *The Tumbleweed,* and in high school he wrote his second, *The Vigilante.* It was also during this time that he first became acquainted with Salmon, Idaho, staying toward the end of the road at the Golden Boulder Orchard and taking his first steps to manhood.

Jonas has lived in six cities in France, in Mesa, Arizona, and explored the United States extensively. He has fought fires for the Bureau of Land Management in five western states and carried a gun on his hip in three different jobs.

In 1987, Jonas met his wife-to-be, Debbie Chatterton, and in 1989 took her to the altar. Over some rough and rocky roads they have traveled, and across some raging rivers that have at times threatened to draw them under, but they survived, and with four beautiful children to show for it: Cheyenne, Jacob, Clay and Matthew.

Jonas has been employed as a Wells Fargo armored guard, a wildland firefighter, a security guard for California Plant Protection and Inter-Con, and police officer. He is now retired after almost twenty-four years of proud employment as a municipal firefighter for the city of Pocatello, Idaho, and works full-time as an armed private security officer guarding the federal courthouse under contract with the security company Paragon.

One of Jonas's greatest joys in life is watching his second son, Clay, become a recognized writer of much talent in his own chosen field, that of fantasy and science fiction, with his current series *The Descendants of Light* now in print. There is no greater compliment a son could give to his father than to follow in his footsteps.

Books by Kirby Jonas

Season of the Vigilante, Book One: The Bloody Season
Season of the Vigilante, Book Two: Season's End
The Dansing Star
Legend of the Tumbleweed
Lady Winchester
The Devil's Blood
The Secret of Two Hawks
Knight of the Ribbons
Drygulch to Destiny
Samuel's Angel
The Night of My Hanging (And Other Short Stories)
Russet

Savage Law series
1. *Law of the Lemhi, part 1*
   Law of the Lemhi, part 2
2. *River of Death*
3. *Lockdown for Lockwood*
4. *Like a Man Without a Country*
5. *Thunderbird*
6. *Savage Alliance* (forthcoming)

The Badlands series
1. *Yaqui Gold* (co-author Clint Walker)
2. *Haunted Shadows* (forthcoming)

Legends West series
1. *Disciples of the Wind* (co-author Jamie Jonas)
2. *Reapers of the Wind* (co-author Jamie Jonas)

Lehi's Dream series
1. *Nephi Was My Friend*
2. *The Faith of a Man*
3. *A Land Called Bountiful*
4. *Shores of Promise* (forthcoming)

Gray Eagle series (e-book format only—forthcoming in print)
1. *The Fledgling*
2. *Flight of the Fledgling*
3. *Wings on the Wind*
Death of an Eagle (e-book and large format softbound)

Books on audio

The Dansing Star, narrated by James Drury, *"The Virginian"*
Death of an Eagle, narrated by James Drury
Legend of the Tumbleweed, narrated by James Drury
Lady Winchester, narrated by James Drury
Yaqui Gold, narrated by Gene Engene
The Secret of Two Hawks, narrated by Kevin Foley
Knight of the Ribbons, narrated by Rusty Nelson
Drygulch to Destiny, narrated by Kirby Jonas

Available through the author at www.kirbyjonas.com

Email the author at: kirby@kirbyjonas.com or write to:

Howling Wolf Publishing
1611 City Creek Road
Pocatello ID 83204